THE CASE OF LUCY B.

Dr Theodore Levin rose to his feet when Lucy Bending came into his office. He thought her the most beautiful little girl he had ever seen. No, not a little girl. A miniature woman.

He reached into the open desk drawer, switched on the tape recorder.

'Lucy, you love your mother and father, don't you?'

'Of course.'

'And because they love you, they want you to be happy and grow up to be a beautiful, healthy, well-adjusted woman. You know what "well-adjusted" means, don't you?'

'It means you don't have any problems.'

'Well . . . not exactly. It means that you're able to handle your problems. Now your parents feel you *do* have a problem.'

'Oh, I know what it is. They think I love too much.'

She raised both hands and swept her long, softly gleaming hair back from her temples. The movements were graceful, lovely, so pure it was difficult to think of them as coquettish or provocative.

'What do you mean by love too much?'

'Just being nice.'

'Are you nice to everyone?'

'Not everyone. Some people are mean and spiteful.'

'Do you know any men who are mean and spiteful?'

'Nooo,' she said thoughtfully, 'not really.'

'Do you kiss men you like?'

'I like to love people.'

'Men, Lucy. Mostly you like to love men.'

'Yes, Doctor Ted,' she said seriously, 'that's true.'

By Lawrence Sanders:

THE ANDERSON TAPES
THE PLEASURE OF HELEN
LOVE SONGS
THE FIRST DEADLY SIN
THE TOMORROW FILE
THE TANGENT OBJECTIVE
THE MARLOW CHRONICLES
THE SECOND DEADLY SIN
THE TANGENT FACTOR
THE SIXTH COMMANDMENT
THE TENTH COMMANDMENT
THE THIRD DEADLY SIN
THE CASE OF LUCY B.
THE SEDUCTION OF PETER S.

THE CASE OF LUCY B.

Lawrence Sanders

NEW ENGLISH LIBRARY

First published in the USA by G. P. Putnam's Sons, and simultaneously in Canada
by General Publishing Co. Limited

First published in Great Britain in 1983 by New English Library

First NEL Paperback Edition April 1984

NEL Books are published by
New English Library,
Mill Road, Dunton Green,
Sevenoaks, Kent.
Editorial office: 47 Bedford Square, London WC1B 3DP.

Made and printed in Great Britain by
Hunt Barnard Printing Ltd., Aylesbury, Bucks.

British Library C.I.P.

Sanders, Lawrence
  The case of Lucy B
  I Title
  813'.54[F]   PS356.9.A5125

  ISBN 0 450 05597 3

PART I

1

The office was half-nursery. One sunlit wall painted with moon-jumping cows and fiddle-playing cats. A deep bookcase jumbled with toys, games, puzzles, stuffed animals. And on the ceiling, pasted stars.

The man planted behind the desk stared through percolator-top glasses. A snarled salt-and-pepper beard framed rosy lips. His nose was a smudge; dainty ears pressed close to a heavy skull.

His hunched body loomed forward, neck sunken in rounded shoulders. Cigar ashes drifted across an atrocious tie and the lapels of a rumpled black suit so shiny it looked like it had been oiled and polished.

'Mrs Bending,' he said, his voice a throaty rumble, 'Mr Bending, suppose you sit there . . . and there. I must start off by confessing that I am a habitual cigar smoker. Of course, if it offends you, I won't light up. Ma'am?'

'No, that's all right,' the woman said nervously. 'Go ahead, doctor.'

'You, sir?'

'Fine with me, doc. Filter-tips are my vice.'

'Thank you.' He took a dark cigar from an open desk drawer, began to strip cellophane carefully away. 'My name is Doctor Theodore Levin. It is spelled L-e-v-i-n, but pronounced Levine, for reasons I have never been able to understand. You are Mrs Grace Bending and you, sir, are Mr Ronald Bending. Your daughter's name is Lucy, and you have been referred to me by Doctor David K. Raskob, pediatrician, of Boca Raton. Do I have my facts correct?'

'Yes, doctor,' the woman said stiffly. She was twisting her wedding band, around and around.

Levin lighted his cigar with a wooden kitchen match scratched on the underside of his desk. He turned the cigar slowly in pursed lips. He blew a smoke cloud toward the pasted stars.

'Now then . . .' he said. 'I have found it best for all concerned if I explain at the beginning exactly how I practice so there can be no possible misunderstanding. As I told you on the phone, ma'am, my fee is a hundred dollars an hour. That is a professional hour; forty-five minutes to be exact.'

'Beautiful!' Ronald Bending said with a loppy grin.

His wife snapped at him: 'Ronnie, be quiet.'

The doctor looked at them, woman to man and back again, with a fiercely benign smile.

'This initial interview,' he continued gently, 'of forty-five minutes at the usual fee, is to give you an opportunity to explain the nature of your daughter's problem. At the end of this meeting, I may tell you that I feel I can be of no assistance. It sometimes happens. In such a case, I may be able to suggest other psychiatrists who might be able to help.'

The woman's eyes squinched with anguish. 'But Doctor Raskob recommended *you*.'

'I appreciate that, ma'am, but your daughter's problem may be better handled by another. Please let me be the judge of that.'

He paused a moment while Ronald Bending lighted a cigarette, using a gold Dupont lighter. Bending then sat back negligently, crossed his knees, adjusted the crisp crease in his trouser leg. He was wearing tasseled cordovan moccasins, burnished to a high gloss.

Dr Levin went on: 'In the event I feel tentatively that I might be of help, I will require an initial interview with your daughter, uh . . .'

'Lucy.'

8

'Yes, with Lucy. After meeting and talking with her, I will be able to give you a final decision on whether I believe I can be of help and will accept the case.'

Bending's face reddened. He jerked forward angrily. 'See here —'

'Ronnie,' his wife interrupted, 'please! We understand all that, doctor.'

'And you wish to continue?'

'Yes.'

'If I accept your daughter for psychotherapy, I will inform you as to the frequency of visits I recommend. Once or several times a week. The first regular visit, or sometimes the first two, will be given over to a complete physical examination, conducted by my associate, Doctor Mary Scotsby. There will be additional billing for X-rays and laboratory analyses.'

'Now see here,' Ronald Bending said, lips pulling tight, 'Raskob has been Lucy's doctor since she was born. He has all the tests; he can tell you anything you want to know.'

'I prefer to conduct my own examination, sir.'

'Oh Jesus!' Bending said disgustedly, and leaned forward to jab out his cigarette butt in the big marble ashtray on the doctor's desk.

'Ronnie,' his wife said, her voice strangled, 'will you please let me handle this? We understand, doctor, and we'd like to go ahead.'

'A moment . . . In the psychiatric treatment of a child of — how old is she?'

'Lucy is eight years old.'

'In the treatment of a child of eight, it is sometimes necessary to meet also with her parents, siblings, if any, and even, on occasion, her teachers, friends, neighbors, and so forth. These interviews are for the usual professional hour and billed at the usual fee. I want all this to be clearly understood before you decide to continue.'

Bending threw his hands into the air and rolled his eyes in comical disbelief. 'Grace, this could cost a fortune!'

'We want to go ahead, doctor,' she insisted.

Levin inspected the husband without expression.

'Sir, if you have any objections, or if you feel you cannot carry the, uh, financial burden, I may be able to recommend agencies that –'

'No!' Bending said at once. 'No agencies. We'll go on with this.'

'You're certain in your own mind?'

'Hell no, I'm not certain. But I'll go along.'

'And you, ma'am?'

'Yes. Positively.'

'Very well. Now just one additional fact of which you should be aware . . . This interview – and all interviews in the future, with Lucy, with you, and others – is being recorded on a tape recorder.'

Bending blinked with surprise. 'What's the point of that, doc?'

'To maintain a history of treatment and provide a handy referral to past interviews. To enable me to review the case when the patient is absent and perhaps discover things that were not immediately apparent during the actual interview.'

Bending was back to his lopsided grin. 'I hope you keep the tapes locked up!'

'I do indeed. In a fireproof, burglarproof vault. They will be heard only by myself and my associate, Doctor Scotsby. You still wish to continue?'

'Yes, doctor, we do.'

'You, sir?'

'Yes.'

'Very well. If I agree to accept Lucy as a patient, I will ask both of you to complete questionnaires that will provide me with most of the needed basic information: date and place of birth, family medical history, education, employment, and so forth. At the moment, I think we should concern ourselves solely with the reason for your being here. What, precisely, is Lucy's problem?'

Husband and wife glanced at each other. She fidgeted; he blandly lighted another cigarette, then examined the burning tip.

Silence expanded, filled the room. The doctor waited patiently, squarish hands clasped loosely over his bulging vest. His cigar had gone out; the butt rested on the edge of his scarred desk. He looked calmly at the Bendings, and said nothing. Finally . . .

'Uh, Grace,' Ronald Bending said, staring off into space, 'you tell him.'

She started with a rush: 'Doctor, our Lucy is a beautiful little girl. When you see her, I think you'll agree she is just lovely, and very intelligent and – and poised for her age.'

'Smart as a whip,' Ronald Bending drawled.

'She is very popular with her friends, both girls and boys, and her teachers love her. There is nothing mean or malicious about her. And her brothers just dote on her.'

She stopped. Silence again. Dr Levin waited a moment, then said, 'And . . . ?'

'Well, for the past three years, about, since she was five, she – Ronnie, wouldn't you say it's been for the past three years?'

'Maybe longer. Maybe since she was four.'

'Doctor, she has become increasingly, uh, affectionate Hugging and kissing all the time. Hanging on to people. She's become very, uh, physical, and is always touching and stroking. Sometimes in a vulgar way.'

'And . . . ?'

'Well . . . that's it, doctor.'

'I see . .' Levin leaned forward over his desk, looming again, hunched and burly. He spoke to both of them, but he locked stares with Ronald Bending. 'You have described to me a very loving, well-adjusted, outgoing little girl. Is that the impression you wish to give me?'

'Grace, for God's sake,' Bending burst out, '*tell* him!'

'Doctor, it's . . .' Her voice trailed away.

'Oh Christ!' her husband said furiously. 'Doc, it's more

11

than just being affectionate. She's – well, she's always coming on. Not with her kid friends or brothers. But with me and any older men we invite to the house. She's always holding their hands, kissing, and petting them. At first it was cute. Now it's become an embarrassment. She's all over every man like a wet sheet. She wants to sit on their laps. She squirms between their legs. You've seen young hounds that grab your shins in their paws and rub up and down? She's just like that.'

'Ronnie!'

'Grace, it's true and you know it. What the hell's the point of paying for professional help if we don't tell the truth? Doc, Lucy is a beautiful, intelligent little girl. That *is* the truth. But she acts like a sex maniac. I mean it. She touches men between their legs – if you know what I mean. She twists around on their laps and strokes their thighs and wants to kiss. Older men. Always older men. Sometimes, I swear to God, she acts like a little hooker. Touching them up, laughing, really trying to excite them. I include myself, except that now I try to hold her off. Not reject her, you understand, but trying to let her know she's doing the wrong thing. But every time we have a male visitor, someone older than, say, eighteen or so, she starts coming on with them. It's so obvious that all our friends know about it. We joked about it at first, but it's gone beyond the joking stage now. Let me tell you what happened when –'

'Ronnie! Please don't.'

'Yes, I've got to say it. We had a lot of people in for a Labor Day cookout. It lasted all day – a pool party. Things got kind of drunk later that night. I went into the kitchen to get more ice, and here was – here was this good friend of mine backed up against the sink. Drink in one hand, cigarette in the other. Lucy was standing between his legs and rubbing him up. He was wearing slacks, and she was rubbing his, uh, penis through the cloth. With both her little hands. Listen, he was stoned, I admit it, but also I swear it wasn't his fault. I'm not even sure he knew what was going on, but Lucy knew. Oh yes! He wasn't seducing her; she was seducing him. And when I came into the kitchen, she turned, gave me a great big gorgeous smile, and said, 'Hi daddy!' as if what she was doing was the most natural thing in the world. I mean there was absolutely no realization that what she was doing was wrong. I yanked her out of there, cracked her behind, and sent her upstairs to bed. Maybe I shouldn't have done that, but I was so pissed off I wasn't thinking straight. Then I kicked his ass out of the house. But I know, I *know*, it wasn't his fault. It wasn't his idea; it was her idea. She came on to him. That's the way she is.'

'I see,' Dr Levin said. He leaned back in his scuffed swivel chair. Slowly, deliberately, he relighted his dead cigar. He placed both thick hands on the desk top, palms down. He turned his searchlight eyes to Grace Bending. 'Ma'am, is what your husband told me correct?'

She lifted her chin, poked slender fingers into her sun-streaked chignon. 'Well, ah, of course I didn't see that particular incident, but I believe it. Yes, that's the way she acts with men. It's so distasteful. Disgusting. Kissing them and petting them and touching them. It's horrible enough in our own home, doctor, but what worries me, uh, us, is what might happen away from home. If some man picks her up . . . We can't be with her every minute. I just don't know . . .'

Suddenly she was weeping, hunched over and biting a knuckle. Her shoulders shook. Little snuffling sounds came from her. Ronald Bending looked at her ironically.

'Please, ma'am,' Levin said, 'try to control yourself.'

'We're not exaggerating, doc,' Bending said stonily. 'That's the way she acts. We've tried talking to her, explaining that she's annoying people. We've tried spanking her and sending her to her room without supper. We've tried everything we can think of. But she just doesn't seem to understand that what she's doing is wrong. She just keeps doing it. And she's really beautiful, with a great little body.

So a lot of our friends welcomed her, uh, attentions – until they realized what was going on. Now some of them won't come to our house. It's just too embarrassing. Doc, may I ask you a question?'

'Yes.'

'Have you ever heard of anything like this before? Have you ever treated a little girl who acts like that?'

'Sir, Lucy's problem, as you describe it, is not unique, I assure you. There is literature on the subject. And yes, I have treated a similar case in the past.'

'And you cured her?' Grace Bending asked, looking up with teary eyes.

'You must pardon me, but I cannot discuss another case with you any more than I would discuss Lucy's case with anyone else.'

'But you can cure her?'

'I don't like that word "cure," as if your daughter had some dreadful disease. I don't "cure" my patients; I provide psychotherapeutic treatment and try to adjust their behavior to acceptable standards. For their good, and for the good of society. If you want me to guarantee success, no, I cannot do that; no medical doctor or psychiatrist can. All I can do is tell you that your daughter's behavior is not as outlandish or reprehensible as you may think, and the possibility of change and improvement does exist.'

'Then you'll take her on as a patient, doctor?' Grace Bending said hopefully.

'We'll see, ma'am, we'll see.'

'Well, what's the next step?'

'I think I should speak to Lucy

2

The rusted air conditioner whined steadily, but the motel room smelled of roach spray and spent passions. A bent venetian blind on the west window could not be closed tightly; the beamy Florida sun printed a ladder across Jane Holloway's naked back. Ronald Bending traced shadow and light with a gentle finger.

'How do you get an overall tan?' he asked her.

She lifted onto her side, stretched across him for the cigarette pack. Ribs pressed glossy skin.

'You've asked me that before,' she said. 'Several times.'

'And you've refused to answer – several times. I tell you things.'

'Nothing important,' she said. She rolled onto her back, blew a plume of smoke at the cracked ceiling.

'Tacky dump,' she said.

'You picked it,' he said mildly. 'It doesn't make any difference, does it?'

'No.'

The mildewed walls were a map of strange worlds. Every flat surface in the room bore a tattoo of cigarette burns. In the bathroom, a vending machine dispensed condoms in three colors. The sheets were stiff as sacking, the towels lacy from years of laundering.

From outside came the grind of a powered lawnmower and the whiz of traffic on I-95. They heard the crunch of steps on the gravel parking lot and a woman's high-pitched giggle. A radio was playing somewhere, too faintly to distinguish the song, but they could hear the driving pulse.

'What about the all-over tan?' Bending asked again.

She turned her head to stare at him. 'Persistent bugger, aren't you?'

'Just envious. I'll tell you something important if you'll tell me how you get the tan. Deal?'

'Depends. Let's hear your news first.'

'Well . . .' Bending said, lighting his own cigarette, 'Grace and I finally went to a psychiatrist in Fort Liquordale this morning. About Lucy.'

'You should have gone years ago.'

'I suppose.'

'Is he going to take her?'

'He wants to talk to her first.'

'That figures. What's he like?'

'The shrink? Seems like a no-nonsense guy.'

'Young? Old?'

'About my age,' Bending said. 'Maybe a few years older. Short. Stocky. Beard and thick glasses. Young Doctor Freud. He's supposed to be a good man.'

'How much, Turk?' she asked curiously.

'Hundred bucks an hour. Which is forty-five minutes.'

'Jesus. He better be a good man.'

'All right, that's my trade. Now how about your tan?'

She touched the indentation of her waist, pressed the hardness of her thigh. She felt the flatness of her abdomen, stroked her shoulder. He waited patiently. Finally she said:

'I have a friend in Plantation with a roof terrace above everything around. I suntan in the nude up there a couple times a week. No one can see me.'

'Except helicopter pilots and the people in the Goodyear blimp. Who's the friend?'

She didn't answer.

'Man or woman?' he asked.

'Man.'

'Do I know him?'

'I don't think so.'

'What's his first name? You can tell me that, can't you?'

She considered a moment. 'His first name is Randolph,' she said.

He looked at her, blinking.

'My God!' he said. 'Not the senator?'

'Ex-senator.'

'Whatever. Jane, he's got to be eighty!'

'Pushing.'

'What does he do – beat you with his truss?'

She showed her teeth. 'Nothing like that. He's never touched me.'

'Then what does he *do*?'

'Just looks. Looking can be a pleasure, too, you know. I see you staring at the creamers on the beach in their string bikinis.'

'Yes,' he said, nodding, 'that's true. And he's never touched you?'

'Never.'

'What do you get out of it?'

'A perfect tan. Some good stock tips. Ripe gossip about local political bigwigs. Who's doing what to whom. Did you know there's a pillar of the community, who shall be nameless, who gets it off with little black sambos?'

'Big deal,' he said. 'I know a pillar of the community who gets it off with alligators.'

She struck him on the shoulder with a clenched fist. 'You're impossible.'

He agreed.

He swung his legs out of bed, padded to the dresser. He took two Cokes from an insulated bag, just large enough to hold a six-pack. He popped the tabs, came back to bed.

Ronald Bending was a stretched, farmerish man. Hair sun-bleached brown. Ruddy complexion. Laugh lines at the corners of his eyes. A voice curdled with irony. Outsize gestures, almost theatrical. Eyes of faded blue. His body was all angles and edges. Skin a bronzy red above and below the white outlines of his swimming trunks.

He put one of the cold cans of Coke atop her stomach.

17

She gasped and plucked it away. They lighted new cigarettes and sipped and smoked, smoked and sipped.

'Did Luther Empt say anything to Bill?' he asked her. 'About a meeting tonight?'

'If he did, I don't know about it. Why?'

'Luther called me at the office, wants me to come over for a drink. Wouldn't tell me what it's about, but he sounded excited. As excited as Luther can get.'

'That man's a lump.'

'A smart lump. I take it he's one you've missed.'

'You take it correctly.'

'I know where he gets his jollies.'

'Not from his wife, that's for sure. Did you ever try that, Turk?'

'I tried,' he admitted. 'Got nowhere.'

'You're too old for her,' she advised.

'Too old?' he protested. 'I won't be forty till March. She's got to have a few years on me.'

'Two, to be exact.'

Then they were silent. All this talk about age was disquieting. You rarely spoke of growing old, and death was taboo. You tanned your skin and played golf or tennis. You dressed young, listened to young music, danced young dances. Youth was where it was. Time was the enemy.

'You know who she has eyes for?' Jane Holloway asked. 'Teresa Empt?'

'I didn't think she had eyes for anyone,' he said. 'I thought she had Rose's lime juice in her veins.'

'Eddie,' she said.

'Eddie?' he burst out. 'Your Eddie?'

'That's right.'

'But the kid's only sixteen.'

'Going on twenty-five. You know how he's built.'

'Teresa Empt and Eddie? You're crazy!'

'Am I?' she said lazily. 'We're having a cookout next week. Keep an eye on her. You'll see I'm right.'

'Does Eddie know anything about this?'

18

'Probably. But Bill doesn't.'

'Does Bill know anything about us?'

'Doesn't know and couldn't care less.'

'I hope you're right. Does he own a gun?'

'No. Do you?'

'Sure. And so does everyone else I know. So when all the dingoes start moving up from Dade County we'll be able to protect the sanctity of our homes and the chastity of our women.'

'The first time you try to use it,' she said, 'you'll probably shoot off your whatzis.'

'Probably,' he said cheerfully. 'And then where will I be?'

'Nowhere,' she said. 'You'll end up in a wheelchair like the senator. Just looking.'

She smiled at the image and handed him her cigarette butt and empty can of soda.

Her hair was a silver-white trimmed to a brush cut, an inch long atop her head. Florida women looked at her strangely, but she didn't care. Her dark eyes glittered.

Small, hard breasts were bosses. Hip bones stretched tanned skin. Her hairless body gleamed, arms and legs like peeled willow wands. Her face had been lifted once.

Everything about her was tight. Nothing was soft or saggy. She could grip a man with muscles within her and make him cry out. She used reddish brown polish on her fingernails, and gold on the nails of her long, prehensile toes.

She saw Ronald Bending glance at his wristwatch.

'Do we have time for another?' she asked.

'You're beautiful,' he said with a clownish smile.

'I know,' she said.

3

The terrace faced the beach, ocean, the Bahamas and, eventually, Morocco. A melon moon popped from the sea, rose swiftly, made a path of dark dazzles across choppy water. The air smelled of ruttish heat. In the dimness, white pages turned endlessly on the strand.

William Jasper Holloway, a vague and melancholy man, came out onto the terrace carrying two small snifters of brandy. He paused to slide shut the glass door, locking in the air conditioning. He joined his father-in-law at the white wicker table, handing him one of the cognacs.

'I thank you, Bill,' the old man said.

'My pleasure, professor.'

Lloyd Craner had a white mustache and goatee, a knuckle of a nose, the brows and eyes of a grandee. He glowered at the world from a face that belonged on a cigar box. His false teeth clacked.

Between his knees was propped his rosewood cane with a silver toucan's head for a handle. He sat stiffly upright, scanning the sea, daring it. All his movements were precise and calculated. He was determined not to die.

'Nice night,' Bill Holloway offered.

The ex-professor of geology stuck his beak into the snifter, inhaled, then dipped his tongue.

'Ambrosia,' he said. 'I saw a flurry out there a few minutes ago. Some phosphorescence.'

'School of mullet,' Holloway said. 'Maybe.'

'The sea, the sea,' Craner recited. 'A man has not lived until he has known the sea, until he has felt the giant bounds the soul takes upward when the eyes look upon a world without limit, beauty without end. Always, everywhere, the sea rolls forever. Men come and go, and nations, and civilizations. But the sea! That is life, constant, eternal.'

'Very nice,' Holloway said. 'Who wrote it?'

'I did,' the professor said. 'When I was young and innocent.'

'You were never innocent,' his son-in-law said.

The old man showed his teeth and took a swallow of brandy.

'Excellent dinner tonight,' he said.

'Was it?' Holloway said. 'I can't get used to Florida lobsters. They look like amputees to me.'

'Because you're from New England. They may not have claws, but the flavor is subtle.'

'I'll take your word for it.'

'What was the fight about?'

'With Maria? Jane said she had put too much saffron in the rice. Maria told her that in Cuba she had been a great lady who had servants working for *her*. Jane said maybe she'd be happier back in Cuba. Maria told her in explicit detail what she could do with the saffron rice. Too bad you don't speak Spanish; it loses something in translation.'

'Is that the end of Maria?'

'Probably,' Holloway said indifferently. 'She's lasted three weeks; that's par for the course.'

They sipped their brandies slowly. A thick southeast breeze whipped the fronds of palms screening the terrace. They heard the splash of the sea. A vee of pelicans flapped north across the glow of the moon.

'Montana was never like this,' Lloyd Craner said.

'Sometimes I feel I'm living in a travel poster,' Holloway said.

'I thought you liked it.'

'I thought I did. Now I'm beginning to wonder. Too much sea. Too much beach. Too much perfect weather. That damned sun . . . My brain is turning to mush. I used to

21

read eighteenth-century poetry. Now I read the *National Enquirer*.'

'You still play chess.'

'Badly.'

'A game tonight?'

'Sorry, professor. I've got to have a drink with Luther Empt. Some business proposition he wants to talk about.'

'What do you know about him, Bill?'

'Luther? He came down from Chicago about twelve years ago. Started his own business producing slide presentations for corporations and advertising agencies. Then he got into eight- and sixteen-millimeter educational and training films. Lately he's been processing TV commercials and video cassettes. Seems to be a very capable man.'

'Ambitious?'

'Oh yes. Teresa is his third wife. I heard some talk that it was her money that enabled him to expand into the television field.'

'Was she married before?'

'Once.'

'Going to Jerusalem,' the codger said.

'What?'

'That's what we used to call the children's game of Musical Chairs. He's been married three times, his wife twice. Ronald Bending has been married twice, and so has Jane. I never knew there were so many widowed, divorced, and remarried people in the world until I came to Florida.'

'Going to Jerusalem,' Holloway repeated. 'Good name. Florida: the new Jerusalem. Let me get a refill.'

He took the brandy snifters back into the living room. It stretched the width of the house, decorated in shades of beige and brown. He hated it.

Jane was curled into one end of a ten-foot couch upholstered in chocolate velvet. She was wearing a tube of fuchsia jersey, down to her ankles. She was filing her nails, watching their oversize TV set.

'How's the movie?' he asked pleasantly.

'Shit,' she said.

He poured his father-in-law another brandy and himself a double vodka on ice with a squeeze of lime.

'Where's Gloria?' he asked his wife.

'Doing her homework over at the Bendings'. With Lucy.'

'And Eddie?'

'Upstairs. Unless he's gone out the window again. Let me have a gin martini. Lemon peel.'

He mixed the drink and brought it to her. She took the glass from his fingers without moving her eyes from the television. He carried the other drinks out to the terrace.

The moon was higher, paler, smaller. Dimly, in the gloom, they saw a pack of five joggers pounding down the beach. Far out in the darkness, a necklace of red lights moved northward.

'Probably commercial fishing boats,' Holloway said. 'Heading for the Jupiter Inlet.'

'This Luther Empt . . .' Lloyd Craner said. 'You think he's an honest man?'

'As honest as he has to be. Why the sudden interest in Luther Empt?' He paused a moment. 'Good Lord, professor, don't tell me it's his mother. Gertrude? Is it Gertrude?'

'What we used to call a fine figure of a woman,' his father-in-law said softly.

'Going to Jerusalem,' William Jasper Holloway said.

Two vodkas later, he slipped off his canvas moccasins, carried them and, barefoot, scuffed down the beach to Empt's place, only two homes away. The coarse, gritty sand held the day's heat. There were sand burrs and shards of shell. He didn't care. For some reason he could not understand, it was good to feel. Even pain.

He knew he was softer and pudgier than he should have been. He wanted to be as lean and hard as Turk Bending, but only succeeded in being as plump as Luther Empt, yet without his energy and resolve.

He was a medium man, of medium height, with hair and

eyes a medium brown. All his clothes were medium size. He supposed he had a medium mind and, perhaps, a medium soul.

He wore a knotted silk ascot in the open neck of his white, short-sleeved Izod shirt. He always wore an ascot, an affectation that amused his Florida neighbors. And his flower-patterned polyester slacks would have earned a guffaw from his poofy Boston friends.

But that was another world, in another time.

He came up to the Empt place. He leaned against the concrete seawall to brush sand and burrs from his bare feet and tug on his moccasins. He heard murmurs from the terrace and glimpsed the ghostly figures of Luther and Bending standing near the glass-and-stainless-steel table.

William Holloway's home, and Ronald Bending's too, were built on half-acre plots. Luther Empt had a full acre of waterfront property – and what that might be worth stunned the mind. But of course Empt had bought it ten years ago. Still . . .

The house, like most of the others on the beach, was stuccoed cinder block built on a concrete slab anchored to pilings driven deep into the sand. Most of the other homes had shingled roofs. Empt's had red Spanish tile set in a fish scale pattern.

The lawn facing the highway was beautifully maintained. There was a formal garden, Olympic-size swimming pool, a gas-fueled outdoor barbecue grill. The house itself had been featured in *Architectural Digest*. The article was titled 'Florida Gold Coast Villa.'

'That makes you a villain,' Bending told Empt.

Luther had forced a laugh.

Holloway walked up the short flight of stairs from the beach. His stairs were wooden. Bending's were cinder blocks. Empt's were slabs of coral rock.

The three men shook hands and got themselves seated in low canvas slings. Luther had put out a bucket of ice cubes, bourbon, scotch and vodka. There were crystal glasses, slices of lime, pieces of lemon peel.

'I'm not going to wait on you bums,' Empt said. 'Help yourselves.'

'I may get stoned,' Bending warned, pouring bourbon over ice.

'Go with it,' Empt said. 'I'll see you home.'

'The last time you told me that,' Bending said, 'I ended up sleeping on the beach.'

The two men laughed, and Bill Holloway felt left out. He poured a heavy vodka on ice and squeezed a wedge of lime. Empt was drinking warm scotch.

'What's the occasion, Luther?' Holloway asked.

He sat back with his drink. He could see through the big picture window. Teresa and Gertrude Empt were playing backgammon on a low cocktail table in front of a brick fireplace. The only fireplace Holloway had ever seen in south Florida.

'Lemme give you some background,' Empt said. 'When I came down here from Chicago, I had some good ideas but not so much cold cash. None of the local cracker banks would stake me. Including yours, Bill.'

'You had no track record,' Holloway said equably.

'True enough,' Empt said without rancor. 'Anyway, I ended up at a bank in south Miami. The name don't matter. At the time it was capitalized for about fifty million and was handling an annual cash flow of about five hundred mil. What does that tell you?'

'Mob money,' Bill Holloway said.

'Or cocaine cash from Colombia,' Turk Bending said.

'Or both,' Empt said, nodding. 'But who gives a god-damn as long as it's green? They gave me a loan. Stiff vigorish, but I paid back every cent. And that was the only time I had any dealings with them. I got rolling, and now I'm A-number-one with the local banks. Am I right, Bill?'

'Correct,' Holloway said, although it wasn't *quite* correct. He leaned forward for more vodka.

'About a month ago,' Empt continued, 'I got a call from a VP at the Miami bank. He said a couple of good old boys had a business proposition they wanted to talk to me about. He could vouch for them, *mucho dinero*, and would I listen to their pitch? I said sure, send them up. We met in my office. We talked for maybe three hours, then drove up to Palm Beach for dinner at the Breakers. All in all, I was with them almost six hours.'

'Mob?' Holloway asked.

'You guessed it. That's who they were, but you couldn't tell. I mean, no pinkie rings or dese, dem, and dose talk. Conservatively dressed. Quiet-spoken. Polite. No threats. Very, very smooth. But not soft, if you know what I mean. It was plain they had looked me up. They knew my bottom line and who's holding my paper.'

'What did they want you to do?' Bending said. 'Run white slaves over to the A-rabs?'

'Not exactly,' Empt said. 'To explain what they wanted, I gotta get technical on you. Better have another drink.'

They helped themselves and settled back. Empt was silent a moment, frowning. He was a slow-moving, slow-talking, slow-thinking man.

He had the hard, massive face of a Wehrmacht colonel. Gray hair in a flattop cut. Small, meaty ears set close to his clippered skull. Shrewd coal eyes. A stiff mouth with folds from the corners to his chin.

He was wearing a guayabera shirt to conceal his belly. In swimming trunks, he looked like he had swallowed a cannon ball. His ponderous shoulders, back, arms, chest were covered with a thick black pelt.

He hunched forward in the sling chair, powerful forearms resting on his knees. His white shirt and white duck slacks gleamed in the dusk. He loomed, monumental in his solidity. His hands always seemed clenched into fists.

'I'm gradually switching from film to video cassettes for training and educational movies,' he said in his raspy voice. 'Eventually I'll be taping everything. It's the coming thing,

26

no doubt about it. Everyone says so. Right? The price of video recorders and players will be down to five hundred in another year. Right now, you can buy old movies on tape for thirty to sixty bucks. In that range. That price will probably come down, too.

'But the whole industry is in an uproar. Different systems, noncompatible. Video cassettes and video disks. No standardization. Like LPs when they first came out. All sizes, shapes, speeds. Now the goddamned Japs have announced a video cassette no longer than an audio cassette. Everyone's rushing to get in on video tape. Everyone agrees it's going to be a billion-dollar business. And you know what? I think everyone's full of shit.'

He sat back smiling secretly, arrogant.

'What does that mean?' Bending said. 'You're going bankrupt?'

'Not me,' Empt said with a coarse laugh. 'I got a sweet business. Educational and training cassettes and disks for corporations, schools, the government. I can't miss. But when people talk about a billion-dollar business, they're talking about a mass market, like for LP records, eight-track tapes, and audio cassettes. So I ask: What? What? Where's the billion-dollar market? Turk, what's the best movie you ever saw?'

'The best? I don't know . . . maybe *Gone with the Wind*.'

'All right, *Gone with the Wind*. Would you pay, say, fifty bucks for a video cassette to watch on your small TV screen? Fifty bucks? For Christ's sake, how many times can you watch *Gone with the Wind*? Bill, you're the music nut. Would you pay fifty bucks to watch the New York Philharmonic play Beethoven on your TV set?'

'No . . . not really,' Holloway said, finally getting interested. 'There's no particular advantage in *watching* an orchestra play. The sound is everything. In fact, seeing the orchestra would probably be a distraction. Hearing a good stereo LP or tape is all you want, or need.'

'Right!' Empt said. 'And what about opera and ballet.

On the TV screen the singers and dancers come out a few inches high, and you lose all the effect of the big sets. So what does that leave for the billion-dollar market?'

'Individual stars?' Holloway suggested. 'Performers like Liza Minnelli or Sinatra. Las Vegas comedians.'

'Fifty bucks so you can keep watching some sad-ass comic tell dirty jokes?' Empt said. 'Maybe once, but how many times could you watch it? You'd know all the gag lines. What I'm getting at is who'd want to *own* those tapes and disks? Even if the price comes down to ten dollars, I just don't think the market is there. Let's have another round.'

They leaned to fill their glasses. Holloway could feel the vodka working. He was beginning to sweat. There was a rosy glow that softened everything. No more rough edges. These were splendid fellows.

'Maybe the answer is like a lending library,' Turk Bending said. 'You rent a video cassette or video disk. You want to see a certain movie or football game, say, and you rent it for a day, a week, whatever. From a catalogue.'

'Maybe,' Luther Empt agreed. 'Maybe that's the answer. But rentals are no billion-dollar market. All I'm saying is that there's not going to be any great rush to buy cassettes or disks of movies, plays, sporting events, orchestras, operas, or ballets. Oh, there'll be a market with the gadget crowd and maybe the rock-and-roll groupies. But the potential isn't as big as everyone thinks. Except for one thing.'

'Porn,' Bending said promptly.

'You son of a bitch,' Empt said with heavy good humor, 'you're way ahead of me. But you're right. Pornography. Blue films on tape cassettes or disks, played through your TV set in the privacy of your own home. Now *there's* a market.'

'Enter your mob guys,' Holloway said wryly.

'Right,' Empt said. 'They're no dumbbells. They're in it already as far as eight- and sixteen-millimeter films go. Plus

28

books and photos, of course. Now they want to get into TV cassettes and disks. They've already got a production, processing, and distribution setup in LA. They want to do the same thing on the east coast.'

'Why Florida?' Holloway asked.

'Because they think they own the state. And maybe they do. Because the weather is great for movie production. Because taxes are low, low, low, and these guys are very law-abiding. And because distribution from, say, Miami to the big cities east of the Mississippi is a lot easier than from LA. Also, the talent for porn is here. Plenty of young creamers ready to spread their pussies. Directors and cameramen. Writers and set designers. And if they're not here, they can fly down from New York in less than three hours. Florida is perfect for this business. After all, *Deep Throat* was made here. And they could run the finished stuff up to Long Island or Boston by boat, just the way they do with coke and hash, if they don't want to truck it up or fly it up.'

'And they think the market will be that big?' Holloway asked.

'They *know* it will be that big,' Empt said definitively. 'Porn is something that the guys who get turned on by it can watch over and over. So they'll want to *own* it. Collect a library of the stuff. And they'll pay top dollar.'

'What do they –' Holloway started to say, but then Luther Empt exploded a great roar of fury and disgust. He struggled out of the canvas sling and stood swaying, pointing down with a trembling finger.

'Look at that bastard!' he shouted. '*Look* at him!'

They looked. A giant cockroach had climbed up the concrete, over the edge of the terrace. Its brown carapace gleamed in the glow from the picture window. Feelers moved languidly. It scuttled this way and that.

'Shee-it,' Turk Bending said, 'that's nothing but a palmetto bug. Can't hurt you.'

He rose gracefully, moved quickly, and with his bare foot

29

scraped the bug off the terrace back down to the beach.

'No use trying to kill the mother,' he said. 'You need a jackhammer to dent them. Let him run away and play.'

'I hate those bastards,' Empt said, shuddering. 'They're so fucking ugly. Lemme get us some fresh supplies.'

Holloway and Bending grinned at each other in their host's absence. It was comforting to discover another man's weakness.

'Bugs and snakes don't bother me none,' Bending said. 'You?'

'Not really,' Holloway said, finishing the bottle of vodka and trying to remember how much had been in it when he started. 'I can do without the Portuguese men-o'-war, but they're easy to avoid.'

Bending looked at him narrowly.

'Nothing much bothers you, does it, Bill?'

'That's right,' Holloway said uncomfortably, hoping for deliverance.

It came with Empt's return. He brought unopened liters of vodka, scotch, and bourbon, and a tub of fresh ice cubes.

'Woo-*eee*!' Bending said, exhaling. 'I may be a wee bit late at the office tomorrow.'

They poured themselves drinks with the exaggerated care of men who feel their coordination slipping. They settled back in their slings. Holloway noticed Luther Empt kept glancing nervously at the spot where Bending had kicked the palmetto bug off the terrace.

'Where were we?' Empt said. 'Oh yeah . . . They told me about the production, processing, and distribution facility they want to set up in south Florida.'

'What did they want you to do?' Bending asked. 'Be the top honcho?'

'That's right,' Luther said, not without pride. 'Run the whole shebang. No, that's not right. They would handle distribution and marketing. I would be in charge of production and processing. I'd deliver the finished product to them, packaged and ready for point-of-purchase sale. All

30

the money I wanted – within reason, of course – and all the technical help I needed. They said they could practically guarantee I'd have no trouble with John Law. But if it bothered me, they'd put a million in escrow to cover my legal fees if I got in a bind. That's the way they talked: million this and million that. Like it was popcorn.'

'Wow,' Bending said enviously.

'What did you tell them?' Holloway asked curiously.

'I told them thanks, but no, thanks. I said that first of all, I had no experience in porn, didn't know the market, and didn't know the winners from the dogs. They said no problem, they could provide a staff to make sure the product came up to snuff. So then I told them I just didn't have the balls for it. I've got a reputation around here, and I didn't want to risk it. Teresa would have my heart and liver if she found out. You know how she is. The house, the garden, the society columns, the charity teas, the story in *Architectural Digest*, and all that stuff. Teresa would kill me. Let alone what my mother would say. So I told them no soap.'

'How did they take it?' Bending said.

'They took it fine. No strain. Maybe I was just one guy on their possibles list. They made motions like they were ready to leave, but I didn't want to see them go. I guess all that big-money talk was getting to me. Turk, are you sure those goddamned bugs can't bite or sting?'

'I'm sure.'

'Yeah. Well, you know, as long as I've been hustling I've followed what I call "Luther K. Empt's Three-B Law." It guarantees financial success, but they don't teach it at Harvard or Wharton.'

'What does the K. stand for?' Bending asked.

'Konrad.'

'And what's the Three-B Law?' Holloway asked.

'Bullshit Baffles Brains. Every time. So I figured I'd sing a song for those mob guys. I told them they were trying to invest in my weakness, not in my strength. I told them I know shit-all about the production of porn. But when it comes to processing, I know as much about it as anyone south of New York. I'm talking about the conversion of film to tape, the reproduction of tapes into cartridges and cassettes, the technology of video disks, and so forth. So why not, I said, get someone else to shoot the goddamn stuff, do the actual production, and I'd take over the technical end.'

'There goes my dream of stardom,' Turk Bending said.

'I figured this way,' Empt went on. 'In case the law did move in, I'd be in a hell of a better position if all I had was a factory full of automated machines than if I had a studio full of naked creamers sucking every cock in sight, including Dobermans and donkeys. That makes sense, don't it? I could even claim I didn't know what was on the tapes; I just took them in and made copies. Who the hell has the time to inspect every negative they develop? Bill, what do you think?'

'I don't know,' Holloway said slowly. 'I don't know all that much about obscenity law. I think you're probably right that as merely a processor, your culpability would be less than that of the producers and sellers. But there'd still be risk.'

'Of course there'd be risk. But the money!'

'Better talk to a lawyer, Luther,' Bending advised.

'I did,' Empt said. 'But that's getting ahead of my story. Come on, drink up. All this gabbing makes me thirsty.'

The moon was high now, to the south, sailing through a serene sky. Occasionally they saw the lights of an airliner letting down for the Fort Lauderdale airport. Occasionally a cloud, no larger than a puff of smoke, drifted, dissipated, vanished.

They were not conscious of the noise of waves slapping the beach, or the rustle of palm fronds. The tropical world was there, but they didn't feel it, didn't sense it.

'They looked at each other,' Luther Empt continued. 'The mob guys. That's when we went to Palm Beach for dinner. They picked my brain, and I let them. Technical stuff. Video cassettes versus video disks. They wanted to know which I thought would be the most popular. I told them I didn't know, and no one else did either. In my business, I'm getting ready to go both ways. I told them that in their business, they better hope it was video disks because tapes are too easy to pirate. Any garage mechanic can copy a TV tape. They laughed and said they had some experience with guys pirating their eight- and sixteen-millimeter films, making duplicate prints from the original, but they said those problems had been solved.'

'Oh sure,' Turk Bending said. 'And the guys who tried it are now walking around on the bottom of the Atlantic Ocean wearing cement boots.'

'Probably,' Empt said, shrugging. 'Those guys play hard-ball. But I told them that the big problem with video tapes wouldn't be with pirates trying to peddle copies; it would be with the average joe who buys a porn cassette. Then he calls in a neighbor who's got a player, too, and it's the easiest thing in the world for the neighbor to rip off a copy on a blank tape. Get it? You buy porn, and I copy it for my library. Then I buy, and you tape my cassette. There goes your billion-dollar market. So I told these guys they better pray that video disks make it big, because it's practically impossible to copy a disk – for the average guy anyway. Now you're getting into laser technology and expensive equipment.

'Anyway, that's mostly what we talked about at dinner. Technical stuff, and how I'd be the sole processor of their east coast production. They said the proposition sounded good to them, and they'd present it to their people and get back to me. And that's how we parted. They paid for the dinner. I had a great red snapper.'

There was a pause.

'Is that the end of it?' William Holloway asked, hoping.

'Oh hell no!' Luther Empt said boisterously. 'While I was waiting for them to get back to me, I called Lou Manata –

he handles my legal stuff – and told him what the problem was. He made some calls and got me the name of some hotshot attorney in New York who specializes in obscenity and pornography law. So I called him, made an appointment, and flew up for one day. I laid it right on the line to him and asked him what the risk was.'

'I hope he told you to forget it,' Holloway said, emboldened by the vodka.

'Just the opposite,' Empt said smugly. 'He said anyone who claims to understand obscenity and pornography law in this country is a goddamn liar. It changes every time the Supreme Court opens its mouth. Every state has its own laws, every county, city, town, and village. It's a mess. But he said that in the situation I outlined, his best judgment was that the risk to the processor would be minimal. His exact words: "The risk is minimal." If I was producing the fuck-'em-and-suck-'em tapes, or transporting them across state lines, the risk would be much more. But as strictly a nuts-and-bolts guy, a processor of an existing product, the legal risk would be minimal.'

They drank again. More slowly now because when they looked up, the stars seemed to be swirling, the sky revolving, the whole dark dome of the cosmos tilting in a magical way.

'They came back to me,' Luther Empt said in a thickened voice. 'They said their people had okayed it. They wanted to hire me. Set up a separate processing corporation. They'd own it; I'd work for them. I said fuck that. I've been an independent too long to go back to the nine-to-five routine. I guess they expected that; they were ready with a fallback offer. I could have my own business, and they'd work on a contract basis. That's what I wanted, so I agreed. Then they showed me the numbers. I almost died. I had no idea the porn industry was that big. I'd need a new factory, machines, more people. With the output they were talking about, I figured it would take an investment of at least a mil to tool up.'

'A million?' Holloway cried, his voice breaking.

'On the strength of a mob contract?' Bending asked.

'No, no,' Empt protested. 'To prove they're serious, they're willing to give me a quarter-of-a-million loan. Straight ten percent. Can you believe that? Only a straight ten. Strictly a loan. No piece of the action. I thanked them and told them I'd get back to them.'

Then, Luther Empt said, he went home, sat down with a pocket calculator, and started figuring the numbers. His original guess of a million was close to the mark. Maybe, he said, it would be nearer nine hundred thousand, but with inflation and overruns, a million would be a safer estimate.

With a mob loan, that meant he had to come up with $750,000. He said he could raise that if he put everything he owned into hock: his business, physical plant, his house, his wife's jewelry – everything. But he admitted he was getting a little long in the tooth to take that kind of gamble.

'That's why I asked you to come around tonight,' he concluded. 'How about each of you taking a third? That means a quarter of a mil each. That, plus the loan, will give us our nut. Each of us will own one-third of the corporation, or the partnership if that's what the tax attorneys recommend. I hate calling this a "sure thing" because Skid Row is filled with guys who bet on a sure thing. But it's the best chance I've seen since I was running a Three-card Monte game in east Chicago.'

Holloway and Bending leaned forward to pour fresh drinks. Luther's pitch had climaxed so abruptly that they were stunned. Both were addled by drink, but sober enough to know that at the moment, they couldn't think straight.

'Look,' Empt said, 'don't get me wrong. I don't expect an answer this minute. I just want you to think about it. Okay? I know both of you can come up with that kind of loot without hurting too much. That's why I asked you. If you decide yes, that's fine. If it's no, then no harm done, and we're still good drinking buddies. I'm in the process now of making up a presentation. One for each of you. All the numbers.

'The way it's shaping up,' he said, 'we'll get our money back in about twenty months to two years. After that, it's Treasure Island. Well, you look over the numbers and make up your mind. Of course, if you decide to come in, I'll make sure you meet the mob guys and go over their line of credit. They said they'd have no objection to that. Well, what the hell, enough about business. Now let's do some serious drinking.'

Holloway was thankful that the monologue had ended. It wasn't that Luther Empt was especially ungrammatical or vulgar in his language. But his raspy voice was loud and harsh, his city accent grated on the ear, and just his energy and forcefulness were wearing.

Also, Empt had asked for a decision. In recent months, William Jasper Holloway had striven to reduce his decision making to a minimum. Jane ran the house, and his Executive VP pretty much ran the bank.

Which was the way Holloway wanted it. More and more he felt the need to simplify his life, reduce his existence to essentials. It was from a growing distaste. He recognized that.

Food had lost its flavor. Sex had lost its savor. That sweaty coupling. Ridiculous, really, when you analyzed it. The joys of fatherhood were foreign to him. What was left? He had no talent for fun.

But now, suddenly, he had a decision of some import pushed in his face. Empt was correct: he could easily afford the investment of a quarter of a million dollars. It wasn't the money that disturbed him; it was the choice he was being asked to make. Just when he was doing so well in molding a choiceless and neuter world.

So he was happy that Empt's argument had come to an end. Luther, and Turk Bending, too – men like that daunted him. They seemed so sure, so totally without doubt. They went barging through life, sweaty and roaring. He had learned long ago that he could never be like that. He had ceased trying.

He thought dully that he was quite drunk, but comforted himself with the hope that the other two were in the same condition. They were telling Polish jokes now, and he laughed when they laughed, not bothering to listen.

It was in the middle of one of Turk Bending's anecdotes that, in a hazy dream, Holloway saw the feelers, head, and then the shiny body of a palmetto bug appear over the edge of the terrace.

He held his breath, watching it move cautiously toward the light. It moved in short darts, pausing, waving its antennae, then scampering on at an angle.

Luther Empt's sling chair went over with a crash. The big man cursed hysterically, fought the canvas, struggled to his feet. He stood panting, mouth open, eyes bulging.

'I'm going to get that cocksucker,' he yelled. 'I'm going to *get* him!'

He stumbled to the glass door, slid it open with a clang, rushed inside.

'My, my,' Turk Bending said happily. 'It's turning out to be quite an evening.'

He and Holloway watched the antics of the palmetto bug. It moved in quick rushes, tacking back and forth, but heading toward the opened glass door.

'Let him go,' Bending said, laughing. 'He gets inside, Luther will burn down the house.'

'Maybe we ought to kill it,' Holloway said.

'Naw,' Bending said. 'Give Luther that pleasure. He probably went for a hammer.'

Not a hammer. Empt came charging back onto the terrace. He held a flashlight in one hand. In the other, he brandished an enormous revolver, heavy, polished, wicked.

'Holy Christ!' Turk Bending said.

He and Holloway struggled out of their chairs.

'Where is he?' Luther screamed. 'Where? I'll blow that bastard to hell. Where did he go?'

He switched on the flashlight, swept the beam about. The palmetto bug darted out from under Empt's fallen chair, scuttled swiftly, disappeared over the lip of the terrace.

'I'll get him, I'll get him!' Empt yelled, and went pounding down the steps to the beach.

The other two men rushed after him.

'Get it away from him,' Bending said to Bill Holloway. 'That cannon's a three-five-seven Magnum. He'll blow his fucking leg off.'

'*You* get it away from him,' Holloway said. 'The man's demented.'

By the time they hit the beach, Luther was searching around the sand and coconut palm roots near the seawall. He was bent over, stalking the bug.

'Come on, you fucker,' he growled. 'Come on, you little piece of shit. Show your ugly head.'

In the beam of the flashlight they saw the bug run swiftly from the wall toward the open sea. Luther Empt aimed and fired. It sounded like a bomb.

A spurt of sand sprayed up in front of the sprinting bug. It changed direction, began zigzagging back toward the seawall.

'Luther,' Bending yelled, 'you're too drunk to hit the ocean. Gimme that goddamned piece.'

But Empt went blundering after the bug. Finally it halted, feelers moving wildly. The hunter approached cautiously, lowered his gun until the muzzle was a few inches from the bug. He pulled the trigger.

The bomb went off again. The sand exploded. The bug was gone. There was a small crater in the beach.

'Got him!' Luther Empt shrieked triumphantly. 'I got him! Did you see that? I blew that fucker away!'

'Give me that,' William Jasper Holloway said, twisting the revolver from Empt's grasp. 'Just give me the gun, Luther.'

The weapon was unexpectedly solid, heavy in his grasp. Holloway flourished it over his head.

'Hey, hey!' he shouted. 'Look at me! I'm John Wayne. Watch out, you lousy varmints. I'll blow you away!'

He went capering down the beach, waving the revolver over his head, laughing and hiccuping.

'Oh for God's sake,' Bending groaned, and ran after him.

Holloway sprinted for about twenty yards, then stopped, panting. He brandished the gun. It felt like a piece of fine machinery, oiled and efficient. He looked around for a suitable target.

His head tilted back. He saw the lemon moon still riding the night sky. He raised a wavering arm, tried to sight on that glowing sphere.

'Goodbye, moon,' he screamed, and pulled the trigger.

The jolt traveled down hand, wrist, arm, shoulder. The gun went flying up, free, and then into the sand.

'You fucking idiot!' Turk Bending yelled at him, coming up and grabbing the revolver. 'You're lucky if you didn't sink a boat on the Intracoastal. Now do everyone a favor and go home. I'll get Luther to bed.'

He stalked off, carrying the gun. Holloway stood swaying in the darkness, looking up to where the moon cruised on calmly, untouched.

'Goodbye, moon,' he repeated softly.

He looked around, recognized dimly where he was, and went staggering toward his own house. Once he fell, going down onto hands and knees on the sand.

'Good Lord,' he said aloud, 'I *am* drunk.'

On the beach in front of his home, he decided to go into the sea. Just dunk, not swim. Just get wet and cold and sober. He went floundering down to the water. Fully dressed, still wearing his moccasins, he waded into the Atlantic Ocean. It wasn't all that cold, but it shocked him awake. He didn't try to swim or even to paddle. He just waded steadily, trying to stay upright, moving out until the water was up to his neck, and waves were smacking his face.

He blinked, gasped, spluttered, spat. He shook his head. Unaccountably, he felt to make certain his soaked wallet was still on his hip.

He spread his arms, rose a few inches from the sandy bottom, then came back down as waves passed under him. He bobbed and bobbed, seeing the soft tropical night, the black sea stretching forever.

Suddenly he thought he might wade on. To England, or Portugal, or Africa. Just walk until the salt was in his mouth, nose, his eyes, and his hair would float free. He would just walk into it, striding purposefully until it took him.

He was close to it, close, but a larger wave spun him, arms pinwheeling, and he saw the lights of land, of his own home.

Straining, bending forward, he waded to shore. There was an undertow, not strong, but enough so that he felt the fingers pulling him back. He pushed against it, lifting his knees higher.

He came plunging out of the surf, stumbled, fell, stood, scuttled onward just like that poor, doomed bug. Then he was on dry sand, dripping, chest heaving, the lights of home a blur through a film of salt. The sea and his own tears.

He tried for a sob, but all he could manage was a giggle.

4

Teresa Empt, contained and glacial, came out onto the terrace shortly after midnight. She closed the glass door to the darkened living room carefully behind her. She lifted and straightened the canvas sling chair her husband had overturned.

She stood at the terrace railing – fancifully ornamental ironwork salvaged from the balcony of a demolished New Orleans bordello. A white nylon peignoir whipped about her long legs. The night wind had an edge, smelled crisply of salt.

Sky swept of clouds. Stars glittering. White froth rimming the ocean. Palm fronds rustled steadily, a sibilant whisper. It seemed to her that she might be the last person on earth.

It had been what she termed a gauche evening. Definitely gauche. Early on, she had played backgammon with her mother-in-law. Gertrude persisted in calling her 'Dearie.' There wasn't much Teresa could do about that, but Gertrude had compounded her offensiveness by winning three games.

Teresa Empt did not take losing lightly.

She had been aware of the three men drinking on the terrace. Bragging about their business deals, she supposed, and telling their coarse jokes. Once Luther had come through the living room for more whiskey and more ice. He didn't speak to his wife or mother.

Then, later, after Gertrude had gone off to bed, Teresa had curled up on the couch. She sipped sherry from a Baccarat glass and leafed through a copy of *Vogue*.

Suddenly there was a crash from the terrace. She looked up to see the door flung open. Her husband came charging through, his face wrenched with fury.

'Luther –' she had started, but he had paid no attention to her.

He reappeared a few moments later, carrying a flashlight and a gun. The revolver, she knew, was kept in the desk of his downstairs study.

'Luther –' she said again, and again he paid no heed.

She thought he looked murderous. She rose gracefully to her feet. She stood motionless, one hand clenched over her heart. She heard shouts and, a few minutes later, the sound of two shots. A few minutes after that, there was a third explosion, this one fainter.

He's dead. That was her first reaction: Luther was shot and dead. She thought immediately that she'd have to buy black. She had no suitable black gowns in her wardrobe, and knew she'd have to shop on Worth Avenue for something elegant.

But then Luther and Turk Bending came stumbling in from the terrace. Bending was carrying the gun, and had one arm about her husband's waist, half-supporting him and dragging him forward. Bending was grinning.

He told her everything was all right, no one had been hurt. Luther had just been shooting at a palmetto bug. Bending said he'd get her husband to bed. She watched the two drunken fools go staggering up the stairs. Then she went to the marble-topped sideboard and poured herself another sherry.

When Bending came downstairs, he reported that he had dumped Luther onto his bed, and had taken off his shoes, but not undressed him. She thanked Turk, but didn't offer him a drink. After he left, she had turned off the lights and wandered out onto the terrace.

It wasn't the first time her husband had behaved in such a crude manner. She knew why she endured it. The answer was simple: this place was paradise. *Paradise*.

She was from Iron Mountain, Michigan. It was an ugly, brutally frigid place where all the women read confession magazines, watched Phil Donahue on television, and exchanged recipes for Apple Pan Dowdy.

Her first husband was a dear, sweet man, and a totally ineffective lover. When he died unexpectedly of a heart attack at the age of thirty-eight, she had been agreeably surprised to find herself heiress to almost a half-million dollars in Triple-A-rated commercial bonds and tax exempt municipals.

Her husband had not accumulated this fortune; he had been an only child who inherited, and now it was all hers. She moved immediately to Florida.

She knew at once it was paradise, the place she wanted to spend the remainder of her life. The only drawback was the equivocal status of unattached women of her age in south Florida; there were so *many* widows and divorcees. She was not accorded the respect and admiration to which she felt her beauty and wealth entitled her.

She met Luther Empt at a cocktail party following a polo match in Palm Beach. He asked her to dinners and beach parties several times. She did not think him physically repulsive, exactly, but he certainly wasn't her type. She accepted his invitations because she enjoyed the almost forgotten experience of being squired.

Never would she admit to herself that she was lonely.

When it became evident that his attentions were more than casual, she wisely had him investigated by a private detective agency that specialized in discreet inquiries of that nature.

Everything he had told her turned out to be true: He was in the process of obtaining his second divorce. He had a total of five children by his two wives, all the children in custody of their mothers.

His net worth was estimated at slightly less than $300,000, but he owned his own successful business, producing and processing training and educational films. He had the reputation of being a hard, shrewd businessman who was willing to gamble on his hunches.

There was talk, the investigator reported, that Luther Empt hoped to expand into producing and processing video cassettes and disks. But his plan required more capital than local banks were willing to lend on his current assets.

In the end, it was not his energy, wealth or business acumen that persuaded her to accept his proposal; it was the overgrown acre of beachfront property and the rather ramshackle home he owned south of Boca Raton.

She saw at once what could be done with it. She could create a showplace. That home could become one of the glories of Florida's Gold Coast, a palace in which even the ashtrays would reflect her impeccable taste.

When the proposal came, she was ready with a list of demands. It was more a meeting of lawyers than of lovers. Her conditions:

It was to be a sexless marriage; they would have separate bedrooms. He would be allowed complete freedom with the proviso that his extramarital affairs were conducted with discretion and resulted in no public scandal.

The refurbishing of the home and grounds were to be totally her responsibility, with no interference on his part. The renovation expenses were to be split fifty-fifty. Running the household, including the hiring and firing of servants, was also to be in her domain.

In return, she agreed to cosign his notes, putting up her bonds as collateral. However, these securities would remain in her name, and the income therefrom, approximately $50,000 annually, would be hers alone. In addition, he would provide $25,000 a year for day-to-day household expenses.

He accepted these harsh terms with remarkable alacrity. He made only one counter demand: that his widowed mother be allowed to continue to reside in the beachfront home. After several moments of consideration, Teresa assented.

All in all, this marital contract worked out well. Luther's business was expanded and flourished. The house was redone with a new red tile roof. An Olympic-size swimming pool was installed. Slowly, over a period of several years, the showplace was created. Teresa was satisfied with the results of her labors.

The presence of Luther's mother, though frequently annoying, had proved to be less of a burden than anticipated. Gertrude, a short, plump, roguish woman, rarely interfered in the redecoration or domestic routine of her son's home. Teresa was the acknowledged mistress of the Empt villa, except in bed.

In this area, Luther had kept his word. He never physically forced himself upon her. In public, his demeanor towards her was as affectionate and gallant as his rude nature allowed.

Soon after their marriage, Teresa had learned from commiserating friends that Luther had been seen here, there, everywhere with a variety of women known in south Florida as 'creamers': young, nubile, tanned, addicted to the skimpiest of string bikinis and obscene T-shirts.

None of these liaisons seemed to last long, and as Teresa accumulated the testimony of witnesses, she came to realize what Luther was doing: he was hiring a succession of professional and semiprofessional bodies, paying for his pleasure but forming no lasting relationship.

Teresa approved.

Her own sex life was somewhat more complex. She had recognized since youth that she was not as intensely sexual as other girls her age.

But she was not totally without physical passion. Since moving to Florida, she had been conscious of a growing thaw. An ice dam was melting. The blazing sun, sapphire sea, caressing breeze, glimmering beach – all worked subtly to free her repressed appetite.

Now she masturbated briskly every Tuesday afternoon following her weekly visit to the beauty salon where she had her long sable hair shampooed and styled. And a manicure, pedicure, and bikini wax treatment.

More than that, she found herself strangely and powerfully attracted to Edward Holloway, the sixteen-year-old son of Jane and Bill. She was shrewd enough to realize that at his age, he was probably as unsophisticated sexually as she. That was part of his appeal.

But mostly it was his physical beauty that stirred her. Tall and muscular, but slender, he wore his sun-bleached blond hair almost shoulder-length. He moved with careless grace. His bronzed skin had the look of satin: soft, gleaming. It would be a delight to feel. To taste?

She had watched from this very terrace as he rode his surfboard. The nimble body crouched, long hair flung in the wind, body glistening with spray. She thought he would smell fresh and young, uncorrupted. Fantasies bloomed.

So Teresa Empt, standing on the balcony of her palace, alone in the darkness, dreamed her febrile dreams. And all about her the fertile land seemed choked with the scent of growing things. The nurturing ocean was there, the sweet wind, endless sky.

She left paradise reluctantly to retire to her empty bed. But the vision went with her. Of beauty, youth, and hope. Naked in her locked bedroom, she felt firm breasts and tight thighs. She thought she might be blossoming like some tropical plant: brilliantly colored, scented, turning toward the quickening light.

5

Dr Theodore Levin rose to his feet when Lucy Bending came into his office – which was more than he had done for her parents. He thought her the most beautiful little girl he had ever seen. No, not a little girl. A miniature woman.

Shapely. Tall for her age. No evident baby fat. Clear, almost luminous features, with an enchanting smile of bright innocence. Long, flaxen hair without curl or wave. Her skin was particularly limpid.

She had a quality of steady repose, with a look of alert attention. Eyes a bluish-gray. Lips full and artfully bowed: a burning carmine. Her movements were well-coordinated, almost precise. She exhibited no signs of fear, resentment, or petulance.

Dr Levin found himself smiling broadly.

'Please sit here, Lucy,' he said hastily, gesturing toward the chair alongside his desk.

'Thank you,' she said. The voice was clear, low-pitched, without quaver.

'Comfortable?' he asked.

'Oh yes.'

He leaned forward to inspect her. She was wearing a party frock of eyelet cotton lined with blue. A darker blue sash encircled her waist. Bracelet of small auger shells. Strapped sandals of white leather over anklets. She carried a small plastic purse on a brass chain.

'I like your dress, Lucy,' he said.

She looked down as if surprised, plucked at her ribbon sash. 'Oh, this old thing . . .'

47

He sighed, settled back in his swivel chair. He reached into the open desk drawer, switched on the tape recorder.

'Lucy,' he said, 'I know you've been to a doctor several times. In fact, it was Doctor Raskob who suggested I see you. Do you like Doctor Raskob?'

She smiled sweetly. 'He's so funny. He gives me a lollipop every time I see him.'

'Does he now?'

'I never told him, but I hate lollipops. They rot your teeth. So when Doctor David gives me a lollipop, I take it home and give it to Harry. He's my kid brother. He loves lollipops. He's so fat.'

Dr Levin straightened in his chair. 'Well now, you make me feel a little better because I have no lollipops to give you.'

'That's all right. I'm too old for lollipops.'

'But I *am* a doctor, a special kind of doctor.'

'I know that. You're a shrink.'

'Where did you learn that word, Lucy?'

She looked around the office curiously. 'Oh, I don't know . . . All the kids use it. Like a witch doctor, you know, who shrinks people's heads. That's why they call them shrinks.'

'I hope you don't think I'm a witch doctor who shrinks people's heads.'

'Oh no. That's silly. My goodness, you can't shrink a person's *head*.'

'Of course not. What I do, Lucy, is talk to children, just talk, and if they have any problems, then sometimes by talking we can solve them.'

'I don't have any problems.'

'Well then, that's a problem *I* have, and I hope you'll be able to help *me* solve it. You see, your parents feel something is bothering you, and they asked me to talk to you about it.'

She looked at him steadily. 'Nothing is bothering me.'

'Lucy, you love your mother and father, don't you?'

48

'Of course.'

'And you know they love you?'

'Sure.'

'And because they love you, they want you to be happy and grow up to be a beautiful, healthy, well-adjusted woman. You know what "well-adjusted" means, don't you?'

'It means you don't have any problems.'

'Well . . . not exactly. Everyone has problems. But being well-adjusted means that you're able to handle your problems, to solve them by yourself. Now your parents feel you *do* have a problem. Can you guess what it might be?'

She frowned, blinked, bit her lower lip. She lowered her head, stared intently at her dangling feet. Then she looked up, her face cleared. She beamed at him. He thought she might be a consummate actress, but he could not be sure.

'Oh, I know what it is,' she said. 'I bet I know. They're always after me about it. They think I love too much. Isn't that silly?'

'What do you mean by love too much?'

She did not reply. Her eyes drifted away to the painted wall, the bookcase of toys and games, up to the pasted stars. Dr Levin waited patiently for a full minute, then tried again . . .

'Well, Lucy? You haven't answered my question.'

Her eyes came back to him. She tilted her head. 'Your name is Theodore, isn't it?'

'Yes. My first name.'

'Theodore,' she said, giggling. 'That's a funny name.'

'I agree! But most of my friends call me Ted.'

'Can I call you Doctor Ted?'

'Of course. I'd like that.'

'If your friends call you Ted, and I call you Doctor Ted, that makes us friends, doesn't it?'

'I'd like very much to be friends with you.'

'Me, too.'

Silence again. She raised both hands and swept her long,

49

softly gleaming hair back from her temples. Then she shook her head to let the tresses fall freely down her back. The movements were graceful, lovely, so pure it was difficult to think of them as coquettish or provocative.

'You haven't answered my question, Lucy,' he said gently. 'What did you mean when you said your parents think you love too much?'

'Oh . . . you know,' she said vaguely. 'Just being nice.'

'Are you nice to everyone?'

'Oh no. Not everyone. Some people are mean and spiteful.'

'Can you give me some examples – of people who are mean and spiteful?'

'Mrs Gower at Sunday School – she's always yelling at us kids, and she never smiles.'

'Anyone else?'

'Miss Mackinroydt at the library. She gets mad when we, uh, you know, sort of whisper.'

'Do you know any men who are mean and spiteful?'

She considered that. 'Nooo,' she said thoughtfully, 'not really. I can't think of any men who are mean and spiteful. Just women.'

'So you can be nice to men?'

'Oh sure. I like some of them better than others but, well, you know . . .'

'Do you kiss the men you like?'

'Well,' she said, lowering her eyes and smiling secretly, 'some of them are so funny and sweet, I wouldn't mind kissing them.'

'Lucy, does it embarrass you when I ask you questions like that – about kissing?'

She was startled. 'Of course not. Why should it?'

'No reason. I'm glad it doesn't. But hasn't your mother spoken to you about kissing boys?'

'I don't kiss boys,' she said primly. 'Except my brothers, of course. But those don't count. Those are just family kisses.'

'But you kiss men?'

'Sometimes.'

'Did your parents tell you that you might be annoying the men you kiss?'

'They told me, but I don't see how.'

'Do you touch men, Lucy? Stroke them?'

'You mean like petting? Yes, it's so funny; they get all red and giggly. Like tickling – you know?'

'Do you think the men enjoy the, ah, tickling?'

'Oh yes.'

'Do *you* enjoy it? Doing it?'

'I like to love people.'

'Men, Lucy. Mostly you like to love men.'

'Yes, Doctor Ted,' she said seriously, 'that's true.'

He tried hard to remain expressionless, but didn't quite succeed. Her innocent frankness had a perfume, a scent of sweet youth, flowers, and an unspoiled world. For the first time, he wondered if corruption might be part of his job.

'You know, Lucy,' he said, 'some people – some men don't like to be touched.'

'I don't see why not.'

'Some men are like that; they just don't want to be touched. Do you have your own bedroom, Lucy?'

'Of course.'

'How would you like it if someone, say your brother, came into your bedroom and rummaged through all your private things? You wouldn't like that, would you?'

'I wouldn't care.'

'Most people would. We want a certain part of our lives to be private. We want to hold back a little bit of ourselves, *for* ourselves. Don't you ever want to be alone?'

'All alone? By myself?'

'Yes.'

'No, Doctor Ted, I don't believe I do. I don't like being by myself.'

'Does it frighten you?'

'I just don't like it.'

'Are you frightened when you sleep by yourself?'

'Well, my goodness, that's *sleeping*. So how can you be frightened?'

He envied her. His own sleep was a wrestle with terror. Al Wollman, his occasional analyst, had suggested that his dread of sleep was a fear of losing control over his reasoned, structured life. Levin thought that a simplistic explanation.

One of his worries sprang from his acknowledgment of psychiatrists' high suicide rate. Most laymen, he supposed, believed psychiatrists fell apart under the weight of other people's problems.

Dr Theodore Levin had another theory.

He feared that a psychiatrist's life force gradually leaked out. It was expended on sympathy, understanding, the obsessive need to heal and help create whole lives. Other people's lives. But always from the outside. Always the observer. Then one day he would wake up and discover that he himself was empty, drained.

That was one reason Levin did not welcome sleep. The horror persisted that he might awake to find himself a hollow man.

'Have you ever had bad dreams, Lucy?' he asked.

'I used to, when I was a little kid, but I don't anymore.'

'Are you getting tired of this? Are we talking too much?'

'Oh no. I like this. I like you.'

'Thank you. I like you, too. I really want to help you, Lucy.'

'I'm sure you do, but I don't know how. I mean, I really don't need any help. Do I?'

'Let's get back to what we were talking about before . . . Suppose a man came to visit at your house. A friend of your parents. Would you be nice to him?'

'If he wasn't mean and spiteful, I would.'

'You'd pet him? And kiss him?'

'Yes, and love him.'

'Would you sit on his lap?'

'I might.'

'Why would you do that?'

'Because it's nice and cuddly. I like that.'

'Would you touch him between his legs?'

'I might.'

'Why would you do that?'

'That's when men get red and giggly, like I said. They like it.'

'How do you know?'

'I just know.'

He stared at her. There was a surety about her that daunted him. He had never before seen it in one so young. Her mother had called her 'poised.' She was more than that; she was knowing and certain.

In addition to her flirtatiousness, he thought he detected an unadmirable slyness about her. It wasn't as deliberate as deceit, but there was a foxiness beyond her years. He didn't want to imagine how age and experience might enlarge and fix this gift of cunning.

He asked: 'Do you know what men have between their legs, Lucy?'

'Of course, silly.'

'What do they have?'

'A peter and nuts.'

'How do you know that?'

'*Everyone* knows that. My goodness, Doctor Ted, I'm not a child.'

'Has your mother told you how babies are born, Lucy?'

'Some. And some I learned in school. And some the other kids talked about.'

'Suppose you tell me, Lucy – how does a baby get born?'

'Don't you know?'

'I'd like you to tell me.'

'Well, a man has this peter between his legs, and he puts it in the hole between his wife's legs, and then a baby comes out.'

'Has a man ever tried to put his peter in your hole, Lucy?'

'That's silly! My goodness, I'm not old enough to be a wife.'

He could not decide if that was the ingenuous reply of a female child of eight, or the ironic answer of a mature woman. There was nothing in her wide blue eyes to suggest that she might be mocking him. Still . . .

'But you like to touch a man's peter?'

'Sometimes. If he's nice. I don't see what's wrong with it.'

'Did I say it was wrong, Lucy?'

'Well . . . my mother is always saying it's wrong.'

'And your father?'

'Sometimes. But mostly my mother.'

'Do you trust me, Lucy?'

'Trust you?'

'Do you think I'd lie to you?'

'Nooo . . .'

'If I told you that kissing men and touching them the way you do is wrong, would you believe me?'

'Well . . . you'd have to prove it.'

'I see. Lucy, I think we'll end this now. I want to tell you that I've enjoyed meeting you, and I thank you for answering all my questions so honestly.'

'Will I see you again, Doctor Ted?'

'I'll let your mother know. She'll tell you.'

'I hope I see you again. You're very nice. Your beard is so funny.'

'Why is it funny?'

'It's so bristly. You're not mad at me, are you? Because I said your beard is funny and bristly?'

'Of course I'm not mad at you. It *is* funny and bristly.'

'I love you, Doctor Ted.'

6

Their combined age was more than a century and a half –
but they were peppery. Scoundrels, both of them.

'Good morning, Gertrude,' Professor Lloyd Craner
called, tipping his white, wide-brimmed Panama hat.

She looked up at him and grunted.

He leaned elegantly on his cane, punched into the dry
sand. She was grubbing about in the surf with a long-
handled net. Her legs and feet were bare. The hem of her
skirt was sodden, but she didn't care.

'Shelling again, I see,' he observed.

'No,' she said, 'I dropped a dime, and I'm looking for it.
Wanna help?'

He smiled genially and gazed out to sea. A dazzling
morning. But a solid block of rain, about two miles out, was
moving slowly southward.

'Ten-minute squall out there,' he said.

Gertrude Empt glanced up, shaded her eyes, stared.

'It'll miss us, perfesser. Probably hit Lighthouse Point or
Pompano Beach.'

She came trudging out of the ocean, carrying her net and
a plastic grocery bag.

'Any luck?' he asked.

'Half-a-dozen whelks. Four olives. A couple of nicked
sea fans.'

When she came closer, he hefted her bag of treasures,
peering at the wet shells.

'I'll take the brown olive,' he said.

'Fat chance,' she said, and he laughed.

They strolled along together. Without shoes, she barely came to his shoulder. Beneath her loose, flower-printed shift, her body was stocky, tanned, firm. He had seen her in a bathing suit. He had noticed.

Her skin had the translucent purity some fortunate older women achieve: a smooth porcelain gloss. Her dark brown eyes were snappy. Gray, wiry hair was pulled back with a barrette. Her teeth were her own, and she showed them frequently in a wisenheimer grin.

'Beautiful morning,' he offered.

'They're all beautiful,' she said.

They paused to watch two early-morning joggers go pounding by. The woman was in her late twenties, tall, erect, lithe, and muscular. Her companion was a potbellied older man, bandy-legged. His face was reddened with effort, his chest pumped in and out as he strained.

'He's ready for cardiac arrest,' Professor Craner commented.

'A lot of shitheads in Florida,' Gertrude Empt said.

'True,' he agreed. 'But then there are a lot of shitheads everywhere. One must pick and choose one's companions.'

She glanced at him a moment. 'If you say so, perfesser.'

They sauntered on, stooping to examine a dead blue that had been savaged by barracudas. There was a piece of timber covered with barnacles; a cork float that had once been painted red; a clump of bleached coquinas that weren't worth picking up.

'Looks like we'll get a raise in Social Security next summer,' he said.

'Looks like,' she said. 'The more the merrier.'

'How's your health?' he asked suddenly.

She stopped, and so he stopped. She turned to face him, her expression boldly scornful.

'I know you old Florida geezers,' she said. 'The next thing you'll be telling me about your BM.'

'I'd never mention it,' he assured her. 'I was just making a polite inquiry about how you're feeling.'

'Hah,' she said.

They strolled on.

'I'm feeling fine,' she said finally. 'Thanks. You?'

'Tip-top,' he said. 'You happy living in your son's home?'

'What's this?' she demanded. 'Twenty Questions?'

'Just trying to make conversation,' he said mildly.

'Am I happy in my son's home?' she repeated. She flipped a palm back and forth. 'So-so. Are you happy living in your daughter's home?'

'So-so,' he said. 'I like Bill. Still, it's not like having my own home.'

'I know what you mean, perfesser,' she said. 'Boy, do I know.'

'I get a pension,' he said, staring straight ahead. 'Almost four hundred a month. In addition to Social Security.'

'I got a nice block of Ma Bell,' she countered. 'Not a lot, but enough to make me feel independent.'

'That's the way I'd like to be,' he said. 'Independent.'

She gazed up at the pellucid sky.

'Not many cheap rental properties around,' she said thoughtfully.

'Not many,' he said, nodding. 'But when you get off the beach, on the other side of the waterway, there are reasonable places. Some of them not so bad. And sometimes you can work out a deal with a motel on an annual rate. I've been looking into it.'

She stopped again, and again he stopped. They faced each other challengingly.

'What are you getting at?' she said.

'You,' he said.

She stared at him. 'What would I want with an old fart like you?'

'Beats the hell out of me,' he said.

She laughed and punched his arm lightly.

'You're okay, perfesser. I'll think on it.'
'Do that,' he urged.
Before they parted, she gave him the brown olive.

7

Saturday morning dawned blunt, the sky oysterish, with a variable wind at fifteen knots. The sea was choppy. Rain clouds scudded across the horizon, and a waterspout was reported off Delray Beach. There was talk of canceling the Holloways' cookout.

But then, toward 11:00 A.M., patches of blue showed, the sun burned through. The temperature rose to 84° F, and pelicans appeared. The wind still gusted, but now it was welcome. Someone said a shark had been sighted off Boynton Beach, but no one got out of the sea.

The festivities started on the beach shortly before noon, mostly for the children, with hot dogs, Cokes, and junk food available on the Holloway terrace. The Holloway and Bending kids were there, of course, and about twenty others from up and down the beach. Most were in the eight-to-fourteen age group. A few younger, a few older.

Wayne Bending, twelve, was the first one out, carrying his short surfboard with a nylon cord to be attached to his ankle. He was wearing cutoff jeans, sun-bleached and sea-faded. He propped his board against a palm and hunkered down in the sand to wait.

He watched his brother and sister wander over. Harold, five, was carrying his newest electronic game. It was programmed with song melodies, and the crazy kid stood in the middle of the beach punching buttons like mad.

Lucy stepped delicately down to the water and stuck in a tentative toe. She turned toward Wayne and did a burlesque shiver. Which was a lot of bullshit, Wayne knew; the water still held its summer heat.

Wayne Bending acknowledged his sister's physical beauty. He also knew she was as nutty as a fruitcake. And so was his kid brother, Harry. And so were his mother and father. The whole Bending family, Wayne reflected mournfully, was nutty – and that probably included him.

He looked up the beach and saw Mrs Empt come out on her terrace. She was wearing a white two-piece bathing suit. Not a bikini, but her belly button showed. It was, Wayne knew, an insy.

When he looked in the other direction, he saw Eddie Holloway coming toward him, trailed by his kid sister, Gloria. She was only a year older than Lucy, but she was wearing the world's smallest bikini; the bottom part looked like an eyepatch.

Gloria went down to the water to join Lucy who, at her mother's insistence, was wearing a modest one-piece suit in a peppermint stripe. The two girls immediately began whispering and giggling. Wayne looked away in disgust.

Edward Holloway came up and leaned his surfboard next to Wayne's.

'Doesn't look fabulous,' he said, jerking his chin toward the ocean.

'Not what I'd call incredible,' Wayne agreed.

Eddie sat down alongside him and took a pack of cigarettes from the hip pocket of his surfing trunks. They lighted up and puffed importantly. Wayne craned around to stare at the Empts' terrace.

'She's there again,' he reported. 'Mrs Empt. Looking at you with binoculars.'

'Silly bitch,' Eddie Holloway said, combing his long blond hair with his fingers.

'She's hot to trot,' Wayne assured him.

'If her brain was as big as her tits,' Eddie said, 'she'd be a genius.'

The two boys laughed and pushed each other. They finished their cigarettes, watching the other kids coming straggling from homes up and down the beach. They inspected the girls coldly.

'Who do you like, Eddie?' Wayne asked.

'Barbara Fleming. That diaper suit turns me on. She's ripening nicely. Give her another year . . .'

'How about Sue Ann?'

'All ass, no jugs. Jesus, this is going to be a dull day with all those brats around.'

'Imfuckingpossible,' Wayne said, nodding.

'Let's give the drink a try,' Eddie said, flicking his cigarette butt away. 'It looks like shit, but you never can tell.'

They carried their boards down to the ocean and paddled out. But the waves were too short and choppy for a decent ride. So they came back to their palm tree. They grabbed a Frisbee away from one of the younger kids, spun it back and forth for a while, then gave up.

'Wait here,' Eddie Holloway said. 'Be right back.'

He went to the rear of his own home and returned in a few minutes with four cold cans of beer wrapped in a towel.

'I say, old boy,' Wayne Bending said. 'Good show.'

'Any experienced cat burglar could have done it,' Eddie said, shrugging. 'The drunks are beginning to gather back there.'

They popped the tabs, and sipped their beers solemnly, belching occasionally. Most of the kids had gathered on the Holloway terrace, and were wolfing hot dogs and stuffing their mouths with potato chips, cheese crisps, and cream-filled cup-cakes.

'Wanna frank?' Eddie asked. 'There's plenty. With pickles, onions, relish, and all that crap.'

'What're you having tonight?' Wayne asked.

'Steaks.'

'I'll wait for that. I'm not hungry right now. The beer and all . . .'

'Yeah,' Eddie agreed. 'Beer bloats you. I prefer a good scotch and Pepsi any day, but I've got to sneak it. Listen,

61

kiddo, this day is going to be a disaster; I can feel it. After dinner, suppose I clip a couple of joints and we turn on?'

'Suits me. Can you get them okay?'

'Sure. When my mother is busy with the party. She keeps a dozen or so in her diaphragm case. She'll never miss a couple. This is top-grade grass, the real stuff. We'll fly.'

'Sounds good,' Wayne Bending said. 'When?'

'I'll give you the signal and we'll cut out.'

'Whatever you say, Eddie.'

They opened their second beers. They watched Teresa Empt walk slowly along the beach in her two-piece suit. Her long black hair swung loosely down her back. She didn't turn her head to look at them.

'You gotta admit, Eddie,' Wayne said, 'it's not a bad piece.'

'Good lungs,' Eddie admitted, 'but who needs it? I wonder if she gives head?'

'Would you like a little of that?'

'Depends,' Edward Holloway said judiciously. 'Maybe once. For laughs.'

'I gotta pee,' Wayne said.

'Let's take a swim and you can piss in the ocean. The fish won't mind. Then we'll go around to the pool and see what the old farts are up to.'

Adults began gathering about 3:00 P.M. in the pool and patio area between the Holloway home and highway A1A. A rank growth of tropical foliage hid the party from the road. By 4:00 P.M., there were eight cars parked on the crushed shell driveway, and there were a dozen people in the pool.

Maria, who had not been fired, was serving, along with John Stewart Wellington, the Empts' black houseman who had been borrowed for the occasion and who insisted on being addressed by his full name.

By 5:00 P.M., most of the kids had moved around to the pool from the beach. Jane Holloway had invited twenty adults and had ordered enough food to feed thirty, knowing how friends liked to bring friends. Some of the guests also brought bottles, and some brought chilled mangoes, melons, or pastries.

The bar, set up under a big umbrella on the patio, had the usual selection of whiskeys, mixers, and soft drinks. Beer and wine were also available, and there was a large pitcher of strawberry piña colada and one of the banana daiquiris. Bill Holloway served as bartender, and was his own best customer.

Some of the adults who had been in the pool went into the house to change back into slacks or shorts and shirts, but many men and women continued wearing their bathing suits. The bar began to get a big play. A few of the men clustered around a portable TV set to watch the last quarter of the Hurricanes' game.

There were bowls of potato chips, salted peanuts, chunks of sharp cheddar, and a tub of iced olives, radishes, carrot sticks, cherry tomatoes, cucumber chunks, peppers, celery stalks. At 6:00 P.M., John Stewart Wellington brought out an enormous platter with five pounds of boiled and peeled shrimp on a bed of crushed ice.

A caterer had been hired to prepare and serve the dinner, which would consist of broiled New York strip steaks, baked yams, and a mixed green salad with hearts of palm. The caterer's truck arrived at 7:00 P.M. The chef, wearing a high toque blanche, began to spread charcoal in the Holloways' brick barbecue.

Jane Holloway, having planned and arranged for all this, left the work to the hired hands and mingled with her guests on the patio, in the pool, at the bar. She detested domestic chores and intended to enjoy her own party.

She was wearing a maillot of black stretch nylon, cut very high on the thighs and very low in back. She was sleek and shiny as a seal. During the afternoon she drank Perrier water with a lime squeeze. Then she switched to white wine.

About 5:30, Ronald Bending sought her out and held a

light for one of the thin brown cigarillos she habitually smoked.

'Good party,' he said.

'Is it?' she said, looking around. 'I guess. Thanks for bringing the shrimp. Was that Grace's idea?'

'That's right,' he said, smiling. 'I wanted to bring booze. How about you and me taking a walk down to the beach?'

She looked at him with wide, unblinking eyes. 'Why would I want to do that?'

'Something I want to talk to you about,' he said. 'Won't take long. A few minutes.'

She considered a moment. 'All right. It'll give your wife something to worry about.'

He followed her along the chattahoochee walk that led from the patio around the house to the beach. He watched her haunches move slinkily under the smooth suit. He watched the ripple of muscles in the backs of her thighs, the way her suave calves bulged. Nice, he thought. Really nice.

They waded into the ocean up to their knees, and watched a flotilla of sailboats beat against the wind. There was no one nearby in the sea, no watchers on the shore.

'Well?' she asked.

'Listen, Jane,' he said hoarsely, 'have you got any joints?'

'Jesus Christ!' she said wrathfully. 'Is that what you dragged me out here to talk about?'

'No, no,' he said hastily. 'That's not it. But it just occurred to me I might like a toke later, and I'm out.'

She sighed. 'I've got some upstairs. I'll get you one after dinner.'

'Thank you,' he said gratefully. 'I'll pay you back. Jane, did Bill tell you anything about Luther Empt's proposition? When we went to his place for drinks?'

'The shootout at the O.K. Corral?' she said. 'The whole beach heard about that. Bill's going to buy a gun.'

'You're kidding!'

'No, he really is. He told me so.'

'What the hell for?'

She shrugged.

'Maybe he wants to take another shot at the moon,' Bending said.

'Maybe.'

'Did he tell you what Luther wanted?'

'He blabbed something about processing movie films or tape cassettes. I really wasn't listening. He wasn't making much sense. I've never seen him so stoned.'

'Luther's got an offer from some mob guys to process their pornographic video cassettes.'

'Oh-ho.'

'He wants to set up a corporation. Him, me, and Bill. Equal shares. A quarter of a million each. Plus a loan from the mob to total a million capital. Did Bill show you the presentation Luther made up?'

'No.'

'Well, Luther gave him a copy. Get a look at it. Jane, it's a gold mine. More money than you've ever dreamed of.'

'What about the legal angle?'

'Minimal risk,' Bending said. 'That's what the lawyers claim. We wouldn't be producing the stuff or distributing it or selling it. Just processing it. A mechanical job.'

'So?' she said. 'Why are you telling me about it?'

'You know Bill – he needs nudging. You can talk him into it. Hassle him. Jane, I want to get in on this, and we need Bill. My God, he can afford it. Easily. You know that.'

She sloshed around in the shallows, walking in circles, her head down. Her arms were folded. She gripped her elbows.

She looked up at him suddenly. 'What's in it for me?' she demanded.

'Jesus, Jane, you'll be rich!'

'We're already rich.'

'I'm talking about *rich* rich.'

'And I'm talking about what's in it for me personally.

You're talking about *Bill* getting rich. What do I get out of all those big numbers? Me? Personally? If I talk Bill into going along?'

He looked at her admiringly. 'You're a tough cookie.'

She smiled tightly.

'What do you want?' he asked.

'A piece of the cake, a slice of the pie. Not a big piece; I'm not greedy. But *something*.'

'How about like, uh, a finder's fee. Some cash. If Bill comes in.'

'How much?'

'I don't know. I'd have to talk to Luther to see if he'll play along.'

'Before you do that, let me get a look at the presentation to see if it's as good as you say.'

'It's better. Believe me.'

'I'll let you know.'

'Next week? At the motel?'

'Maybe. Give me a call. Now let's get back to the party.'

'Don't forget the joint,' he said, and began plodding after her in the soft sand.

Tables for four were set around the pool deck, with one long trestle table for the children. Tablecloths were paper, but the food was served on stoneware plates. Adults received stainless steel cutlery; the children were provided with plastic implements.

Each table had bowls of salad, condiments, arrangements of fresh hibiscus, crown of thorns, and birds of paradise. There were bottles of wine for the adults, soft drinks for the children.

Eddie Holloway and Wayne Bending had learned how to beat that system a long time ago; they disappeared briefly at regular intervals to fill empty Coke cans with stolen beer. They kept the fake colas in plain view on the table before them. If the younger kids were aware of what was going on, none of them dared snitch.

One of the caterer's men came around with pad and

pencil to take orders: how many rares, medium-rares, and well-dones. The expert barbecuer set to work while a hired accordionist strolled among the tables, playing 'Lady of Spain.'

Eddie Holloway, elaborately bored, sat at the head of the children's table. He had been charged with the job of maintaining discipline among the younger children, but he knew it was a hopeless task. He made no effort to halt the shouting, pushing, or the throwing of food.

Wayne Bending sat next to Eddie. Next to Wayne was his brother, Harry, and Wayne had promised his mother to help Harry cut up his steak. But the nutty kid was such a food freak that he grabbed up his steak and gnawed on it like it was an apple or something. Wayne gave up in disgust.

Most of the boys sat in a group at the head of the table, most of the girls sat side by side at the other end. Gloria Holloway was at the foot of the table with her best friend, Lucy Bending, on her right.

Gloria was a haughty, snippety girl whose dark brown hair was permed once a month into a cap of tight curls. She had a highly developed sense of social caste, but her supercilious manner was somewhat marred by a missing upper incisor.

She was skinnier and bonier than Lucy, and the development of her body had convinced her that she had a splendid career as a high-fashion model awaiting her. But as the two girls ate their dinners, ignoring the tumult about them, Gloria told Lucy she had changed her mind.

'I am going to be a famous actress of stage, screen, and TV,' she announced. 'First of all, you get to travel all over the world, and you can keep the clothes they give you to wear in movies and things. Also, you get all kinds of proposals from rich men, and when you make like, you know, a commercial, well, every time that commercial is on television, you get paid again, so you make millions of dollars.'

'Who told you that?' Lucy asked curiously.

'My father. And he should know.'

'My goodness, I should think so. Being a banker and all.'

Gloria's eyes glazed over, and she leaned close to Lucy.

'Listen,' she said in a low voice, 'last night I came past my parents' bedroom, and they were in there, and the door was closed. I could hear, but not exactly. I mean, I didn't catch all the words. They weren't fighting, but mother's voice was louder. I couldn't hear daddy at all. And I heard mother say, "You're important, you know you're important, so why don't you go to a doctor?" Isn't that strange?'

'Definitely,' Lucy said, chewing her steak thoughtfully. 'Definitely strange. If you're important, why do you have to go to a doctor?'

'I don't know,' Gloria confessed. 'That's why it's so strange. I mean, important people like the president and judges and movie stars and all, they don't have to go to doctors – do they?'

'I don't think so.'

'Well, anyway, that's what I've decided to be: a famous actress. With scads of clothes and all the shoes I want. A bigger house than this old one. With a lot of servants to do the work. You know, cook and clean up and all. Maybe a big boat.'

'And cars,' Lucy added enthusiastically.

'At least two,' Gloria said. 'Maybe more. I'll be married, I suppose, to a very rich man. Older, you know, because he's in love with me. But I'll have boyfriends, too. Do you want the rest of my steak? I can't finish it.'

'No, thanks, I'm full. But pass it up to my brother Harry; he'll eat it. He finishes everyone's food.'

Gloria passed her unfinished steak up to Harry, who greeted it with glistening eyes behind his thick, horn-rimmed glasses. The two girls sat back with folded hands, waiting to be served dessert.

It was dark enough now to switch on the Japanese lanterns strung from the boles of bottle palms framing the Holloways' pool. After dessert had been served and consumed, the tables were cleared and pushed back. The caterer's men packed up their chairs and equipment, and departed. The accordionist went to his well-deserved rest.

Bill Holloway brought out two portable speakers connected by long cords to the hi-fi equipment in his library. He put on a tape of disco music, and some of the younger couples and children began to dance on the pool deck and on the band of lawn surrounding it.

Turk Bending sought out the hostess.

'Good dinner,' he said. 'I ate myself sick.'

'And now you want that joint,' Jane Holloway said.

'No, no,' he said, lowering his voice, leaning close to her. 'That's what I wanted to tell you: I don't need the joint. Tom Janssen brought some coke.'

She brightened. 'Good stuff?'

'He says so. He's got it in his car. The white Jaguar. Want a snort?'

'Sounds good to me.'

'We don't want to go there in a gang. Just sort of wander over, one by one, casual-like.'

'Who's snorting?'

'You, me, Tom, Luther Empt, and Tom's creamer.'

'The kid in the red diaper suit?'

'That's the one.'

'Tom better tell her she needs a shave.'

'Maybe he's figuring on chewing it off,' Bending said, grinning wolfishly.

So Jane Holloway didn't go up to her bedroom for a stick of marijuana. Which was fortunate, because if she had, she would have caught her son Edward rifling her bureau drawer.

Eddie had signaled Wayne Bending by jerking his head toward the Empt home. Wayne had nodded and drifted off into the darkness. He left it to Lucy or his mother to get Harry home. The kid had eaten so much he was sleeping sitting up in a chair, gripping his favorite pocket calculator. Wayne figured he'd be all right if he didn't topple over.

He moved slowly out of the lantern light glimmering on the surface of the pool. Then he began trotting. He came to the highway and jogged along the verge of A1A until he came to the white gravel driveway leading to Luther Empt's home.

The entrance was guarded by two big gates of wrought iron, but they were never locked. Wayne slipped through, closing the gate behind him. He stayed in the shadows of royal poinciana and tulip trees as he made his way onto the grounds. Dimly, muted, he could hear the music from the Holloways' pool party. By now, he thought sourly, the grown-ups would be getting bombed and feeling up their friends' wives. Someone fully dressed would fall, or be pushed, into the pool, and everyone would laugh hysterically. It was sickening.

Wayne was a stocky, squarish boy with a long torso and short legs. His shoulders were bunchy, his neck thick. He wasn't much to look at, he knew, but he could throw a football farther than any of his friends, and only Eddie Holloway could beat him at arm wrestling.

Sometimes he wondered if he really was his father's son. He obviously didn't have his father's good looks, and it seemed doubtful if he'd ever have his height. Also, his father was fair-haired, cheerful, and made out with women like a bandit. Wayne was dark and dour, and girls never gave him a second glance.

He found the place he was looking for: a spidery wood latticed gazebo Teresa Empt had erected on her well-manicured lawn near a fine stand of pink, yellow, and white frangipani. The gazebo was octagonal, topped with an open-worked cupola. Inside were two chairs and two loveseats of cast iron in a Victorian grape-and-vine pattern, painted white.

The gazebo was rarely used by the Empts, unless newspaper or magazine photographers were expected. But Eddie Holloway and Wayne Bending used it, to smoke pot, drink a beer, or just talk. One of these nights, Eddie kept saying, they would bring a couple of cunts there and make out like mad.

The cast-iron chairs and loveseats might have been decorative but without cushions they were hell to sit on. Wayne Bending squatted on the hard-packed sand floor, facing the Empt house. There was a dim light on downstairs, but he supposed everyone was still at the Holloways' party.

He sat there in the sand, hunched over and brooding. Wayne Bending, at the age of twelve, had had it. It was all so finky. Everything was. He wanted to set fire to the world. He could burn, pillage, kill; he didn't care. Nothing made sense.

What was so awful, what fueled his anger, was the gap between what people said and what they did. It was obvious to him that everyone lied. Everyone cheated. Everyone screwed everyone else. No one was faithful, to anything or anyone. People were shit; he recognized that, and it infuriated him.

Look at his father . . . And his mother . . .

He heard a low whistle and straightened up. Eddie Holloway came sauntering in, his blond hair gleaming. Wayne could see his teeth shining.

'Get them okay?' he asked.

'No sweat,' Eddie said, sitting down alongside Wayne. 'I would have copped a couple more, but she's only got eight left.'

'Won't she notice these two are missing?'

'Maybe,' Eddie said, shrugging. 'If she does, she'll think Maria lifted them. Jesus, what a night. That party was the pits; the *pits*. Let's light up, and away we go.'

That was another thing that depressed Wayne Bending.

He had smoked marijuana twice before with Eddie Holloway, and it hadn't *done* anything for him. He had followed Eddie's instructions, inhaled deeply, held the smoke in his lungs, and waited. Nothing. He had watched Eddie get high and felt a vague panic at his own lack of response.

71

Because he wanted Eddie – the best-looking guy on the beach, the most popular and coolest – to think well of him, to like him. Because he wanted to be Eddie Holloway's best friend. So he had faked it.

He had rolled his eyes, slumped limply. He murmured, 'Oh man, that's cool, that's really tough.' He mimicked Eddie's high, pretending a euphoria he didn't feel.

That made him just as finky as everyone else, didn't it?

So they lighted up, dragged away, grinned vacuously, and told each other how great it was to get out of it. They smoked slowly, but soon enough they were down to tiny roaches they could not hold without burning their fingertips.

Then Eddie lay on his back, stretched his arms wide. He giggled, and drummed his heels lightly on the packed sand.

'Oh man,' he murmured, 'this is it. This is *really* it.'

Then Wayne Bending, for reasons he could not understand, rolled onto his side. He propped himself up and leaned over Eddie Holloway. He brought his face slowly close and kissed Eddie on the lips.

It lasted. Not long, but not a short time either. Then Eddie rolled his head away and stared into Wayne's glittering eyes.

'You nut,' he said, laughing softly, 'what do you think you're doing?'

8

Former Senator Randolph Diedrickson was living out his days in a home that resembled a New England merchant's mansion more than an antebellum plantation. It was all white fretwork and gingerbread trim, with gables, dormers, bow windows, and a stained-glass fanlight over the doorway.

The senator, confined to a wheelchair by rheumatoid arthritis, had an elevator installed in this rambling and somewhat fusty manse. So he was able to get around easily (the wheelchair was battery-powered), but spent most of his time in his upstairs study or on the sundeck at the top of the house, three stories up.

Since the house was centered in a three-acre plot, and the nearest neighbors inhabited ranch-type dwellings, the senator achieved complete privacy on his sundeck. He frequently assured visitors he felt close to God up there. He said this with a straight face, and they never knew whether or not he was serious. The majority decided he was.

Most mornings he spent dictating his memoirs into a tape recorder. He had spent thirty-six years in the Congress of the United States, and believed his recollections of events during those stirring days would be of interest to historians.

The tapes were later transcribed by a full-time, live-in secretary (white, male) who worked in the second-floor study. This amanuensis also made complete sentences and corrected the grammar of the senator's ramblings. He had already amassed 800 pages, and they were only up to 1956.

In addition to the secretary, a cook-housekeeper and a houseman, wife and husband, both black, also lived on the premises. They were kept busy; the senator did a great deal of entertaining and frequently had sleep-over guests.

The senator met Jane Holloway when she and her banker husband had attended a fund-raising cocktail party in the senator's home for the benefit of a local Democratic candidate. Jane Holloway, at the senator's invitation, had become a regular visitor. Without her banker husband.

Their relationship had endured for almost two years, and had proved mutually rewarding. Most of their time together was spent on the sundeck atop the house. During these visits, the door leading to the interior was kept locked. Only the senator had the key.

The sundeck itself was an approximate ten-by-eighteen-foot duck-boarded area. Half of it was shaded by a fringed canvas awning; the senator avoided direct sunlight since in addition to arthritis he suffered from actinic keratosis.

There were wheeled lounges up there, with canvas pads, and comfortable cushioned captains' chairs. There was also, under the awning, a completely equipped rattan bar. A telephone enabled the senator to make and receive outside calls or, by pushing buttons, communicate with his secretary in the study, the cook in the kitchen, or the houseman in the downstairs parlor.

On a hard, diamond-bright Monday morning, the sun fierce, Jane Holloway lay naked on a beach towel spread over the canvas pad of one of the lounges. She had oiled her body, including fingers and toes, and had two pads of cotton Vaselined to her closed eyes.

Beneath the couch, in the shade, were her suntan oil, a towel, leather-strap sandals, and a half-finished glass of iced tea. She also had a small transistor radio there, but had switched it off when her host began to speak.

The senator sat in his wheelchair in the shade, a thin cotton shawl draped over his knees. He wore a lightweight pink sports shirt, with a matching cardigan. On his massive skull was perched a rumpled white fishing hat, wide-brimmed, with grommets for ventilation.

He had been an enormous man, somewhat shrunken now, but he still had the presence to awe. His face hung in pendulous folds, jowls, wattles. A roadmap of burst capillaries wandered across his mottled cheeks and bulbous nose. The hands gripping the arms of the wheelchair were spatulate and spotted.

When he spoke, his voice was strong, orotund, with a moist, fruity texture. A Washington, DC, reporter had once written that 'every word spoken by Senator Diedrickson sounds like it has been dipped in honey and hung up to dry with a golden safety pin.'

'There is a bank in Martin County,' he intoned. 'A chain of banks, I should say. Listed on the American Exchange. Shortly, within a month or so, it will be the target of a takeover attempt.'

Jane Holloway stirred. 'Yes?' she said.

'The attempt will fail,' the senator rumbled on, 'and the stock will return to its usual level. But when the report of the intended takeover gets about, I believe we may anticipate an eight- to ten-point run-up. I suggest you buy as soon as possible. I have made a note of everything you need to know. Please use the broker I recommend. His discretion is assured.'

'Thank you, senator,' she said gratefully.

'My pleasure, dear,' he said.

'Now there is something I'd like to ask you,' she said. 'I need your advice.'

'Of course,' he said. 'You know I am always at your disposal. Nothing gives me more true gratification than to assist my friends.'

She told him about Luther Empt's proposal. As she spoke, his smoky, somewhat bloodshot eyes never left her body. His gaze moved over her like a swab, from her short, silvered hair to her gilded toenails. The stare paused briefly

75

at the clean pucker of her navel and the small, trimmed bush, soft as down.

She told him she had studied the presentation Luther Empt had given her husband. She told him of Turk Bending's efforts to secure her aid in convincing her husband to come in on the deal, and her demand for a reward if she did. She told the senator everything.

'What do you think?' she said, when she had finished her recital.

He didn't reply at once. She took the greased pads from her eyes and dropped them to the deck. She rolled onto her stomach, turned her head and pillowed it on one forearm so she could look at him. She spread her legs. Sunlight gleamed dully on her oiled buttocks.

'This Luther Empt,' the senator said, 'is he a Jew?'

'I don't know,' Jane Holloway said. 'I don't think so. Polish or Ukrainian – something like that.'

'Do you know the names of the men who approached him?'

'They're in the presentation, but I don't recall. I do remember that one of them is named Rocco. His first name.'

The senator made a sound deep in his heavy chest, half-snort, half-grunt.

'During my illustrious career in the United States Senate,' he said, no irony in his voice, 'I had but one ironclad rule: Never do business with a man named Rocco. However . . . It would help, my dear, if you could provide the names of these men. Then I would make private inquiries to ascertain if they are indeed who they purport to be.'

'I'll call you when I get home,' she said, 'and give you the names. But what do you think of the proposition generally?'

He sighed. 'Do you know the annual income of the pornography industry in this great nation of ours?'

'Millions, I suppose. Probably hundreds of millions.'

'The last number I saw,' he said slowly, 'was six billion.

76

That's *billion*. Annually. Oh, the money is there; no doubt about that. But there is one slight drawback that may give you pause.'

'The legal –' she started, but he interrupted.

'In this case, I agree with the attorneys consulted: the legal risk is minimal. No, I am referring to the character of the men who have presented the proposal.'

'The mob guys?' she said. 'I think Luther Empt can handle them. He's a hard man.'

The senator laughed mirthlessly.

'A hard man, is he? My dear, neither you nor Luther Empt knows what hard is. These representatives of what is called "organized crime" – although it has been my experience that they are frequently as disorganized as American industry or government – these men are of a hardness beyond your ken. What do you suppose might happen to Empt, or Ronald Bending, or your husband, if these men decide they are being deceived, or cheated, or even just overcharged?'

'I don't know,' Jane Holloway said. 'Would they kill?'

'Nothing as crass as that, my dear,' the senator said. 'One day the man they wanted out would simply disappear. He would be here, and then he would be gone. The world would be as if he had never been. There would be no letters, no threatening phone calls. He would just vanish, never to be heard from again. His body would never be found.'

Jane hunched her shoulders and shivered. 'So you think I should just tell Bill to forget about it?'

'Oh no,' the senator said. 'Large returns require large risks. And in this case, the returns can be very large indeed. Get those names for me and I'll see what I can discover about their bona fides.'

'Thank you, senator,' she said. 'And now I think I better be getting home.'

She rose to her feet, stretched gracefully, bent and twisted. She knew his hooded eyes never left her.

She padded over to him and knelt on the rough duck-boards in front of his wheelchair. She whisked the cotton shawl away. With practiced fingers, she unzipped his fly. She delved within and deftly withdrew his cock from under-drawers and trousers.

'Look at that thing,' the senator said sadly. 'It is an antique, my dear. That is a genuine antique you fondle.'

'Now, senator,' she said, leaning forward, 'don't get maudlin.'

His eyes squinched shut. His speckled hands gripped the armrests tightly.

She had told Turk Bending the truth; the senator never touched her.

9

Mrs Grace Bending was a stalky woman, erect to the point of stiffness. Clear features, complexion unblemished. Sharply cut profile. A wan, distant smile. Very controlled, but with an effort.

When she entered the office of Dr Theodore Levin for the second time, she was wearing a severe, man-tailored suit of white linen. Neckline closed with a flowing scarf of silk printed with tiny forget-me-nots. Semi-opaque hose. Low-heeled pumps.

During her first visit, her long, sun-streaked hair had been piled atop her head in a braid, precisely coiled. Now it was down, hanging like pale snakes.

Then she had been nervous and brittle, gnawing her lower lip in moments of stress. Now she was somewhat thawed, sitting far back in the chair the doctor indicated. She crossed her knees. Good legs, he noted. No jewelry. No discernible perfume.

'Doctor,' she started, 'I was glad to hear you have decided to accept Lucy.'

He nodded. 'I hope it didn't occasion any, ah, family disagreement?'

'No, not really. We finally agreed it was best. And Lucy told me she likes you. You *do* think she has a problem?'

'Oh yes,' he said, sighing. 'A problem exists. I cannot even begin to discuss possible causes or possible solutions or even frequency of visits until we have the results of her physical examination. It will be scheduled for next week – if that is satisfactory to you.'

'Yes, that will be all right. After school would be best. You said your associate, a woman, will do the exam?'

'Doctor Mary Scotsby – that is correct. We have been associated for several years. She is, of course, an MD. Mrs Bending, I think I have all the basic information necessary from the questionnaires you and your husband completed. However, there are some additional things I need to know about Lucy.'

'Yes, doctor?'

'Does she wet the bed?'

He thought he saw her frail smile falter, and there was a brief collapse in her patrician manner. He recalled the adjectives she had used in the first interview to describe her daughter's behavior: 'vulgar . . . distasteful . . . disgusting . . . horrible.'

'No,' Grace Bending said shortly. 'Not now. She did. In the past.'

'When was this?' he asked. 'At what age?'

'Up to about three or four years ago. Then she wet the bed regularly.'

'How often?'

'Perhaps two or three times a week.'

'But not recently?'

'No.'

'Not at all?'

'No.'

'It simply stopped?'

'Yes.'

He pondered that. He supposed such an abrupt and complete cessation of enuresis was possible, but he didn't think it likely. Still, this mother would have no reason to lie – unless she found the whole subject so revolting that she refused to discuss it.

'Mrs Bending,' he said, 'these exhibitions of, ah, passionate attention on Lucy's part are never to her brothers?'

'No. Never.'

'Or boys her own age or slightly older?'

'Not to my knowledge. Only with older men.'

'Have her menstrual periods started?'

'Doctor! She's only eight years old!'

'Mrs Bending, you would be surprised to learn at what an early age some female children begin their menses. To your knowledge, does Lucy masturbate regularly?'

'Absolutely not.'

'Occasionally?'

'Never!'

He was surprised at the heat of her response. She was, he decided, either a liar or remarkably unobservant. This woman had come to him because of her daughter's abnormal sexuality, which she recognized. But now she was denying her daughter's normal sexuality. He found that intriguing, and possibly significant.

'I noted Lucy is not a nail-biter. Does she have any other personal habits you feel I should know about? That might assist in analyzing her condition?'

'No, I can't think of any.'

'Eat well? A good appetite?'

'Oh yes.'

'Is she taking any drugs? Particularly mood-altering drugs, such as tranquilizers or amphetamines for hyper-activity. Anything of that nature?'

'No. A children's-strength aspirin once or twice, but nothing stronger.'

'She does well at school? She is a good student?'

'Yes.'

'Does she read? I mean other than school assignments? Does she read for amusement or entertainment?'

'Oh yes. Lucy is a great reader. Very advanced for her age. She brings books home from the library at least once a week.'

'You review the books she brings home?'

'Of course.'

'Of course. How much television would you say she watches? Hours a day.'

'Perhaps one or two hours a day. More on week-ends.'

'Have you noticed any preference? In the type of shows, I mean.'

'Nooo, not exactly. She seems to enjoy, uh, family sagas. "The Walton Family." "Little House on the Prairie." That sort of thing. Very normal.'

Very normal, he thought mordantly, except for one teensy-weensy quirk: she likes to stroke men's pricks.

He recalled the first interview. Grace Bending had been the dominant one, the leader. At first. 'Let me handle this.' She had said that twice to her husband. And he had been almost hostile – at first.

But when he got them down to the nitty-gritty, it was the husband who said what had to be said; the wife couldn't bring herself to it.

And now, again, she was blocking. Oh, she had thawed a bit. She was opening up. But not enough. He sensed a reserve there, deep and unyielding. It would take time to break through.

'Mrs Bending, does Lucy have any particular friends? Boys or girls of her own age?'

'Lucy has many friends,' she said briskly. 'A little girl, Gloria Holloway, who lives next door, is probably her best friend.'

'And boys?'

'Many, but no one in particular.'

'Any crushes? On special teachers or friends?'

'No, no crushes that I'm aware of.'

'Does Lucy keep a diary?'

'My goodness, what an odd question. No, not to my knowledge.'

He noted that 'my goodness.' Lucy had used the same phrase in her interview. But it was hardly unusual. Girls frequently mimicked their mothers' speech patterns, just as boys did their fathers'. But under the circumstances, 'my goodness' seemed particularly inapt.

'Has Lucy ever used language that, ah, you felt was not appropriate?'

'Dirty words, you mean? No, Lucy has been taught better than that.'

'Never a "damn"? Never a "hell"?'

'Oh, perhaps. Once or twice. But not frequently.'

'And never anything but "damn" or "hell"?'

Grace Bending blushed. 'Once she said, "Shit." But only once.'

'Uh-huh. But not sexually oriented obscenities?'

'No. Never.'

'Mrs Bending, how would you characterize Lucy's relations with her brothers?'

'Well . . . they get along. Rather well, as a matter of fact. Sometimes there's squabbling, but that's to be expected.'

'Of course.'

'And sometimes the three of them gang up against my husband and me, but it's never been anything serious.'

'Could you give me an example?'

'Oh, they might object to a TV program we want to watch or a movie we want to see. But generally, there's very little unpleasantness. All my children are well-mannered.'

'You are fortunate.'

'I thought so.'

'But you don't now?'

'It's this thing with Lucy. It has me very upset.'

Her answer angered him, though he was careful not to show it. He guessed her concern for her daughter's behavior might be rooted in how that conduct affected *her*.

He wanted, if not to humble her, to remind her of her humanity.

'Mrs Bending,' he said softly, 'my questions about Lucy have been preliminary probing. In the sessions to come – with her, you, your husband, Lucy's brothers – we'll try to dig a little deeper. But for the moment, let me switch gears here and talk to you about *you*.'

'If you wish.'

'You're an intelligent woman, and I know you understand that whatever I may ask you is for one reason only: to help resolve Lucy's problem.'

'I know that, doctor.'

'Good. Mrs Bending, how would you characterize your marriage – as happy, average, or unhappy?'

'Oh, happy. I am very happy. I don't mean it's perfect. What marriage is? But I'd say that, all in all, it's a happy marriage.'

'No serious disagreements, arguments, or conflicts that might affect Lucy?'

'No. None.'

'You and your husband have been married – how many years?'

'Fourteen. Fifteen in December.'

'The first marriage for both of you?'

'For me. My husband was married previously. Once.'

'And you have lived in your present home for how many years?'

'Almost ten. We came to Florida ten years ago.'

'You and your husband have your own bedroom, of course?'

'Of course.'

'Double bed or twin beds?'

'Doctor, I don't see what –'

'Please answer my question,' he said sternly.

She was cowed. 'Twin beds.'

'The children's bedrooms are on the same floor?'

'Yes.'

'Each child has his or her own room?'

'Yes.'

'Which child has the bedroom closest to yours?'

'Lucy. Then Harry. He's my youngest boy. Wayne's bedroom is at the end of the hall.'

'Each has an individual bathroom?'

'Lucy has her own. Harry and Wayne share a bathroom.

But there's another across the hall, connected with the guest room. It can be used in case of, uh, emergency.'

'A large home.'

'It's a beautiful home!'

He suspected it would be an immaculate home. Silver polished. Ashtrays dusted. Rugs perpetually vacuumed. She would watch the television commercials intently and read the family service magazines. No soap spots on the glassware. No odors in the bathrooms. She would be proud of the gleam on her kitchen floor.

He was tempted to ask how many times a day she bathed.

Instead, he said: 'Let me see . . . you are three years older than your husband?'

'That's correct.'

'How did you meet?'

'We were introduced by mutual friends.'

'But you didn't grow up together? Not childhood sweethearts?'

'Oh no. Nothing like that.'

'Lucy mentioned a Sunday School teacher. She attends regularly?'

'Yes. She and Harry.'

'Do you attend church regularly?'

'Yes.'

'Your husband?'

'No. He plays golf.'

'And your older son?'

'Wayne? No, he no longer attends church regularly.'

'Is – or was – this a matter of contention between you and your husband – his refusal to attend church? And Wayne's absence?'

'Not contention exactly. We discussed it at length. Several times. Then I realized it was hopeless trying to force my beliefs on my husband and older son. So I let them go their own way.'

Her tone of self-abnegation amused him. He was beginning to understand this woman. He thought she might have a strong martyr complex. He pitied her husband.

'Mrs Bending, how would you characterize your sexual relations with your husband?'

'I don't understand what you mean, doctor.'

'Would you say they are satisfactory? Ecstatic? Unsatisfactory? Repellent to you?'

'Satisfactory,' she said primly. 'My physical relations with my husband are satisfactory.'

'You are both relatively young, apparently healthy and vigorous – how often do you have intercourse?'

'Doctor, is this absolutely necessary?'

'Mrs Bending, I am fishing, I admit it. I am trying to amass as much information as I can, hoping that somewhere I may find a clue to Lucy's behavior. I would not be doing my job if I didn't ask, and you might be lessening our chances of success if you refused to answer.'

'Well . . . all right then. But I find all this very embarrassing and – and distasteful.'

'I appreciate that. But your cooperation is essential.'

'Very well.'

'How often do you and your husband have sexual intercourse? Once a week?'

'Less.'

'Once a month?'

'Perhaps. It depends . . .'

He wanted to ask: 'Depends on what?' She did not strike him as a woman who sold her favors, in one way or another, to her husband or other men. She was too asexual for that. But, he admitted, she might surprise him.

He thought her physically attractive. Breasts, hips, thighs – they were all there, swaddled in garments. But they were all belied by her spiky aloofness. She seemed determined to deny passion. Because it did not exist, he wondered – or had it been drained?

'How would you characterize your husband, Mrs Bending? Affectionate? Loving? Passionate? Or cold, withdrawn, unfeeling?'

'Well, my goodness, he can be all those things at different times. He's human, you know.'

'Of course. But which of those adjectives would you select as describing his true nature?'

'Would you repeat them again, please, doctor?'

'Affectionate? Loving? Passionate? Or cold, withdrawn, unfeeling?'

'I'd say my husband is an affectionate man.'

'A good husband and father?'

'Yes.'

'A real family man?'

'Ah . . . not exactly.'

'Is your husband faithful to you?'

'I think you better ask him that, doctor.'

'Are you faithful to him?'

'Always! Forever! Since the day we met! I have never played around.'

'I see. One final question, Mrs Bending . . . It is of a particular intimate nature, and if you don't wish to answer at this time, I can well understand your reticence. When you have intercourse with your husband, do you achieve orgasm?'

'Uh . . . I think so.'

'Thank you. And now I see our time is up . . .'

PART II

1

Luther Empt wanted to hold the meeting in the conference room of William Holloway's bank, but Bill said he did not feel that would be prudent.

Later, Empt said disgustedly to Turk Bending: '*Prudent*, for God's sake! Here we're talking about a million-dollar deal to process porn, and this guy is talking prudence! If it wasn't for that bimbo he's married to, I'd figure him for a nelly.'

Bending, prudently, did not reply.

So Empt rented a suite at the Hibiscus Motel on Federal Highway. He arrived early, with bottles, and ordered up extra glasses, mixers, and plenty of ice. The meeting was scheduled for 9:00 P.M. Luther hoped it would be over by midnight at the latest.

Bending and Holloway drove over in the latter's Mercedes saloon. They didn't talk much during the trip. Bending was figuring what investments he would have to liquidate to come up with a quarter of a million. William Jasper Holloway was wondering what the hell he was doing there.

He had been prepared to give Luther Empt's proposition a vacant, meandering rejection – more a banker's shilly-shallying than a forthright 'No!' On paper, the proposal looked good. But Holloway simply didn't want to complicate his life with new endeavors.

Besides, he told his wife, they had sufficient money for their needs, now and for the foreseeable future. That statement enraged her and she went to work on him.

She listed their current expenses, which were not inconsiderable. She reminded him that the children would require college educations – and who knew what that might cost by the time they were ready? She spoke darkly of the possibility and financial drain of catastrophic illness.

When she began to talk like that, he knew he was defeated; she would have her way. Her vigor and resolve would wear him down. She would never give up. And she had a hundred ways of making his life a hell.

When he entered the motel suite Luther had rented, all of Holloway's objections to this enterprise were revived.

Later, Ronald Bending said that it reminded him of Van Gogh's 'The Night Café.' There were the same ugly and evil colors: dirty yellows and sickly greens, washed with acid. Dead reds. Lights haloed: a miasma swirling in that dread room.

Even the shadows were faded. And over all, a hopeless stillness, a lonely quiet that had its own smell: sweet and piercing. It was, Holloway decided when he saw it, a room to vanquish hope. He headed immediately for the bottles and poured himself a heavy vodka.

Their guests arrived shortly after nine o'clock. Introductions were made, everyone was seated and served with drinks, Turk Bending acting as bartender. They chatted idly a few moments, about the weather, pro football, the stock market.

Then Luther Empt got down to business. He spoke loudly, rapidly, in his harsh city voice. The two visitors listened intently, not revealing by gesture, movement, or expression, their reactions to Empt's proposals.

Rocco Santangelo was the taller of the two. He was lofty, whip-thin, beautifully shaved, and wearing a navy blue suit of raw silk. No jewelry, but shirt, tie, and pocket handkerchief were monogrammed. He was obviously no stranger to facials and manicures.

Jimmy (not James, but Jimmy) Stone was shorter, bulkier. He wore a somewhat baggy three-piece suit of slate gray gabardine. His bullet head was topped with a brush of blond hair, stiff as stubble. He didn't have Santangelo's polish, but he had a craggy presence, sitting motionless with clumpy hands gripping thick knees.

William Holloway found the two men disturbing. It was their closed faces, the deadness of their stares. He supposed they were men with friends, families, loves. But those empty eyes gave nothing back.

Empt started by saying that the three of them were prepared to contribute $750,000 to a new corporation. He hoped their visitors were still willing to advance a quarter of a million dollar loan to the project. At ten percent interest.

Santangelo said the loan was available immediately. And should overruns or unexpected expenses require it, 250 additional jacks would be available at the same interest rate. 'Jacks' was the word he used.

At that point, Santangelo withdrew two folded letters from an inside pocket and handed them to Empt. Luther read the pages and passed them on to Bending and Holloway.

They were 'To Whom It May Concern' letters of recommendation from the presidents of commercial banks in New York and Miami. They stated that the bearer, Mr Rocco Santangelo, and associates, were personally known to the signatories as trustworthy men of financial probity.

Both letters also stated that the undersigned would welcome personal inquiries into the credit rating of the aforesaid Mr Rocco Santangelo, and associates.

William Holloway read these paeans with some bemusement. He recognized the name of the New York banker, although he didn't know him personally.

But he had played golf occasionally with the Miami man at state banking conventions. He remembered him as a frosty, somewhat remote character. Not at all the type he would have suspected of dealing with Rocco Santangelo.

Empt said that the bankers' letters were welcome, and he hoped that as soon as the corporation's charter was granted, Mr Santangelo would be willing to sign a sales contract.

Mr Santangelo then looked inquiringly at his associate.

Jimmy Stone said, 'No,' in a voice so low it could hardly be heard.

Whereupon Santangelo turned back to the three partners and explained that, because of the nature of the business, a signed contract would not be necessary.

'If we stiff you,' he said earnestly, 'what are you going to do – call in the law and tell the judge we haven't paid you for this wet pussy shit? He'll kick your ass out of court.'

They saw the logic of that.

Santangelo said there would be no signed contracts, letters of intent, or business correspondence. All orders, agreements, complaints, and inquiries would be made verbally.

In addition, Santangelo said, the initial quarter of a million dollar loan, and all subsequent payments for merchandise, would be made in cash.

'It's simpler that way,' he explained.

He must have seen something in their expressions, because he went on to say that what they chose to reveal of their income to the IRS was their decision to make. But, he said, there were to be no invoices, bills of lading, statements, or any other written documents indicating the nature or scope of the business.

'You see,' he said in his rich, assured voice, 'our relationship must be based on mutual trust. You treat us right; we treat you right. One hand scratches the other. We're willing to show our good faith by handing over a quarter-mil, bingo, like that. This could be a very nice little deal for you, so it's silly to argue about signed contracts and all that bullshit.'

Luther Empt said, well, perhaps a signed contract would not be absolutely necessary, but he would feel a lot better if the loan was made available before the new factory was contracted for and equipment ordered.

Santangelo said, of course, the money could be handed over at once. Tomorrow, if Empt desired.

'And we won't even ask for a receipt,' he said, showing his teeth.

Luther said that sounded good to him, and everyone had another drink.

Then Luther said that as soon as the corporation charter came through, and an office was established, they would get rolling on the physical plant in west Broward County.

Santangelo asked whom Empt had in mind as architect and general contractor for the factory.

Luther replied that there were several good local firms he had dealt with before. Rocco Santangelo said that he would like to recommend a Miami-based builder with whose work he was familiar. His prices were reasonable, and he always met schedules.

Luther said he would prefer to give the work to contractors he knew in Palm Beach County.

Santangelo said he really would consider it a personal favor if Empt would agree to use the Miami builder.

Empt said that was out of the question. He said that he and his partners were risking three times the amount being loaned by Santangelo, and associates, and they had to be allowed to make business decisions they felt to be in their own best interests.

Santangelo said that was true, but in this particular case, he had to insist that Empt and his partners defer to his wishes. There were reasons he could not go into, but employing the Miami builder was essential.

Empt, beginning to bristle, said no, absolutely not. They would select their own builder.

Then there was silence. At that point Holloway thought the whole deal was about to fall apart. Santangelo's eyes were, if possible, colder and emptier than before. And Empt's face was bright with his stubborn anger.

But then Ronald Bending spoke up boldly. If he wasn't nerveless and amused, that was the impression he gave.

'Gentlemen, I really don't believe you appreciate what is at stake here.'

The two visitors slowly turned to him.

'South Florida is not New York,' he told them. 'It's a lot of little towns, and the counties are just as important. Everyone knows everyone else. We all take in each other's laundry. All the money people know one another or have mutual friends. Now you go to build something – a house, a factory, a swimming pool, whatever – you go to local people. A friend, or a friend of a friend. That's how you buy your car and insurance. That's how you spend your money. You understand? It's all local. Then not too many questions are asked. No one gets too curious. No one gets envious. You're paying your dues. Bill, am I right?'

'That is correct,' Holloway said.

'Now then,' Turk Bending went on smoothly, 'we bring in a Miami builder and all the local people get sore. "What's wrong, we're not good enough for you guys?" That's what they'll say. Then they'll start asking, "What the hell are you building out there anyway?" And a lot of these guys are in local politics. We'll need favors – you know? Permits and variances and so forth. So what's the sense of getting their balls in an uproar? Let's face it: we're not building a public library; we're going to process porn. So doesn't it make sense to keep a low profile? And we do that by spreading the bucks around locally. We don't want to get our neighbors sore at us before we even get started.'

The three partners looked at Rocco Santangelo. He turned his head to his companion.

'Okay,' Jimmy Stone said in his low, lifeless voice.

After that, they all relaxed and had another drink. Arrangements were made for delivery of the $250,000 in cash to Empt. They were given a Miami telephone number where messages for Santangelo could be left. He promised to return their calls promptly.

Empt suggested that while the new factory was being erected, and equipment ordered, he could start processing porn films in his existing facility. This would, he said, serve as a trial run and provide valuable experience for the time when they would go into full production.

'We'll start with cassettes,' he said. 'Then, if the new disk players catch on, we'll add disk processors. The important thing is to stay on top of the market, but not put all our eggs in one basket.'

Santangelo approved of this cautious approach and said he'd have a print of a new porn movie delivered next week. It was a twenty-minute film in color, called *Teenage Honey-pots*.

The meeting ended soon after that. Everyone shook hands genially and promised to stay in touch. It was only a few minutes after eleven o'clock.

They had a final drink after the visitors left. Empt clapped a meaty hand on Bending's shoulder, called him 'old buddy,' and said he had handled the matter of the local builder in masterful fashion.

'Like I told you,' he said, laughing, 'Bullshit Baffles Brains.'

'Luther,' Bending said, 'what I told them was true. We want to keep a low profile on this thing, and the easiest way to keep everyone happy is to spread the loot around so none of the locals start asking questions.'

'Ahh,' Empt said roughly, 'who gives a good goddamn what those turd-kickers think?'

William Holloway drove Bending home. Again, both men were silent with their own thoughts.

It was a balmy night, cool enough to turn off the air conditioner and run the windows down. As they drove eastward, they lost the moist, humid land odors and smelled the pungent freshness of the sea. It came into view molten and heaving, rippled mercury in the nightglow.

William Jasper Holloway felt a vague distaste for this melodramatic scene. It was all, land and sea, too exuberant. It offended his New England sensibilities. In all the State of Florida, there was no decent restraint.

He longed for order and tradition. He would have welcomed limits. Discipline, punishment, and guilt. But he found himself loose, a man involved with *Teenage Honeypots*, and he could not puzzle out the path that had brought him to this place.

It was said that in a new Ice Age, all of Florida would be submerged. Holloway found sour satisfaction in that prediction. He didn't want to think that the same catastrophe would drown his beloved Boston. It was enough to wish for the day when all this dreamy indolence would disappear.

2

All of Luther Empt's women, wives and whores alike, were
as brassy as he. They all haggled. He was not an introspec-
tive man; it never occurred to him that he sought out such
women. But he was happy with the cost-counters, the
women who could work a deal. He respected them.

It simplified things. It saved him from such intangibles as
affection, responsibility, love. It brought his personal relations down to the bottom line. Numbers. Profit or loss.
Something he could understand.

He was smirky after the meeting with the mob guys. It
was going to be a sweet deal. And it ended before midnight.
Plenty of time . . .

He carried the unused whiskey down to his white Cadillac Seville. Then paid the bill at the motel desk with a credit
card. It would all be billed to the new corporation. No fool
he. Shortly before twelve, he was heading south on Federal
Highway, windows down, a tape playing soft rock. He
loosened his tie, opened his collar.

'Tomorrow *der vurld*!' he shouted in a thick German
accent, and laughed uproariously.

He had, he figured, been to every raunchy pickup joint in
Palm Beach and Broward counties. And sometimes as far
south as Dade. He was heading for one of his favorite
haunts now: a nude dancing dive west of I-95 on Atlantic
Boulevard. He usually scored there.

It was traditional Florida Honky-Tonk. Splintered wood
floors. Topless barmaids. Neon beer signs. Plastic tables.
Crashing jukebox. Waitresses with black net opera hose. A

rough crowd of rednecks, tourists, hustlers, drug pushers – the lot. Luther Empt loved it: the smoke, noise, the smell – everything.

He was smart enough to know he was a man of crass tastes and vulgar appetites. The fancy Palm Beach cocktail lounges were bullshit. His home – the 'Gold Coast villa' – was bullshit. This place, where men came to find women they could fuck, was the real thing. Everything else was bullshit.

He shouldered his way to the bar. He ordered a double Cutty from a barmaid whose naked breasts looked like underdone flapjacks. Then he stared around to check the action. He didn't even glance at the nude go-go dancer who was stroking her appendicitis scar in rhythm to 'I Want to Love You, Baby.'

There were creamers at tables and at the bar. Some he had bought before. When they caught his eye, he waved negligently. He rarely purchased the same body twice. If Luther Empt had known that his wife considered south Florida a paradise, he would have agreed with her – but for a different reason.

There were two well-dressed women sitting alone at a table. Middle-thirties, he guessed. Out-of-towners. All gussied up, stiff in brocaded, off-the-shoulder gowns. Plenty of gold and pearls. Money there, he reckoned; they were trying to appear amused and superior.

Empt had been to a cocktail party following a jai alai match at Dania. There was a buck-toothed Britisher holding forth at the bar. He was a tall, gawky man, not sober, who seemed to have an endless store of anecdotes, most of them pointless to Luther. But he remembered one of them . . .

The Englishman had said that, years ago, there was a fine, haughty duchess in Britain who, at a grand ball, was approached by a well-known and very wealthy rake. The libertine, quite seriously, asked the titled lady if she would go to bed with him for a million pounds.

100

She considered a moment, flushing, then said, 'Yes.'

'Will you do it for two pounds?' the man asked.

'Sir!' she cried, drawing herself up. 'What do you take me for?'

'We have already established that, ma'am,' the rake said. 'Now we're trying to determine the price.'

Luther Empt thought that was one of the funniest, truest stories he had ever heard. He believed it implicitly, since it confirmed what he already knew. All women had their price. Marriage or cash – what difference did it make?

Now, looking at the two elegantly clad tourists, he wondered what their price was. He suspected it was the other way around; they were looking for beachboys, for young cock, and they would pay. Well – why not? Money, money, money. Was there anything else?

He turned back to the bar. Down toward the end, making her way slowly toward him, was a young woman, a girl, really. Limping on one withered leg. Not a creamer, oh no, but a broken bird, wistful and hopeful.

He looked in the back bar mirror. He saw his hulking figure, brutishly handsome, and was not displeased with the image. His eyes moved to the reflection of the crippled girl.

She was dragging herself slowly along, stopping at each man or group of men at the crowded bar. Most of them were drinking beer on ice. She spoke repeatedly with a determined smile, and was answered with a hard laugh, a shake of the head, or blank-faced silence.

She accepted these rejections without rancor and moved on. Empt watched her approach with mild interest Perhaps, he thought, she was cadging a drink or soliciting funds for some phony charity. When she stood, finally, at his shoulder, he swung around on his bar stool to inspect this waif.

A coffin-shaped face framed in black, shiny hair. Parted in the middle, falling straight in gleaming wings, the heavy mass of hair was her most attractive feature, but made her pale face seem narrower. The face of a drowning woman.

The eyes were dark and glittering, the nose small, lips thin. The body was slight, almost frail. She wore a man's white shirt, clean enough, and a wraparound skirt of denim cinched with a straw belt. Sandals on bony feet.

And then, of course, there was the withered leg. Not puckered or scarred or anything like that, but atrophied – a skin-covered bone.

She looked at Luther Empt, with a brave smile.

'May I accommodate you?' she asked softly.

He almost yelped with laughter. He thought he had heard every whore's pitch, but this was something new.

'Accommodate me?' he said. 'How?'

'Any way you like,' she said, still smiling. 'Any way.'

He leaned close to her. 'How much?'

'Twenty. An hour.'

He made up his mind at once, and for the rest of his life he could not have said why.

'Wait for me outside,' he said in a low voice. 'Five, ten minutes.'

She nodded and turned away. In the bar mirror he watched her move haltingly to the door. So thin! A wisp. He finished his drink slowly. No way was he going to be seen leaving with her.

He was already ashamed of his decision, calling himself a randy fool. He consoled himself with the thought that it might be a laugh, something different, a story to tell in the locker room at the club.

He paid his bill and left, casually, strolling. Outside, he looked about and saw her standing in the shadow of a clump of palms. He went over to her, lighting a cigarette as he walked. She was happy to see him.

'I was afraid you were going to stand me up,' she said with a timid smile.

'Now why would I want to do that?' he said, and took her fragile arm. 'My car's over here.'

'We can go to my place,' she offered. 'In Pompano. Not far.'

'No, thanks,' he said. He never went to their homes or apartments. Too much chance of a husband or boyfriend barging out of a closet with an iron in his fist. 'I know a motel close by. Television on the ceiling.' He laughed without mirth.

He wasn't lying about that. And, at extra cost, you could have a waterbed and porn movies. He didn't go for that stuff. A plain, hard bed was all he wanted. He didn't need aids. Or fantasy.

'What a beautiful car,' she breathed, sinking back into the leather-covered seat.

'Yeah,' he said, 'not bad. What's your name?'

'June,' she said. 'What's yours?'

'Bill,' he said, deriving a perverse amusement from using Holloway's name.

The motel room was sparsely furnished, but clean. The air conditioner worked. The towels were thick. There was a strip of paper across the toilet seat, absolutely proving the bowl had been sanitized. The drinking glasses were inserted in little paper bags.

'This is nice,' she said, looking around.

'Yeah?' he said, surprised, wondering what she was used to.

He made certain the door was locked and chained, the venetian blinds tightly closed. No one was lurking in the bathroom or closet; he checked.

'You want the lights on or off, Bill?' she asked.

'On,' he said. He wanted to see this skeleton.

'You want me to take my clothes off?'

'Yes.'

'You want me to do it, or do you want to do it?'

'You do it,' he said, touched by her anxious complaisance.

He took a twenty from his wallet and handed it to her. He always paid in advance. The deal sealed.

'Thank you, Bill,' she said gratefully. 'You're very nice.'

'I am?' he said.

103

He sat in the single armchair and watched her undress.

My God, he thought, she's a child.

He had guessed her age at about twenty-five, twenty-seven – around there. But now, seeing the slender, almost unformed body emerge, he had a sudden surge of fear that she might be underage.

'How old are you, June?' he asked.

'Twenty-three,' she said. 'Next month.'

He felt better. 'You have a nice body,' he said.

She smiled shyly. 'I don't have very much up here,' she said apologetically.

'That's all right,' he heard himself say. 'Don't worry about it.'

She was so white, so white. A tint of pink at the nipples, an ebony triangle below her soft belly. But the rest of her untouched by the sun and even, you might think, by the air, for the skin was so fine, with the milkiness of tissue grown in the dark.

She came over to stand before him naked, head bowed, arms down straight at her sides: the penitent child asking forgiveness. The sable hair covered her face, fell forward to mask her tender breasts.

He put a hand awkwardly on her bony hip. Her skin was cool, limpid. Her flesh surrendered, not resisting his fingers. He thought it might hold his imprint.

'June,' he said hoarsely, 'are you too cold?' And wondered at his solicitude.

'No,' she said, 'I'm all right. Do you want me to undress you?'

'I'll do it,' he said, standing. 'You get into bed.'

But she sat on the edge of the bed and watched him with grave eyes. By the time he removed his shorts, he was almost rigid.

'You're very big,' she said.

He didn't answer; that was a whore's gambit.

He stood in front of her. She took his penis in a gentle hand.

'Bill,' she said seriously, 'I can get on my back if that's what you want. Really I can. But I can't pull my knees all the way up. My leg – you know? But I can get on my hands and knees easy, and you can do it dog fashion. If that's all right with you. Bill? If not, I can lay on my back.'

'Dog fashion is, is –' he said, and then something caught in his throat. He stood there, trying to breathe. His fingers were entangled in her glossy hair.

She touched him lightly. She stroked him. She smoothed him. She looked intently at what she was doing, then looked up at his face with widened eyes.

She must have seen something there, for she stopped her caresses, stood, turned, and kneeled on the bed. She bent far forward, put forearms and then her cheek against the blanket. She brushed her hair away from her face; her eyes rolled back to watch him.

He moved closer until he was standing between her ankles, one normal, one shrunken, hanging over the edge of the bed. He put his hands on her hips and looked down at the suppliant body.

Stalky neck drooped forward humbly. Shoulder bones poked. Spine a string of stones. A waist he might encircle with his big hands. Lyre flare of hips. Buttocks of gloss.

He ran a finger down her back, touching each of those stones. She shivered.

'Can you spread your knees?' he said throatily. 'A little?'

She did, and he touched her, exploring. Her dark eyes closed, a bit, and the pale lips parted.

'Oh,' she said dreamily. 'Oh. Thank you.'

It was so unlike him, and he knew it: to be gentle and caring. Always, before, he had been a grab-and-tussle man, intent only on his own pleasure.

Now he was tender and concerned, feeling her, his cunning fingers seeking her out.

'There?' he asked. 'There?'

'A little higher,' she murmured. 'Oh yes, Bill. There. Yes.'

He felt moisture, the slickness, and pressed forward. She reached behind her with one hand to guide him. He entered her. She breathed a sound: half-moan, half-sob, all bliss.

'All right?' he asked.

Her head nodded on the blanket, eyes closed now. He worked away slowly, holding her hips, looming over that meek body, bent in submission.

Once, when he almost withdrew, she cried out and begged, 'Don't go away from me.'

So he moved tight to her, grinding, and she moved in tiny little lurches. He started, stopped, started, stopped, until he could no longer stop, and with eyes squinched, mouth stretched wide, punished her with his weight and strength.

When he spent, he thrust his pelvis forward, arched his back, and howled soundlessly at the ceiling. Then, shuddering, emptied, he fell forward, collapsing from the waist to cover her with his heavy torso and bury his face in that mass of hair. It smelled of almonds.

He felt the frantic pound of his heart: a frightening stutter. He gulped air, huffed it out. His body burned with fever, and deep in his gut he felt a stirring, almost a hot tickle, as if a finger flicked him there.

After a few moments he said anxiously, 'Are you all right?'

She nodded, eyes open now, and said, 'Please don't go away from me. Not yet.'

'Am I too heavy on you?'

'No. You're beautiful. Just stay where you are. Just for a minute. Please.

So he lay awkwardly atop her, his hairy legs thrust out behind him, toes snagged in the shag rug. He thought he must be crushing her, but she made no complaint. Instead, she reached back with both hands to pull him closer, tighter to her.

Finally, he touched a finger to the tip of her nose. When the dark eyes turned to look at him, he said, 'I'm going to get up now.' She nodded.

He rose with some difficulty, staggered and almost fell. He went into the bathroom and closed the door. He looked at himself in the medicine cabinet mirror. His fleshy face was flushed, a little, but there was no obvious sign of what he had felt, no transfiguration.

He washed his face, armpits, genitals with one of those minuscule cakes of motel soap. He dried, urinated, and came out into the bedroom. She was standing by the bed.

'I'll just be a minute,' she said, giving him a wistful smile. As she passed him, before he could stop her, she grabbed up his hand and kissed his hard knuckles. Then she went into the bathroom.

He should have dressed. He should have been ready to leave when she came out. He should have driven her back to the honky-tonk or wherever she wanted to go. He should have dumped her.

When she came out of the bathroom, he was seated on the edge of the bed, still naked. He held out another twenty.

'Here,' he said, not looking at her. 'Another hour.'

She took the money hesitantly, but she took it. She got into bed. They both lay back, side by side, not touching.

'What's wrong with your leg?' he asked gruffly.

'I was born with it.'

'They couldn't fix it?'

'No. I don't know. Maybe. Anyway, nothing was done.'

'Tough,' he said.

She turned onto her side, cuddled close to him, kissed his meaty shoulder.

'Do you like me, Bill?' she asked.

'Yeah. Sure.'

'I like you. Very much.'

'I'm old enough to be your father.'

'I never had a father.'

His laugh was a snort. 'Everyone had a father.'

'I mean I never knew mine. He ran away from home when I was just a little kid. But I couldn't run,' she added sadly.

This conversation disturbed him. 'How you doing?' he asked her. 'I mean money-wise. You get by?'

'Oh yes. I don't need much.'

'No children?'

'Oh no. I've never been married.'

He was about to tell her that she didn't have to be married to have children, but shut his mouth. She moved closer, put her lips to his ear.

'Do you know what I'd like to do?' she whispered.

'What?'

'I'd like to make love to you. Please?'

'All right.'

'You just lay there,' she said. 'Close your eyes and pretend you're asleep. Okay? You know, like I just sneaked into your bedroom. You pretend you're asleep and don't even know I sneaked into your bedroom. And you won't even move or anything, and I'll make love to you.'

A nut, he thought. A sweet nut.

'All right,' he said again.

'Close your eyes,' she said. 'Don't open them. Okay?'

He shut his eyes. He lay slackly, arms at his sides.

Her fingertips touched his brow, stroking. Traced his face, pressed tenderly against his closed eyes. His jawline. Beneath his chin. A light touch. A butterfly touch. Behind his ears. His neck.

He heard a slight creak of the bedsprings. Then a wet, warm tongue was in his ear, squirming. He clenched his fists to keep from moving. Cat's teeth bit gently at the lobe, lips sucked greedily.

Cool fingers drifted down over shoulders and chest, tugging gently at his thick hair. Cool fingers fluttered across his stomach, pried into his navel. Cool fingers caressed his hips, slithered down to his heavy thighs.

108

And all so slowly, slowly and lovingly, that he thought it a dream, and he was really asleep. He willed the dream to last forever.

Lips and a loving tongue followed the fingers, and he felt himself begin to harden and lift. A soft hand was between his legs, a hot mouth was about him, wet and sleek.

He kept his eyes resolutely closed. He felt the heat withdrawn, momentarily, as hair as light as feathers swept back and forth over his face, nipples, torso, groin, legs. He felt himself straining up into the air.

Then the seeking mouth was back, tongue busy. He didn't touch her. Never once did he touch her. He heard her gasps, heard his own stertorous breathing. He felt the speeding rhythm of his own heart, felt the deep demand grow and grow and grow.

She was so slow, so deliberate. It was a sweet punishment not to be endured. And when he could no longer endure it, and spurted, she devoured him, gulping noisily, sobbing, wailing, and he could not believe this was a whore's feigned passion. Then:

'I swallowed every drop!' she cried triumphantly.

Later, moving as if drugged, they washed again. They dressed slowly without speaking, but smiling timidly at each other.

When they were back in the white Cadillac, he asked where he could drop her.

'Where we met?'

'Oh no,' she said. 'I'd like to go home. Please? It isn't far.'

It was east of Federal, a few blocks north of Atlantic Boulevard. There was a huge supermarket and, behind it, blocks of small, neat homes, some with boats on trailers parked in the driveways. June's place had a lime tree in front and a border of dwarf palms.

'I don't have the whole house, of course,' she explained. 'But I have my own little apartment. Really just a sort of bed-sitting room, with my own bathroom. Best of all, I

109

have my own entrance around at the side, so I can come and go as I please.'

'What about cooking?' he asked her.

'Mostly I eat out,' she said, and he figured that meant McDonald's, Burger King, Lum's, and Long John Silver.

He had parked on the verge, killed his lights. They sat in the darkness while she told him all this. She hugged his arm to her small breasts.

'Will I see you again?' she asked.

'Sure. Why not?'

'I have my own telephone,' she said brightly. 'Will you take my number?'

'Of course.'

He searched in the glove compartment, and wrote her number on the edge of a Mobil roadmap.

'You'll call?' she said. 'Please?'

'Sure.'

'I want to thank you,' she said primly, 'for a lovely evening. I enjoyed it.'

A nut, he thought again. A sweet nut. Now he was bringing her home from the prom. He rolled onto one hip, dug his wallet from the opposite pocket, fished out the third twenty of the night.

'Here,' he said, thrusting the bill into her hand. 'Get yourself something pretty.'

'Thank you, sir,' she said gaily. 'I do appreciate that.'

Just as his initial decision to go with her had been unthinking, so now did he bend forward suddenly to kiss her whore's lips. And what kind of an idiot did that?

'Oh!' she cried. 'Oh Bill!'

Then she had her arms about his neck, was pulling his head close, her mouth glued to his. He resisted a moment, then surrendered. He held her tightly. He strained to her, tasting her soft, yielding child's mouth.

She pulled away, stared at him in the gloom. 'You'll call?'

He nodded dumbly. Then she was out of the car. She shut

the door gently. She bent down to look through the open window. She kissed her palm, then blew it at him. He waved. She limped slowly around to the side of the house. Then she was gone.

He drove home at two in the morning with a dull, brooding hurt, like a hound puzzling over a kick from a stranger. Those luminous eyes – he couldn't understand what had happened, was happening to him.

Nothing in his varied experience with brash creamers had prepared him for this. She might be twenty-three next month, but she was a child, a child-whore. And she was, he thought mournfully, a year younger than his oldest daughter.

A whack, no doubt of that. Something wrong there. Her gears had slipped. Not a lot, but some. She had a breathy, gee-whiz way of talking. She called him 'Sir' and said, 'Please.' And he loved it. Why not admit it – he loved it.

Well . . . maybe not *loved* it, but it stirred him. She stirred him. She excited him. A gimp. He was hooked on a gimp. What the hell was going on?

He could understand weakness that masqueraded as strength, and take advantage of it. But here was a frank, abject vulnerability, the soft-boned pup turned belly-up, begging a caress. It made him shiver to remember that tender white back bowed before him as if she were praying, worshipping.

He shook his big head angrily. There was nothing she wouldn't do; he was convinced of that. Suck my toes, lick my ass, and all the rest. And if he brought a bunch of guys over for a round of corn-on-the-cob, she'd do that, too.

He never would, of course. Still . . .

He had never articulated the principle of money as power, though he sensed it. But now, struggling with thoughts and emotions too complex to comprehend, he glimpsed that more than money was involved here. A link of sorts had been forged. She had grabbed him by the *cojones* and wouldn't let go.

111

He resolved to forget it, let it end. It was, as he had anticipated, a laugh, something different, a story to tell in the locker room of the club. A wild night. A funny memory. Let it go at that.

He had to get out of his car to open those stupid wrought-iron gates leading to his place. He saw there was a single dim light burning in a downstairs room. He parked the Cadillac in the big carport next to Teresa's black LTD. He locked up and started for the house.

Then he went back and took the Mobil roadmap from the glove compartment.

3

Teresa Empt and Grace Bending were both homemakers – but in different ways.

Teresa saw her home as a showplace, a brilliant stage set. Having created it, brought her vision to reality, she was content to delegate the maintenance to employees. She was more curator than housewife.

To Grace, her home was an environment, castle of the family, school for her three children. It was a sanctuary. Almost a church. Domestic chores were a comforting duty. There was an element of expiation she did not recognize.

Early in October, Grace and a maid hired by the hour from a temporary employment service went through the Bending home like a typhoon. Broom and mop, vacuum and dusting cloths, soap and cleansers, waxes, polishes, disinfectants, and room deodorizers.

When they finished shortly before 2:00 P.M., the house shone, freshly linened, smelling like an apple orchard. Grace showered, changed her underclothing, donned a newly laundered white polyester pantsuit. She sat down to relax for an hour. Then it would be necessary to fetch Harry and Lucy from school. Wayne would get out later and take the school bus.

The Bending home was neither as luxurious as the Empts' nor as flamboyant as the Holloways', but Grace believed it to be decorated in better taste than both. It was – well . . . more traditional perhaps, but it was quiet, dignified, and everything matched.

For instance, the couch on which she sat was covered

113

with a toile de Jouy print on an off-white muslin. The same fabric covered an armchair and was used in the long drapes at the picture window and glass doors to the terrace.

The remainder of the living room was vaguely eighteenth-century French, with touches of gilt, cherubima and floral reproductions everywhere. Even the television set was in a white cabinet that Grace had decoupaged herself with vines, cabbage roses, and butterflies.

Sitting quietly in this artificial conservatory, blonde hair tied back with a pert bow of blue yarn, Grace Bending welcomed the moment of silent reflection when she might ponder her children's problems and her problems with her husband.

She was convinced that Ronald didn't have any problems; he rode the crests like a triumphant surfer.

When the front doorbell rang, she made a small moue of discontent. Not because of the interruption of her gloom, but because of the chimes themselves. They sounded 'Shave and a haircut, two-bits.' Ronald had insisted on installing that vulgar signal.

Looking through the judas of the oak door, she saw a completely bald, giant colored man, light-colored, no more than beige, but undeniably Negro, standing straight, sparkling cordovan attaché case at his feet. He wore a suit of black alpaca that shone in the sun, clean white shirt, black tie narrow as a ribbon.

She opened the door to the length of the restraining chain.

'Yes?'

'Ma'am,' he said, the voice a deep, thrilling diapason, 'I surely do apologize for disturbing you. I would like to speak to you regarding the health and well-being of you and your loved ones.'

'About what?' she asked suspiciously, talking through the gap in the chained door.

'Vitamins,' the giant said, showing a mouthful of thirty-two white teeth. 'Food supplements. The road to regenerative good health, to a happier and, yes, a more rewarding life.'

'Sorry,' she said. 'We already take vitamins. All of us. All we need.'

'No, ma'am,' he said gently. 'Not all you need. Are you totally aware of the demands of nutrition? Alfalfa pills? Soya? Folic acid? Essential additions to today's energy-deficient diet. May I have a moment of your valuable time, ma'am? Please keep the chain on your door. I wish only to leave with you a few brochures in four-color on glossy paper which you may study at your leisure.'

When she didn't answer, he stooped swiftly, opened that gleaming attaché case and withdrew a bundle of pamphlets which he poked through the door gap, and which she took.

'Yours to study at your leisure, ma'am,' he repeated in that resonating voice. 'And if they are of nominal interest, may I request you to hand them on to others? Ma'am, I represent Good Life, Incorporated, a nonprofit organization devoted to improving the eating habits, life-style, and nutritional morality, you might say, of all living Americans. To further these aims, we –'

As he rumbled on about vitamin deficiency, the impossibility of achieving a balanced diet with processed foods, and the absolute necessity for supplements to prevent frambesia, bilharzia, and the fantods, Grace observed him closely.

He was a comfortably plump man, about fifty, she guessed. He had an eggish head, a body with a pear's outline, and a belly like a sweet, round muskmelon. But despite these disconcerting resemblances, there was no denying his dignity.

He boomed the glories of alfalfa pills, and her eyes fell to the opened attaché case. There, nestled amongst packets of four-color, glossy paper brochures, was a black, leather-bound volume, the cover bearing a gold cross and the legend: Holy Bible.

'What is your name?' she said sharply, interrupting his monologue.

'Osborn T. Fitch, ma'am,' he said softly.

She slipped off the chain and held the door open for him.

'I am Mrs Grace Bending,' she said severely.

He bowed his bald head gravely.

In the living room, holding his unlatched attaché case in both arms, he looked about with admiring eyes.

'A splendid home, Mrs Bending,' he caroled. 'Just splendid. I see love everywhere.'

She glowed.

He was seated, and accepted a glass of cold water, though she had offered a cola. 'No dope, thank you, ma'am,' he said.

He started again on the alfalfa pills, and again she interrupted him.

'Why do you carry a bible in your case, Mr Fitch?' she demanded.

He looked at her with a small smile.

'Have you been born again?' he asked.

'No. I'm not sure what that means. I'm a churchgoer. Presbyterian. I've heard of born-again Christians, of course. But I don't know exactly . . .'

'Discovering the Lord Jesus Christ,' he cried. 'To rededicate your life to Him, and to find therein riches you have never known, dreams you have never dared, a new life of humility, happiness, and glory.'

It wasn't the words so much as that plummy voice . . .

'Are you a preacher?' she said.

'Not ordained,' he said humbly. 'No, Mrs Bending, I am not. I have no official position, as you might say. I do conduct a very informal, ah, group. I hesitate to use the word "church."'

'Tell me about it,' she said.

He told her. It was a gathering of born-agains that met twice a week. Usually at the home of one of the members, or occasionally in a store, a garage, once in a parking lot.

116

'It is very informal,' he said, his deep voice bubbling with laughter. 'Very unstructured. Blacks and whites. All ages. We might have fifty at a meeting. One night we had three. We may sing a hymn. We may testify. If a brother or sister wishes to testify, so be it.'

'But what do you *do*, Mr Fitch?' she said.

'We support and comfort each other in the faith. We counsel and offer love. We do what we can. Visit the sick, the afflicted, the lonely and despairing. No monetary contributions are required or requested. Members do contribute: money, clothing, such things as hot water bottles and frying pans, as required. As I said, it is very unstructured, and we mean to keep it that way.'

'And you are the minister or preacher?'

'Oh, no, ma'am. I neither minister nor preach any more than any of the other members. Perhaps you might call me a moderator. Yes, true, I endeavor to moderate. That is my role. I will read from the Holy Book on occasion. To offer solace to those of us who suffer, and forgiveness to those who sin. We make no effort to convert others unless they express interest first.'

'How long has this, ah, group been in existence?'

'About a year. We started with four members. Now, as I said, we might have fifty at a gathering.'

'Whites and blacks you said?'

'Oh yes, ma'am. Our youngest member is nine, our oldest eighty-six. I say "members," but there is no list, no registry. We are all equal in the love of Jesus. That is what we feel.'

'Yes,' she said, examining her fingernails.

There was silence a moment. Then:

'Mrs Bending,' he said gently, 'would you care to attend one of our gatherings? I assure you that you would be most welcome.'

She considered. 'It would be difficult, Mr Fitch. I have a husband and three young children. Your meetings are held in the evening?'

'Yes, ma'am. Most of our people are working folks.'

'It would be hard for me to get away. I do, once a week, attend an evening prayer meeting at my own church.'

'And what day is that, Mrs Bending?'

'Every Wednesday night.'

'The next time we plan to gather on a Wednesday evening, I could call you. If you wish . . .'

'Just to observe,' she said sharply.

'Of course, ma'am,' he intoned. 'Just to observe.'

Before he left, she ordered a bottle of 100 alfalfa pills.

4

Ronald Bending, jaunty, even breezy, plopped into the chair across the desk from Dr Theodore Levin. He lighted a cigarette with theatrical flair. He looked with some amusement at the bookcase of dolls and games.

'What's with the toys, doc?' he asked.

Dr Levin switched on his tape recorder.

'I sometimes ask my young analysands to select a doll, toy, or game to play with. Their choice occasionally offers a clue to their behavior.'

'You mean if a kid picks a popgun or rubber tomahawk, it proves he's aggressive?'

'Something like that.'

Bending made a snorting sound. 'Too bad you don't have a life-size Barbie Doll. I might be interested.'

'Would you?'

'Just kidding, doc, for God's sake.'

'Uh-huh,' Levin muttered, busily peeling the cellophane from a black cigar, piercing it, lighting it slowly with a wooden kitchen match.

Bending viewed this ritual with a thin smile, then pointedly looked at his wristwatch.

'How long do you figure it will take, doc? I don't mean your lighting your cigar or this session today, but getting Lucy straightened out?'

'Would you object if I addressed you as Ronnie?'

Bending took a deep breath and blew it out, lips fluttering. 'Yes, I would. I don't want to make a federal case out of it, but my wife is the only person who calls me Ronnie. I hate it. Ronnie, for Christ's sake! Makes you think of a freckle-faced kid with two front teeth missing.'

'I'd be happy to address you as Ronald, if you'll call me doctor instead of doc.'

'Sorry about that. What the hell – let's go for broke; my friends call me Turk.'

'Turk? How did you get that name?'

'Haven't the slightest. But it's been Turk since my college days. What do your friends call you – Ted?'

'Yes.'

'Well, why don't we make it Ted and Turk?

'That's agreeable to me.'

Bending settled back comfortably, as if he had won a debate. Levin stared at him, eyes goggly behind thick glasses. As usual, he hunched forward, neck hidden in rounded shoulders. Bending endured the inspection calmly.

'Have you told your wife?' the doctor asked.

'What?' Bending said, startled from his pose. 'Told her what?'

'How you feel about the name Ronnie?'

'Have I ever! But getting that woman to change her ways is like getting the Sphinx to yawn. So I finally gave up; just too damned much trouble arguing about it. When she drops dirt on my coffin, she'll say, "Goodbye, Ronnie." Well, enough about names; let's get back to my question: How long do you figure Lucy's treatment will take?'

Levin sighed noisily. 'I cannot give you an accurate prediction.'

'How about an estimate? A rough estimate?'

'A minimum of a year. Possibly – probably longer.'

Bending gloomed into space as he worked out the financial consequences.

'At one session a week, figure about five grand a year – right?'

'About.'

'Well . . . I guess I can swing it. It's going to hurt, but it's

120

worth it if you can get Lucy back on the tracks. You think you can, doc – uh, Ted?'

'I think I can. But as I told you at our first meeting, I cannot guarantee success.'

'So, in effect, I'm gambling the five grand?'

'Or more,' Dr Levin said with some relish.

'Or more. Okay, let's do it. She's such a terrific little girl, I want her to have every possible chance.'

'Very commendable.'

'You're a snotty bastard, you know that, Ted?'

'I meant it sincerely. I have always found that sarcastic people are very quick to ascribe that characteristic to others.'

'You're right, and I apologize. I have a big mouth. It's gotten me in a lot of trouble.'

They looked at each other with half-smiles. A little more relaxed now, but the wariness persisted. Levin pondered how he might thaw the adversary relationship he saw as blocking what he wanted revealed.

'Turk, I see by your questionnaire that you are president of a printing company. What kind of printing do you do?'

'Mostly financial statements and annual reports.'

'That sounds interesting,' the doctor said politely.

'Not very. And don't ask for stock tips. It's against the law to divulge insider information.'

'I won't ask. How did you get into that line of work?'

'I studied fine arts. I wanted to be a serious artist.' A twisted grin. 'Ain't that a laugh? But I drifted into commercial illustration and graphic design. From there it was a short step to layout and typography. Now I run a printing plant. Who'd have thunk it?'

'Do you still paint or draw – for your own enjoyment?'

'Nah. I've got a wife, three kids, two cars, a mortgaged home – and now this thing with Lucy. Who's got time for painting? I had to give up all my wacky dreams. Ah shit, that's not fair. Grace wanted me to go on with my painting.

What happened to me is my responsibility. *I* decided to throw away my paintbox.'

'What decided you?'

'I was no good. Or not as good as I wanted to be. Ted, how is all this bullshit about me going to help Lucy?'

Levin sat back, splayed his hands flat on the desk top. He was finding this interview difficult. Not for the first time he reflected that he was better with children than with adults.

But he did know that frequently adults opened up simply because they enjoyed it. Someone expressing interest seemed to be a new experience for them. Which meant that, even after years of marriage, they were unable to talk to their mate.

'As I explained to your wife, I am trying to collect as much information as possible about Lucy, her parents and siblings. Perhaps I'll learn something that will help explain Lucy's behavior and give me a lead on how to resolve her problem.'

'All right,' Bending said, nodding. 'That makes sense to me. Fire away.'

'Turk, would you say yours is a happy marriage?'

'Wait a minute, Ted. Hold it! I'm talking to you in strict confidence – right? I mean, you don't repeat what I tell you to Grace, and you don't repeat to me what she says?'

'That is correct.'

'Okay then. Now about our marriage . . . It has its ups and downs. About average, I suppose. Better than some, worse than some.'

'You've been married for how many years?'

'Uh, let's see . . . Thirteen, I think. Around there.'

'How did you and Grace meet?'

'I picked her up at the Metropolitan Museum in New York. At a Degas exhibit.'

'Your wife is a college graduate?'

'That's right. Radcliffe. I went to Brown.'

For some reason Levin could not analyze, it was difficult

122

for him to see this man as a college graduate who once had dreams of becoming an artist.

Bending was a bundle of contradictions. An obviously 'masculine man' – the type Levin usually found difficult to relate to – but with an ironic and sometimes bitter wit.

'Turk, do you have any shared interests with your wife? In addition to your children and home?'

'You mean like hobbies?'

'Hobbies, sports, perhaps attending art exhibits or the theatre?'

'Nooo, I can't really think of anything. Well, we both like to entertain. She plays a pretty fair game of tennis, and occasionally we play mixed doubles. But that's about it. I usually work late and sometimes on Saturdays, so we don't have too much time together.'

'Does your wife object to the long hours you work?'

'No. I think that secretly she's happy to have me out of the house.'

'Why do you think that?'

'I don't know – just a feeling.'

'Do you drink, Turk?'

'Sure, I take a drink. Why – are you going to offer me one?'

'No. Would you characterize yourself as a light, social, or heavy drinker?'

'Social, I guess.'

'Does your wife drink?'

'One or two weak highballs at a party. That's about it.'

This line of questioning, the psychiatrist reflected mournfully, was getting him nowhere. He decided to push ahead boldly, to determine as soon as possible the limits of this man's candor.

'Turk, how would you characterize your sexual relations with your wife?'

'Nonexistent.'

'What do you think is the reason for that?'

'A lot of reasons. My working hours, for one thing.'

'And . . . ?'

'I don't really think Grace is particularly interested in that part of married life.'

'You mean she rejects you?'

'No. Never.'

'Then why do you feel she has no interest in sex?'

'Are you married, Ted?'

'Divorced.'

That was a deliberate falsehood, and not the first time Levin had uttered it. He had never been married but, as he had explained to Dr Mary Scotsby, the lie helped establish rapport. A husband or father with a wife or child in therapy was not apt to accept the expertise of a bachelor.

'Unethical, yes,' Levin told Dr Scotsby, 'but let's not get into a philosophical discussion of whether or not the end justifies the means. All I can tell you is that my falsehood serves its purpose.'

'Well then,' Bending said, 'if you've been married, you must have learned that there are a hundred ways of knowing when your wife isn't interested. She doesn't have to tell you she has a headache.'

'Has your wife always had a lack of interest in sexual relations?'

'God, no! She used to be too much for me.'

'So her, uh, coolness is a recent development?'

'Fairly recent.'

'How recent?'

'Say about, oh, three or four years.'

'But would you say that Grace is a good wife? Other than the sexual estrangement between the two of you?'

'Yes, she's a good wife. Keeps the house squeaky clean. A great cook.'

'And a good mother?'

'A marvelous mother.' Bending sounded sincere.

'Has Grace been faithful to you?'

'I think you better ask her that.'

124

'And have you been faithful to her?'

'Ted, are you sure this is going to help Lucy's treatment?'

'I'm sure.'

'Well, I won't lie to you; there have been a few times in our marriage when I've strayed.'

'How many times?'

'A few.'

'More since your wife has shown a lack of interest in sex? More infidelity in the last three or four years?'

'You really go for the jugular, don't you?'

'You haven't answered my question.'

'Yes, possibly more in the last three or four years.'

'Is Grace aware of these affairs?'

'No. I don't think so. And even if she was, I don't think she'd object. Might even be relieved.'

'Why do you say that?'

'Just a feeling I have.'

When Dr Theodore Levin started his practice, he had been inclined to give weight and importance to analysands' statements: 'It's just a feeling I have.' Or, 'My instinct tells me so.' Experience had taught him that 'feelings' and 'instincts' were frequently mask-words for prejudices and desires.

'Turk, do you think your children are aware of their parents' sexual, ah, enmity to each other?'

'I wouldn't call it enmity. I still think Grace is a damned attractive woman. I hope she still thinks I'm not completely repulsive.'

'Perhaps "enmity" was a poor choice of words. Will you accept "indifference"? Would you say that you and your wife are sexually indifferent to each other?'

'I guess so, Ted. I guess we're indifferent, as far as bed goes.'

'Do you think your children are aware of this?'

'Of course not. How could they be?'

The psychiatrist stifled a sigh. It was hopeless trying to convince parents how much their children knew of the 'secret' life of the master bedroom. Not knew intellectually, but sensed, felt, and were so influenced.

'Your older son – that's Wayne, isn't it?'

'Yes.'

'He's twelve, isn't he?'

'That's correct.'

'Have you been responsible for his sex education?'

'What there was of it. Believe me, Ted, he knows everything – or thinks he does. He sure knows a hell of a lot more than I did at his age.'

'And the younger boy?'

'Harry? He's only five. He hasn't asked any questions yet. Too busy making radio sets. The damned kid's a genius.'

'And what about Lucy's sex education?'

'I left that to Grace.'

'Lucy never asked you questions?'

'A few times. I told her to ask her mother. Do you have any children, Ted?'

'Twin girls,' Levin said, lying smoothly. 'Their mother has them. I see them for a month out of every year.'

What began as a simple lie ('I was married; I am divorced') had escalated into a blooming fantasy. With some pleasure, Dr Theodore Levin had added to and embellished the basic falsehood.

Now he was divorced, with twin daughters he visited every year. He could describe the mythical wife and the mythical children. Even the home in which they had once lived, the domestic routine, the crises and the picnics.

He had confessed this fantasy to his own analyst, Al Wollman, who had stared at him a long moment.

'You're nuts,' he said finally.

'Well, Ted,' Bending was saying, 'you wouldn't believe how smart kids are about sex these days. I mean, they get it in biology courses at school and sometimes in special sex education instruction. With films yet! Last year Wayne brought home a booklet from school that had everything in

126

it: drawings of a man's joint, a woman's cooze . . . just everything. So they don't have to ask as many questions as they used to. Thank God.'

'But when Lucy asked you questions, you sent her to her mother?'

'That's right.'

'When Lucy became, ah, overly loving with you, how did you handle it?'

'I told you. I tried not to reject her. I didn't get angry or wallop her or anything like that. I just made it plain that she was annoying me, that I didn't like what she was doing.'

'And she stopped?'

'Yes.'

'How did it affect her attitude toward you?'

'As far as I can see, it didn't. She's still affectionate, but in a normal way. She kisses me every morning at breakfast, and throws her arms around me if she's up when I get home. But she doesn't try to feel me up or grope me. And she doesn't come onto my lap unless I ask her. My turning her off hasn't made her hate me, if that's what you think.'

'But she continues her hypersexual behavior with other men? Friends and visitors?'

'Yes.'

Levin put his cigar butt carefully aside. He sat back, hands laced across his belly. He stared down at his intertwined fingers, reflecting on the endless variety of the human animal.

'Turk, do you think your sons are aware of Lucy's, ah, unusual conduct?'

'Not Harry. Probably Wayne. Yes, I'd guess Wayne knows what's going on.'

'Has he ever said anything about it?'

'Not to me.'

'Have your sons ever seen Lucy naked?'

'Only Wayne, and not since she was a little baby.'

'Have your children ever seen you and your wife naked?'

'Good God, no! What a question! Oh, wait a minute . . .

127

Wayne and I play golf together occasionally at the club. He's seen me naked in the locker room. But not the other kids.'

'Not Lucy?'

'Certainly not! Goddamn it, Ted, what are you getting at?'

'I'm not getting at anything. I'm just asking questions.'

'You don't think I've exhibited myself to Lucy, do you?'

'Have you?'

'No!'

'Have either of your sons?'

'They better not! I'd break their goddamned necks!'

'Well, I think our time is up. Thank you for your patience. You've been a big help.'

'I have? I'll take your word for it.'

5

Starting around midnight, a series of sharp squalls swept eastward from the Naples–Ft. Myers area on the west coast. They flooded the Everglades, then slammed at east coast communities from Miami north to West Palm Beach.

Streets were hubcap-deep, lawns soggy, the beach itself gullied into miniature rivers and tributaries. The sky was low, roiling and muddy, with lightning flashes like far-off photographers' bulbs. Thunder did not crack, but rumbled and grumbled all morning.

Then, around noon, the front passed through; rain ceased, the sky began to clear. People ventured out, tentatively at first, then with more confidence. Patches of blue appeared, a bloated sun burned through the haze. By 2:00 P.M., it was a perfect day, and the world was drying.

Wayne Bending, sitting alone on the rear benchseat of his school bus, watched eagerly for a glimpse of the sea. He hoped the storm had left a strong swell running. Then he might get in some late-afternoon surfing.

But the ocean, when he glimpsed it, was a disappointment. It was high, but choppy and rough; small waves crested several times before they spilled onto the beach. No surfing. And even a swim didn't seem too attractive.

His mother and Lucy and Harry were in the living room, eating peanut-butter-and-jelly sandwiches and drinking milk from lap trays. They were watching some dopey TV show with puppets and a real-life guy wearing a fireman's suit. Wayne nodded coldly in return to their greetings, and went directly to the kitchen.

He made himself a thick ham-and-Swiss-cheese sandwich on rye bread, slathered with mayonnaise. He took that, a can of Coke, a handful of chocolate-chip cookies, and went up the back stairs to his own bedroom. Inside, he locked the door, switched on his radio to a rock station, and kicked off his loafers.

In bed, his back against the headboard, he ate his sandwich and cookies, gulped his Coke and, not listening to the music, decided he might as well be dead.

Since that night of the Holloways' party, he had not spoken to Eddie. He had only seen him once, from a distance, and even then Eddie had turned away. Wayne was convinced that Eddie was avoiding him, disgusted with any guy who would kiss another guy, even after smoking a joint.

Why had he done such a stupid thing? It was the grass; he was sure of that; it had zonked him without his being aware of it. Everyone said pot made a sex maniac out of you. He had just felt this tremendous urge, and he had done it, and he was lucky Eddie hadn't hit him.

But now Eddie had time to think about what had happened, and it probably sickened him. He probably thought Wayne was a screaming fag, and he wanted nothing more to do with him. Maybe Eddie had told the other guys what Wayne had done. The thought was enough to shrivel Wayne's insides, and he felt like weeping.

He finished his food and wiggled down until he was lying on the bed, head on the pillow. He stared at the ceiling and thought about death. He supposed it was like sleep, just like sleep, only you never dreamed, and you never woke up.

Thinking such somber thoughts, he felt himself growing drowsy. He let go, went along with it, hoping he might never wake up. But just before he was completely out, the bedside phone shrilled. His entire body jerked as if he had been pierced with one of those long steel needles his father used to barbecue chunks of beef.

The phone was Wayne's own, his private phone in bright red, a gift on his twelfth birthday. He had his own number and was listed in the book, like most of the other guys he knew. He rolled over and grabbed for the handset.

' 'Lo?' he said in a sleepy voice.

'Hey man,' Eddie Holloway said, 'how they hanging?'

Wayne came awake abruptly, swung his feet onto the floor. He sat on the edge of the bed, clutching the phone so tightly that he saw his hand trembling.

'This and that,' he said as casually as he could manage. 'What's doing?'

'Dull dull dull,' Eddie said cheerfully. 'I was hoping there'd be some surf after the storm, but no luck. Where you been keeping yourself?'

'Here and there,' Wayne said lightly. 'Going off my nut with the bullshit around here.'

'Yeah,' Eddie said, 'you're singing my song. Listen, dumbo, the old lady got in a new shipment. I guess the shrimp boat landed. Dig?'

'Oh yeah. Sure.'

'So how's about you and me turning on?'

'Suits me. When?'

'Tonight. Nine. Can you make it? Same place.'

'No sweat.'

'I'll bring an old blanket,' Eddie Holloway said. 'The ground's still damp. Listen, can you lift some sauce?'

'Uh . . . maybe. Yeah, I think so. I'll try.'

'You're my main man,' Eddie Holloway said. '*Hasta la vista, mi amigo*. I just learned that today. It means "Up yours, Charlie." '

'Yeah,' Wayne said, laughing. 'I know where you're from.'

Then he went downstairs to the living room where his mother, Lucy, and Harry were still watching the boob tube.

'Hi, gang,' Wayne Bending said brightly.

As usual, his father didn't show up in time for dinner.

131

Out shagging some quiff, Wayne figured, but he couldn't have cared less. As long as he paid the bills.

There was pot roast with vegetables, a salad with creamy garlic dressing, and key lime pie for dessert. His mother, as usual, insisted on saying grace before they began eating.

Wayne thought that was funny, a woman named Grace saying grace. But he couldn't have explained exactly where the humor was.

After dinner, he helped clear the table. He stacked the dishwasher. He put the linen napkins into their proper initialed plastic rings. He even took out the garbage.

He stalled around until his mother shepherded Lucy and Harry upstairs. Lucy could bathe herself, but Harry had to be watched in the shower. Then they'd be put to bed. Wayne figured he had an hour before his mother came downstairs again. Now if only his father didn't show up unexpectedly . . .

He went to the kitchen cupboard where his mother kept empty jars, used pieces of aluminium foil (smoothed out and neatly folded), plastic containers, string, and old wire ties.

He selected an empty pint mayonnaise jar. He took it back to his father's liquor cabinet in the living room. There were three full and sealed liters of vodka, and one opened liter that was three-quarters filled.

Working quietly, swiftly, carefully, Wayne filled the pint jar from the opened bottle and tightened the jar lid. He took the vodka bottle into the kitchen and filled it to its original level from the cold water tap. He replaced the bottle in its former position in the liquor cabinet.

He took the pint jar of vodka outside and concealed it behind a dwarf palm. Then he came back and settled down in front of the television set. When his mother came downstairs, he was watching an educational film on Channel 2 from Miami. It was about the wild dogs of Africa.

He got up, turned off the TV. 'Dull stuff,' he commented. Then he stretched, elaborately casual. 'Well, I better go upstairs and hit the books. We got a math quiz tomorrow.'

'If you get hungry,' his mother said, 'there's some pie left. But leave a slice for your father.'

Upstairs, safely locked in his own bedroom, he didn't glance at his homework. He lay on the bed, stared at the ceiling, listened to a program of country-and-western songs. He kept the radio turned low so crazy Harry wouldn't complain the noise was keeping him awake.

Wayne thought about meeting Eddie Holloway in the Empts' gazebo at nine o'clock. This time he was determined there would be no replay of his dopey behavior. No kissing. Nothing like that.

They would just smoke a joint, sip a little vodka, get a little high. They'd talk. Maybe about surfing, boats, women – whatever came up. Eddie was a cool guy to rap with.

Wayne was flattered that Eddie had picked him for a special close friendship. And it was special. Eddie always had a bunch of guys and young creamers hanging around him, but he had selected Wayne Bending for these private pot sessions in the gazebo. That was something.

Thinking about Eddie Holloway like that, Wayne suddenly realized he was getting an erection. He jumped from the soft bed hastily. He stalked about the room, hands shoved in his hip pockets. Shaken, he tried to breathe deeply, wondering what the hell was happening to him.

At about a quarter to nine, he took his English-Spanish dictionary and went down the front steps to the living room. His mother was seated in a pool of light from a floor lamp. The TV set was on, but she was peering through wire-rimmed glasses at the knitting in her lap, counting stitches.

She hadn't heard him, and he stood there a moment, staring at her. His mother wasn't a bad-looking woman, he acknowledged, but she could have done a lot more with herself. More makeup, for instance. A classier hairdo. Brighter clothes. She was kind of drab. Not like Eddie's mother, who really came on.

133

She looked up from her knitting, smiled. He came into the room.

'Listen,' he said, speaking rapidly, 'I just got a call from Eddie Holloway. He's got a Spanish test this week, and he left his dictionary in his locker at school, so I said I'd lend him mine.'

'Is he coming over for it, dear?' she asked.

'Uh, no. I said I'd bring it over and sort of, you know, quiz him on words and phrases. I mean, he's got all his stuff spread out and all, so it would be easier if I went over there.'

'How long will you be gone?'

'Oh, like an hour or two. Shouldn't be later than that.'

'All right, dear,' she said. 'Maybe you should wear your nylon jacket.'

'Nah,' he said, 'it's still warm.'

He went out through the kitchen door. He retrieved the jar of vodka from behind the dwarf palm. He walked rapidly out to A1A, ready to dart into the bushes if the headlights of his father's car turned into the driveway.

He stayed on the verge of the highway until he came to the Empts' place. The big iron gates were yawning wide; the ground floor of the main house was brilliantly lighted. There were several cars parked in the driveway. Wayne figured they were having a dinner party. Old lady Empt liked to entertain.

He slipped through the trees to the gazebo. The cast-iron benches were dry, still warm from the afternoon sun. He bent to feel the packed sand floor. The top inch or so was warm, but when he prodded with a finger, he could feel cool dampness below. So he sat on one of the hard benches, holding his dictionary and jar of vodka. He waited for Eddie.

He sat there for almost ten minutes. That was Eddie: a cool guy; he was never on time. While he waited, Wayne watched the big house and saw figures moving back and forth across the lighted windows. He could hear, rising and fading, the sound of music. Once the sea breeze brought a burst of muted laughter.

He hoped no bombed guest would stagger out to investigate the gazebo. The thought of that happening angered him. This was his secret place. His and Eddie's.

Holloway showed up eventually, sauntering. He was wearing jeans and a cotton T-shirt hacked off raggedly so his midriff was bare. This was a style a lot of the guys had swiped from the practice clothes of pro football players. Eddie had a rolled-up blanket clamped under one arm.

'Hey, Bending,' he said, 'what are you doing here in the dark – fluffing your duff?'

'*Quién sabe*, mother,' Wayne said, and Eddie laughed.

'That kid sister of mine,' he said, spreading the worn blanket on the sand. 'That Gloria – she's something else again. Now she wants an evening gown. Can you beat that? A nine-year-old brat wanting an evening gown?'

'What did your folks say?'

'Ah, shit,' Eddie said, 'I walked out on the argument. Instant hysteria. Kicking and screaming. Who needs that bullshit? But she'll get it. Just to keep her yap shut. You bring any booze?'

'Pint of vodka,' Wayne said, holding up the jar.

'Beautiful,' Eddie said. 'Just gorgeous. Slip me a fix.'

They sat on the blanket, handed the opened jar back and forth. Eddie took a deep gulp and said, 'Oh man.' Wayne tried a small sip and coughed on it.

'Warm,' he said. 'I should have put in some ice. Maybe a piece of lime.'

'Nah,' Eddie said. 'It goes down smooth the way it is. Now for dessert . . .'

He had the cigarettes tucked inside the cuff of one of his socks, swaddled in toilet paper. He unwrapped them carefully.

'New brand,' he announced. 'They got a thin wire pressed into the paper. So when you get down to the roach, you can hold it on the end of the wire. Ain't science grand?'

They lighted up, lay back, stared through the latticed roof of the gazebo at a night sky that went on forever. Eddie combined drags with sips from the vodka jar, but Wayne was content with the marijuana.

'You know Tony Sanchez?' Eddie asked lazily. 'A red-headed cat? He works at a gas station up in Boca on Saturdays.'

'The football guy?'

'That's the one. Quarterback, but not first string. Anyway, he's got a fourteen-foot Hobie Cat he wants to sell. It's kinda beat up. Needs work, but the sheets are okay. Jesus, I'd love to buy that mother.'

'What's he want?'

'He's asking a thousand, but I think I can get him down. Nine hundred, maybe. You got any money, dumbo?'

'About a hundred,' Wayne said humbly. 'In my savings account.'

Eddie Holloway laughed harshly. 'That's a hundred more than I got. I spend it as fast as it comes in. Ahh, shit. I wish I owned that boat. What a high that would be.'

This time Wayne was convinced the pot was getting to him. No finkery now. He lost track of time. The world softened, hard edges blurring. The night seemed blander, almost fluffy, and there was a hum in the air. He reached across Eddie for the jar of vodka and took a swallow. This time he didn't cough.

He leaned across Eddie again and pressed the jar back into the sand so it wouldn't tip. He was stretched across Eddie, looking down at him.

Eddie had his eyes closed. His hand was up in the air, holding the joint: a tiny, glowing beacon. Eddie was really a sharp-looking stud with his long, sun-bleached blond hair, his movie star face. And the gleaming skin a coppery tan.

Wayne put a palm lightly on Eddie's bare midriff, covering flat stomach, perfectly round belly button.

'Hey man,' Eddie said sleepily. 'This is a new kick – right?'

Wayne set his own cigarette carefully aside, poking the wire down into the sand. He turned back to Eddie. He bent over him, pressed his lips to the skin of ribs and stomach. Warm satin. Soft. Sun-scented.

'Oh yeah,' Eddie breathed. 'Don't stop now.'

Thoughts thundering, desire inchoate, Wayne fumbled at Eddie's belt and fly with frantic fingers. What . . . What . . .

'Ohh,' Eddie murmured. 'Oh yeah. Yeah.'

He knew what to do. He knew exactly what to do. Without training or experience. And that thought would puzzle him for the rest of his life.

It was sweet, so sweet. It was comfort, relief of his anguish, balm for his hurts. He nuzzled, panting, Eddie saying, 'Yeah, yeah,' with his pelvis beginning to move just as Wayne felt his own gush of tears and something else.

And when it was over, he was certain Eddie would kick him away, beat him to pulp. 'You filthy fag!' But Eddie lay relaxed, slowly puffing his toke. And with one hand he stroked Wayne's hair, and he said throatily, 'Nice. Nice. The greatest.'

Then they kissed. They kissed! Wayne was so thankful, so grateful. It wasn't the end. He laughed aloud with happiness.

'You nut!' Eddie said affectionately, and put a hand on Wayne's balls, squeezing gently. 'You're really a dumbo – you know that?'

Wayne nodded, giggling. He relighted his roach, and they shared it because Eddie had finished his. They they sipped what was left of the vodka, handing the jar back and forth.

Once Eddie took a sip of warm vodka, then pressed his lips to Wayne's and spit the warm stuff into the other boy's mouth. Wayne thought that was the most important thing that had ever happened to him. It was a pledge, the sealing of a compact.

Finally the vodka was gone, but neither of them moved.

They lay side by side, staring dazedly up through the latticed roof. They heard the far-off sounds of talk, laughter, the growls of motors as the Empts' guests departed.

'Listen, you bastard,' Wayne said. 'You really want that Hobie Cat? The one Tony Sanchez wants to sell?'

'Sure, I want it, dumbo,' Eddie said. 'I told you I did, didn't I?'

'Well . . .' Wayne said, plotting, 'you know Mrs Empt's got eyes for you.'

'So?'

'So she's got all kinds of loot. They're loaded. My father says so.'

Eddie was silent a moment. Then:

'You think she'll pay cold cash for my hot bod?'

'Why not?' Wayne said. 'If you work it right. You know, play her along. Get her hooked.'

'Like a grouper,' Eddie said, laughing.

'Just like a grouper,' Wayne said, laughing. 'You can do it. Sink the hook and play her. Give her a taste and then tell her, Gee whiz, I'd really like to buy this swell boat.'

'You think she'll go for it?'

'Come on, man,' Wayne said, suddenly feeling dominant and superior. 'Of course she'll go for it. I did, didn't I?'

They both broke up, trying to stifle their screams of laughter, wrestling, rolling on the blanket. Then they lay apart, panting.

'But how do I explain it to my parents?' Eddie asked. 'Suddenly I turn up with this boss boat. How do I explain where I got the loot to buy it?'

'How much allowance do you get?'

'Twenty a week,' Eddie said. 'I've been working on the old man to give me a raise to twenty-five.'

'Okay,' Wayne said, 'here's what you do . . . You get the cash from old lady Empt – right? You buy the boat. Then you tell your folks that Sanchez agreed to take ten a week. And you fix it up with Tony so he'll back you up. He'll do it if you give him the thousand he's asking. Also, it will help you get a raise in your allowance from your old man. Does that make sense or doesn't it?'

Eddie bent over him, stroked his cheek tenderly.

'You know, dumbo,' he said, 'you're not so dumb.'

6

Something strange was happening to William Jasper Holloway.

And he knew it.

About a year ago, he had started talking to himself. It hadn't happened suddenly, overnight. It had come on gradually.

For instance, a year ago when he was seated in his private office at the bank and needed to go out onto the tellers' floor for some reason or other, he would simply rise, walk to the door, open it, and exit. Just like anyone else.

Then he found himself planning his moves. Commanding himself. 'Now you will get up. You will walk to the door. You will turn the knob and open the door. You will walk out onto the floor.' All in silence. All in his mind.

This period lasted a while, this stage of silent orders. And then, when he was alone, he discovered he was voicing the commands aloud in a low but firm voice: 'Stand up. Walk to the door. Turn the knob. Now open the door. Now go out onto the floor.'

And not only at work. Whenever he was alone he spoke to himself aloud: 'Turn right at the next light. Take a new bar of soap from the cupboard. Write to Tallahassee re the tax return.'

The next step, a recent one, was a self-dialogue, spoken aloud, during which he debated, sometimes even argued with himself.

'Luther Empt wants you to play golf on Saturday.'

'I don't know if I want to go.'

140

'Maybe you should.'

'What for?'

'To see what's happening with the new factory.'

'I don't care. And I don't feel like playing golf on Saturday. Especially with Empt. The man's an animal.'

'You need the exercise. Fresh air.'

'I'll play a bad game. Drink too much afterward.'

He knew it was happening. He knew he spoke aloud to himself when alone, but it didn't frighten him. He found it almost amusing. He went along with it. Where was the harm?

His decision to purchase a handgun was the result of one of these voiced dialogues:

'What do you need a gun for?'

'Empt has one, and Turk Bending.'

'But why do *you* need one?'

'Crime is increasing. Protect the family, the house.'

'You don't know how to handle a gun.'

'I can learn. It's simple: you point and pull the trigger. I did it with Luther's gun that night on the beach. It felt good. Maybe I won't buy a gun as heavy as Luther's. Just a small one.'

'You'll go to a gunshop and some redneck will laugh at you. He'll see you don't know a damned thing about guns. He'll be contemptuous, rude.'

'So what? I'll treat him coldly. I'm the customer. I'll get a good gun and insist he shows me how to use it. I'll be firm and definite.'

So, convinced, he went to a gunshop on Federal Highway. The clerk turned out to be no redneck at all, but a vested executive type who spoke William Holloway's language. He didn't even ask his customer's reasons for wanting to purchase a firearm.

'Sir,' he said unctuously, 'if your experience with handguns is limited, may I suggest this truly beautiful and efficient weapon? It is a Colt Detective Special, a six-shot, thirty-eight-caliber, all-steel revolver with a two-inch barrel. Total length: six and three-quarter inches. Total weight: only twenty-one ounces. May I call your attention to this snag-eliminating ramp front sight, ejector rod shroud, and wraparound grips of checkered walnut? Just handle this beauty, sir, and judge the heft.'

Obediently, though somewhat gingerly, William Holloway took the gun into his palm.

'It is unloaded, sir,' the clerk said gently. 'I assure you.'

Emboldened, Holloway gripped the weapon tighter. He swung it up, aimed at the far wall.

'Feels fine,' he said confidently.

'Oh yes indeed, sir. Light, but with sufficient up-front weight to provide perfect balance. And small enough to provide convenient concealment at home or carried in your car, as conditions warrant.'

'All right,' Holloway said, 'I'll take it.'

'Very good, sir,' the clerk said. 'Now this model is available in blue or nickel finish.'

'Uh . . . nickel would be nice. And I'll need some bullets.'

'Of course, sir. And may I show you some very handsome holsters to add protection and prestige to your purchase?'

So, after showing identification, signing documents, and learning about the waiting period, William Jasper Holloway paid for gun, bullets, black leather holster. He was assured the firearm came with cleaning kit and a pamphlet providing information on loading, firing, and maintenance.

He returned to the gunshop three days later and picked up his purchases. It was almost 3:00 P.M., and he decided not to return to the bank. On the drive home he had one of his dialogues:

'Well, I did it!'

'I still don't see why you need a gun.'

'Protection. Reassurance. Confidence.'

'You'll be careful with it?'

'Of course.'

'It can kill.'

'I know that.'

'It can kill.'

'I said I knew that.'

'It can kill.'

'Oh shut up!'

Jane and his father-in-law were out somewhere, the kids were at school, and only Maria was at home, banging pots around in the kitchen and singing a Spanish lament in a reedy voice.

Holloway poured a heavy vodka over ice, added a squeezed wedge of lime. He took the drink and his purchases up to the master bedroom and locked the door from the inside. He sat on the edge of the bed and examined his treasures.

He inspected the gun closely. It seemed to have a light, smooth film. He sniffed it and smelled oil, steel, wood. It was really, he decided, a precise, polished piece of machinery. It filled his hand, compact and solid. It felt good.

He read the instructions. He made certain the weapon was unloaded. He aimed at the opposing wall, sighting along the front ramp sight. His hand was steady. He pulled the trigger. It resisted more than he thought it would, but then there was a satisfying click.

'Bang,' he said softly.

He repeated this process, aiming at the bedroom door and the pillow on his wife's bed. Each time he said, 'Bang. Bang.'

He sat there, revolver dangling casually from one hand, while he took several sips of his iced vodka. Then, consulting the instructions again, he loaded the chambers, handling the bright cartridges with slow, exaggerated care. He eased the loaded cylinder back into place.

'Now it can kill.'

'I know that.'

Keeping his forefinger carefully outside the trigger guard, he reaimed at his three targets: the opposing wall,

bedroom door, pillow on his wife's bed. His repeated
'Bang! Bang! Bang!' was louder now.

'Why not you?'

'Why not?'

Still with his finger carefully away from the trigger, he
pressed the muzzle of the gun to his chest. To his genitals.
Then, mouth stretched wide, he inserted the short barrel of
the weapon between his teeth.

He withdrew it, tasting not the oil or polished steel of the
gun but something as bitter as an old penny. He stared at
the precisely turned and manufactured machine in his
hand. Power. His.

He moved to the window with a zany smile. Through the
palm fronds he saw glittering sea, gleaming beach. Men,
women, children sporting in skimpy, brightly colored suits.
Holloway could almost smell the brine, suntan oil, sun-
baked flesh.

South Florida was a painted harlot, doused with dime-
store perfume. Too crass, too importunate, too gaudy.

Still keeping his finger outside the trigger guard, William
Jasper Holloway aimed his new gun through the closed
window. At the palm trees. Beach. People. Sea. Florida.
World. Life.

'Bang,' he said in a low voice. 'Bang.'

7

'Regarding the case of Karen J,' Dr Theodore Levin said pontifically, 'I listened to the tapes and I think you're handling it exactly right.'

Dr Mary Scotsby nodded. 'It seems to be a textbook case of kleptomania.'

'I concur. You don't happen to have another bottle of this wine, do you?'

'I do, but I have something better.'

'No, no, this will do fine. You know my vulgar tastes.'

She went into her kitchen and brought back another bottle of the cheap California burgundy they had been drinking. Levin broke the seal and filled their glasses. Scotsby curled up in one corner of the corduroy-covered couch. Levin sat solidly in a worn wing chair.

They were both wearing bathrobes. Hers was a pale yellow chenille. His was an old-fashioned flannel with an all-over carpet design and a cord sash. His fleshy feet were bare. She was wearing frolicsome mules with blue pompoms.

'It's really a very raw wine, Ted,' she said. 'I only buy it for you.'

'I know,' he said. 'I have no palate at all. Probably all those cigars I smoke. I can't taste anything.'

'I hope you tasted that curry tonight.'

'*That* I tasted,' he said, smiling wanly. 'You saw me sweating, didn't you? Mary, can we talk about the case of Lucy B?'

'If you like.'

'You listened to the tapes?'

She nodded.

'Any immediate reactions?'

'I think you're handling the parents very well. They're opening up. I have a feeling that Lucy has you buffaloed.'

He thought about that.

'You may be right,' he said finally, sighing. 'An extraordinarily beautiful little girl. I thought she looked like a miniature woman. Did you get that impression?'

She frowned a moment, biting her lower lip. 'Yes, I'll go along with that.'

'When you examined her, did you notice if her breasts were overdeveloped?'

'For a child her age? Perhaps they were. Not the breasts of a woman, you understand, but more like the breasts of an adolescent. The nipples were well defined, almost erectile.'

'Uh-huh.'

She stared at him through her wire-rimmed glasses. 'What are you getting at, Ted?'

He shifted his bulk in the soft armchair. He took a gulp of his wine.

'I've been anxious about something,' he said. 'For some time now. The case of Lucy B has brought it to a head. Briefly, I've been wondering if my entire approach to psychotherapy is too parochial. I've been thinking that perhaps I should give more weight to other factors. Sociological. Cultural. Physiological.'

'Physiological? Lucy appears to be in perfect health.'

'Mmm. Still . . .'

She waited patiently for him to continue. She was a rawboned woman, taller than he, with bony shoulders. Awkward arms and legs, long feet. Her breasts were small and muscular; rib cage and pelvic bones pressed fair, freckled skin.

They had showered an hour ago. Her face, washed free of makeup, was clear and shining. Brown hair was pulled

146

straight back from her high brow and fastened with a plain gold barrette.

It was a sharp face, nose and jaw jutting. Pale lips were thin. Small, convoluted ears hugged the skull. No lines, wrinkles, or crow's-feet. The eyes gave nothing away. A stretched neck, and then the hard bones of her chest.

'When I came down here about ten years ago,' he said slowly, 'I became aware that the cases I was getting were different from those I treated in Denver. I was seeing more deviance and perversion. More aberrant sexual habits. I've been wondering why this should be so.'

'The climate,' she said wryly. 'It is tropical, you know.'

'Oh yes,' he said seriously, 'I do believe that's a factor. The total environment. Hot sun, glorious beach, relaxed outdoor living. It's difficult to resist pleasure as a way of life. But I think other factors are involved. For instance, since you've been down here, have you ever met anyone who was born in Florida?'

'No.'

'I have. One old man. But everyone else is from somewhere else. So you have this feeling of rootlessness. No one really belongs, in the sense of having family that's lived here for generations. No foundations. When you go to a foreign country, you have a tendency to cut loose. I think it's a very human reaction, in a new and strange place, to slough off old rules, old repressions and constraints.'

'I concur,' she said, staring at him with steady, unblinking eyes.

'And another factor . . .' he went on. 'Al Wollman and I were talking about why the children down here, and particularly the young girls, seem so physically mature for their age. I'm sure you've seen twelve- and thirteen-year-old girls on the beach with the bodies of eighteen- to twenty-year-old women. Very well-developed breasts. Tall. Well-defined waists, hips, buttocks.'

'And with heavy makeup,' Scotsby said. 'Some of them look like young hookers.'

147

'Yes,' he said. 'Al thinks it may be due to the fact that so many go on the Pill at a very early age. All those estrogens. Plus the fact that so much of our meat, especially chicken, has been treated with growth-accelerating hormones. Plus the current fad for vitamins and food supplements. Does all this sound completely nuts to you?'

'Well . . . no,' she said cautiously. 'Not completely.'

'So now we have several factors – environmental, sociological, cultural, physiological – all of them adding up to a speeding of maturation, and particularly amongst infant, latency, and adolescent children.'

'And you feel you haven't been giving these factors sufficient weight in your diagnosis and treatment?'

'I think it's a very real possibility. Now let's get back to the case of Lucy B. Ten years ago, in Denver, I would have pigeonholed her as middle latency.'

'Ted, Bornstein subdivided latency into two phases. Lucy could be early-latency or late-latency.'

'Did you read Pandey's paper dealing with prelatency, latency, and postlatency? So now we have three phases. But my point is that, due to accelerated growth caused by the factors I mentioned, Lucy B, in spite of being eight years old, may not be a latency child at all, but in an early stage of adolescence.'

'An interesting theory, Ted.'

'Latency, according to Freud, is a sexual lull, a period of genital anesthesia with a definite decline in masturbatory activity between the ages of about five to ten or twelve. Her mother says Lucy does not masturbate. Do you believe that?'

She looked at him. 'If her mother is telling the truth, and Lucy doesn't masturbate, that doesn't help your theory, does it? It would indicate that Lucy *is* a latency child. Is that why you don't want to believe Grace?'

'Possibly. But I think now that Grace may be telling the truth, and Lucy does not masturbate. Not because she's a latency child, but because she has discovered a sexual practice that gives her more pleasure than masturbation. An adolescent practice.'

'Exciting older men?'

'Yes.'

'On the tape, she said she doesn't think she's doing anything wrong. Do you believe she really feels that way?'

'Wrong? Mary, what does "wrong" mean in this case? It's not "wrong" to her; it's pleasure.'

'Sexual stimulation?'

'Of course. Plus a feeling of mastery, of power. She can make men become "red and giggly." She likes that. Right and wrong have no meaning for her in this connection. Good and bad would be closer to the mark. But not good and bad in the ethical sense, but what results in pleasure or pain.'

They were silent a moment. Levin leaned forward to refill their wineglasses. He badly wanted a cigar, but she would not let him smoke in her apartment.

'Ted,' she said, 'if what you said is true – about the growth-accelerating factors that have made Lucy an adolescent instead of a latency child – then why aren't there many other little girls like her? Her case is unique, in my experience.'

'Why?' he said bitterly. 'Why? We always come back to that, don't we?'

'On one of those tapes – the first one, I think – you mentioned a similar case you treated. Was that the truth?'

'Do I ever lie?'

'Do you really want me to answer that?'

'No, that won't be necessary. Yes, I treated a similar case. About seven years ago. It's in the file. The girl's name was Betty or Barbara – something like that.'

'Was it resolved?'

'In a manner of speaking. It turned out to be incestuous corruption by her father.'

'Yuck!'

'A very trenchant, scientific observation – yuck.'

'That's the way I feel. What happened to Betty or Barbara?'

'The family broke up. Divorce.'

'Not what you'd call a complete success.'

'It was a solution. The best under the circumstances.'

'You think something similar may be the reason for Lucy's hypersexuality?'

'Mary, at this stage I just don't know. I've got to learn more about her parents and her early childhood.'

'And then what? Her parents' parents and *their* child-hood?'

'Possibly.'

'It never ends, does it?'

'Well, it's limited by the time you can devote to a single analysis. You can't go back to Adam and Eve, though it might help to talk to them.'

He struggled out of the wing chair, plopped down on the couch close to Dr Mary Scotsby. He put a heavy arm across her shoulders.

'Now let me ask you a question,' he said. 'Do you think it's possible that Grace doesn't know whether or not she's had an orgasm?'

'Yes, I think it's possible, Ted. It's not so unusual amongst women who have had only one man in their lives.'

'Have you had an orgasm?'

'Of course,' she said. 'You know, and I *know*.'

He laughed. 'So much for previous experience.'

She laughed too, and punched his knee lightly. 'You bastard, you tricked me. Ted, do you think Grace could be a religious fanatic?'

'I'd guess not. Just a very conventional woman with traditional beliefs. I'll bet that home of theirs is *shining*. Neat as a pin. She's a real Mrs Craig.'

'Who is Mrs Craig?'

'Before your time, my dear, and it would take too long to explain.'

'You're insufferable. You know that, don't you?'

'I've suspected it.'

They kissed.

'How have you been sleeping lately?' she asked.

'Not so great.'

'Lucy B?'

'Mostly. I'm convinced that those contributing factors I mentioned may have pushed her into premature adolescence. But they don't explain what triggered the hypersexual behavior. As you pointed out, other female children don't act that way. Something caused it. *Something*.'

'Ted, do you want to sleep over?'

'Yes. Please.'

8

About a mile north of the Holloways, Bendings, and Empts, there was a blank stretch leading from A1A to the sea. It was an alley, called a public access road, that allowed auslanders to reach the water.

On the highway end, there were parking spaces (with meters) for a dozen cars. Then the access was paved part of the way, this section provided with a shower. Then sand to the ocean's edge.

The access was the meeting place for Eddie Holloway's crowd. They called themselves the 'Wild Bunch,' or usually just the 'Bunch.' They gathered almost every late afternoon, and usually on weekend nights. They were mostly highschoolers, ages about fifteen to nineteen. They arrived on bikes, skateboards, in pickup trucks and a few sports cars.

Most of the boys, and some of the girls, were surfers. They drank beer, mostly, but sometimes strawberry wine and vodka. Marijuana. Occasionally speed and downers. They tossed Frisbees and, in the fall, footballs. Usually they just horsed around.

Sometimes, especially on Friday and Saturday nights, the Bunch made a lot of noise and impeded traffic on A1A. Homeowners unfortunate enough to live near the access frequently called the police. It didn't do much good. The dope was stashed before the cops got out of their cars, and the booze always belonged to those of legal age. So?

The girls usually wore bikinis or diaper suits. The guys wore cutoff jeans and maybe T-shirts with the sleeves

152

ripped out. No one wore shoes, except cool running Adidas with colored stripes.

This year the in-word was 'blast.' You having a good time? A blast. Last year the word was 'gas.' The year before, it was a 'bomb.' Whatever they called it, it was the same. There were thick hibiscus bushes bordering the access road. Late on Friday and Saturday nights, that could be a blast.

Edward Holloway dropped his cherry in those bushes. A bomb! And one night Sue Kellerman gave two jocks hand-jobs, one in each fist. A gas! And how about that round-robin night – two highschool cheerleaders and the basket-ball team. A boss blast!

One Saturday afternoon, just for kicks you know, and the weather being lousy, they decided to have a contest: who could boost the most valuable merchandise. They scattered to shoplift stores from Pompano to Boca. Then they gathered at night. Tony Jergens won; he had lifted a twelve-inch portable TV set. Crazy? A blast!

Eddie was right in there with the Wild Bunch, smoking the funny cigarettes, drinking the sweet wine, grab-assing all the creamers. He was well liked. They called him a cool stud. 'Hey, where's the stud?'

But suddenly the stud wasn't there. He was alone, walking the beach near his home. Sometimes he spent late afternoons sitting on the sand, staring moodily out to sea. Not quite. He was watching the comings and goings of Mrs Teresa Empt.

He thought he had her routine down pat. On good, sunny days, at about 4:30 to 5:00 in the late afternoon, she came out onto her terrace. She usually wore her white, two-piece bathing suit, a conservative bikini. But you could see her soft belly and the bulge of her big jugs.

She spent about ten minutes on the balcony anointing herself with suntan oil, though by that time the sun had lost its strength. Then she would step down the coral rock stairs to the beach and start walking south through ankle-deep surf. Past Eddie Holloway. She always walked in his direction. One day he sat north of her house, and that day she walked north.

(That Wayne Bending! He was only twelve years old, but he was a smart little bastard!)

'Afternoon, Eddie!' Teresa Empt would call out as she passed him.

'Afternoon, Miz Empt,' he would say, and give her a smile. He tried to make the smile kind of sad, so she would think something was bothering him.

As she walked away from him, down the beach, he would watch her – and damned if he wasn't getting a hard-on. Not only big jugs, but an ass that didn't end. Great legs. Good tan. And she didn't slop like so many old dames. She was solid. And that long black hair. A blast!

The afternoon he selected was hot and muggy for October. The westering sun seemed to hang there, not wanting to go down, and there was a milky haze about it. The air was thick and sticky. Even the ocean seemed to have an oily film; it heaved and rolled but never broke. Breathless. The whole world was breathless.

'Afternoon, Eddie!' Teresa Empt called out.

He scrambled to his feet.

'Miz Empt,' he said desperately, 'could I walk along with you for a way?'

She was startled, then pleased.

'Of course you can, Eddie,' she said, smiling. 'I'm just taking my afternoon constitutional.'

He didn't know what the fuck she meant.

'Yeah,' he said, falling in step alongside her. 'Well, I should walk more – you know? Keep in shape.'

'You look in pretty good shape to me, Eddie,' she said roguishly, glancing sideways at him. 'I imagine you get plenty of exercise.'

'Yeah,' he said. 'But still . . . you know . . .'

They walked down the beach, side by side. Then he realized what a big woman she was. As tall as he, or maybe

154

even a little taller. And she moved smoothly, striding out on firm thighs. She was all right, he thought. She kept herself nice. A hunk. If he could get into that, it wouldn't be a drag.

'I like your hair, Eddie,' she said lightly. 'You don't bleach it, do you?'

'Huh?' he said. 'Oh, you mean like with chemicals? Nah, nothing like that. It's just the sun and the salt water.'

'Yes,' she said, 'I thought so. You're in the water so much. I've watched you surfing.'

'Yeah,' he said, 'I dig surfing.'

'And you have a luscious tan,' she said.

The word 'luscious' frightened him, pleased him, emboldened him.

'Well, you have a great tan too, Miz Empt,' he said. 'Darker than mine.'

'Yes,' she said, 'but not as . . .'

She didn't finish, and he couldn't guess what she had started to say.

'I'm not going to walk very far, Eddie,' she said. 'Just to the inlet. Then I turn around and walk back.'

'Whatever,' he muttered.

'Eddie,' she said, turning her head to look at him, 'is something bothering you?'

He heaved a deep sigh. 'Miz Empt, I got a confession to make to you.'

'A confession?' she said, laughing tinnily. 'My, that sounds serious.'

'Well, it is,' he said, staring out to sea. 'To me anyway. It's been bothering me, and I've been hoping to get a chance to talk to you about it. I hope you won't laugh at me.'

'I won't laugh at you, Eddie. I promise. What is it?'

'Well, you know that, uh, like a little latticed shed you have on your place? The white one?'

'The gazebo?'

'Yeah. Near the road. Well, you know your gates are

155

always unlocked and, Miz Empt, I've been going there at night. To the gazebo. And like I'm trespassing, and it's been bothering me, so I figured I better tell you about it and all.'

She was silent a moment. They walked along, kicking at the frothy surf. He glanced at her briefly. Her head was lowered, the long black hair fell about her face. Then she swept it back with her fingers so it fell loosely onto her strong, tanned shoulders.

'You go there alone, Eddie?' she said in a quiet voice. 'Or to meet someone?'

'Alone!' he cried. 'Always alone, Miz Empt, I swear to you. I mean, I don't *do* anything there.'

'But *why*?' she said. 'Why do you go there?'

He had come prepared with answers.

'Miz Empt,' he said solemnly, 'sometimes I just have to be alone. I mean with my family and school and all, I just have to get off by myself and be alone for a while. I just sit there and think. That's all I do, Miz Empt, I swear it – just sit and think. But then I realized I really have no right to be there, and it's been bothering me, so I figured I better tell you about it. I'm sorry, Miz Empt.'

'Oh Eddie,' she said, turning toward him, 'there's nothing to be sorry about. I think you've done a fine thing to tell me about it, and I respect your honesty.'

'Listen,' he said hoarsely, 'if you want me to stop going there, just say the word and I'll never go again, I swear it.'

She laughed lightly. 'I really don't see what harm you're doing. As long as you don't have any wild parties or anything like that.'

'Miz Empt, I've never been there with *anyone*. I mean, it's like a secret place – you know? Where I can be by myself and think.'

'Yes, Eddie,' she said gently, 'I understand. Well, you just keep going there. I have no objections at all.'

'Gee, thanks, Miz Empt,' he said gratefully. 'I really appreciate that.'

They reached the inlet and turned back. It seemed to him that she had moved closer. Occasionally the backs of their hands brushed, bare arms touched.

'Oh look!' she said, put fingers on his warm shoulder, turned him toward the sea.

There, twenty yards offshore, two skin divers came lurching out of the water. They were wearing black wetsuits, with masks, tanks, flippers. Weighted belts about their waists, knives strapped to their legs.

Teresa Empt laughed uncertainly. 'They look like denizens of the deep,' she said.

'Yeah,' Eddie Holloway said, not quite sure what 'denizens' meant. 'They probably been out to the reef. Lots of good shells and coral out there.'

Her hand slipped lingeringly from his smooth shoulder. They resumed their homeward walk.

'Do you go to the gazebo every night, Eddie?' she said, looking straight ahead.

'Almost every night, Miz Empt.'

'About what time?' she asked in a shaky voice.

'About nine o'clock,' he said, and thought exultantly: Got her!

9

'You know what I saw last week?' Lloyd Craner said. 'At the Boca Mall? A woman with a goiter.'

'No kidding?' Gertrude Empt said. 'My God, I haven't seen one of those in fifty years. When I was a kid, it was all goiters, infantile paralysis, and chicken pox. None of that anymore.'

'No,' he said shortly. 'Now all the sickness is in their heads.'

'You can say that again, kiddo,' she agreed. 'Where are you taking me?'

'To a motel,' he said.

'Oh, you mad, impetuous fool,' she said. 'We'll register as Mr and Mrs Smith, you'll hustle me into a room and try to get in my bloomers.'

'*Bloomers*?' he said, laughing. 'I haven't seen *those* in fifty years.'

When he had retired, and had decided to accept his daughter's invitation to live with them in south Florida, Professor Craner had driven down from the small Montana college town in his ancient, high, bulge-bodied Buick.

He took it easy – the trip lasted three weeks – and he figured he averaged about eight miles to the gallon. But he didn't care; he had the money and the time. He reckoned the two were running out at about the same rate, and he was satisfied with that.

He still had the Buick. It was in mint condition, and every so often some antique car nut would offer him ten times what he paid for it. But he wasn't interested. He thought of it as good, dependable, comfortable transportation. He didn't want to think of it as a museum piece.

Now he and Mrs Empt were luxuriating in the front seat, driving sedately south on A1A. They paid no attention to the stares their ancient conveyance attracted. The windows had been cranked down; the early afternoon breeze smelled young and hopeful.

'I've been exploring,' Craner said. 'Stopping here and there to get an idea of rents on an annual basis.'

'I haven't made up my mind yet,' she said sharply.

'Of course you haven't,' he said mildly. 'Didn't expect you had. But it doesn't do any harm for you to look, does it?'

'Guess not.'

'Just to see what you think of the appearance of the place . . . It's south of Lighthouse Point. Near the Fourteenth Street Causeway. On the west side of the Intracoastal.'

'Right on the Waterway? Lots of bugs and smells and crazies revving their boat engines.'

'Oh no,' he said. 'Not *on* the Waterway. Closer to Federal Highway. Near the Pompano Fashion Square.'

'That's nice,' she said. 'I'm so interested in fashion – as you can tell by the way I dress.'

'Convenient for buying bloomers,' he said, and they both laughed, and she poked him.

When they got there, he pulled off onto the verge, and they inspected the motel without getting out of the car. He pointed out the features: twenty-two units in two one-story buildings. Swimming pool. Shuffleboard court. Neat landscaping. Metal lounge chairs on the trimmed lawn. Everything seemed freshly painted in pink.

'What do you think?' Craner asked casually.

'Not too bad,' she said grudgingly. 'Pink I can do without, but I guess I could get used to it. Looks like it's kept up okay.'

'Spotless,' he assured her. 'It's owned by a retired New Jersey cop and his wife. They got a black who does repairs, runs the mower, and things like that. About a third of their units are rented year-round, and they do very well on seasonal bookings. The same people keep coming back year after year.'

'That's what they told you, perfesser,' she said cynically.

'That's right,' he agreed. 'That's what they told me.'

They sat in silence, watching the motel. People in swimming costumes came out to the pool. A couple began a game of shuffleboard. Two men flapped their newspapers on lawn chairs.

'Kids?' Mrs Empt asked.

'A few,' he said. 'None of the permanent residents have children, but the snowbirds do. It seems to be a quiet place.'

'Lots of old farts,' she observed.

'Younger than us,' he said gently.

'And how much are they asking for this palace?'

'They have two different efficiency units available,' he explained. 'On a yearly basis, the smaller unit is three hundred a month. That's one room, kitchenette, bathroom. Cramped. I don't recommend it. The larger efficiency has a small living room, separate bedroom, also small, a bathroom, a kitchen large enough for a table and chairs. That's four-fifty a month.'

'Mmm,' she said. 'Maid service?'

'Not for the units rented on an annual basis, unless you want to pay extra. Would you like to look at the apartments?'

'Not right now.'

'All right,' he said equably, starting the engine. 'Let's go get some lunch. I found a nice place right on the Waterway, down near Atlantic Boulevard. We can sit outside at an umbrella table and watch the boats go by.'

'Screw the boats,' she said. 'Can you get a drink?'

'Of course.'

'I could use one.'

They lunched on a concrete dock, six feet from the

water's edge. Their faces were shaded by a fringed table umbrella. The patio bar was getting a big play, mostly from boaters off moored outboards. But only a few of the tables were occupied.

She had a beer and he had a Gibson on the rocks, both drinks served in soft plastic glasses. Then they both had rare hamburgers, french fries, and small salads. They ate swiftly and silently. Then they had another drink.

They sat placidly. They watched the roistering drinkers at the bar who thought youth was permanent. They watched the boats go by on the Waterway. They watched their perky waitress chatting up the single customers. It was pleasant to see it all, and understand.

'When did your wife die?' Mrs Gertrude Empt asked, almost lazily.

'Ten years ago,' he said, just as indolently. 'Three years before I retired. On a Saturday. I was home, and she was going out to a bridge game. She said to me "Don't forget to take the roast out of the oven." Then she went into the hall and I heard this terrible thump. She was gone when I got out there. Heart.'

'My old man didn't go sudden like that. Just downhill. His liver. The booze got to him. Eventually.'

'What did he do, Gertrude? His work?'

'Construction. Foundation work. He worked hard and brought home a good dollar. When he wasn't on the sauce. But he was all right.'

'Is Luther your only child?'

'No. I got a married daughter in Texas and another daughter in California. God knows what she's doing. She never writes except to ask for money.'

'Those things happen,' he said. 'Jane is my only child.'

'Uh-huh,' she said. 'She's doing okay. Married to a banker and all.'

'Yes,' he said. 'How about another round?'

'Why the hell not?' she said. 'Let it all hang out.'

He was wearing his white suit; white Panama and cane on

161

an empty chair. His white mustache and white goatee jutted. Fierce eyes were squinched against the glare off the water. He sat erect, his back not touching the chair.

'What were you a perfesser of?' she asked him idly.

'Geology.' He smiled briefly. 'Foundation work.'

'Yeah,' she said with a slow grin. 'I get them, don't I?'

She turned her head to watch a motor launch maneuver alongside the dock. He stared at her. She sat solidly in her printed cotton shift, and he thought her a strong, vital woman. She had been around the block twice, he imagined, and there wasn't much that could shock, dismay, or frighten her.

'Gertrude,' he said carefully. 'I'm serious about this thing. About you and me.'

She turned back to look at him with her snappy brown eyes.

'I know you are,' she said. 'I know you're serious.'

'As long as you know,' he said. 'Take your time; I'm not rushing you.'

She didn't answer. They had two more drinks and he drove extra carefully on the way home. They decided they had better take a long stroll on the beach to walk off the alcohol, and so they did.

By that time the sun was dipping; the light was a rich apricot. Her bare legs were the color of tea, and his face was smoothed and glowing with the radiance. And the Gibsons. They walked along slowly, and they talked.

What didn't they talk about! Penny candy. Following the tar wagon down the street and chewing on a gob of the hot, gummy stuff to whiten your teeth. Packing a snowball around a stone.

They chivied each other and laughed a lot. Once she goosed him.

10

Dr Theodore Levin had declined an invitation from Dr Mary Scotsby to share a spaghetti dinner in her apartment. Instead, he locked himself into his own cluttered penthouse atop a nineteen-story condominium on the Intracoastal Waterway.

He showered and donned a flannel bathrobe, duplicate of the one he kept in Mary's apartment. Then he put an Isaac Stern on the tape deck, opened a bag of Pepperidge Farm mint-flavored Milano cookies, and poured himself a waterglass of Gallo Hearty Burgundy. He lighted a cigar. Then he got down to work.

At home, he was the most disorganized of men, and he knew it, despaired of it, and never reformed. His books, pamphlets, and papers were stacked higgledy-piggledy in wall-to-wall bookcases, tossed onto chairs, piled on the floor, tables, bureaus, desk. It took him longer to find what he wanted than to read it.

By midnight, he had pored through whatever he could find on the sexual pathology of latency children, including papers by Pandey, Kay, Anthony, Fraiberg, and Kaplan. He found no reference to a case exactly like Lucy B's. But that was hardly unusual; the literature of psychotherapy rarely included cases that were 'exactly alike.'

Then, the wine, cookies, cigar, and Isaac Stern finished, he poured himself a small brandy and went out onto his rarely used terrace. He took off his robe. He spread it across a webbed plastic chair so his softly fleshed body

163

would not be imprinted with a waffle pattern.

The cool night breeze felt good on his bare skin. It was like taking an air bath. He slumped, laced fingers across his furred belly, and contemplated the night lights of Fort Lauderdale.

He could make out the blaze surrounding the airport, the glow of a racetrack in the distance. And in between, necklaces and garlands of lights. Beacons on tall buildings. Steady lights. Flashing lights. Twinkling lights. And on the black scar of the Waterway, green and red lanterns of slowly moving boats.

Noises were muted. Airliners coming in or taking off. Street traffic below. Occasionally boats hooting for a bridge to be raised. But these were background sounds, aural wallpaper. Over all was the stillness of a clear, gigantic night, stars forever, and space that hummed gently if you listened for it.

He was convinced that his analysis of Lucy B was correct. Despite her age, she was not a latency child at all, but in the early stages of adolescence. The world had changed, was changing at an accelerating rate, from the days when Papa Sigmund had set down the age limits of latency.

If he was right, if Lucy was already an adolescent, that would account for the end of genital anesthesia, for reactivated sexuality. But valid or not, his thesis could not account for her particular aberration.

That, he supposed sadly, had been triggered by an infant or childhood experience that he could not, at the moment, imagine. He saw it in terms of a trauma, a psychic wound, that had set her on her way.

He grunted with displeasure at his own romantic maunderings, and took a gulp of brandy. He knew how rarely psychopathy could be traced to a single incident, one cataclysmic happening that determined a life. Usually, people were bent by repeated experiences, a whole distorted youth.

But still, the single momentous and violent psychic

hurt was not alone the stuff of opera, myth, novels, and Shakespeare's plays. Rapes, murders, seductions, treacheries – these things did occur in real life, and he would ignore them at his peril.

He looked down at his podgy, middle-aged body, white, slack, and woolly with hair, and wondered, not for the first time, why he had selected the profession he had.

It seemed to him that there were certain occupations – psychiatrist, policeman, gynecologist, judge, and perhaps even priest – that automatically disqualified those who sought them. They demanded an ambition and conscious choice that guaranteed failure. What normal man or woman would seek such callings?

It was a dilemma Theodore Levin had never been able to resolve. Sighing, then draining his brandy, he lurched awkwardly to his feet. He pulled on his robe, went back inside. Seated at his desk, he began to make brief notes on how best to handle the following afternoon's session with Lucy B.

She appeared in his office promptly at 4:00 P.M. He thought he had steeled his heart against the attraction of her physical beauty. But he found himself greeting her with a smile that stretched his face.

That afternoon she was wearing tight jeans, sneakers, and a checked gingham shirt with the sleeves rolled up on her pliant arms.

'Hi, Doctor Ted!' she said.

'Good afternoon, Lucy,' he said, as gravely as he could, and motioned her to the armchair which he had pulled around to the side of his desk.

They chatted a few moments about her schoolwork and her plans for the weekend. He saw her eyes wandering to the toys and games piled in the bookcase. He switched on the tape recorder.

'All those are for the children who come to talk to me,' he explained. 'Go ahead, take a look at them.'

Obediently, she rose and walked slowly down the display. Once she poked a teddy bear in its fat stomach and laughed.

'Do you like that?' he asked her.

'It looks just like you,' she said, giggling. Then she came back to her chair.

'Nothing you'd like to play with?' he said. 'You can, you know, if you like.'

'No, thank you,' she said formally. 'That's kid stuff.'

'The dolls, too?'

'I don't play with dolls, Doctor Ted. My goodness, I'm not a child.'

'No dolls at home?' he persisted. 'Not even one? An old favorite?'

'I have a Snoopy dog I like,' she said. 'But I don't play with it. He just sits on my dresser.'

The most important thing in his profession, he knew, was learning to ignore the inconsequential. But the most difficult thing was deciding what was meaningless. He was like a homicide detective with too many clues.

'Lucy,' he started, 'the last time we talked, you said you loved your parents and they loved you. Is that right?'

'Of course.'

'Do you think your mother and father love each other?'

'My goodness!' she said with a dazzling smile. 'That's a silly question.'

'Why is it silly?'

'How can you know if someone loves someone else? I mean, they could say they do and act like it, but you can't tell for sure, can you?'

He admired her perspicacity.

'If you believe that, Lucy,' he said gently, 'then how can you be sure your parents love you?'

'You're mean and spiteful,' she cried immediately, 'and I hate you.'

Suddenly she was weeping. Sitting there upright, little hands gripping the armrests of the chair, she turned her face directly to him and let the tears stream. She wept silently, no sobs or snuffles, just quiet, dignified grief.

He slid the opened box of Kleenex across to her side of the desk and waited patiently. Finally the tears stopped, she dabbed at her eyes delicately with a tissue.

'I must look a mess,' she said.

'You look fine,' he assured her. 'But why did you cry?'

'Because of what you said about my parents not loving me.'

'Lucy, I didn't say they don't love you. I just asked you how you knew it.'

'Well . . .' she said slowly, 'if I tell you something, will you promise not to tell anyone?'

'I promise.'

'And specially not my mother and father,' she said, laughing shrilly. 'If they found out I told you, they'd just kill me.'

'I won't tell them.'

'Well . . . you see . . . my mother isn't my real mother. My real mother is dead. She was killed dead in a tragic car accident.'

'When did this happen, Lucy?'

'A long time ago.'

'How long?'

'Oh, maybe five years ago.'

'You were just a little girl then? Three years old?'

'Yes.'

'But you remember your mother? Your real mother?'

'I certainly do. She was beautiful and loved me very much. I *know* she did, Doctor Ted, because she was always telling me so, and hugging me and kissing me and all. And some nights she would take me into her bed so I could get to sleep, you know. And telling me she loved me best of all in the world. But then she got killed dead in this tragic car accident. Well, my poor father has to go to work every day and all, so he married this woman to, you know, take care of us kids. But she's not our real mother, but you promised not to breathe a word of this.'

'I won't, Lucy,' he said heavily. 'I never tell anyone what you tell me in this room.'

'Good,' she said. She took a round mirror out of her little plastic purse and examined herself critically, turning her head this way and that.

He watched her closely, seeing the grace, the pride of a mature woman.

He thought it best not to follow up on her fantasy at this time. He would leave it for another session when he could determine how much she remembered of the daydream, if it was completely formed and recurrent or something she had devised on the spur of the moment to justify her tears.

'Lucy,' he said, 'do you recall when we were talking before about how babies are born?'

'I remember. You asked me how, and I told you.'

'That's right. You know I'm a doctor, Lucy, and doctors know all about girls and boys and men and women.'

She looked at him, puzzled for a moment. Then her face cleared.

'Oh, you mean naked? Without any clothes on?'

She was so quick.

'Correct,' he said. 'Doctor David has examined you when you didn't have any clothes on, hasn't he?'

'Of course.'

'Of course he has. And so did Doctor Scotsby. We're all doctors, Lucy, and there's no need to feel ashamed or embarrassed when a doctor examines you.'

'I'm not ashamed or embarrassed, Doctor Ted.'

'Good. And sometimes doctors have to ask very personal questions. So they can help you. You understand that, don't you?'

'Sure.'

'Do you know what masturbation means, Lucy?'

'Masti –?'

'Masturbation.'

'I think I've heard the word, but I'm not sure what it means.'

'Well, it means giving yourself pleasure. Making yourself feel good. I don't mean by eating or swimming or having fun or anything like that. I mean physical pleasure. Making yourself feel good inside your body. By touching yourself.'

'Oh.'

'A girl might touch herself between her legs –'

'Or put her finger in her hole,' she said breathlessly. 'Gloria Holloway does that. She told me so.'

'Do you do that, Lucy? Put your finger in your hole?'

She leaned toward him, almost whispering.

'Once. I did it once.'

'Did you like it?'

She leaned back and smiled secretly.

'It felt good, at first, but then I got scared.'

'Why were you scared?'

'It just felt so – so funny. I thought maybe I was dying. So I stopped.'

'Why did you think you were dying?'

'Well, I got all dizzy. And I couldn't catch my breath. That part of it scared me. And then I couldn't get my finger out. It was like it was caught in there, like maybe it was cut off. That's why I was scared.'

'And you only did it once?'

'Just that one time. And I'm never going to do *that* again, I assure you. I told Gloria, but she said she doesn't care. She does it all the time. She likes it.'

'Did you ever see her do it?'

'No, I never did. But sometimes she does it in the ocean, you know, when we're swimming together. Then she tells me, "I'm doing it!" '

'Did she ever ask you to do it for her? To use your finger? In her hole?'

'*My* finger? Oh no, I never did that.'

'If she did ask you, would you do it?'

She stared at the stars pasted on the ceiling.

He waited a while. When she didn't answer, he made no

effort to force a response. But when she lowered her eyes to his and spoke, it was something totally unexpected.

'There's a book in the library,' she said, smiling brightly, 'and it tells what names mean.'

He had learned long ago that with juvenile analysands, it was best to let them run. To zig and zag. When they fell silent, he could provide direction and lead them. But it was more profitable to follow their turns of conversation and alterations of mood. Sometimes a world was revealed.

'A book that tells what names mean?' he said ruminatively. 'A dictionary?'

'No, silly. *Names*. What your *name* means. Lucy means "light." And I looked up Ted, but it was under Theodore, and do you know what Theodore means?'

'What?'

' "Gift of God." Isn't that nice?'

'Do you believe in God, Lucy?'

'Well, of course. *Everyone* believes in God.'

'What do you think God looks like?'

'Well, He's this old man, kind of nice, you know, and smiling, and He's got a beard.'

'Like my beard?'

'Oh no. God's beard is a *big* beard, and it's white. And sort of, you know, soft and silky. Not like yours.'

'Would you like to sit on God's lap, Lucy?'

She looked at him, wide-eyed. 'Can you do that?'

'If you could, would you like to?'

She pondered. 'I might. I guess I would. Because He's nice and knows everything, doesn't He?'

Levin was in terra incognita here, and didn't know how to proceed. He was fishing and he knew it. But he assured himself that nothing would be wasted.

'Do you go to church, Lucy?'

'I go to Sunday School.'

'Do you like it?'

'Ohhh . . . it's all right. I like the pictures.'

'Pictures?'

'In our books. There's this man with arrows stuck in him, all over. And they chopped off heads and arms and legs. Ugh!'

Afterward, he would never quite understand why he said it, because he had decided to put off any reference to her fantasy to a later session, but now it suddenly seemed important, and he asked it . . .

'Chopped off their heads and arms and legs?' he said. 'Like your mother in that tragic car accident? Your real mother?'

'Yes,' she said, nodding.

And there it was: castration. Plain as plain could be, and he wondered why he hadn't guessed it before. He was confounded by the possibilities. Penis envy, he decided, because he was the kind of man who wanted to put a label on everything. It had to be penis envy.

And when she excited older men, squirmed on their laps, it was the priapic vitality she sought. She coveted that virile member, having been deprived of it at birth, or having lost it. Her hypersexuality was a frantic effort to get back her own.

But how to account for her fantasy: the dream of her mother castrated? Did she believe her mother possessed of a penis and she, Lucy, had been robbed of what was rightfully hers: the power of the phallus?

'Lucy,' he said, 'have you ever thought of what you'd like to be when you grow up?'

'A doctor,' she said promptly. 'I want to be a doctor.'

But she was so clever he could not be sure if she was telling the truth or trying to curry favor.

'Why do you want to be a doctor?'

'So I can examine people and cure them.'

'Don't you want to get married?'

'Ohh . . .' she said thoughtfully, 'I might and I might not.'

'Wouldn't you like to have a husband, a home, children? You could do that and still be a doctor, you know.'

171

'I don't think so,' she said suddenly. 'I don't think I want to get married. I'll just be a doctor and help people. Like there'll be this man dying of this horrible disease, and I'll examine him and find out what it is, and cure him because no one else in the whole world can do it, and he'll want to marry me, but I'll say no, I've got to help people. Like that.'

'Yes,' Dr Theodore Levin said, 'that's very admirable.'

'Or,' she said, 'like someone got a head or an arm or a leg chopped off, and I could sew it back on, and it would be just as good as new. Can they do that, Doctor Ted?'

'Well . . .' he said cautiously. 'Fingers sometimes. A hand or foot. I think they've done an arm. But it's still experimental, Lucy.'

What am I doing? he thought desperately. I am sitting here discussing microsurgery with an eight-year-old disturbed child. Is this significant? For her or for me?

'Well, I could do it,' she said firmly. 'I'll sew on a head, and it will be just as good as new.'

He stared at her. He was daunted by her complexity.

'Lucy,' he said tentatively, 'how do you feel about talking to me?'

'How do I feel?'

'When I first spoke to you, you said that you didn't have any problems, that nothing was bothering you. Do you still feel that way?'

She looked at him – oh, how she looked! The bluish-gray eyes alert and thoughtful. Full lips pursed. Golden head cocked slightly. She was judging him. He was convinced of it.

'I like to talk to you, Doctor Ted,' she said quietly.

'I'm glad to hear that, because I like to talk to you, too.'

He didn't say that she had slid around his question, met his direct query with a compliment. She was there, and she wasn't there. Each time he came closer, she eased away. Where did that cunning come from?

'Well, Lucy, I think our time is up.'

When the door closed behind her, he thought mournfully that Mary Scotsby was right: the child had him buffaloed.

PART III

1

They were in that fleabag motel. Squally rain clattered against the windows, rattled off the roof. They were naked in bed, clammy bodies clasped languidly. Not a bad way to spend a wet November afternoon.

Ronald Bending took his mouth from her engorged nipple.

'You like money, don't you?' he asked.

Jane Holloway opened her eyes, looked at him.

'I give you a ten for technique,' she said, 'and about a three for passion.'

'And you thought I was just another pretty face,' he said, grinning.

'Well, what's with the question about money? What's that got to do with anything?'

He lighted cigarettes for them. Then he sat up in bed, hugging his gawky knees.

'You want to know how I figure you?' he said.

'Sure,' she said, looking at him curiously.

'Some I know,' he said, 'and some I've guessed. I figure you're a woman with a sharp eye for the main chance. I figure you ditched that first husband of yours because you decided he was a loser. He was never going to be anything but a pencil-pusher in that rube town bank. Twenty Gs a year tops. Then you met William Jasper Holloway and decided to move onward and upward. So now you're in Boston, married to a guy with old money. But Boston is too cold and stuffy for you, and you don't like Bill's la-di-da friends. You want to be where the action is. So you con him into moving to sunny Florida. Maybe a little mattress extortion there.'

'Bastard,' she said tonelessly.

'And then,' he went on, 'you're in the land of palm trees and year-round Bain de Soleil. You can wear those obscene bikinis of yours every day of the year if you want to, everyone's screwing up a storm, all the grass and coke you could want, and everywhere you look there's another chance to make money. Like meeting Senator What's-his-name, playing the market, keeping a safe deposit box your husband doesn't know about, and generally living the good life while the bucks pile up. Not your family's bucks, or your husband's, but *your* money. That's about it. How close am I?'

'Close enough,' she said, her smile bleak. 'I thought you were a lightweight. Now I think you're a mean ass-hole.'

'As mean as they come,' he said, not without pride. 'Originally I was a Kentucky mountain boy. Can't get much meaner than that.'

'Well,' she said, 'if you know – or guess – all that about me, why ask if I like money?'

'Let's have a dope,' he said.

He got them two cold Pepsis from his little insulated bag. They sat up in bed, drinking, smoking, listening to the rain thrum against the thin motel walls.

'I had an idea,' he said slowly, 'and wanted to try it out on you.'

'So? Try me.'

'It's just a rough idea – I haven't worked out the details yet – but it goes like this: That deal that Bill and I are in on with Luther looks like it's going to be a real money machine. The mob guys came up with their quarter-million loan without blinking. The factory to process the porno films into TV cassettes is coming along. Luther already has one film and is figuring ways to bring down production

178

costs. We're thinking about getting into video disks. The mob guys keep pushing. They say the market is getting bigger every month. There's zillions in it.'

'So what's your idea?'

'Well . . .' he said, staring at the opposite wall, 'Bill and I and Luther each have a third. Of everything. Luther's taking fifty grand for the first year to honcho the whole thing and get the production line rolling. He didn't even ask for an employment contract. Bill and I control two-thirds of the stock, and . . .'

His voice trailed away.

'And,' she said, with a harsh laugh, 'why not wait till Luther has the whole thing set up, then freeze him out. That leaves you and Bill as equal partners.'

He took a deep breath. 'Yeah. Something like that. I don't know exactly how it could be done, but with Bill and me controlling two-thirds of the voting stock, it shouldn't be too difficult. As I told you, it's just a rough idea. What do you think?'

'I thought Luther was a friend of yours.'

He turned to look at her. 'A *friend*? Who the hell has friends anymore? Everyone has acquaintances; that's all. Well? What do you think?'

'Mmm,' she said, staring at the scabby ceiling, 'it's possible. Where do I come in?'

'Look,' he said, 'you got a nice piece of change for convincing Bill to come in on this deal, didn't you? There'd be an even bigger fee if you can con Bill into going along on this.'

'No dice,' she said. 'I want a piece of the action. For myself alone, in my name.'

'Well . . .' he said cautiously, 'maybe that could be worked out. How big a piece?'

'Say ten percent,' she said. 'Forty-five to you, forty-five to Bill, ten to me.'

'That would give you and Bill a controlling interest.'

It was her turn to look at him. She put the can of cola

aside. She took his testicles into her chilled hand, gripping him tightly.

'Not necessarily,' she whispered, staring into his eyes.

Then, stirred more by avarice than passion, she was all over him with lips, tongue, teeth. His can of Pepsi dropped to the floor to gurgle out, while he tried to meet her onslaught.

'Jesus!' he groaned. 'Take it easy!'

'Ten percent!' she hissed in his ear. 'Ten percent!'

She ground him down and drained him. She emptied him out and left him nerveless and whimpering. Then she rolled away, lighted another cigarette, and watched him panting, gasping for breath.

'Let me think about it,' she said coldly. 'There's no rush, is there?'

He shook his head.

'You'll want to wait until the factory is finished,' she told him, 'and Luther has all the production bugs worked out. And you'll have to find someone who can run the business after Luther is gone. So nothing has to be decided for at least a couple of months – right?'

'Yeah,' he said. 'Right. No dummy you. I didn't think about finding someone to run the factory after Luther is out, but that shouldn't be too hard. So what do you say? Are you in?'

'For ten percent?' she said. 'I'll think about it.'

He nodded, got out of bed. He staggered a moment, put a hand on the mildewed wall to steady himself. He made his way over to the dresser, popped the tab on another can of Pepsi.

He turned his face upward and poured half a can of the cold cola onto his face, neck, shoulders, sweated torso. The liquid fizzed in his sun-streaked hair, dripped off his chin, ran in wandering rivulets down his ruddy thighs.

'You nut,' she said, watching him.

He was over to the bed in two swift strides. He poured the rest of the Pepsi onto her hard breasts, flat stomach,

180

tight thighs. She lay there and let him drench her, making no effort to avoid the stream.

'Now what?' she said, looking at him.

He shook the remaining drops onto the shaved vee between her legs.

'Now I lick it off,' he said.

'Get to it, boy,' she said, dark eyes glittering.

2

William Jasper Holloway believed that something happened when more than two men gathered. Two men, in
their relationship and communication, might be capable of
delicacy, understanding, restraint. But rarely could three
men (or more) resist coarseness, a thickening of the spirit, a
dulling of perception and sympathy.

So it was during a late evening gathering on Ronald
Bending's terrace. They had come together in the darkness
to hear a progress report from Luther Empt. Bending had
put out bottles and ice, and they were sitting around with
their shoes off, enjoying the booze and the cool November
night wind.

'I swear to God,' Empt said, 'I think we're going to come
in under budget. The slab is in, and the cinder blocks are
going up. Got delivery today on all the window and door
frames. There's a little slippage in the schedule, but nothing
serious. Maybe we'll top out a week or ten days late, but we
can live with that.'

'Perhaps,' Holloway said hesitantly, 'we should have
hired a general contractor.'

'Nah,' Empt said. 'Why pay the money? I can put that
thing together. It's just a glorified shed.'

He didn't mention the kickbacks he was getting from the
architect, carpenter, plumber, electrician, and all the rest.
He figured Bending and Holloway guessed he was chisel-
ing; they went along with it because they were content to
leave the donkey work to him.

'Luther,' Turk Bending said, voice athrob with sincerity, 'you're not neglecting your own office, are you? Bill and I know how hard you've been working on this thing, and we appreciate it. But we wouldn't want your own business to suffer. Right, Bill?'

'What?' Holloway said. 'Oh. Yes. Right.'

'Not to worry,' Luther said, pouring himself another belt and thinking these were okay guys. 'I've got my plant set up so it practically runs itself.'

'Oh?' Bending said casually. 'Got a good Number Two man, have you?'

'The best,' Empt bragged. 'I'm lucky to have him, but don't tell him I told you so; he might hit me for a raise.'

Bending laughed heartily. 'Who's that, Luther?'

'Ernie Goldman. He's a hell of a tech. There's just one thing wrong: he loves to play the ponies, and he's always in hock to the sharks. He's into me for about three months' advance. But let him lose his shirt at the track as long as he does his job.'

'Ah well,' Bending said lightly, having discovered what he wanted to know, 'we all have our little vices.'

Then they discussed a fishing trip they might take down to the Keys. Charter a boat, just the three of them, no women allowed, stock up on booze and beer, and go down for a long weekend. Maybe try for bonefish.

'I've never netted one of those suckers,' Empt said angrily. 'Had them on the line a dozen times, but they always spit the hook.'

'Shrimp,' Bending said authoritatively. 'That's what you need for bonefish – shrimp.'

'What the hell do you think I was baiting with?' Luther demanded. 'A knockwurst?'

He pulled on his moccasins, heaved himself to his feet. He scrubbed his scalp with his knuckles, stretched, yawned, belched.

'Don't let me break this up,' he told the other two, 'but I gotta split. Paperwork to do.'

He waved to them and stalked away, lumbering down the beach. They watched him go.

'Paperwork, my ass,' Bending said. 'He's fishing for creamers tonight.' He clapped Bill on the shoulder before going into the house for more ice.

He was right about the paperwork; Luther Empt had other plans.

He had resisted for almost a week. Then he had called the number jotted on the margin of his tattered Mobil roadmap. June had been happy to hear from him; he could tell by her voice; she wasn't just giving him the old come-on.

He said brusquely that he'd like to see her again, but he didn't know when he'd be able to make it. Without his suggesting it, she volunteered to stay in her apartment every night until 9:00 P.M., waiting for his call. If he hadn't called by then, she'd figure he couldn't manage it.

He was pleased.

He had called her before he went over for drinks at Bending's place. Now he didn't even re-enter his home, but went around the house to the carport. He headed south on A1A in the white Cadillac Seville. He was as excited as a kid on his first date.

He was almost twenty minutes late, but she was waiting on the little porch of her private apartment. He pulled up and blinked his lights. He watched her hurry toward him in her broken, scuttling walk, and he wondered what the hell he was doing.

He opened the door for her; she slid in awkwardly, turned to him. Then her arms were around his neck, her cheek pressed to his.

'Oh Bill,' she said breathlessly, and he was startled until he remembered that was the name he had given her.

'How you been?' he asked gruffly.

'All right,' she said. She put her hand to his face. 'You look tired. Have you been working hard?'

Teresa had never asked him that. This girl's concern made his throat go dry.

'Listen,' he said, 'I thought we'd take a little drive. Not a motel.' He added hastily: 'I'll pay for your time.'

'That's okay,' she said happily. 'I don't care.'

'I just want to talk,' he said, and she hugged his arm and snuggled closer to him.

He came off the Atlantic Boulevard bridge, made a sharp right, and parked on the concrete lot bordering the Intracoastal. There were several other cars there; fishermen were standing patiently on the lip of the Waterway. What they might catch that was worth eating, Empt couldn't guess.

He switched off the motor and lights; they sat quietly in the gloom. Her head was on his shoulder. He was happy and didn't know why.

'I've been thinking,' he said hoarsely, 'and there's something I want to talk to you about . . .'

He had worked it out like a business contract, being the kind of man he was, and figured it wouldn't cost him a cent. He could carry her as a regular employee of his own company or of the new corporation he had formed with Bending and Holloway.

If his accountant didn't like that, he could pay her from petty cash. Or pad his personal expense vouchers. There were half-a-dozen ways it could be finagled, but however it was done, it wouldn't be coming out of his pocket. Not a penny.

'I'll pay you two hundred a week,' he said rapidly. 'Cash. No paper. You won't have to declare it if you don't want to. If they catch up with you, I'll pay your tax and penalties. Can you live on two hundred a week? Net?'

'Yes,' she said in a low voice.

'In return,' he said, his voice thick, 'I want you to stop hustling. No one but me. Understand?'

He felt her head nodding against his shoulder. He reached sideways, touched her breast through the thin stuff

185

of her blouse, then took his hand hastily away.

'Now listen,' he said, 'that doesn't mean you can't go out. I won't see you every night. Maybe only two or three times a week. And I'll give you advance notice. I mean, I don't want you just sitting home waiting for me.'

'I'll wait,' she said.

'Go out,' he said. 'Enjoy yourself. But when I call and say I'm coming over like tomorrow night, I want you there. Okay?'

'Yes.'

'Can we, uh, meet in your apartment?'

'Oh yes. The people I rent from don't care. As long as we don't have any noisy parties or anything like that.'

'We won't,' he assured her. 'But no hustling. In your apartment or anywhere else. All right?'

'Yes.'

'Then you agree? It's all right with you? What the hell are you crying about?'

For her shoulders were shaking, her head bowed. Soft, whimpering cries were coming from her. He put an arm clumsily around her bony shoulders, pulled her closer.

'You'll take care of me?' she said in a piteous voice.

'That's what I've been telling you,' he said, almost angrily. 'I'll take care of you.'

'Oh,' she said. 'Oh oh oh. Bill, I'm so happy.'

'That's another thing,' he said, staring through the windshield at the motionless fishermen. 'My name's not really Bill. It's Luther. L-u-t-h-e-r. Luther.'

She laughed timidly. 'My name's not really June. It's May.'

He turned to look at her. 'Not June but May? Why not April?'

She didn't understand his weak joke, but he hugged her to him.

'Do you want me to call you Luther?' she asked.

'Whatever.'

'Would you be mad if I called you "daddy"?'

'Why daddy?'

'Because you're going to take care of me, and my real daddy never did.'

I've really got a nut case here, he thought. I'm really asking for it, tying up with this crazie.

'Call me daddy,' he said, 'if you like.'

'Daddy,' she said softly, falling slowly out of his encircling arm, slipping down sideways until her head was in his lap. 'You'll be my daddy and I'll be your little girl.'

'Something like that,' he said.

He sat there, suddenly feeling so sad. His heavy hand began to stroke the mass of shiny black hair, smoothing it back from her temples. He combed it with his fingers, touched the warm scalp beneath with his fingertips. She purred with pleasure.

'I haven't had such a great life,' he said to the world. 'I've had to hustle since Day One. So I know what you've been through, May. My old man got busted up on a construction job when I was ten, and then it was out on the street for me, helping to keep the family together. Oh, I went to school and all that, but I also worked my ass off. Ran errands. Sold papers. Made deliveries. I had two sisters, and they worked just as hard, waiting for the day they could get out of that house. The whole place smelled of my father dying. He was a lush. Then he finally did die, which was a blessing, and the girls got married and moved away. Then it was just mom and me. I never stopped running. It was like a habit by then – you know? Anything and everything. Anyway I could turn a buck. I envied kids my age who could go to college and then waltz into a good job while I was scrambling. Then I discovered a great truth: most people are stupid. I mean they're *stupid*, May. All those college guys, the ones in the big offices, they got no street smarts, and I could take them. In any deal, I could take them. Once I realized that, I got a lot more confidence and I started moving. Now things are really coming my way. But no one did it for me, no one did me no favors. I did it all myself.'

'Daddy,' she murmured.

'Ahh, what the hell . . .' he said. 'Someday we're all going to be dead – right? So get it while you can. I truly believe that. You and me are going to have some laughs together, aren't we, May?'

She nuzzled her face into his groin. He moved her gently away and lifted her upright.

'I better get you home,' he said.

'Will you come in with me?'

'Well . . . maybe just for a few minutes. You got anything to drink?'

'I have some beer.'

'Okay. I'll leave you some extra money; you pick up some Cutty Sark scotch. That's what I usually drink. Keep Cutty in the house.'

'Cutty Sark,' she repeated, memorizing the name. 'I'll buy some tomorrow.'

'That's my girl,' he said.

Her apartment was a shock: one big room filled with houseplants. Every size, shape, color, scent. Aloe, fern, African violets, coleus, several varieties of begonia, ivy, philodendron, laurel, spider plants, and much, much more.

On the windowsills, tables, dresser, bookcase. On the floor, in planters, in wall brackets, even on the toilet tank in the tiny bathroom. The atmosphere was warm, humid, scented, cloying.

'Jesus Christ!' Luther Empt said. 'This place is a fucking jungle!'

'They're my children,' May said, looking about fondly. 'I love them and they love me. I talk to them every day.'

'Yeah,' Empt said. 'Great. How about that beer?'

He sat in an armchair, the back and seat upholstered but the wooden armrests worn bare of varnish. A frond of asparagus fern, hung from the ceiling, tickled the back of his neck.

'You really can't stay?' she said.

'Not tonight. I've got things to do.'

'Is it all right if I get ready for bed?'

'Sure,' he said. 'I'm leaving as soon as I finish this.'

She went into the bathroom and closed the door. He sat solidly, gulping his beer from a can, looking around the growing room and shaking his head.

It wasn't, he saw, much of a bed. A sofa really, with pillows. No headboard or footboard. But it would do, he supposed. The small kitchenette was clean. It would be a neat little place if it wasn't for all those crazy plants.

She came out of the bathroom barefoot, wearing a thin cotton nightgown. One of the shoulder straps had broken and was fastened to the bodice with a safety pin.

She looked at him timidly. 'Was the beer all right?'

'Sure,' he said, setting the empty can on the floor alongside his chair. 'I guess I was thirsty.'

'Would you like another?'

'No, thanks. Next time get light beer, will you? I've got to lose some weight.'

'You look fine to me, daddy,' she said.

She sat on his lap, wriggling around until she was comfortable. Her head was on his shoulder. His arm was around her shoulders, covered with her long hair.

Through the nightgown he could feel the heat of her child's body. The jutting bones. Looking down, he could see the softness of her small breasts, the little pink nipples.

Holding her, feeling her, he felt peculiarly sexless. But he felt a warm, milky affection he had not known since he held his infant daughters on his knee, stroked their fine hair, smelled their fresh, innocent perfume. So clean. So sweet. A knife in the heart.

'Do you want me to do anything, daddy?' she whispered.

'No,' he said. 'Just let me hold you a few minutes.'

'I'll do anything you want; you know that. I want you to be happy.'

'I am,' he said, wondering if he was.

He slipped his free hand down the neckline of her

189

nightgown. He held one of those frail breasts lightly. It felt like a bird, fluttering in his palm.

'May . . .' he said.

'What?'

'Don't you have any family?'

'No,' she said, 'they're all gone.'

'No brothers or sisters? No uncles, aunts, cousins?'

'Someplace,' she said. 'I don't know where. I don't care. I like it when you hold me nice and loving like that. You're so sweet. I knew you were sweet the moment I saw you. I knew you'd never hurt me.'

'No,' he said, 'I won't do that.'

'Some men do,' she said sadly.

'I know,' he said.

'Does it bother you?' she asked. 'About my leg?'

'Of course not.'

'I wish I could be perfect for you. I feel bad about that.'

'Don't feel bad,' he told her. 'I like you just the way you are.'

'Could we go out some night?' she said eagerly. 'We could go somewhere where we wouldn't be seen. You know?'

'Sure,' he said. 'We could do that. Drive down to Dania maybe. Hollywood. Maybe even Miami.'

She sighed contentedly. 'I'd like that. And some night I'll cook you dinner. I'm not very good, but I can make steaks and chicken and easy things like that.'

'Sounds good,' he said. 'I'm not fussy about my food. Steak or chicken would be fine.'

'Do you love me?' she asked suddenly.

He didn't answer.

'I know you don't,' she said. 'That's all right. I didn't expect you to. But could you say it? I'll know in my heart of hearts that you don't really mean it, but I'd like to hear you say it. No one's ever said that to me.'

'I love you, May,' he said in a wispy voice.

She hugged him tighter. She grinned fiercely.

'Oh, how I love you, daddy! I'll be ever so good to you, you'll see. I'll do everything you tell me to. I'll obey you and never be naughty. You'll see. I'll love you every way you want.'

He took his hand from her breast. He tilted up her chin. He kissed her child's lips, as chastely as a father. Her eyelids slowly closed. Her pale face became clear and serene. They sat motionless, mouths pressed and yielding.

He had the sense of coming home. This warm, lived-in place was familiar. He felt easy here. He could kick off his shoes, if he liked, or open his belt. And the odor of the damp earth and growing plants was not unlike the smell of his drunken father dying. Even May, with her torn cotton nightgown, reminded him of his mother and sisters.

He thought of the house Teresa had put together. Glass, marble, stainless steel. Abstract paintings on the walls, and not a comfortable chair in the joint. Everything was hard, cold, as impersonal as an office. He belonged here, with the sagging armchair, sofa bed with pillows, rag rug on the splintered floor. This was his kind of place.

She took her mouth from his, kissed the tip of his nose.

'Do you know what I want to do more than anything in the world, daddy?'

'What?'

'Dance. I'd love to go dancing. I can't, of course, because of my leg, but I'd love to. I dance all the time when I'm alone. It's not real dancing, I know, because I'm not with anyone, but I love to pretend. Would you like to watch me dance, daddy?'

'Maybe I'll have another beer,' he said hoarsely, 'and then I'll watch you dance.'

'You won't laugh at me?'

'I won't laugh. I promise.'

She brought him a beer, then switched on a little transistor radio in a cracked red plastic case. She turned the dial until she found a station playing a slow instrumental: Noel Coward's 'I'll See You Again.'

191

She began to move slowly about the room, thin arms held out, wrists cocked, fingers curled just so. Her head was back; long tresses streamed. She tried to swoop and glide, dip and turn.

He gulped his beer and watched her gravely. Her eyes were half-closed, lips parted. She moved in a dream all her own, off and floating. Arms waved like feelers. Hair flickered like black flame. He saw her dancing brokenly, dragging her leg, and lost.

The music ended. She stopped. He put his beer can aside and applauded softly.

'That was beautiful,' he said. 'Just great.'

She came over to him, eyes shining. She stood before him, lifted the hem of her nightgown to her waist.

'Kiss me, daddy,' she said. '*Please.*'

He leaned forward, pressed his face against her soft belly. She held the back of his head, pulling him closer. The nightgown tumbled down about his shoulders, and he was hidden there, alone and secret in that fragrant tent.

He smelled her and tasted her. She was young, fresh, free of taint. He dreamed she was a virgin, pure, uncorrupted, and he owned her.

It wasn't love, he convinced himself. He could endure the thought of losing her. But if he did, he'd want another child-woman exactly like her.

It never occurred to him that this might be the nature of love: the image but not the object.

3

Dr Theodore Levin was continually surprised and saddened by the number of children he treated who were soured and embittered. Youth, he felt, should be a time of curiosity and delight, the world opening up, life bright and limitless. But so many of his young patients already seemed ancient, weary, without hope.

When Wayne Bending slouched into his office, Levin guessed at once that this boy was one of the defeated. He could hardly believe this dark, dour youth was the son of Grace and Ronald, brother of Lucy.

Wayne was short for a twelve-year-old, stocky, with hunched shoulders and short legs. There was truculence behind his slouch. And on his face, not a sneer, but a carefully arranged implacableness, a mask presented to a hostile world.

Levin got him seated and switched on the tape recorder. The boy still hadn't met his eyes, but stared at a spot over the doctor's head.

'Wayne,' he said, 'thank you for coming in. I am sure you know that I am Doctor Theodore Levin, and I am treating your sister, Lucy. I hope you will be able to help me.'

The boy didn't reply.

'Are you aware of the reasons why your parents brought Lucy to me for counseling?'

Wayne shrugged.

Levin leaned forward, hands clasped on the desk. He had hoped the movement would bring the youth's gaze down to his. It didn't.

'Wayne, Lucy has a serious problem. It's going to take her cooperation, and the help of her parents and brothers, to find the best way to, uh, deal with her problem. I'm sure you want to do everything you can to assist.'

'The kid's a nut!' the boy burst out, fidgeting fretfully in his chair.

Levin sat back, laced fingers across his middle. He regarded the brother solemnly.

'Why do you say that?'

'She's always doing nutty things.'

'Like what?'

'You know,' Wayne said, almost accusingly. 'The reason my folks brought her to a shrink. She's always feeling up old guys.'

'Anything else?'

'Telling stories all the time. Crazy stories. And she swears they're true.'

'Wayne, you're old enough not to take the storytelling too seriously. I imagine that when you were Lucy's age, you told stories too. I know I did. But as we grow older, we learn not to tell other people our dreams and fantasies. That doesn't mean we don't have them. But we keep them to ourselves. Don't you create stories or dreams or fantasies you don't tell anyone about?'

The boy didn't answer.

'I'd like to hear some of your stories, Wayne.'

'I don't have any.'

'No matter how wild or crazy they might be,' Levin persisted. 'I'd like to hear them.'

Wayne hunched forward, hands clasped tightly. 'Listen, doc, Lucy is your problem, not mine. I don't have to tell you anything.'

'That's true. But if it will help Lucy? You love your sister, don't you?'

He shrugged again. 'I guess.'

'How do the two of you get along?'

'Okay.'

'Do you spend much time together?'

'What for? I see her around the house, at mealtimes – like that. We don't hang out together, if that's what you mean.'

'Who *do* you hang out with, Wayne?'

'Friends.'

'Boys your age?'

'Some. Some a little older. I don't hang with kids.'

'Girls? Do you have any girlfriends?'

'A few.'

'Anyone special?'

'No. How the hell is all this bullshit going to help Lucy?'

'I don't know,' Levin said equably. 'I'm just trying to find out as much as I can about the Bending family. That makes sense, doesn't it?'

The boy shrugged.

'Wayne, what grade are you in at school?'

'Seventh.'

'Do you like school?'

'It's all right.'

'How are your grades?'

'I get by.'

'No special problems?'

The boy jerked. 'Like what?' he asked suspiciously.

'Problems at school,' Levin said blandly.

'No. No problems.'

'How about at home? Anything there bothering you?'

'No.'

'No problems at school, no problems at home, plenty of friends . . . You've got a wonderful life, Wayne.'

Now the youth was staring at him.

'And you're full of shit,' Levin thundered, slapping the desk with a crack of his palm that made the boy jump. 'Don't tell me everything is sweetness and light. Don't give me this crap about not having any problems. *Everyone* has problems. And because you're too goddamned stubborn to

195

talk about them, you're making your sister's treatment that much more difficult. Is that what you want?'

'So I have problems,' the boy said, almost shouting. 'They're none of your fucking business.'

'They *are* my business,' Levin shouted back, 'if they affect Lucy's happiness.'

'They got nothing to do with Lucy.'

'Let me be the judge of that.'

'Screw you!' Wayne cried.

They sat there and glowered at each other.

'What makes you such a snot?' Levin demanded. 'Whoever did anything to you?'

'Who? Who? Everyone – that's who! You sit there on your fat ass and think you know everything. Shit, you haven't got a clue.'

'Give me a clue.'

'Why the fuck should I? You'll just dump on me like everyone else. Why should I trust you?'

Good question, Levin thought. Why should *anyone* trust him? But having started this charade of anger, and convinced it was the only way to break through, he had no choice but to continue.

'Well, why the hell should I trust *you*?' he said hotly. 'All you've told me so far is probably a lot of bullshit. You say you have friends. Maybe that's a goddamned lie. Maybe you're so fucking mean you haven't got a friend in the world, and –'

'I do so too!' Wayne screamed, leaping to his feet. 'I got a better friend than you'll ever have, you fat turd. A friend who really likes me, and he's the only one I can trust and talk to, but not you, you stupid, fat fuck.'

Then, fighting it but not able to hold back, he began to cry. He fell back into his chair, snuffling, drawing the back of his hand across his streaming eyes.

'All right,' Dr Levin said. 'All right now.'

'Son of a bitch,' the boy said bitterly. 'You miserable shit. I haven't cried since I was eight. You lousy bastard.'

196

'It's not so bad to cry,' the doctor said coolly. 'Nothing so terrible about it. Who's the friend?'

'Who?'

'The friend you can trust and talk to.'

'Just a guy. A guy I know.'

'Your age? Or older?'

'Older.'

'How old?'

'Sixteen, I guess. What difference does it make?'

'I'd like to hear about him.'

'Why?'

Levin sighed. 'Because I'm a mean, miserable, fat, stupid fuck – that's why.'

Wayne's tear-streaked face wrenched into a lopsided grin.

'And because I want to be your friend, too,' Levin went on. 'And I want you to trust me. So I want to know what kind of a guy could be a friend to a shithead like you.'

The boy didn't flinch, and Levin thought that was the way to talk to him: insults, profanity, with tenderness hidden, sentiment camouflaged. Everything casual, obscene, cynical.

'He's just this guy I know,' Wayne Bending said. 'His name's Eddie Holloway. He lives near me. A big, blond guy. Good-looking – you know?'

'Gets the girls, does he?'

'A stud,' the boy vowed. 'A fucking stud. But cool – you know? A great surfer. I go surfing with him all the time. He's better than me, but I can throw a football farther than he can.'

Levin shook his head as if in puzzlement.

'I don't know,' he said. 'A cool, good-looking stud like that, with all the girls he wants, what the hell does he hang around with you for?'

'He likes me,' Wayne said defensively. 'And . . .'

'And what?'

'I'm smarter than he is,' the youth said, lifting his chin.

197

'That's God's own truth. In lots of ways I'm smarter. He's a klutz when it comes to school. And other things. So I give him advice sometimes.'

'About what?'

'Oh . . . this and that.'

'And he takes your advice?'

'Sure.'

Levin switched gears on him. Sometimes this verbal shock therapy worked.

'Ever take a drink, Wayne?'

'A beer now and then.'

'You smoke pot?'

'I tried it once. It didn't do anything for me.'

'You on any other drugs? Uppers? Downers? Coke?'

'No.'

'What do you and this Eddie do together? Besides surfing?'

'Oh . . . you know. Just fart around.'

'Ever go on a date with him? With girls?'

'No.'

'The two of you ever have a girl together? You know – just farting around?'

'No.'

'Does this Eddie have one special girlfriend?'

'No,' Wayne said, moving restlessly. 'He plays the field.'

'Uh-huh,' Levin said, watching the boy wriggle nervously in his chair.

This talk about Wayne's best friend and girls was disturbing him. That wasn't unusual. A boy in early adolescence was torn between male bonding and reawakened sexuality. But Levin wondered if that's all it was: normal growth, normal change.

'Wayne,' he said, 'have you ever been with a girl? Ever screwed a girl?'

'No.'

'Ever seen a girl naked?'

'Once. The girls at my school, in the shower room of the

198

gym, you know, they pushed this girl out and wouldn't let her back in. She didn't have any clothes on. A joke, you know. I saw her. A lot of guys saw her.'

'Have you ever seen your mother naked?'

'Christ, no!'

'Lucy?'

'Not since she was a little baby.'

He had, Levin reflected, learned a great deal about Wayne Bending in a short time. But nothing much that illuminated Lucy's problem. Wayne's disillusionment was *another* problem. Not serious, yet, and not one he was being paid to solve.

Still, he was nagged by the notion that this boy's deep disenchantment and his sister's hypersexuality might possibly spring from the same source. Hardly unusual to have two siblings react in different psychopathic ways to a common traumatic experience.

'Wayne,' he said, 'you're a smart asshole, I can see that. I'm not trying to butter you up; I really think you've got a brain. The fact that Eddie Holloway, an older guy, takes your advice just goes to prove it. All right, here's a chance to use your brain. Why do you think Lucy acts the way she does?'

'You mean feeling up old guys?'

'Yes.'

The boy thought a long time. Or pretended he was thinking. Levin couldn't be sure which. But then, when Wayne finally spoke, he looked directly at Levin with a frank and open manner, and the doctor was certain he was dissembling.

'What I think,' he said, and then cleared his throat. 'What I think is that the kid is a nyfomaniac.'

'A what?'

'Nyfomaniac.'

'You mean nymphomaniac?'

'Yeah. Like that.'

'Where did you hear that word?'

'Oh . . .' Wayne said vaguely. 'Around.'

'Do you know what it means?'

'Sure. A woman who wants to do it all the time.'

'And you think Lucy is a nymphomaniac?'

'Sure,' the brother said, looking wide-eyed at the doctor. 'What else could it be?'

'Lucy is only eight years old. Not old enough to do it all the time, even if she had the opportunity, which she doesn't.'

'I know that,' Wayne Bending said wisely. 'But she *wants* to. Don't you get it?'

'Mmm,' Dr Levin said. 'An interesting theory. I'll have to look into that. Wayne, I think our time is up. Thank you for coming in and talking to me.'

'Anytime,' the boy said briskly. 'You going to straighten out Lucy, doc?'

'I'm going to try.'

'She's a pisser, isn't she?' the brother said, shaking his head in wonderment.

The moment the door closed, Dr Levin switched off the tape recorder and lighted up a cigar. Fifteen minutes before the next patient, an obnoxious little boy who had thrice set fire to his own home.

But Levin did not want to think about him. He wanted to reflect on Wayne Bending, a sad boy whose melancholy had probably already turned to despair, and from there to frustration and fury.

Levin knew the progression well: it was his own boy-hood. And he had been raised in a large, warm, loving family environment. So much for a happy childhood. No guarantee of adjustment and a sense of self-worth.

Like Wayne, he had been physically unattractive. Short, stumpy to the point of deformity. Low-browed and glower-ing. A squeaky voice. Helpless at sports. He couldn't walk through a room without bumping into furniture. And girls laughed at him.

He had gone through the same sequence Wayne was

200

enduring: misery to hopelessness to hostility. He had been rescued by a ninth-grade teacher, a fierce, old maiden lady who had recognized his intelligence and had convinced him that he could do, be, anything he chose.

So he *knew* Wayne Bending, just as he remembered the young Teddy Levin, the clumsy kid with nothing going for him but a good brain and a raw sensitivity.

Wayne Bending was hiding something; Levin was convinced of it, recalling how he concealed his innermost terrors. That talk of a 'nyfomaniac' was designed to confuse or mislead. Wayne knew, or guessed, the cause of Lucy's behavior. But he wasn't talking.

Which could possibly mean that the revelation would be too painful or might pose a threat to Wayne personally. What was the boy hiding?

Sighing, Dr Theodore Levin pressed a button on the intercom. A signal to the receptionist to send in the juvenile pyromaniac.

4

For two nights following his walk on the beach with Mrs Teresa Empt, Edward Holloway had arrived at the gazebo promptly at 9:00 P.M. He sat on the worn blanket he brought along, hugged his knees, and waited. Nothing.

'You blew it, dumbo,' he complained to Wayne Bending. 'She ain't going to show.'

'Sure she will,' Wayne said confidently. 'She asked you what time you got there, didn't she?'

'Yeah.'

'So she'll show. Have a little patience, for God's sake. She's just trying to prove she hasn't got the hots for you, that it means nothing to her. So she's stalling awhile. But she'll show up.'

'You think so?' Eddie said. He respected Wayne's knowledge of how old people thought and acted. 'Well, I'll give it another couple of nights. Then screw it.'

'She'll show,' Wayne assured him. 'And don't, for Christ's sake, hit her with the loan for the boat the first time. Act the nice, innocent, tender boy. Play her along. When you get her hooked, you can go for the loot.'

'I know what to do,' Eddie said, aggrieved. 'If she shows, she's dead meat. Mamma mia, those jugs!'

On the fourth night, Eddie made his usual preparations. He washed his armpits. He changed to a clean pair of yellow bikini underpants. He combed his long blond hair carefully. Then, when it was plastered into place, he tousled it with his fingers.

He went out the window of his bedroom, blanket under

his arm. He ran lightly over the shed roof of the kitchen, then dropped to the ground. It spared him the hassle of exiting through the living room and scamming his parents about where he was going.

She showed. About twenty minutes after nine. He saw a light flash on briefly in the rear of the big house. Then it went out, and he could see a white figure walking toward the gazebo. Moving slowly. Sort of wandering.

Eddie Holloway grinned. That Wayne Bending! He was some kind of genius.

She came up to him, arms folded, gripping her elbows. She had a white cardigan thrown across her shoulders. The ruffled, high-necked blouse was white. The pleated silk skirt was white. She was dressed like a fucking *lady*!

'Why, Eddie,' she said, laughing timidly, 'you really do come here, don't you?'

'I told you, Miz Empt,' he said sincerely. 'I sure hope you don't mind.'

'No, I don't mind. But isn't it too cool for sitting tonight?'

'Not really,' he said. 'I brought along this old blanket to keep out the damp. It's a nice night.'

'Yes,' she said, looking up at the stars. 'It is, isn't it? A divine night.'

'The benches are kinda hard without cushions, Miz Empt. Would you like to sit here for a minute?'

He moved aside politely.

'Why, thank you, Eddie,' she said. 'Maybe just for a minute.'

She folded gracefully down onto the blanket, tugging her skirt over her bare knees. She fussed with the cardigan over her shoulders, so the tied empty sleeves fell across her front. She sat with knees to one side, back erect. He caught a whiff of her perfume.

'Tell me, Eddie,' she said conversationally, 'how are you getting along in school?'

'Okay,' he said. 'I mean, I'm not great brain or anything like that, but I'm not flunking. About average, I guess.'

'Maybe you have too many outside activities,' she said in a teasing tone.

'Nah.'

'Don't you date a lot, Eddie?'

'Well . . . now and then.'

'No special girl?'

'Not really,' he said, voice troubled. 'I'll tell you, Miz Empt, the girls I meet mostly don't interest me. I mean, all they want to talk about is rock groups and movies and all that bul – stuff like that.'

'Well, they're young, Eddie,' she said lightly. 'Aren't they?'

'Yeah,' he said. 'Too young for me. I'd like to meet a girl, a woman, I can talk to about serious things.'

'Like what?'

'Oh . . .' he said vaguely, 'you know. Like what we're going to do with our lives and so forth.'

'It is a problem, isn't it, Eddie?'

'You can say that again.'

He lay back supine, hands clasped behind his head. He was wearing a short-sleeved shirt, the tails outside his jeans, the front unbuttoned low enough to show his hairless chest. And around his neck, a long black shoelace from which dangled a shark's tooth, gleaming against tanned skin.

'Sure is a nice night,' he said. 'Must be a jillion stars.'

'Yes,' she said in a low voice. 'It is nice.'

'Like I told you,' he said. 'That's why I come here. It's so secret. Away from everything.'

'It isn't as cool as I thought it would be,' she said throatily, the words catching.

She untied the sleeves of her cardigan. She folded the sweater neatly, put it carefully aside. He glanced briefly, saw the ruffled blouse had no buttons, no zipper. Son of a bitch! A pullover, unless the zipper was on the back.

She moved, bringing up her knees. She was facing him. If he turned his head, he swore, he'd be able to see up to her

204

cooze. She bent forward to rest her head on her knees. The long hair streamed down over the white skirt. He reached out to touch her hair, just for an instant, then clasped his hands behind his head again.

'You sure have pretty hair, Miz Empt,' he said.

'Why, thank you, Eddie. But don't you think it's silly for you to keep calling me Mrs Empt? You can call me Teresa. If you like . . .'

'Yeah,' he said, 'I will. But only when we're alone. You know? I mean, when other people are around, I'll still call you Miz Empt. Okay?'

'You're very understanding,' she said, laughing shakily. 'For such a young boy.'

He turned to look at her.

'I'm not so young,' he said.

She dived on him. That was the way he described it later to Wayne Bending: 'The fucking cunt *dived* on me!'

One moment she was sitting quietly there, knees drawn up, head bowed, and then suddenly she uncoiled and pounced. Her long body fell upon his, driving out his breath, and a frantic mouth was seeking his, a hot, wet tongue was darting wildly, forcing his lips.

He didn't even have time to take his clasped hands from behind his head. She was all over him, stroking his hair, then one hand ramming up under his shirt to rub his stomach, pinch his nipples.

'Hey,' he managed to gasp. 'Hey. Take it easy.'

She wouldn't take it easy. She acted like she wanted to devour him. She bit his lips, sucked his neck, raked his bare torso with her fingernails. It really hurt. And all the time she was making crazy noises, little cries, moans, some words he couldn't understand.

He feared she had gone off her gourd, and he was scared. He got his hands free, pinioned her arms. He held her as tightly as he could until she stopped threshing about and lay still, face turned away from him.

They lay that way in silence for a few moments. Her big

jugs were pressed into his chest. One of her knees was between his thighs, pressing into his nuts. But she just lay there motionless. Like she had fainted. Or died. He didn't know what to do.

'I'm so sorry,' she said quietly. 'I'm so ashamed.'

Then he knew what to do.

'Oh Teresa,' he said, trying to get a groan into his voice. 'Teresa, don't be sorry. Don't be ashamed. Don't you think I've been wanting to, uh, kiss you? I see you on the beach in your little white suit and tanned skin and long hair and all, and I go bananas. I mean, I dream of you all the time. I truly do. Kissing you and all. Maybe that's why my marks aren't so good. Because I think about you at school, at home, at night in bed. All the time.'

He felt her body stiffen, then relax into him.

'Really?' she said breathlessly. 'You feel that way? Really?'

He rolled her away, not without some effort because she was a big woman. Then they were on their sides, facing, so close their noses almost touched.

'I get all hot when I see you,' he whispered. 'Last week I had a wet dream all because of you.'

'Did you?' she said, laughing gaily. 'Oh Eddie, how *nice*!'

He kissed her. Nose, mouth, chin, neck. Then back to her lips, his tongue wagging.

'That's called a French kiss,' he told her.

'I know,' she said.

They kissed, they kissed. Her hand snaked down to his crotch, felt him.

'Oh my,' she said.

'See what you do to me?' he cried. 'I told you. Didn't I tell you?'

He cupped a big breast through the white silk blouse. He could feel a bra. The tit felt like a rock. He put his lips to the cloth.

'Please,' he moaned piteously.

His fingers found the zipper at the back of her blouse. He

fumbled, but couldn't get the damned thing started.

'Let me do it,' she said stiffly.

She pulled away from him, sat up. Reaching behind her with a dexterity he admired, she unzipped the blouse and shrugged it off. She shook it free of wrinkles, folded it carefully, set it atop the cardigan sweater.

She pulled down a side zipper on the skirt. She raised her hips, slid the skirt down from her legs. She flapped it once, folded it neatly, stacked it on the blouse and sweater. Then she lay back on the blanket, arms outstretched, staring at the stars.

She was wearing a white half-bra that bulged her breasts. Her bosom, Eddie thought, looked like a baby's ass. And below, little white bikini panties. There were sharp suntan marks across abdomen and thighs made by her bathing suit. Her legs were long and hard. She hadn't taken off her high Wedgies.

The half-bra had a front closure; Eddie had no trouble there. When he parted it, those glorious appendages surged free. Thank you, God, Eddie said silently. He put his mouth to her breasts. He lipped her nipples, big and sweet as gumdrops.

'Oh my God,' she murmured. Then: 'So good,' she kept saying. 'So *good*!'

He was trying to keep his cool, but it wasn't easy. She had to help him slide the panties down. Then she was wearing nothing but those crazy Wedgies, but he figured, What the hell . . .

He started to unbutton his shirt, but she pushed his hands away.

'Let me do it,' she said. 'I want to do it.'

So he lay back obediently and let her undress him. She wasn't so neat with *his* clothes, he noted. Just wrenched them off and flung them aside. She was very intent, determined, and he let her do what she wanted, wondering if all old women were as horny as this one.

When he was bare-ass naked, she just moved him over on

207

top of her. Recalling the scene later, he realized how strong she was: just lifted, rolled, clutched, and there he was, between her legs.

He fumbled around, and after a few moments her cool fingers guided him. He was not practiced, not experienced. But he was young, crude, ferocious, hard. Which apparently was exactly what she wanted.

Her knees rose. Ankles and Wedgies locked behind his back.

'Do, do, do!' she said.

By that time, Edward Holloway had lost his cool completely, and was bucking and plunging like a demented mustang. His hands were yanking on her ass, and her hands were yanking on his, and if the apocalypse had arrived just then, both would have yelped, 'Wait! Wait just one fucking minute!'

He slipped out, he slipped back in. He chewed on those wondrous jugs. She tugged his hair and tried to gnaw through his carotid. They banged and squirmed, mumbling at each other. They pumped, both going, 'Hah! Hah!' as if they had slain dragons.

She wouldn't let him roll away, but clutched him so tightly that his ribs ached. He could feel her throb, deep, a pulse that gradually diminished. She was so hot. And wet. And bottomless. She was a well. He could drown in there.

Finally she let him withdraw and roll free. He lay on his back, trying to live. The stars were whirling through the latticed gazebo roof. He wondered where he was, had to think a moment to recall his name, the place, the date – he was that broken.

'Do you have a phone?' she said.

'What?' he said, startled. 'What? Oh yeah, I have my own phone. In my own name. I'm in the book and all.'

'Good,' she said coldly. 'I'll meet you once or twice a week. Maybe more. I'll call you ahead of time and let you know when.'

'Well . . . yeah,' he said faintly. 'That's great.'

But this wasn't going so great. It was taking a switch he hadn't figured. And neither had Wayne Bending, that fucking genius.

'Well, yeah,' he said. 'Sure you can call me. That'll really be super.'

She must have caught something in his tone, because she rolled onto a hip and bent over him.

'You liked it, didn't you, Eddie?'

'Oh God, yes,' he moaned. 'Great. Really heavy.'

'More,' she murmured in his ear. 'There'll be more.'

She told him what 'more' might include. He shivered. This old dame could kill him; it was possible. He had never heard a woman suggest such things. Fear pierced him. She was a fucking barracuda.

She lay back, close to him, holding his hand.

'Ohh, wasn't that nice, Eddie?' she said softly.

'Oh yeah. Nice. The greatest.'

'Different from your young girls?'

'You better believe it,' he said. 'Different and, and, and . . . well, you know, *different*.'

'We're going to have fun together, aren't we, Eddie?'

'Oh yeah,' he said. 'Fun.'

'Your body is so beautiful,' she said. 'So beautiful.'

She turned back to him again, and her tongue got busy. He would have appreciated a little intermission right then, but she wasn't having any. He protested, but it did no good. She wanted to explore him, as if she had never come upon such a treasure before. She poked and prodded, caressed and nipped. Out of the trees. Off her branch.

'Teresa, Teresa,' he said despairingly.

'I love the way you say that,' she said. 'You understand about the phone calls, don't you?'

'What?' he said.

'Try to concentrate, Eddie. I'll call you beforehand and tell you when we can meet. Try to bring another blanket; this one smells.'

A fucking ball-breaker!

'Sure, Miz Empt,' he said. 'Uh, Teresa.'

'You don't have anything to smoke, do you, Eddie?'

'Uh, no, I don't, Teresa. Not right now.'

'I don't mean regular cigarettes. I mean pot. Grass. You understand?'

'Oh yeah. Sure. I haven't got any right now.'

'But you've smoked it?'

'Oh yeah.'

'Can you get some? For us?'

The opportunity was too good to pass up.

'I think I can,' he said cautiously. 'But it'll cost. You know? And I can't handle it, being on an allowance and all.'

'Don't worry about it,' she said. 'I'll bring you money. Will twenty be enough?'

That was more like it.

'Twenty will be fine,' he assured her. 'I'll get us some good stuff.'

She took him in her arms. She hugged him. She ran a palm down his chest, down his abdomen. She eased a fingertip into his navel and stirred gently. Then she looked up at his face.

'Do you like that, Eddie?'

'I like everything you do. You're the sexiest woman I've ever met.'

'Sexy?' she said, laughing softly. 'I've never thought of myself as a particularly sexy woman, but perhaps you're right. It just took the right man to bring it out.'

His ego soared. He had really given her a superbang. Short, but super.

'My first husband wasn't much of a lover,' she said, wriggling closer to him. 'I just adore cuddling, don't you? He went through the motions, but you could tell his heart wasn't in it. Or maybe he just didn't have enough experience. I know I didn't; I was a virgin when I was married. Hold my boob, Eddie. And I really wasn't interested in sex. It didn't seem all that wonderful to me. But when he died, and I moved to Florida, I began to change. And lately, the last few years, I've been thinking about it more and more. When I see what's going on, what everyone's doing, I think, why shouldn't I? No one takes it all that seriously, do they? Put your hand down here, Eddie. As far as Luther goes, it really means nothing to me. He goes his way and I go mine. It's a very modern marriage. You can move your finger if you like. Life's so short. You're very young and don't believe that, I'm sure, but it's true, and you'll realize it as you grow older. So you must live your life to the fullest, I've become convinced of that. You don't know what I'm talking about, do you? Yes, that's nice. Just a little higher. Yes, right *there*. So when I saw you on the beach and surfing, so handsome, with your lovely body and blond hair flying, I knew I had to have you. Some way, somehow, I had to have sex with you. You don't think I'm awful, do you? And then, when you told me about coming here to the gazebo almost every night, I knew it was the answer. Of course, no one, absolutely *no* one, can know about this, or I'll be ruined in the community. So I'm depending on you to be very, very discreet, and not tell a soul. Oh yes, I love that. Go a little faster. You're so young and sweet. My God, if my friends knew what I was doing, they'd just *die*! But I'm not going to tell a soul, and I don't want you to either. Eddie, I hope you don't think of this as a one-night stand, like some of your creamers I'm sure. I want this to be a long, loving relationship. Now kiss my breasts. Oh, what a lover you are!'

He had listened to this monologue with growing dread. And now, head lowered, sucking desperately at her nipples, he wondered how long he could endure.

He raised his face to look at her.

'Some nights I might not be able to make it,' he said hoarsely. 'You know? I mean, homework and all . . .'

'I understand, Eddie,' she said. 'But surely we'll be able to get together two or three nights a week.'

'I guess,' he said mournfully.

211

She laughed, and he was convinced it was a crazy cackle, and maybe she really was off the wall.

'Oh, we're going to have such *fun* together,' she said, almost gurgling. 'You'll teach me and I'll teach you. We'll just do *everything* together.'

He would have been terrified by that prospect, but all the time she was talking, she was playing with his pud, squeezing it, flipping it, yanking on it like it was a goddamned rope or something, and she was ringing a church bell.

So, willy-nilly, he found his body responding. He became engorged, and she peered at the stone-white shaft gleaming in the darkness.

'It's mine,' she said. 'Isn't it all mine, Eddie?'

'All yours,' he said in a strangled voice.

'I don't want you to give it to anyone else. Is that understood, Eddie? I want it all for myself. Promise?'

'I promise.'

'And now,' she said, 'I think I shall give it a little kissy. Just one.'

When she raised her head, she looked at him anxiously . . .

'Can you do it again, Eddie?'

'Sure,' he said with a bray of insane laughter. 'Why not?'

5

Ronald Bending awoke late on Saturday morning, swaddled in a sweat-damp sheet. He blinked sticky eyes, tasted a flannel tongue. Shafts of sunlight struck through the east windows. He squinted against the glare, fumbled for cigarettes on the bedside table.

He sat naked on the edge of the bed, yawning and smoking. He slept naked: another argument with Grace, even though they had separate beds.

'It's so *gross*,' she told him.

She was using that word more and more. His smoking was gross. His drinking was gross. His jokes were gross.

He had reminded her that when they were first married, everything had been loose, free, uninhibited, pagan. When, he wanted to know, had all the things they shared and loved become gross? She hadn't answered. Because they both knew.

He lifted an arm and sniffed at his bicep. He grinned feebly, remembering the girl from the bank. Her scent was still on him. What a wild one she had been. A tattoo, for God's sake! Yes, a little blue butterfly just below her navel. That was Florida for you: tattooed teenagers.

He finished his cigarette. He went into the bathroom, showered, and shaved. He curried hair and skin carefully with oils and lotions. He coaxed his body to youth, pampering it. But when he inspected himself in the mirror, he saw age there, grinning.

He pulled on swimming trunks, then white duck jeans, a short-sleeved polo shirt. He went bouncing downstairs,

213

barefoot. He smiled at his first sight of the beach through the picture window: shining sand and a platinum haze over the water. Turner would have loved that beamy light.

No kids around, but Grace was in the kitchen, busy with an open cookbook, pots, pans, a flour sifter. Ronald felt so good that he kissed the back of her neck. She waved him away with a floury hand, not looking at him.

'What time did you get in last night?' she demanded, studying the cookbook.

He knew a ribald answer to that, but forbore.

'Late,' he said, pouring himself a mug of black coffee from the burping percolator. 'I told you the accountant was coming in.'

'Was the accountant about eighteen or nineteen?' she asked, still bending over the cookbook. 'A dark-haired girl in a tight sweater? That's who Myra Webster saw you with last night at Julio's.'

God bless Myra Webster, he thought.

'That was the accountant's assistant,' he said glibly. 'Mary Something. He was busy with the books, so I took her out for a bite to eat. Then we went back to the office.'

'I don't really care,' she said, turning to the electric range. 'There's orange or tomato juice. If you want toast and eggs, you'll have to make them yourself.'

'Coffee will do me fine,' he said.

He held the mug in both hands, leaning against the countertop and watching his wife move purposefully about the kitchen. Not for the first time, he wondered who she was.

A strand of blondish hair had escaped the barrette, and dangled on her cheek. Her face was serious, intent. There was a smudge of flour on her nose. Occasionally she bit her lower lip.

The body, he acknowledged, was still good. But stiff and unyielding. He remembered when it was supple and eager. She hadn't aged so much as tightened. Flesh had hardened; the spine had frozen.

In their early days together, he had done some charcoal sketches of her. Nudes. Quick drawings that caught her sinuosity. They were the best things he had ever done. About five years ago, she had come across the drawings in an old file and burned them.

'Well!' he said. 'Where are the kids?'

'Out,' she said. 'On the beach, I guess.'

'And what are your plans for today?' He was trying very hard to be pleasant.

'What do you care?' she said bitterly.

It always came to this: stinging each other with words.

He tried again:

'Is there anything you want me to do? Uh . . . shopping? Need anything from Publix?'

Finally she looked at him. Turning to face him directly. Wooden stirring spoon in one hand. The other hand a bleak fist.

'Yes,' she said loudly, 'there is something I want you to do. I'm going to a meeting at noon. I want you to come with me.'

'A meeting?' he said cautiously. 'What kind of a meeting?'

'A group.'

'What kind of a group?'

It all came out in a rush. Being Born Again. The Lord Jesus. Whites and blacks together. Saved. Confession and forgiveness. The sympathy and understanding of fellow sinners. Giving and absolution. Repentance and a new life.

'I'll pass,' he said blithely. 'Not my cup of tea.'

'You have sinned,' she said darkly.

'Haven't we all?'

'Ronnie, I don't ask much of you, do I?'

'No,' he had to admit.

'I'm asking you now. Just this once . . . Come with me. Meet Mr Fitch. Talk to him.'

'Who?'

'Osborn Fitch. Our shepherd. A marvelous man.'

215

'I'm sure he is, Grace. Last year it was that Indian swami, or whatever. And the year before that, the Korean with the gold earring. Look, we've been through this before. Many times. You do what you want to do. But don't expect to drag me into this bullshit.'

'You're going to burn in hell!' she screamed at him, so loudly that he started and slopped coffee onto his hand.

'Yes, well,' he said, 'that's possible. But I'm not going to go through hell while I'm still alive. Not if I can help it.'

He slammed the coffee mug into the sink, stalked out. He was convinced she was getting loonier every day, and wondered how much more he could take.

He stripped off jeans and shirt on the terrace, then went trotting down to the sea. Slow rollers were coming in, the water reasonably clean and cold enough to shock. He ran in determinedly, plunged, and swam out with a strong crawl.

The first five minutes were an ache. But then he slowed, steadied; muscles loosened. He swam far out, turned onto his back. He floated, arms and legs spread wide, chest arched, and let the waves take him. He closed his eyes against the noon glare.

He lay like that, bobbing, melting, until his breathing was back to normal. Then he backstroked to shore, feeling muscles pull as he reached high over his head to row the ocean past.

He waded ashore, palmed water from his hair and face. Born Again: that was the way he felt. Lucy and Gloria Holloway came running up to him.

'Daddy!' Lucy said excitedly. 'Look what Gloria's got!'

The nine-year-old Holloway girl who, Turk Bending thought, looked like a young harridan, displayed a brightly colored carton labeled 'Kiddie Kosmetics.'

'Lipstick, rouge, powder, and eyeshadow,' she said authoritatively. 'My mother bought it for me.'

'Very nice,' Bending said, nodding.

'We're going to put it on,' Lucy said. 'Aren't we, Gloria?'

216

'Me first,' Gloria said coldly. 'You can help.'

'Then me?'

'If there's enough.'

'Beautiful,' Bending said. 'A couple of glamor girls.'

They giggled and ran up the beach to the Holloway home. Ronald watched them go, their brown legs flashing, tight little rumps churning. He thought he could get twenty years for what he was thinking. Not for doing anything, but just for *thinking* it.

He trotted around to the side door of his own home. He used the outside tap to wash sand from his feet. Then he went into the kitchen, leaving wet footprints on the tile. Grace was gone, for which he was thankful.

He took a gallon thermos jug from under the sink, rinsed it out, and dumped in a trayful of ice cubes. Then he padded into the living room for vodka. He opened a fresh bottle and hoped this one would have more kick. The half-filled bottle he had just finished had tasted curiously watery.

He dumped half a liter of vodka into the thermos, then added a generous dollop of Rose's lime juice. He capped the jug and swirled it around and around in both hands. A giant cocktail shaker.

He found some clean plastic glasses in the cupboard, took those and the thermos jug, and started for the beach. But then he had to come back for a big beach towel, cigarettes, lighter, and a white terry cloth hat.

He finally got settled on the beach, on dry sand but near the water. He sat on his beach towel, put on his hat, lighted a cigarette, and drew an icy gimlet into a plastic cup from the little spigot on the thermos jug. He could feel the sun already baking his shoulders and back.

He held his drink up to the ocean, world, life.

'God bless,' he said aloud.

The gimlet was tart, bitingly cold, and so good he almost sobbed with delight.

His wants were simple, he assured himself. This was all

217

he needed: hot light, cold drink, a cigarette, and the view. Not so much of the sea, but of the passersby splashing along in the surf.

The creamers! The parade of creamers. All ages, all shapes, all sizes. He loved them all. Some, true, he loved more than others, but his artist's eye saw merit in all. In their maillots, two-piece suits, diapers, bikinis, string bikinis. Patches of white, black, purple, blood red.

Blondes, brunettes, redheads. Strutting, strolling, jogging. Or wandering, prancing, almost dancing across the strand. A frieze of women. And if you couldn't find joy in that, you were one of the breathing dead.

Item: A twelve-year-old in a black G-string supported by gold chains. A tiny bra covering budding breasts. Blonde pigtails braided with black ribbon.

Item: An older woman, solid and secure, with a zoftig body in a sleek white maillot cut high on the thigh. Hemispherical breasts and artfully coiffed hair piled atop her head like a wedding cake.

Item: About thirty, tall, rangy, with an athlete's body. A no-nonsense stride, muscles oiled and gleaming. A stern face and eyes blanked with mirrored sunglasses. Calves bulging . . .

Item: William Jasper Holloway, shuffling barefoot through the wash, slacks rolled up to his knees. Face vacant and lips moving.

'Hey, Bill,' Bending called.

Holloway looked up slowly, features forming. He came over, loomed, stared down. He tried a smile.

'Turk,' he said. 'What's new?'

'I'm new,' Bending said breezily. 'Plant your ass and have a shot from this wonderful pot.'

Holloway sat down clumsily on the corner of Bending's beach towel. He accepted the plastic cup of gimlet in a trembling hand. He took a deep swallow, closed his eyes, drew a heavy breath, opened his eyes.

'Yes,' he said. 'Thank you. I should have done that two

hours ago. I thought a walk would help, but it didn't. Gimlet?'

'Yes.'

'Fine. Just fine. How are you, Turk?'

He held out his empty cup, and Bending filled it again.

'I'm surviving,' Ronald said. 'Putting in my usual Saturday afternoon of bikini-watching.'

'Anything good?' Holloway asked without interest.

'It's all good. All of it.'

They were silent, watching three young girls saunter by, kicking through the surf. One of the three had a marvelous suntan: golden, glowing, burnished.

'I love you,' Bending said softly. 'Marry me.'

Bill Holloway turned to look at him.

'You never get tired of it, do you?'

'No,' Bending said. 'Never.' Then, as if he felt the need to explain: 'I know that everyone thinks I'm a clown and a womanizer.'

Holloway made a gesture, a wave of his hand.

'It's not that at all,' Bending said. 'Not the sex thing. I don't walk around with a constant hard-on. That's not it. I used to be an artist, you know. Fine arts. Painting. Oil and watercolors. Studied at Brown and at the Art Students League in New York.'

'I know. You told me.'

'Well, I'm not an artist now; I admit it. But some things stick. A way of looking at things. Line. Color. Mass and composition. Tension.'

'Sure,' Holloway said.

They sat in silence awhile. Then Bending offered another gimlet, but Holloway refused. He thanked Turk for the drinks, struggled to his feet, went shambling off to his own home.

Bending lighted another cigarette, tilted the thermos to draw another drink. He watched the women. Hel-*lo* there. I love you. Marry me. Oh sweetheart. Aren't you the chubby one? Swing it, baby. Come live with me and be my love.

It wasn't sex. He repeated to himself: *it was not sex*. It was the artist's eye. Love of grace. It was line, curve, color, mass, hue, proportion, tension, composition. It was perfection that turned his stomach.

The platinum haze hugged the sea. Frothy rollers made their own music. Far out, white sails etched against blurred blue. And close, the glitter of the sand. A kissing breeze. Vaporous sky with a haloed sun. The world perfumed with light.

Hi darling, he said silently to the passing parade. You're beautiful. Love that suit, sweetheart. My, what have we here? Oh God, I can't stand it. Yes, you have a right to strut. I'll see you in my dreams. Look at me and know my heart.

6

Dr Theodore Levin, growly in dark, vested suit and white cigar ashes, invited Mrs Grace Bending to be seated in the armchair facing his desk. He switched on the tape recorder. Then he stared at her.

She was wearing a shirtwaist dress in a pastel flower print. Long-sleeved and buttoned up to the neck. But her good legs were bare, her ropy hair fell loosely. It smoothed her carved features, softened the expression of prim distaste.

'Doctor,' she said, bending forward stiffly, 'are you making progress with Lucy?'

He ignored the question.

'Mrs Bending, in cases of this nature, it is frequently helpful to delve a little deeper into the personal history of the parents. That is what I'd like to do today – to learn a little more about you.'

'If you think it will help . . .' she said doubtfully.

'I think it will. Suppose you just tell me the story of your life.'

'Well . . .' she said with a nervous laugh, 'I am thirty-six years old. I was an only child. Does that mean anything?'

He looked at her. 'It means you were an only child. Please go on.'

'I had a happy childhood. I don't mean that I now remember it as being happy, but at the time, I was aware that I was happy. My father had a very good job with an insurance company. He was an executive in the main office

221

in Hartford, Connecticut. That's where we lived. In a big house. My father's mother lived with us until she died when I was nine. Then there was just the three of us. My father was a handsome man. At least I thought he was. And he was a very kind man. Stern but kind. I mean, he had his standards. My mother, very pretty, was something of a flibbertigibbet, but my father loved her very much. I did too, of course. Let's see . . . well, I really had a very normal childhood. Nothing dramatic happened to me. I did well in school. I was salutatorian of my high school graduating class. Then I went to Radcliffe. In my second year, my mother contracted cancer of the lymph nodes. She was gone in six months. I wanted to drop out of school, but daddy wouldn't hear of it. So I was graduated. I worked for two years in a law office in Hartford. Then I met Ronnie, and we dated for almost a year, and then his divorce came through and we were married. He was separated from his wife when I met him. I mean, I don't want you to think I took him away from his first wife or anything like that. We lived in New York City for a while, and then we moved to Florida about nine years ago. And – and that's about it.'

Levin had listened intently to this recital. Grace Bending had started out haltingly, fidgeting with her wedding band. But she concluded her account with calm restored, voice steady and emotionless. She faced the doctor with chin raised, eyes challenging.

'Is your father still living?' he asked.

'No. He died several years ago. A stroke.'

'You have aunts, uncles, cousins?'

'A few. We exchange Christmas cards, but we are not close.'

'You say you had a very normal childhood. That was your term. Friends?'

'Of course I had friends.'

'Girls or boys? Or both?'

'Both.'

222

'You dated while you were in high school?'

'Yes.'

'And in college as well?'

'Yes.'

'Would you say your experience with men prior to your marriage was extensive?'

'Uh . . . average.'

'You were not a virgin when you were married?'

She glared at him, opened her mouth apparently to make a sharp retort, then closed it so abruptly that he heard her teeth click.

'No, I was not,' she said coldly. Then: 'My husband had been married before.'

'Yes,' Dr Levin said. 'Have you had any problems with the physical side of marriage?'

'Problems? No, I have no problems.'

'In a previous meeting, you told me that you and your husband have sexual relations about once a month. Is that correct?'

'Yes.'

'You are satisfied with that frequency?'

'Yes.'

'Surely you must be aware that once a month is hardly a, uh, hardly an average for married couples of your and your husband's ages.'

'I don't really see how you can set any averages for something like that. My goodness, doctor, it's very personal, and everyone is different.'

'From what you told me about your childhood and youth, I get the impression that you were closer to your father than to your mother. Would you say that is accurate?'

'I loved my mother,' she said stiffly.

'I'm sure you did. But would you say you felt closer to your father?'

She didn't answer, which was answer enough.

'Mrs Bending, were your parents churchgoers?'

'Oh yes. Regularly. My father was a vestryman.'

223

'And you told me that you also attend regularly?'

'Yes, I do.'

Levin had hoped after their previous meeting that she would continue to thaw, to be more forthcoming in her responses. But she now seemed as tight and frozen as during the initial interview. He searched for some way to shatter that chilly composure.

'Mrs Bending,' he said softly, 'have you ever had sexual relations with a woman?'

'A woman?' she cried. 'Of course not!'

'How do you feel about women who are physically intimate with each other?'

'It's disgusting!'

'And men? What about homosexual love?'

'It's so filthy!' she burst out. 'I know what's going on today. You can't pick up a book or see a movie . . . Even on television! It's so ugly and degrading. I can't understand how people can do those things. Like animals! Whatever happened to love and faithfulness between a man and woman? I feel very strongly about that. Very strongly.'

Levin listened to this outburst with his hands clasped on the desk. He goggled at Mrs Bending through his thick glasses, seeing her flushed features, her wild animation that came perilously close to hysteria.

But he didn't interrupt or attempt to calm her. He let her run down, then watched as she took a small square of cambric from her purse and patted at perspiration beading her upper lip and beneath her sharp chin.

He could appreciate how horrendous her daughter's behavior must seem to her. There was a leper in her home, her own guilty offspring. He reflected ruefully that it was Dr Mary Scotsby who had suggested this woman might have a religious mania, and he had rejected that analysis. Now he thought it a thread in the skein.

'Mrs Bending, to which church do you belong?'

'Officially, I am a Presbyterian.'

'Officially?'

'That was my parents' church, I am a registered member, and still attend faithfully. However, I have become interested in other beliefs and faiths and sometimes attend their meetings as well.'

'I see. And you have been doing this for how long?'

'Doing what?'

'Your interest in other beliefs and faiths outside the Presbyterian Church – when did this begin?'

'Oh . . . perhaps four or five years ago.'

'What beliefs? What faiths?'

'I became very interested in Oriental religions and religious practices. Buddhism, for instance. Yoga. And Zen. Recently, I have joined a small fundamentalist group. It is basically Baptist, I believe, but with a more, uh, a more, uh, an approach to personal salvation through confession and repentance.'

'Does your husband share your interest in personal salvation?'

She looked at him hard, thinking he was mocking her, but he was not.

'No,' she said shortly. 'My husband has little interest in religion.'

'Tell me, Mrs Bending, what do you feel is the reason for your present interest in a fundamentalist church?'

'It offers a hope of purification,' she said, staring down at her hands. 'Of cleansing the true believer, washing us free of our sins.'

'You feel you have sinned?'

She raised her eyes to look at him. 'Doctor, we are all sinners. Some worse than others, but none of us is without sin. Yet there is hope of the soul born anew, past mistakes confessed and forgiven. There is hope for a fresh life, of being born again.'

'Have you tried explaining this to your husband?'

'He knows how I feel.'

'And . . . ?'

225

'He laughs at me and goes his own way.'

'Mrs Bending, I would like to make a statement. An observation, really. But before I do, I want to assure you that it is not a judgment. But I would like to tell you my impression, and ask you if you think it is reasonably accurate. Do you understand?'

'Yes.'

'It seems to me that you and your husband have drifted – are drifting apart. You have been married for – how long? Fourteen years? – and apparently it is, or was, a happy marriage. Your husband is successful. You have three children, a fine home. I am sure your relationship was not perfect; human relationships never are. But I get the sense of a growing estrangement. If I am wrong, please correct me. Am I wrong?'

'No.'

'Thank you. The reason I am speaking so frankly to you is that I am trying to determine any possible contributing cause for Lucy's behavior. Could you hazard a guess at the reason for this increasing animosity between you and your husband?'

'It's obvious,' she said with a smirky laugh, 'isn't it?'

'Not to me it isn't, Mrs Bending.'

'My husband is a woman-chaser. Anything in skirts. Or jeans. Or bikinis.'

'Oh? Is this something you suspect? Or know?'

'I *know* it,' she said definitely. 'Without a shadow of a doubt. He has been seen with other women. Girls, really. He stays out to all hours. He comes home smelling of them. Suspect? Oh no, doctor, I *know*.'

'How long has this been going on?'

'From the start. The very beginning. I wasn't aware of it at first. Now I can no longer disregard it. He really makes no effort to hide it. Everyone knows. All our friends.'

'Have you talked to him about it?'

'I've tried. Many times. He denies everything. He lies, lies, lies!'

'Mrs Bending, I am not going to make a judgment on the truth or falsity of your accusations. I have no way of knowing, of course, and my opinion is really not important. What *is* important is that you feel this way, and the growing rancor between you and your husband cannot help but affect your children.'

'They know nothing about it,' she said woodenly.

Levin sighed. 'Mrs Bending, one of my most difficult tasks is convincing parents how much their children *do* know. Children are remarkably sensitive to currents of emotion between their parents. Looks, tones of voice, the presence or absence of gestures of affection – all these things, and more, affect the children. Usually subconsciously. Without analyzing it, or putting it into words, they are aware of the atmosphere of their home. And the home represents their safe haven. The one place where they don't have to worry about the foreign and hostile currents of the world outside. Anything that threatens the security of the home threatens *them*. So, frequently, when they feel that security is diminishing, they react in unexpected ways, seeking security elsewhere.'

'Doctor,' she said tensely, 'are you suggesting that Lucy does, uh, the things she does because of the way my husband acts?'

'The way you *believe* he acts,' he corrected gently, 'and your reaction to that belief. I am not saying the relations between you and your husband are the sole cause of Lucy's disturbance. There may be other, more important factors. At this stage, I just don't know. I am just mentioning to you what I think could be affecting Lucy and the way she acts.'

Levin watched while she pondered what he had said. There was suddenly, in her face, an expression of sorrow and guilt that saddened him. He had seen it before in the features of concerned parents: the shocking realization that they might have created their child's psychopathy.

'We never fight when the children are around,' she said dully.

227

He was very patient. 'It is not necessary for children to witness a fight to be aware of what's going on. Believe me, Mrs Bending, they are more perceptive than you think.'

'And they never forget,' she said unexpectedly.

Then suddenly she was weeping, bent over, face in her hands. He listened to her sobs, an occasional 'God help me' or 'God forgive me.' Levin thought the recognition of her possible culpability would do her no harm. He slid the box of Kleenex to her side of the desk.

Finally she quieted, dabbed at her streaming eyes with a tissue. She opened her purse.

'Pardon me,' she said in a thick voice, stood, and turned her back to him while she inspected herself in a mirror and patted some powder on her cheeks.

Dr Levin thought it was a charming gesture, but wondered at a woman who considered applying makeup such a private and intimate act that it must be hidden from men.

'Mrs Bending,' he said, after she was seated again, 'I am sorry if I upset you. I tried to make it clear that I am not accusing you or your husband of anything.'

'I understand, doctor,' she said, head bowed. 'What do you suggest that I – that we do?'

'Nothing,' he said firmly. 'At the moment. In this case, pretending emotions or an affection you don't genuinely feel is as bad as, or worse than, being honest in your relations with your husband. Perhaps Lucy can be persuaded to accept things as they are, and to be convinced that her personal safety and future are not threatened. We are just in the beginning of this therapy, Mrs Bending. How long has it been – two months? I must ask you to have patience.'

'It's difficult,' she said.

'I know,' he said sympathetically. 'But Lucy's well-being is at stake. And that's what we both want, isn't it? Lucy's well-being?'

'Yes,' she said in a low voice. 'And mine.'
He looked at her queerly.
'I think our time is up,' he said.

7

It was a culture that demanded constant change. New fads, new follies. Clothes, drinks, jokes, cars, restaurants – what's the latest? Even the old welcomed the different.

That year the newest of dishes served at private dinners was called Noodles Alfredo à la Las Vegas. It was the traditional pasta, but with bite-sized pieces of crisp bacon and sautéed veal.

Mrs Teresa Empt decided on Noodles Alfredo à la Las Vegas for the main course of her dinner party. It would be preceded by a seafood cocktail appetizer: chunks of stone crab, prawns, and crayfish. It would be accompanied by a ratatouille and an astringent salad of endive and romaine. Lemon ice and key lime pie for dessert.

The wine, she decided, should be white, a dry California Chablis. Knowing her guests, she was certain they would be well-lubricated with cocktails before sitting down to dinner. A good French Pouilly-Fuissé would be wasted.

Having planned this menu, Teresa hired people to prepare the meal; she had no intention of spending all day in the kitchen. A Palm Beach caterer supplied a chef and assistant. The Empts' black houseman, John Stewart Wellington, would serve.

In consultation with Mrs Grace Bending and Mrs Jane Holloway, it was decided that everyone would dress formally for this affair, the women in long gowns and the men in white dinner jackets. An exception would be made for Professor Lloyd Craner, whose formal wear was an old, rusty black tuxedo with wide faille lapels.

Luther received news of the planned dinner with calm resignation. Since Bending and Holloway were now his partners, he could write off the entire cost of the party as a business expense. He bought sufficient whiskey and wine so there would be enough left over to see him through the Christmas season.

The dinner was held on the last Friday night in November. The weather had been delightful for that time of year, with cloudless days of 75 to 80 degrees, and mild nights in the high 60s. News of an early blizzard up north made everyone happier.

On Friday afternoon, Mrs Teresa Empt drove to her favorite florist in Boca Raton and selected flowers for the party. She chose tall branches of red and white gladioli for the living room, and low arrangements of daisies, sweetpeas, rosebuds, asters, and maidenhair fern for the dinner table.

She also bought a single crimson hibiscus bloom to wear in her hair.

She returned home, placed the flowers precisely where she wanted them. She visited the kitchen to check on the progress of the chef. Then she went upstairs to bathe and dress.

She donned a flowing gown of Siamese silk with a wild poppy print on a jungle-green background. She let her hair swing free, and pinned the hibiscus blossom above her left ear. She put a snake bracelet about the bicep of her right arm.

When she inspected herself in a pier glass, she saw a tall, healthy, suntanned woman, glowing with sultry vitality. There was, she decided, something primitive in the way she looked, and it pleased her. She *felt* primitive as if, finally, after all these years, she had found the molten, mysterious heart of life.

Head high, she swept from her bedroom and slowly, proudly, descended the wide staircase to greet her guests.

*　　　*　　　*

Mrs Jane Holloway wore a tube of black jersey, snug at bosom and hips, suspended from her smooth shoulders by straps no wider than shoelaces. A choker of diamonds about her unlined throat.

Mrs Grace Bending wore a flowered blouse, high-necked and long-sleeved, with a woven straw belt, and an evening skirt of white pleated silk. She was the only woman present wearing hose.

Mrs Gertrude Empt wore what appeared to be a muumuu in a hellish Hawaiian print that included pineapples and Polynesian war canoes. She also sported a double-looped necklace of auger and olive shells, her own handiwork.

Professor Lloyd Craner wore his rusty black tuxedo with an old-fashioned wing collar and a somewhat lopsided black bow tie. He had a small white mum on his lapel, and his mustache and goatee had been waxed to needle points.

William Jasper Holloway, Ronald Bending, and Luther Empt wore white dinner jackets. Holloway's trousers were black, Bending's were a Black Watch tartan, and Empt's were fire-engine red. All three men wore ruffled shirts and oversized butterfly ties. Ruffles and ties were edged with scarlet.

Grace Bending asked for diet cola, but all the others accepted drinks from the enormous crystal pitcher of vodka martinis that Luther Empt had prepared the night before and left in the refrigerator to chill and meld properly without the addition of ice.

Olives, pearl onions, and slices of lemon peel were available for the martinis. And also – very big in Florida that year: a new taste sensation – thin slices of unpeeled cucumber.

Teresa allowed one round of drinks. Then, on a signal from John Stewart Wellington, she shooed everyone into the dining room, telling them to bring their glasses. She seated them at the table with a drill sergeant's precision, making certain wives and husbands were separated.

*   *   *

'Teresa,' Grace said, 'everything was delicious. A wonderful meal.'

'Yeah,' Luther Empt said. 'Tony's Take-out does all right. Next time we're going to try Sambo's. Come on, everyone, drink up. The party's not over yet.'

They finished all the bottles of wine, Ronald Bending and Luther Empt doing more than their share. They had lemon ice or key lime pie. Then the hostess suggested they adjourn to the beach terrace for coffee and postprandial drinks.

A dark, balmy night, no moon, but a painted sky: streaky purple with a glaze of starlight. Moving air touched. They heard the sea's whisper. There was a tanged perfume on the breeze, something foreign and frightening.

'This is what we came to Florida for,' Teresa Empt declared, and watched critically as John Stewart Wellington served coffee.

The ladies, except for Grace Bending, accepted Brandy Alexanders. The men had Brandy Stingers. These sweet drinks brought the evening to a ceremonial conclusion: all rites and customs observed.

'Now we can get down to serious drinking,' the host said. He brought out bottles of vodka, gin, bourbon, scotch. Mixers. A bucket of ice cubes. Glasses of double-walled plastic so drinks would not melt too quickly or drip.

Gertrude Empt and Professor Craner murmured a moment, then rose simultaneously.

'We're going to take a walk on the beach,' Gertrude announced, kicking off her shoes. 'Ta-ta, everyone.'

'Don't do anything I wouldn't do,' Turk Bending called after them. 'And there's nothing I wouldn't do.'

'Oh Ronnie,' his wife said, 'you're impossible.'

He grinned in the darkness, remembering that not too long ago Jane Holloway had told him the same thing.

'Just improbable,' he said.

They sat silently in the soft marrow of the night. Only

233

Grace Bending fidgeted, not trusting this dreamy drunkenness. But she would not leave.

'I do believe,' Jane Holloway said lazily, 'that if I could find my purse, I'd also find a funny cigarette.'

'I'll get your purse,' Bending said.

'Ronnie, you stay here,' his wife said sharply.

'I'll fetch it,' Luther Empt said. 'Great idea, Jane. Support home industry. Florida's largest cash crop.'

The joint was found, brought, lighted. Grace wouldn't touch it, but the others puffed and passed it along.

'Mellow,' Bending said. 'Definitely mellow. Where do you get the stuff, Jane?'

'From my gynecologist,' she said. 'He claims it's the only way he can survive.'

'That business is looking up,' Bill Holloway said.

'Oh-ho,' she said. 'My husband made a joke. Sort of.'

Luther Empt filled their glasses again. 'What the hell,' he said, 'tomorrow's Saturday; we can all sleep late.'

'If we finish these,' Turk Bending said, 'we may never wake up. What a way to go!'

They drank and smoked somnolently, lulled by the beauty of the night. It was a palpable presence. They could feel the velvet.

'Well,' Grace Bending said tightly, 'I think it's about time we go home and see how the kids are doing. Ronnie . . . ?'

'Not me,' he said roughly. 'Run along if you want to. I'm staying.'

Grace sank back into her chair. The others said nothing.

'Party-pooper,' Bending said. 'Won't drink. Won't smoke. Do you the world of good, dearie.'

'You drink and smoke enough for both of us,' his wife snapped at him.

'Hey-hey!' Luther Empt said happily. 'A family fight! What every party should have.'

'Luther, shut up,' his wife said.

'Don't tell me to shut up,' he snarled at her. 'It's my fucking home.'

Insults spread like yawns, one to another.

'I wish I had a fucking home,' Jane Holloway said, 'but it isn't. Maybe Bill will get it up for Christmas.'

'Since when have I been your only source?' he asked her.

'Maybe Bill gives at the office,' Bending said.

'And maybe shrimp can fly,' Luther said. 'Bill, you better try some dark meat and change your luck.'

'I changed my luck,' he said, 'when I married Jane.'

'I made a man out of you,' she told him, 'and you've never forgiven me for it.'

'Jane,' Luther said, 'you better try Teresa's beauty parlor. Her fag hairdresser gives a great bikini wax.'

'I have something better than that,' his wife said smugly.

'A king-size vibrator?' Bending asked. 'I'm thinking of buying an inflated, life-size party doll.'

'Just your style,' his wife said coldly. 'A plastic creamer in a bikini.'

'I dream about them,' he said, 'but Luther gets them.'

'If they're big enough,' Empt said, 'they're old enough. For God's sake, drink up, everyone; the night is young.'

Jane Holloway finished the tiny, glowing roach. She drained her straight vodka. She stood up, pulled a strap off one shoulder. She posed provocatively, hip-sprung.

'I'm going skinny-dipping,' she announced. 'Who's game?'

'Count me in,' Bending said immediately.

'Ronnie!' his wife said.

'Bill?'

'No.'

'Luther?'

'Sure. Why not? How about it, Teresa?'

'All right,' she said slowly.

'This is disgusting,' Grace Bending said.

235

She and William Jasper Holloway sat stolidly in their canvas sling chairs and watched the others undress, giggling.

'All the way down,' Jane Holloway commanded. 'No bras, panties, or jockstraps allowed.'

The four undressed with frantic fingers, scattering garments on chairs, table, the railing of the terrace.

'Jesus, it's cold,' Luther Empt said.

'The water will be warm,' Jane Holloway promised. 'My God, Teresa, if I had your boobs, I'd own the world.'

Then they were naked, laughing, pushing, grabbing at each other. They scrambled down the steps to the beach. Grace Bending and Holloway saw pale wraiths race away into the darkness, darting toward the sea.

Holloway leaned forward to pour more vodka over ice.

'I'm timid,' he offered.

'What?' Grace Bending said.

'I've always been timid,' he said. 'All my life. People know that, or sense it, and push me around.'

'Really?' she said, not interested.

'Surely *you* must feel the same way?'

Now she was interested.

'What way?' she asked.

'People manipulating you. Don't they?'

'I'd like to move someplace else,' she said fervently. 'A better class of people . . .'

He strangled on his drink. 'No such thing,' he said with a bleak smile. 'This is what we've got.'

'I don't believe that.' She bowed forward, peered toward the ocean. They could hear muted cries, hoots. 'What are they doing?' she asked nervously.

'Go on down,' he said cruelly, 'and watch.'

'They're drunk,' she said. 'They don't know what they're doing.'

'Sure,' he said, smiling secretly.

'It's all so ugly,' she said in a tone of wonder.

236

Then they sat in silence, listening to the soft yelping coming up from the beach.

'I hope they get arrested,' she said vindictively.

'Let's take our clothes off,' he said, laughing softly. 'You and me. When they come back, we'll be sitting here bareass naked, quietly having a drink and discussing the International Monetary Fund. What do you say?'

'You're crazy!' she shouted, not realizing he never would. 'What are you getting at?'

'I'm not getting at anything.'

'What have you heard about me?' she demanded.

He was bewildered. 'Grace, I haven't heard anything about you.'

'It's not true,' she burst out. 'Not, not, not!'

'Go home,' he advised her. 'Check on your kids.'

'I hate you,' she said. 'All of you.'

'Yes, well . . .' he said, 'that's understandable. I'm not exactly enamored of us either.'

She stood up.

'Fuck you,' she said, and he was more saddened than shocked.

He watched her stalk away, down the steps, along the sand to her own home. He thought her an inconsequential woman and was glad she was gone. The sick, he reflected, are not interested in the illnesses of others.

Alone, he wriggled down to the end of his spine, propped bare feet on the glass-topped table. He cuddled his drink on his chest, stared open-mouthed at the streaming night sky.

It seemed to him he had behaved well. All evening he had made a determined effort to appear jolly. He had contributed to the conversation, remembered to thank the hostess. He had drunk steadily, true, but not too much. No one could possibly guess . . .

'Why,' he asked aloud, 'did you instinctively and immediately refuse to strip naked and show yourself to the others?'

'Partly physical modesty,' he answered aloud. 'And it

237

may have been a symbolic act. A disinclination, or an inability, to reveal yourself totally. Who you are.'

Longing clawed at him, but for what, he could not say. There was a looseness in his life; he craved a texture. He felt not so much guilt as a sense of cruel waste.

'It is a need,' he said aloud. 'Something to be provided . . .'

'There is no spine,' he added. 'This place . . . Even the palm trees have shallow roots.'

The careless debauchery of the others did not wither him. Only his own growing anomie. There was, tickling, an answer just beyond his grasp. It was something at once painful and just.

A chorus of rude laughter came up from the beach. He thought he could see kicked spume and the squirm of white shadows. There was a vision of dripping marble, wrenched torsos caught and held in a posture of frenzied lust, throats straining.

'Impotence,' he said aloud. 'Physical lassitude. Anxiety without cause. Spiritual sterility. A profound boredom.'

'The symptoms,' he answered. 'But the cause? And more important – the cure?'

It did not exist, he decided, in his relations with wife, children, or anyone else. The malignancy was within, and growing. He knew its sharp teeth and feral grin. It was, he knew, devouring him.

'It is in your mind – is that not so?'

'Yes.'

'Well, you have a good mind; you know that. Use it.'

He brought his feet down. He fished melting ice chips from the bucket, filled his plastic glass. Poured in more vodka. He stood at the railing, looked out over the darkness of the glittery sea.

Slyly, unbidden, the thought crept in that his deepest want might be to live as a virtuous man.

This fancy, a mutter of foreign words, was so strange to him that he could taste but not determine its flavor. It tantalized and touched. He could walk around it, inspect, but he could not recognize it.

'To live a virtuous man?' he asked aloud, puzzled. 'In this day and age? For what reason?'

'For no reason,' he answered. 'An act of faith. An affirmation.'

The stars spun their ascending courses. He heard the dry rustle of fronds. The surge of the sea was in him; he felt its push and ebb. And below, the cinder whirled to a merry calliope tune.

Never had he felt so deeply the mocking strangeness of life, its inexplicableness. The whole world was terra incognita, and its inhabitants condemned to stumbling. Craziness was everywhere, and only the maddest survived.

'What are you going to do?' he asked aloud. 'Live a virtuous life?'

'Explore the possibility,' he replied.

Then naked savages came running at him from the darkness, hugging themselves and mewling. He showed his teeth as they scampered up onto the terrace and danced about him, as if he was the sacrifice.

8

Everyone who knew Jane Holloway thought her a vain woman, but she was not. She had no excessive love of her own person, nor did she derive a sensual pleasure from pampering and adorning her body.

She was proud of her body, true, but in the way the owner of a grand house, a thoroughbred, or a well-made machine might value and respect his possession. It deserved care.

So much for her appearance. When it came to achievements, Jane Holloway felt she had even less reason for vanity. Other women might think her life full, pleasurable, and rewarding. She found that gap between reality and her wants a humbling irritant.

She liked to think she was ambitious rather than greedy. She knew she was possessed of a pawky mind, limitless energy, and a fierce desire for money and power, which seemed to her the levers that moved the world.

She had concluded, without being familiar with the term, that life was a zero-sum game, and she had no intention of being a minus. With such a belief, it was inevitable that all her relationships, even with father, husband, children, should be adversary.

On Monday morning, she slept late, then drowsed awhile, listening to the sounds of Maria getting Gloria and Eddie off to school. She heard her husband depart for his bank in the big Mercedes. She drifted back to sleep again, and finally awoke close to 10:30 A.M.

Before showering, she phoned former Senator Randolph

Diedrickson. The old man said he was suffering from a particularly painful bout of rheumatoid arthritis, and intended to spend the day in bed. But he urged her to come visit him and brighten his life.

'You do me more good than a shot of cortisone, my dear,' he assured her in his fruity rumble.

She showered and groomed herself, applying her brilliant makeup swiftly and expertly. Because the senator would be in bed, and she sitting alongside, she decided to wear a cheongsam of butter-colored silk. It had a mandarin collar, frogs of black braid, and was slit up to the hip on one side.

She wore no undergarments.

Thirty minutes later she was driving south on A1A in her small white Alfa Romeo convertible, the top down. She stopped for a light at Atlantic Boulevard, and a truck driver in the next lane, looking down into her car and seeing her bare thighs, made loud kissing sounds. She gave him the finger before zooming ahead.

She turned west onto Commercial Boulevard and stopped at a liquor store to buy the senator a bottle of Southern Comfort, which he dearly loved. She was at his home a little after noon, and was admitted by Renfrew, the black houseman.

The senator, wearing wrinkled cotton pajamas, sat propped up in an old, dark oak, four-poster bed. A sheet and light wool blanket covered his lap. Scattered on the bed were manuscript pages of his memoirs which he had been reading with the aid of a small magnifying glass.

He accepted the gift of Southern Comfort with pleasure, and asked Renfrew to pour them each a small wineglass of the stuff. Then the houseman departed, closing the heavy bedroom door softly behind him.

It was a cluttered, overbearing chamber with wildly flowered wallpaper, a large collection of framed, autographed photographs, and a wood-bladed ceiling fan that stirred the air without cooling it. The sofa and chairs were carved walnut, upholstered in worn velvet. A dry sink with a white marble top served as a bar.

Jane Holloway pulled up a chair to the right side of the bed, since that was the side where the slit of her cheongsam would open up if she crossed her legs. She lifted her glass.

'To your health, senator.'

'And to yours, dear.'

They talked idly awhile of national and local politics. Diedrickson might be out of office, but he was hardly inactive. Then Jane Holloway crossed her legs. The cheongsam fell open. Diedrickson's eyes drifted downward.

'Senator, about this business with Rocco Santangelo and Jimmy Stone . . .'

'Ah yes . . . And how is that project proceeding?'

'Fine, from what I hear. The factory is on schedule, and those men have done everything they said they would.'

He nodded his massive head. 'I would have expected nothing less. As I told you, my dear, both men are whom they purport to be. They are employed by a very wealthy and capable individual known as Uncle Dom. I have had, ah, certain small dealings with him in the past and can vouch for his probity. He is not a man to be taken lightly.'

'But something has come up that I'd like to talk to you about.'

'Of course.'

She shifted position on the overstuffed armchair. The panel of the cheongsam fell away. The length of her smooth tanned thigh was revealed. The senator never took his eyes from that gleam.

Jane told him of Ronald Bending's suggestion that he and Jane's husband conspire to remove Luther Empt from active participation in the pornographic video cassette processing venture.

'After the factory is completed and in production, of course,' she said.

The senator sighed heavily. 'Never underestimate the

duplicity of your friends, my dear,' he advised. 'And what was your reply to this proposal?'

She answered that she hadn't said yes and she hadn't said no, since an immediate decision was not required. She also told the senator she had demanded a ten percent share for her role in convincing her husband to go along.

'You never disappoint me, dear,' the senator said with a benign smile.

Jane added that Bending had objected to her ten percent, at first, and pointed out that it would give the Holloways a controlling interest. But she had calmed his fears by intimating that she might possibly join forces with him rather than with her husband.

'Very clever,' the senator said, pulling thoughtfully at his rubbery lower lip. 'This Ronald Bending, is he a Jew?'

'No.'

'You are, or have been, uh, intimate with him?'

'Yes.'

'He has money?'

'Not as much as my husband.'

The senator wagged his big head sorrowfully. 'My dear, on several occasions in the past, my avuncular advice has been solicited by young ladies in situations somewhat similar to yours. I have told them all the same thing: "Never fuck a man who has less money than you." However, in this case the damage has been done, and we must devise a plan so that you may profit rather than suffer from your, ah, generosity. Would you mind pouring me just a little more of that soothing elixir? You might also lock the door, that's a good girl.'

She did as she was bidden. She handed him the wineglass of Southern Comfort, then sat sidesaddle on the edge of his bed. The cheongsam gaped. Her bent leg was uncovered. She looked at the senator gravely.

Her face was as hard and smooth as her unlined body. A keen, spade-shaped face, the thinness of the lips painted over with thick vermillion. The eyebrows had been plucked and black-penciled at a slant that gave her a vaguely Oriental look.

Green eyeshadow made her dark eyes more luminous. A blush of rouge accented her cheekbones. People said 'Striking' more often than 'Beautiful.' It was an artful mask of a face, not designed for smiling.

'I think,' Diedrickson said, 'before we even consider what your options might be, it would be wise to discuss fundamental motives and aims. I have always found it lightens the task of decision making wonderfully. Dear, what is it, precisely, you want from life? Money? Financial independence?'

She cocked her head to one side, frowning briefly.

'That, of course,' she said. 'But not only that. What I want is *control*.'

One of his shaggy eyebrows lifted. 'I was not aware,' he said with heavy irony, 'that you had any problems in that area.'

'At home, you mean?' she said. 'It's true that I can more or less get my husband to do what I want. But I am still dependent upon him. Financially, and for – for status. Just as I was dependent upon my father and on my first husband. Things haven't changed all that much. It infuriates me that I cannot control my own life completely. This has nothing to do with feminism, senator. This is *me*. I know my abilities. I know what I am capable of doing. When I say "control," I don't mean only of my own life, my own destiny. I mean control over events.'

'And over other people?' he said shrewdly.

'Well . . . yes, that too. I suppose what I'm talking about is power. The power to make meaningful decisions.'

'Mmm,' he said, sipping at his glass. 'I know that feeling well. Everyone in Washington is infected by it. Being in the right place at the right time with the power to make meaningful decisions. There is no satisfaction in the world like it.'

'Yes,' she said excitedly, 'of course you know. Senator, I

can't endure the thought of living out my life as wife and mother. I don't want to be like most people who seem to have no power – or desire, even – to fashion their own lives. And they end up at their graves saying, "What happened?" That's really what I mean when I say I want control.'

He stared broodingly at her naked thigh, his thick lips going in and out like a feeding fish.

'Power!' he thundered suddenly in his orotund voice. 'Power over people and power over events. You have a taste for it.'

'I suppose so,' she said, sighing. 'But not power for the sake of power. That has no interest for me. But power to get things done.'

'To get what done?'

'I don't know,' she confessed. 'Except that it must be something big, something important. If I don't find it, don't *do* it, then my life will be wasted. I know that.'

'Something big,' he repeated ruminatively. 'Something important. Well, we shall see what we can do about that. Hmm . . . I tell you frankly, my dear, what you say about Bending's suggestion I find somewhat disturbing. Such an action could quite possibly lead to an ugly dispute that might find its way to the courts of law. If that should happen, I assure you that Mister Santangelo and Mister Stone would not be happy. And I hesitate to imagine the wrath of Uncle Dom. He is a man who shuns public exposure like the plague. But perhaps from this nest of nettles we might, with care and attention, extract one perfect bloom. That is to say, dear, we might hoist Mister Bending by his own petard, and by so doing provide you with an opportunity to control.'

She looked at him closely. 'Do you really think that could be done, senator?'

'It might,' he said slowly. 'It just might.'

She held her wineglass in her left hand. Her right hand snaked lazily beneath sheet and blanket, fumbled softly, found its way.

245

'There is time,' she said. 'The factory is still being built. So nothing has to be done immediately. But you'll think about it?'

'I will that,' he said, his old eyes glaring fiercely at her shining thigh.

Her cool fingers worked as she stared at that splendid wreck of a man. The mottled cheeks, the pendulous jowls, the speckled hands lying flaccid on the coverlet.

She had always thought of him with awe. He was a wealthy, cunning, and influential giant who had lived a long time and learned a great deal. He seemed to her outsize, a man who made midgets of other men, who by his very existence revealed their incompetence, superficiality, and puny powers.

Now, for the first time, it occurred to her that she had established a measure of control over this ancient hulk. She had brought him to a state of dependence. Not total, of course. But that, with planning and artifice, might be accomplished.

To test her strength, she spoke to him in a cruel parody of his own speech.

'Senator,' she said briskly, 'shall I endeavor to alleviate your pain?'

'Yes,' he said. 'Please.'

PART IV

1

December began furiously, with three days of northeast squalls that rattled roof tiles and emptied the beaches. A Small Craft Advisory was in effect from Jupiter south to the Keys, and only the most obsessed surfers dared the crumpling eight-foot surf.

Then, overnight, the wind shifted to the southwest, the sky cleared, and white clouds flapped in a lapis lazuli sky as if they had been washed and hung up to dry. Swimmers and shellers came back to the strand. The sun was a beamy blur, and people stretched.

Just as abruptly, the weather soured again. Florida's low clouds pressed down, and a thick, warm wind gusted out of the Caribbean. 'You don't like the weather?' people said. 'Wait five minutes, and it'll change.'

And so it did.

Edward Holloway didn't give a damn about the weather. The old farts were always saying will it rain or won't it, will the sun come out, why doesn't it warm up? But Eddie couldn't care less. There could be a blizzard, and he would laugh. He loved every minute of it. He awoke with anticipation and slept with regret: it was all so satisfying.

He was scamming his way through school, cheating on the tests like everyone else, and his parents were so concerned with their own affairs that they had stopped breathing down his neck – which was a relief. Also, he had grown an inch taller, and the hair around his testicles was getting bushier. Everything was coming his way.

Most important, he was banging this Teresa Empt every

night the weather permitted them to meet at the gazebo. It was a great experience for young Eddie Holloway. So great that the only one he told about it was Wayne Bending, relating in lubricious detail what he did to her and what she did to him.

'Solid meat,' Eddie Holloway said, his voice choked with wonderment at his good fortune. 'You could lose a dime in that belly button. And the snatch? If it had teeth, she could chew me up and spit me over the leftfield fence.'

'Sounds fine,' Wayne Bending said shortly.

'And on top of that,' Eddie said enthusiastically, 'she's good for the dineros. We been smoking some grass, you know, which I clip from my old lady's supply. So I tell her I'm paying twenty for two sticks, and she comes across without blinking an eye.'

'Sounds fine,' Wayne said again.

'So tonight,' Eddie continued, 'if the weather holds, I'm meeting her in the gazebo, and I'm going to make a pitch for the boat. A thousand bucks. Listen, she can afford it. And I think she'll pay up. I mean, she's like hooked on my schlong; I swear it. So tonight we get down to the nitty-gritty, and you better believe she'll pay off.'

'Sounds fine,' Wayne Bending said for the third time.

It didn't rain that night, though the ground under the gazebo was still dampish. Edward Holloway spread a clean blanket, settled down, and waited patiently. He had planned how he would handle this meeting, and had the supreme self-confidence of the brainless young.

She came drifting across the lawn like an eager ghost, pleated white skirt billowing out behind her. Eddie had decided to play it cool. But when she lay down beside him, took his face in her hot palms, and flickered her tongue, he had to groan and grab her. She laughed and let him. She moved. The way she moved drove him bananas. She knew so much, laughing softly.

It was nippy that night, and they didn't take off their clothes. That made it, somehow, more exciting. She wasn't wearing any panties, and he just unzipped his fly. Like they were in the back seat of a car or standing up in a phone booth. Wicked, guilty, dangerous. It was grand.

He didn't know when it had started, or how she had done it, but she had him growling in the busby now, and loving every minute of it. She handled his head by the ears, like it was some kind of a jug, and she gave him orders.

After a good half-hour of this, she would begin to pitch, buck, moan, use language that really surprised him because he hadn't realized that women, especially old ladies, knew those words.

Then she began to shudder, so violently that sometimes it scared him, and he wondered if she might be having a heart attack or something. The shudders increased in intensity until suddenly they stopped. She held his head clamped between her strong thighs. He could hardly breathe, let alone hear.

When she released him, he rolled away, panting as if he had just run a four-minute mile. He tasted her on his tongue and lips. A little like Juicy Fruit. He stared through the latticed gazebo roof at scudding clouds and tried to remember the speech he had rehearsed. It took a while.

'I brought a joint,' he said hoarsely. 'Just one. We can share it. Okay?'

They smoked the cigarette slowly, passing it back and forth. He waited until he felt himself beginning to dissolve, and figured she was probably feeling the same way.

'I wish we could be together more,' he said in a low voice. 'I mean, not just sneaking off to this place to meet.'

'I know, Eddie. I wish we could, too.'

'Not just for sex,' he said earnestly. 'I don't mean that. Just to be with you. Alone. The two of us.'

'You're sweet, Eddie.'

'You don't get seasick, do you? I mean, you like boats, don't you?'

She turned to look at him. 'No, I don't get seasick, and I like boats. Why do you ask?'

251

'I've been thinking,' he said seriously. 'If I had a boat, it would be a good way for us to be together. Alone.'

'What kind of a boat, Eddie?' she asked, taking the roach from his fingers.

'Oh, nothing big. I was thinking about a sailboat. Small enough so you could pull it up on the beach and chain it to a palm tree. Carry four, maybe, but two would be best. Go out on a nice day. Sail around. Have you ever done that?'

'No, I never have. Not on a sailboat.'

'It's the greatest. Out there on the ocean. All alone. Going like a bat out of hell. Nothing like it.'

'Is it safe, Eddie?'

'Well . . .' he said judiciously, 'a catamaran would be best. That's a boat with two hulls. They hardly ever tip over. They got a canvas deck between the hulls. A fun boat.'

'Uh-huh,' she said casually. 'Sounds nice. What does a boat like that cost, dear?'

'Oh,' he said, 'it depends on how long it is. And if it's new, of course. Then it can run into bucks. But a friend of mine, he's got this fourteen-foot Hobie Cat. Really good condition. It needs a little work, some paint maybe, but the sails are okay. The only reason he wants to sell it is because he wants to buy a bigger boat.'

'How much does he want for his boat, Eddie?'

'Well, he's asking a thousand, but I figure he'll come down a hundred for cash. Ah, what's the use of even talking about it. I haven't got near that much.'

She was silent. She took a final puff of the roach and put the tiny stub aside to burn out.

'I'm just dreaming,' Eddie Holloway went on. 'Where am I going to get that kind of money? But I keep thinking of how nice it would be to have that boat, floating around there in the middle of the ocean. I could take you out for a ride, you know, and we'd be all alone. Miles away from anyone. All by ourselves.'

'Do you know how to sail a boat, Eddie?'

'Oh sure. I took classes and everything. I can sail a cat. But what's the use of talking about it . . .'

She turned onto one hip. She smiled at him and patted his cheek.

'Don't give up, Eddie,' she said. 'Maybe it could be arranged.'

'Yeah?' he said eagerly. 'How?'

'Oh, I don't know,' she said vaguely. 'Let me think about it.'

'Jeez,' he said, 'that would be great. You and me all alone, away from everyone.'

She began stroking him through the cloth of his jeans, watching his face.

'Oh my,' she said, 'what have we here? Is this a present for me, Eddie?'

'Yeah,' he said throatily. 'That's for you.'

This was the stage when she wanted him to lie still while she uncovered him, her long fingers working purposefully. The toke was gone, but he still felt the languor and closed his eyes.

He felt her doing things to him. Everything was warm and wet. He heard her moving. He opened his eyes, halfway, and saw her sitting astride him, leaning forward, palms on the blanket at the sides of his head.

She loomed over him, her long black hair falling about her face. She looked fierce and determined, and for a moment he was frightened.

'I'll do it,' she said sternly, beginning to twist. 'Let me do everything.'

And away she went, bobbing up and down like a jockey, occasionally throwing her head back to fling her hair away from her face. Her lips were pulled back from her teeth so it seemed to him that she was grinning as she rode him.

Meanwhile, she was crying out, sometimes so loudly that he feared they might hear her in the house. But he knew there was no stopping her, and after a few minutes he didn't even want to try.

The ululations of Teresa Empt were being overheard. But not in her home. The listener was Wayne Bending, and not only could he hear Teresa, but he could glimpse her frantic gyrations through the gloom. And he could smell the sweetish fumes of the pot they had smoked.

Since Eddie and Teresa had begun their meetings, Wayne had been the silent watcher, sitting far back in a thick stand of shrubs and trees with the syrupy scent of jasmine. He could not hear their words, but their smutty laughter and barks of bliss sounded clearly.

This eavesdropping was so painful to Wayne Bending that he could not have said why he was inexorably drawn to the trysts. Hunkering down on the damp, pungent earth, he sometimes felt like giggling nervously, and sometimes he felt like weeping.

He was wounded by the acknowledgment that the couplings he witnessed were his idea; he had pushed Eddie Holloway into this liaison. But now that it was accomplished, he wanted it finished, over, done.

For it seemed to him that somehow they were mocking him by their intimacy. His own friendship had been devalued. What he had done for Eddie Holloway obviously counted for nothing compared to those breasts, that eager mouth, the grasping thighs.

They were not punishing him deliberately; he knew that. They didn't say, 'Let's screw old Wayne Bending.' There was no intent. But the result was the same.

He had believed there was something special between him and Eddie Holloway, a very special kind of friendship. He had made love to Eddie, or let him make love to him, and there was a sweet surrender there that was proof of how he felt.

And now his special friend was doing all those wild, private things with that old woman, and bragging about it later to Wayne. With never a thought of how his words were tearing Wayne apart.

It was the first time Wayne Bending had tried, really,

truly, to be close to someone. To reveal himself, express his feelings, tell the truth and act honestly with no finkery. He had tried to be himself, to give himself. And this was the result.

Shivering in his hiding place, watching the lovers kiss and touch, grope and stroke, Wayne Bending felt his world falling apart. The pain was so intense that it went beyond weeping.

He wanted to be dead and gone. Out of a world that hurt.

2

The case of Lucy B, Dr Theodore Levin acknowledged, was occupying his time to an inordinate degree. He spent hours listening to the accumulated tapes, reading relevant literature, or just sitting on his apartment balcony, staring blankly at the night sky, and trying to solve the puzzle of this young girl's behavior.

None of his earlier facile explanations – castration complex, penis envy – now seemed sufficient to him. He returned again to the possibility of psychic trauma: a single incident or a series of incidents that had triggered the aberrant conduct.

'Lucy,' he said coaxingly, 'do you remember anything that happened to you when you were younger that made a big impression on you, that you've never been able to forget?'

'You mean,' she said, 'like going to Disney World?'

Once again, he had the feeling that she was playing with him.

'No,' he said, 'not exactly. Something in your private life. Something so important that you've never told anyone about it, that you've kept secret for years and years.'

She appeared to be considering his question seriously, head tilted, bluish-gray eyes regarding him gravely.

'Nooo, Doctor Ted,' she said. 'I can't remember anything like that.'

She was wearing a denim pinafore over a white T-shirt. Her wheat-colored hair had been woven into two long braids, tied with little blue ribbons. Her clear features seemed particularly luminous, glowing with innocence.

'Lucy,' he said, 'you told me your best friend was . . . ?'

'Gloria,' she said. 'Gloria Holloway. She lives right near us.'

'She's older than you?'

'Just a year.'

'What about boys, Lucy? Is there someone special you like?'

She thought a moment.

'There are some boys on the beach who are all right. Freddy Dickson. He's all right. Not too rough, you know. And Ben Hamilton. He's always teasing. Sometimes we play together. Like go swimming, you know. Or just fool around.'

'But no one special boy?'

'Not really. We're always like in a bunch. I've never had a real date, if that's what you mean. Gloria has, but I haven't.'

'Is there one teacher you especially like?'

'Miss Carpenter. She's my homeroom teacher. She has such beautiful eyes, and she never hollers at us. She's really swell. Everyone likes Miss Carpenter. Once she made some fudge and gave it to all us kids. It was very good. Much better than the boughten kind.'

He stared at her, blinking. 'Lucy, who do you love most in all the world?'

'My daddy,' she said promptly. 'And mother. And then my brothers.'

'Do you love your daddy more than your mother?'

'Why do you say that, Doctor Ted?'

'You mentioned him first.'

'I love them about the same,' she said.

'And you want them to be happy?'

'Well, my goodness, of course I do.'

'Then why don't you do what they ask you? Stop annoying men who come to your house by sitting in their laps and touching them.'

257

'Because it doesn't annoy them,' she said with some asperity.

'How do you know?'

'I can tell.'

'Whether it annoys them or not isn't important, Lucy. What is important is that your parents don't want you to do it, and it makes them unhappy when you do.'

'I don't care,' she said, her face suddenly tense.

'You're not going to stop?'

She didn't answer. They sat in silence for a full minute, looking at each other. Finally her eyes lowered, slowly. Long lashes lay upon her limpid cheeks.

'I want to,' she said in a voice so tremulous that he could scarcely hear.

'You want to,' he said gently, 'but you can't?'

'Yes,' she said, prolonging the word into a hiss.

'Why do you suppose that is, Lucy? Why can't you stop when you want to stop?'

'I don't know.'

'Guess.'

'Something makes me do it.'

Levin felt he was coming closer now, that he might be near to a revelation.

'What do you think it is that makes you do it?'

'I don't know.'

'Is it a voice that tells you to do it?'

'No.'

'Is it a feeling you have, something you just have to do?'

'Yes, like that.'

'Because it will make you feel good?'

'Sort of. But they like it, too. I know they do.'

'But that's not why you do it, is it, Lucy? The real reason is to make *you* feel good.'

'I guess,' she said, sighing. 'But it's very mixed up.'

She was right, Dr Levin reflected. And not only *her* motives, drives, dreams, but all behavior. Not for the first

258

time, he despaired of finding adequate explanations of the human enigma.

Part of the problem was vocabulary. Language was simply not subtle and refined enough to identify the delicate nuances of the psyche. What words had been coined had become crass labels that clarified nothing.

The other difficulty went to the foundation of psychotherapy. Could one, by reason, make sense of unreason? Could a rational system of observation, analysis, and theorization understand and explain the irrational? Or could only the mad interpret the mad?

If he believed that, Levin thought, he really should be in another line of work.

He sat back in his swivel chair, hands clasped comfortably across his paunch. He stared at Lucy through his thick glasses, trying to make his expression as sympathetic as he could.

'Lucy,' he said, 'when you get this feeling that you have to sit on a man's lap, or kiss him, or touch him between his legs – well, I wish you would tell me what that feeling is like. I really want to know. Now, suppose you didn't know me. Suppose I was a stranger to you, but your daddy brought me home for a visit. Suppose I'm sitting in your living room, and then you come in and see me sitting there, and your daddy introduces us. What would –'

'Is this like a story?' she interrupted.

'Like a story,' he said, nodding. 'Now suppose you tell me what you'd feel and what you'd do.'

She took a deep breath. 'Well, if I liked you, and I would because you are very nice, and your beard is so funny and bristly, well then, I would love you and want you to love me. And it would feel, I don't know, it would feel good. Warm, you know. So I might hold your hand at first. Yes, I might do that. And if you didn't pull your hand away, I would sort of squeeze it and look to see if you liked that. Then, say, my daddy has to go out of the room because the phone rang and he has to answer the phone. Then we would

259

be alone, and that's better because my daddy would think I'm annoying you, but I know I'm not because you call me "Dear" and "Darling." And you touch my hair. Things like that.'

Levin watched closely, fascinated, as the child became excited by her own fantasy. She inched forward on the chair, leaned toward him. Hands gripped tightly. Face flushed. Eyes glittering. Words spilling out . . .

'That's what you'd say. "Dear" and "Darling." Like that. And I'd say, "I don't care. I just don't care." And you'd say, "Are you sure we're alone?" And then I'd feel you, like maybe I'd be on your lap or maybe standing between your knees. And I'd be feeling you, and your face would get all red and giggly. Then you would touch my legs and under my dress and all, and I'd make these funny noises, and start to unbutton my dress, and I'd say, "Hurry. Hurry." And you'd start to take your pants off, and then . . . and then . . .'

Levin watched her panting, lips wet with saliva, forehead glistening with sweat. Her body was rigid. Her gaze seemed to have turned inward. She sat immobile, frozen.

'And then?' he prompted her.

Suddenly she slumped. Hands unwound. She took a deep breath, moved farther back in the chair. She swung her legs casually. She pulled gently at one of her braids.

'And then?' Levin repeated.

'Oh,' she said with a queer smile, 'then I suppose daddy would come back, and we'd pretend like we had just been talking about things.'

'I see,' he said, but he didn't. Not completely. 'And is that how you always feel, Lucy, and what you think when you touch men and sit in their laps?'

'I might,' she said archly, 'and I might not. You said it was just a story. Gloria and I do that all the time – make up stories. Did you like that story, Doctor Ted?'

'It was quite a story,' he said.

'Miss Carpenter says I have a very good imagination.

260

Sometimes we have to write stories for school, and Miss Carpenter says she likes my stories best of all.'

'I believe it. Lucy, in your story you have both of us saying things. I called you "Dear" and "Darling," and I said, "Are you sure we're alone?" And you said, "I don't care. I just don't care." And then later, you said, "Hurry. Hurry." Did you make that up, Lucy?'

'I think so,' she said, frowning. 'But I may have heard that on television. You know how things stay in your mind, and then you forget where you heard them.'

'Yes,' Levin said, 'that's true. Lucy, in your story, your daddy comes back into the living room, and we pretend nothing happened. Do you think he believed nothing happened?'

She looked at him wide-eyed. 'My goodness, Doctor Ted, how would I know that?'

'But did he behave like he believed nothing happened?'

She pondered a moment. 'Yes, that's how he behaved. Like he believed us.'

She opened the little red plastic purse she was carrying, removed a small, round mirror and examined her face, turning this way and that. Her movements were so similar to those of her mother that Levin couldn't help smiling.

Lucy poked at her hair, rearranged her braids so they fell to the front. Then she replaced the mirror, snapped the purse shut. She crossed her legs, looked at him brightly.

'Would you like to hear another story, Doctor Ted?'

'Oh yes. Very much.'

'Well . . .' she said in a confidential tone, 'there was this man who was very young and handsome. Like a movie star, you know. And he's a doctor. Not a shrink, like you are, but more like a preacher. And he's always helping people. Like if someone hasn't got enough food to eat, well, he gives them food. And he goes to visit sick people and brings them flowers and candy and books to read. You understand?'

'He's a good man.'

'Yes, he is. He helps everyone. Well, he gives everything he has away, so he's very poor. But he doesn't care because all he thinks about is helping people. And he lives underground, like down in a cave, because he's poor, helping all those people and everything, and he can't afford to buy a house. Well, one day he's walking along the street, and he sees this tragic automobile accident. This car hits this beautiful young girl and knocks her down. She is all bloody and everything. And this doctor, he carries her to his cave to take care of her.'

'He doesn't take her to a hospital?'

'No, because where he lives is closer, and if he waited for an ambulance and all, she might just die. So he carries her to his cave because he doesn't have any car, being poor and all. And he closes this big iron door, and they're in there all alone. And he washes her off and brings her fresh clothes, really nice things, and he gives her pills. And she's very sick, but he's very nice with her and loving, so she gets well.'

'Does this man have a wife?' Levin asked.

'No, he's too poor to have a wife. So he's very lonely. My goodness, you can't go around helping people *all* the time. Well, after this beautiful girl is all well again, she sweeps the cave and makes him some delicious meals. And he tells her she is okay now and can leave the cave and go home. But he really doesn't want her to, you know, because he has fallen in love with her, she is so beautiful and all. But she says she has fallen in love with him also, and she doesn't want to leave the cave; she wants to stay with him forever and ever. And he says, "I am sorry, my dear, but I am a poor man and I can't afford to have a wife." And then, guess what?'

'What?' Levin said.

Lucy laughed happily. 'It turns out this beautiful girl is a princess from a foreign country, and her daddy has so much money he doesn't know what to do with it. So they get married and love each other all the time and fix up the cave nice, and she helps him do good things for people.'

She finished and looked at him expectantly.

'That's a lovely story, Lucy,' he said.

'Oh well . . .' she said modestly, '. . . you know. I just made it up. I'm always making up stories. Would you like to hear another one, Doctor Ted?'

'I would,' he said, glancing at his desk clock, 'but our time is just about up. Will you tell me more stories the next time I see you?'

'Oh sure,' she said. 'I like to tell stories.'

When she was gone, he sat slumped at his desk and slowly pulled the cellophane from a cigar. He was satisfied with the session just concluded. He felt progress was being made.

In the second story, Levin supposed, he, Dr Theodore Levin, was the doctor-preacher who helped people. And Lucy B was the beautiful young girl he restored to health and made love to in a cave behind an iron door. The fantasy was a thinly veiled appeal, almost a seduction.

But she also told him the second story, obviously, to divert his attention from the first. And she had tried to convince him of her strong imagination, her skill at story-telling, her penchant for creating characters and situations out of whole cloth.

But he didn't feel her first 'story' fell into that category at all. The detailed incidents were too realistic, the dialogue too adult and believable to be totally the product of her fancy. They came, he guessed, from her memory.

Then, having revealed something she considered secret, unmentionable, and perhaps sinful, a defense mechanism had taken over, and she had hurried to imply that her 'story' was nothing more than a superficial romance.

It was a serious error, Dr Levin knew, to assume the emotionally or mentally disordered were dull- or dim-witted. Usually, quite the reverse.

There seemed to be something in behavioral disturbance that bred devious cleverness. Even in one as young as Lucy

B. There was a cunning there, sharpened by psychologic dysfunction. To hide the guilt, she had built a wall of tricks the therapist had to bring tumbling down.

3

His wife insisted on coming along – another defeat for William Jasper Holloway. He was certain neither Grace Bending nor Teresa Empt knew of their husbands' activities. And even if they knew, he reckoned they would have no interest.

But Jane was familiar with all the plans of EBH Enterprises, Inc. She asked questions, discussed financial details, and even drove out to west Broward County where the new factory was nearing completion on a lonely plot of scrubland.

So when Luther Empt called an evening meeting of the partners and the mob representatives, Jane Holloway announced she would attend. As usual, she wore her husband down with her persistence.

The purpose of the meeting was to view a video cassette of *Teenage Honeypots*, the twenty-minute porn film supplied by Rocco Santangelo and Jimmy Stone. It had been processed in Empt's personally owned facility to develop techniques that would be used when full production began in the new factory.

The viewing was held in Luther Empt's private office, a large room that had been provided with extra armchairs arranged in a semicircle in front of a twenty-four-inch RCA television set equipped with a Sony Betamax cassette player.

Empt had also provided a well-equipped bar and a box of Upmanns. Jane Holloway was introduced to Santangelo and Stone, and all the visitors were introduced to Ernie Goldman, Empt's executive assistant and top electronics engineer.

Goldman was a stick of a man with bent shoulders, a saffron complexion, and an inability to stop blinking. After everyone had settled down around the TV set, he gave a short speech in a reedy, breathless voice:

'The film you are about to see,' he started, then stopped. 'I mean the original film, *Teenage Honeypots*, the one we were given, was not of such great quality. Most of it was shot outdoors and was overexposed. Some of the interior scenes had a greenish tinge. Also, the sound was very bad. A lot of interference. Like you could hear traffic sounds, a police siren, and so forth.

'So when we converted to tape, we used filters to correct the color as much as we could, and enhancers in some places to bring up the reds. Watch the skin tones. That's the best way to judge color reproduction. If the skin tones are realistic, then the rest will probably be okay. We also worked on the sound track to filter out background sound. Anyway, this is the cassette of *Teenage Honeypots*.'

Luther Empt turned out the overhead light, but left on a desk lamp and floor lamp. They all turned their attention to the TV screen. Ernie Goldman switched on the set.

They watched the twenty-minute cassette in silence. Once Goldman started to say, 'Notice the –' but Luther Empt said, 'Shut up, Ernie.'

And once Jane Holloway said, 'How did they get the dog to do *that*?' And Ronald Bending said, 'Maybe they stuffed the girl with Alpo.' No one laughed.

When the cassette ended, Luther switched on the overhead light. They all headed for the bar and refilled their glasses. Then Ronald Bending drew Ernie Goldman over to the TV set, and they ran the cassette again, talking about light streaks, color enhancing, and sound filters.

The others remained standing around the bar, their backs to the television screen.

266

'Well, folks,' Luther Empt demanded in his raspy voice, 'waddya think?'

Rocco Santangelo glanced briefly at Jimmy Stone. 'Mr Empt,' he said, 'I and my associate want to say you've got a work of art here. I mean, we saw the original film, you know, and like your guy said, the color and sound weren't so great. But you made a masterpiece out of it. Right, Jimmy?'

'Right,' Stone said.

'If you can guarantee,' Santangelo went on, 'that when you get in full-scale production, this is the quality of goods we'll be getting, then I can tell you, honestly and sincerely, that we'll be very, very happy, and you'll have more work than you can handle. Am I right, Jimmy?'

Stone nodded.

Santangelo turned suddenly to Jane Holloway. 'What did you think of it, ma'am?'

'I thought the quality was good,' she said. 'But the film itself isn't much. There's no real story, no plot.'

'Well, yeah, sure,' Santangelo said. 'But you got to remember, your average porn freak ain't – isn't interested in any story, like at a regular movie. All he wants is skin – you know?'

'I disagree,' Jane Holloway said crisply. 'Surely you gentlemen aren't the only ones in this business. I would say that you'd be wise to try to make your product different and superior to that of –'

'Nah,' Santangelo said. 'This is strictly a freak market and –'

'Rocco,' Jimmy Stone interrupted in his low, toneless voice, 'let the lady talk.'

'Oh, yeah, sure, Jimmy,' Santangelo said quickly.

'Thank you,' Jane said coldly. 'It seems to me that if you only produce the usual amounts of skin, then your product is no different from that of your competitors. What you should strive for is a quality product that offers something better, something unique. The Cadillac of porn films.

Establish a trademark or catchy name that your customers will remember. Like the MGM lion. And make certain your films have a story or plot that the viewers can get interested in and identify with, in addition to all that sex.'

'Yeah?' Santangelo said. 'And how do we do that?'

'I'm no expert on this,' Jane said, 'but it doesn't seem too difficult to me. Just make certain your scriptwriter, if you have one, which I doubt, or your director, produces a definite story. Look, take the movie *The Sound of Music*. A wonderful film that tells a marvelous story. Now what if that was shot for the porn market, with plenty of nudity and all the things we saw in *Teenage Honeypots*? It would appeal to the freaks in two ways: the kinky stuff they want and a fantastic story that they'll want to watch over and over. Also, a good plot will attract new customers who might not be interested in just porn.'

Rocco Santangelo looked at Jimmy Stone.

'Innaresting,' Stone said.

They talked a few minutes longer, mostly about the future of pornographic video cassettes and disks. Then the meeting broke up.

The mob representatives left first. Then the Holloways and Ronald Bending. Empt and Ernie Goldman cleaned up the office and put the *Teenage Honeypots* cassette in the safe. Goldman said goodnight and drifted away. Empt locked up and went out to the parking lot.

He sat in his white Seville, smoking a fresh Upmann. He was satisfied with the way the meeting had gone. The only thing he regretted was that it had been necessary to bring Bending and Holloway in on such a sweet deal. If he had been able to swing it by himself . . .

But there was more than one way to skin a cat. After they got in production, and the money started rolling in, he'd think about how to cut out his partners. It shouldn't be difficult with such innocents. He knew the business; they didn't. They needed him more than he needed them; that was for sure.

He drove slowly south on A1A to Atlantic Boulevard, the window down. He enjoyed the crispy night air, the taste and smell of his cigar. Most of all, he enjoyed the thought of the woman – the girl – the child – who awaited him. Everything he was doing – the work, the conniving – made sense when he thought of her.

He could not have said exactly why that was. The images he had seen on the TV screen an hour ago – those girls were younger, more attractive, better formed than May. But they didn't turn him on. They were objects, disembodied. That porn film could just as well have been made with animated cartoon characters.

But May was reality. She had warmth, and love for him. He couldn't even come close to understanding his feelings for her. There was the sex, of course; he knew that. But she was a gimp, for God's sake.

So it had to be something else – right? He was still puzzling over it when he drew up before her house and gave the horn a light tap.

She had been waiting for him. He grinned as she came scuttling down the walk, moving like a wounded crab. She lurched onto the seat alongside him, grabbed his face, kissed him on the lips. 'Hi daddy!' she said breathlessly.

He had found a dilapidated rib joint in the black section where he was confident he wouldn't run into anyone he knew. The owners weren't too happy to have him for a customer, but they tolerated him because of May; she charmed them.

They served baby pork ribs with your choice of three sauces: Hot, Hotter, or Hottest. They also made the best home fries he had ever tasted, with plenty of onions. Collards if you wanted them, which he didn't. And icy Rolling Rock beer served in cans; they didn't mess around with glasses.

May and Luther liked the Hotter sauce, and each had two cans of beer with the meal. Neither liked to talk while they were eating. They spread paper napkins across their chests and gnawed ferociously at the succulent ribs. They left a stack of white, shiny bones.

'Want some dessert?' Luther asked her. 'They got pudding or lopes.'

She shook her head, then dabbed delicately at her lips with the paper napkin. 'I'm full up. That was just fine.'

'Want to take a ride?'

'Whatever you want, daddy.'

He asked her what she wanted.

'Let's go home.'

'Okay,' he said.

He left a nice tip for the waitress, and on the way out, he gave the owner an Upmann cigar.

'I thank you,' the black said. 'Come again.' Then, sardonically, 'Tell your friends.'

'Yeah,' Luther said, laughing.

By this time he had become used to the hothouse she lived in, with all those nutty plants. He was glad to see she had spent some of the money he was giving her to fix up the place: a new rug, a bright throw on the sofa, some decent highball glasses. And she had remembered to buy Cutty Sark.

He watched her limping around the little home, busying herself in the tiny kitchenette. She fixed him a Cutty just the way he liked it: two ounces of whiskey over a single ice cube with just a splash of water. When she brought him the drink, he looked up to stare at her face.

He was seeing her frequently, two or three times a week. But when he was away from her, he forgot what she looked like. He could not recall her features, could not see her in his mind's eye.

Perhaps because she was so shadowy. The black, shiny hair, longer and heavier than his wife's, engulfed her thin face. Her features were so small, half-formed like a child's. Only the dark, snapping eyes gave her vibrancy. The rest was dim paleness.

Not only was she physically crippled, but he thought her

270

emotionally flawed as well. There was a simple unworldliness there he considered a disability. For all her days she had circled slowly in the backwaters of life, without direction and without resolve.

She was a willing, an eager victim. She surrendered sweetly, offering thin neck and pallid back without opposition or remonstrance. All of her – body, heart, soul – yielded gladly, happily, as if she were fulfilling her destiny by dumb obedience.

Never before, with wives or whores, had he known such docility. Her total submission was at once exciting and frightening. Exciting to know himself the complete master. Frightening because of an itching curiosity to explore the limits of her compliance.

She went into the bathroom to change, leaving the door open. Following his orders, she had purchased a shortie nightgown of thin white cambric, with a girlish rosebud trim at the neckline.

While in the bathroom, she slowly braided her hair into a single plait, secured at the end with a rubber band. The pigtail was as thick and hard as a hawser, dangling down her back almost to her waist.

Luther mixed himself another drink. He was not impatient. When he was with May, he felt a thawing of all his furies and anxieties.

When she came back to him, she squirmed onto his lap and put a thin arm about his neck. She launched into a long, giggling account of an incident she had witnessed at the supermarket. The bagboy had loaded this woman's shopping bag, and when she picked it up by the handles, the bottom tore and everything fell out!

Empt smiled and nodded, enjoying her pleasure at telling him of this. He kissed her soft neck, nuzzling, smelling her young fragrance.

She lifted his face with her palms, stared into his eyes, suddenly sober.

'What would you like me to do, daddy?'

'Oh . . .' he said, 'I don't know.'

She put her lips to his ear. 'I'll tell you what,' she whispered. 'I'll get into bed and pretend I'm asleep, waiting for you. You know? And then you come home and get into bed with me. And you're ever so quiet and loving so's not to wake me up. And then . . . Do you want to do that?'

'All right,' he said, looking at her strangely. 'If you like.'

She went about the preparations unhurriedly, smiling and humming. Locked and chained the door. Made certain the shades were drawn. Turned off all the lights except the one in the bathroom, and left that door open.

She didn't strip the sofa to sheets and blanket, but instead lay atop the gaily colored throw, using one of the burlap-covered pillows. She lay on her side, pulled her braid free. Her back was to him, bowed. Her knees were drawn up, withered leg hidden beneath her.

He stared at her broodingly in the soft gloom. He wasn't certain what role he was to play in this fantasy. Lover? Husband? Father? He remembered what Jane Holloway had told the mob guys about the importance of story and plot in their skin flicks. A smart lady.

He rose cautiously, tiptoed into the kitchenette to pour a fresh drink. He took a deep gulp and stood there a moment, palms propped on the sink, head hanging. Wondering, wondering . . .

He carried the drink over to the sofa, bent down to look at her. Eyes closed. Lips parted a little. She was breathing deeply. She really could be asleep.

He set the glass aside, tucking it under the sofa so he wouldn't kick it over. He began to undress, staring down at her bare arm, bare leg, both gleaming whitely.

Naked, he sat down softly on the edge of the sofa. She stirred.

'Daddy?' she said drowsily in a little girl's voice. 'Is that you?'

'Yes,' he said soothingly. 'I'm home. Go back to sleep.'

She groaned with contentment, pressed her face into the pillow, her eyes resolutely closed.

He realized, almost with a shock, that he was becoming aroused; this story was exciting him. The child lay curled into a soft ball, unconscious with sleep. And helpless. Did she know him better than he knew himself?

Carefully, tenderly, he drew up the hem of her short nightgown until her bare hip was exposed. There was a half-moon curve. Gleaming highlight. Dusky shadow.

He stared at that small piece of her body as if it might contain all the secrets of the universe, answers to all his questions. It was skin, flesh, gristle, stuff of life. And much, much more . . .

He bent to kiss hard bone pressing soft skin. It seemed to yield, to hold the imprint of his lips. The taste was sweetish, with a tang. Gently, with infinite caution, he lay down beside her, fitting his body to hers. The thick hawser of braided hair lay between them.

At the tip, bound with the rubber band, individual hairs sprouted like a miniature brush. He moved those soft bristles over his own body, peering down to watch what he was doing, and not understanding.

She sighed – in her sleep? – and rolled back and forth a few times as he moved the nightgown up to her waist. Then she lay upon her back but with her head turned into the pillow, an arm thrown across her eyes.

He stared down at her, seeing the whole leg, the shrunken leg, and between, the neat triangle, a patch of black moss.

He moved away from her, rose shakily to his feet. He groped carefully for his drink, found it, took a deep swallow. He stalked about the darkened room, sipping from his glass.

What he wanted, what he really wanted was . . . Was what? Something more than sex. He wanted something absolutely new, never before felt or imagined. He thought that if he could name it, he could find it. But it eluded him.

'What the hell,' he whispered angrily, furious with her, but mostly with himself.

When he came back to the sofa, she had taken off the nightgown and was lying naked, arms and legs outstretched. The pillow was beneath her hips, elevating her rump. The black braid lay along her spine, a plump snake that gleamed and twisted.

He stared down at that pale starfish, spread and waiting. Haunches were tight, back boned, legs roped with tendon. He took a deep breath and put his drink aside.

When he lowered himself upon her, she writhed and moaned piteously in a child's voice: 'Don't hurt me, daddy. Please don't hurt me.'

He paused. He had never hurt her. Never. He knew that, and she knew it, too. He could only guess it was her private fantasy.

Or she was wiser beyond his ken and had decided what might lock him to her, forever and ever.

4

That same evening, while Luther Empt agonized over what was happening to him, his mother, Gertrude, and Jane Holloway's father, Professor Craner, sat placidly on the Empt terrace. They were bundled up against the night's chill, and sipping small snifters of Luther's Italian brandy.

The professor was dressed rakishly in old-fashioned creamy gabardine slacks with a plentitude of sewn pleats at the waist. His open-necked white shirt was decked with a boldy patterned ascot. Over this, he wore a heavy white V-necked fisherman's sweater in a cable knit. The rosewood cane was clasped between his bony knees.

Gertrude wore one of her flowered tents with a drawstring neckline. She had pulled on a moth-eaten wool cardigan (one button missing), and the kind of sashed, wide-brimmed straw hat (decorated with a clump of plastic cherries) that an impecunious duchess might wear to a garden party. As usual, her legs and feet were bare.

Craner looked about serenely.

'Quiet tonight,' he observed. 'Where is everyone?'

'John Stewart Wellington is in his room,' she told him. 'Reading another book about the Battle of Waterloo. That man is just nuts about Waterloo. Luther is at some business meeting or other. He says.'

'And Teresa?' he asked idly.

She didn't answer.

'I didn't mean to pry,' he said apologetically.

'I know you didn't, perfesser. She's not too far from us. On the grounds, in fact.'

'Oh? Taking a walk?'

'Not exactly.' Gertrude paused a long moment. 'She's out in the gazebo. Rubbing the bacon.'

It took him a while to understand. Then he hastily sipped his brandy.

'My goodness,' he said. 'I never would have guessed.'

She grinned at him. 'Don't you want to know who she's doing it with?'

'Not unless you want to tell me.'

'You'll get a charge out of this,' she said, laughing roughly. 'Your grandson.'

Then they both gulped their brandies. They stared out at inky sea, shifting and turning onto the beach. Lights of fishing boats crawled along. There was an occasional flash of a whitecap. They were hardly conscious of the surf's constant pound and splash.

'Jesus Christ!' Craner burst out.

'Yeah,' Mrs Empt said, 'I figured that would throw you.'

'You're sure?'

'Sure I'm sure. I know what's going on in this house. Besides, sometimes when the wind is right, you can hear them.'

'That devil,' the professor said softly.

'Him or her?' she asked, leaning forward to pour them more brandy.

'Gertrude,' he said, 'sometimes I just can't seem to keep up with it. It's a whole new ballgame.'

'Nah,' she said. 'People aren't doing anything that they haven't always done. They just don't make a big deal out of hiding it anymore. No one gives a damn.'

'No one gives a damn,' he repeated, sighing. 'I'm afraid you're right.' He stroked his mustache and goatee reflectively. 'I guess I really don't object.'

'Me neither,' she said. 'To each his own.'

'The boy is only sixteen,' he mentioned.

'If they're big enough,' she said, 'they're old enough. It might be the best thing in the world for him.'

276

'And for her?'

'Her, too. It's a cinch she's not getting any loving from that lummox son of mine.'

He stared at her with a tight smile.

'You don't much like your son, do you, Gertrude?'

She hesitated for a beat or two. 'No,' she said.

'I don't much like my daughter,' he confessed. 'She's all right, I suppose, but she's a stranger to me.'

'It happens,' Gertrude said philosophically. 'God knows I don't know where Luther gets his ambition and drive. Not from me, and certainly not from his father, that's for sure.'

'Are children a blessing or a curse?' he asked her.

'Both,' she answered.

They sat in contented silence. She was sprawled, tea-colored legs thrust out. She wiggled her bare toes reflectively. He sat stiffly, leaning forward from the waist to grasp the silver toucan head of his cane.

'Have you thought about that place we looked at?' he inquired casually. 'The motel near Fashion Square?'

'I've been thinking,' she admitted.

'Good,' he said. 'As long as you haven't forgotten. But in all honesty, I should tell you there's a drawback.'

'What's that?'

'Me,' he said.

'Ah-ha,' she said. 'I knew it. Come clean, perfesser. Spill the beans.'

'I snore,' he said.

'And?'

'I drink prune juice,' he said.

'Big deal,' she scoffed. 'If I had the prune juice concession for south Florida, I'd be a zillionaire. What else?'

'My feet aren't so great. I wear a built-up arch in one shoe, and I've got a painful callus on the other foot. I have to take pills to keep my blood pressure down, no salt, and my liver isn't exactly in prime condition. Let's see . . . what else . . . A touch of arthritis in my hip, I have to wear

277

reading glasses, and the last time I got it up was on May 14, 1968.'

She shouted a laugh.

'Not so bad for an old fart,' she said. 'Want to hear my tale of woe?'

'Delighted,' he said.

'I had a hysterectomy, but I still have trouble occasionally with my plumbing. And the stomach isn't so great. I belch like a maniac, especially in the morning; I'm Tums' best customer. I also had a mastectomy, so I'm titless on the left side. Okay on my last checkup; no signs of spreading. My teeth are store-bought, but my eyes are fine, and my hair's all mine. My ass is sinking, and I've got the Goodyear blimp around my waist. I think that's about all. Scare you off?'

'Not at all,' he assured her. 'I'd be comfortable with another survivor. We might just make a go of it.'

'Maybe,' she said doubtfully.

He looked at her steadily, almost fiercely. 'Gertrude, I would like to live with someone who remembers the same songs I do.'

'We'll see,' she said.

5

The new revolver had been cleaned three times, though it had never been fired. A month after buying it, Holloway had decided it was stupid to keep it in the drawer of the bedside table. He decided to wear it, in the handsome black leather holster he had purchased.

The holster had a safety strap that snapped over the gun, so there was no nonsense of practicing a fast draw. Nothing like that. It was just that the holster and revolver suspended from his belt gave Holloway a pleasant feeling of security and confidence.

More exciting was the feel of the gun when he cleaned it, or just gripped it. There was something sensuous about its oiled gleam, something thrilling in its blunt power.

On a Wednesday afternoon, mid-December, following a two-martini lunch and then three surreptitious nips of vodka from his office bottle, Holloway was bubbling. When alone, he chattered away to himself gleefully, getting good answers to difficult questions.

But by the time he decided to leave the bank, a little after four o'clock, his ebullient mood had shredded away.

The rain didn't help. It had started about 2:00 P.M., with a crack of thunder and strike of lightning, like a curtain raiser. The deluge began. A steady, soaking rain that fell straight down, making a swamp of the bank's landscaped grounds and a pool of the parking lot.

Holloway dashed for his Mercedes, holding over his head the morning's copy of *The Wall Street Journal*. Once inside the car, he started the engine and flipped on the air conditioner. He sat there, gripping the wheel, conscious that his socks and shoes were soaked and squelching.

He made no effort to drive, hoping the downpour might let up. He cleaned a patch of fog from the window and, looking out, imagined that he might be under water, sunk and gone. The grayness was all about him, solid, and he glanced at the floor of the car, half-expecting to see it creeping up.

Nothing had followed that initial crash of thunder, but far up in the murk there were still occasional flashes, lightning like tarnished silver. Holloway sighed, began again his dialogue:

'What happened to your resolution to live as a virtuous man?'

'It wasn't a resolution. Just a decision to explore the possibility.'

'And?'

'It's difficult.'

The difficulty lay, he admitted, not in his willingness, but in the almost total lack of moral choice in his life. His drinking or not drinking could hardly be considered a matter of virtue or vice. Similarly, his involvement in the pornography industry, however peripheral, was simply cold business which did not concern his soul's salvation.

'Piddling stuff,' he said aloud.

'True,' he agreed. 'Nothing meaningful or significant.'

Meanwhile he remained a medium man living a medium life. He longed for drama, a clap of thunder and flare of electricity that might signal theatre of moral import. He wanted to endure a grievous wound or volunteer an extreme sacrifice.

The rain continued. Dreading the drive home, he headed slowly out of the parking lot. The snicking windshield wipers barely kept up with the flood; he leaned forward to peer through the streaked half-moon.

Streets and highways were awash. Stalled cars blocked his way. He maneuvered fearfully, hoping that drivers behind him were moving as cautiously as he. Traffic lights were out, and he waited almost three minutes before daring to turn south on A1A.

There was a delay at Northeast Sixth Street: cars waiting in line for some obstruction to clear.

Dimly, through the streaming window on the passenger's side, he saw a sodden, forlorn figure standing on the verge. The boy was hopefully jerking a thumb southward. Holloway slid across the leather benchseat and rolled the window down a few inches.

'Wayne!' he yelled. 'Wayne Bending! Over here.'

The lad came running. He slipped into the car, slammed the door behind him.

'Jesus!' he said. 'Am I ever glad to see you.'

'What happened?'

'Aw, I missed the school bus and couldn't get a ride. I called home, but no one's there. I decided to hitch, but the guy I was with got flooded out, so I started hitching again. I'm sorry, Mr Holloway, I'm getting the seat all wet.'

'It's only water,' Holloway said.

The line of cars started inching forward again. Holloway leaned to stare through the murk.

'It's a pisser, isn't it?' Wayne Bending said.

Holloway didn't answer. The line of cars stopped again. He turned off the stereo, took a pack of cigarettes from his inside jacket pocket.

'Could I have one of those?' Wayne asked. 'Please.'

'I guess so,' Holloway said, laughing nervously. 'As long as you don't tell your parents I'm leading you astray.'

'They'll never hear it from me,' the boy said.

They lighted up, Holloway holding the match. Wayne handled the cigarette expertly, inhaling without effort. He turned his head away from Holloway, wiped mist from his window, stared out.

'Getting worse,' he reported. 'Shit.'

They sat in silence a few moments. Then they heard the

warbling whine of police sirens. Through the windshield, dimly, they could see revolving red lights.

'Oh God,' Wayne said. 'The cops. That means a crackup or a stalled car. We'll be sitting here forever.'

Holloway opened his window a crack to let the smoke out and help clear the fog from the windows. Wayne Bending watched him, then did the same on his side.

'How are you getting along in school?' Holloway asked with as much interest as he could muster.

'Okay,' the boy said shortly. 'I get by.'

'That's not what I hear,' Holloway said with a tinny laugh. 'I hear you're a hotshot student.'

'Yeah? Where'd you hear that?'

'Around. I wish I could say the same for Eddie.'

'He does all right,' Wayne Bending said.

Holloway turned to look at him. Wayne was examining the burning tip of his cigarette.

'Something wrong, Wayne?'

'Nah. Why do you say that?'

Then the memory returned to Holloway. Not easing its way into his consciousness, but coming back suddenly, with the force of a physical blow, so painful he almost gasped.

An almost identical situation. A young boy and an older man in a car. A Studebaker. Parked in a light rain. The windshield wipers whickering back and forth. The feeling of quiet intimacy.

But this moment wasn't going to end the way that one had. Holloway was certain.

'I don't know,' he said. 'You just look like something's troubling you.'

'I got no troubles,' Wayne said stolidly.

Holloway didn't think the boy handsome. Far from it. The brow was too low, the jaw almost protohuman. Lips were thin, nose a snub. The eyes saved the face: big, widely spaced, of the richest cerulean blue. Shockingly beautiful eyes.

So, despite the other clumsy features and the lumpy

282

physique, the youth was not unappealing. He radiated vulnerability and hurt.

'Mr Holloway,' Wayne said suddenly, 'could I ask you something? Something personal?'

'Well, uh . . .' Holloway said uncomfortably. 'Maybe you should talk to your father about it.'

The boy gave him a sullen glance. 'I can't talk to my father. He's always making jokes.'

'Yes, well . . . All right, what is it?'

There was a long pause.

'It's hard to explain,' Wayne said lamely.

'Take your time. It doesn't look like we're going anywhere for a while.'

'Well, say there's this guy, and he's got a friend. A good friend – you know? And this guy has, uh, done a lot for the friend. Whatever his friend wanted. So this guy figured, you know, he should get something in return. Right? I don't mean money or anything like that.'

'Just friendship,' Holloway said softly. 'He should get friendship in return.'

'Yes. That's right. And the friend knows how this guy feels. Because he's proved it.'

'The guy's proved his friendship?'

'Yes. How he feels. But then, say, the friend goes off. I mean he just sort of drifts away. He finds, uh, someone else. And after a while, he doesn't pay any attention to this guy, doesn't even want to spend any time with him. Well, what I wanted to know is why people act that way. I mean, that's not right.'

Holloway sighed. 'No, it isn't right. And when I tell you that's the way things are, it won't make it any better. Wayne, people change. You, me, everyone. Nothing is forever. The way you feel about someone today doesn't mean you're going to feel the same way tomorrow.'

'I would,' the lad said stoutly.

'Maybe – but I doubt it. Everyone changes. The problems arise when friends, or relatives, or husband and wife change at different times or at different speeds. Understand what I mean? Like the guy you're talking about and his friend . . . The friend is changing, and moving away from the guy. But if he didn't, maybe eventually the guy would change and move away from the friend.'

Wayne pondered that a moment. 'You really think so?'

'I really do. Everyone talks about lifelong friends, but practically no one is one or has one. People drift apart.'

'That's finky,' Wayne Bending said. 'Could I have another cigarette? Please.'

They lighted cigarettes and watched a tow truck move cautiously by in the rain, lights flashing.

He looked at Wayne Bending. The boy had such a woebegone expression that Holloway feared he might weep. He wished there was something he could do, make some physical gesture, to ease the lad's anguish.

'That guy you were talking about,' he said, staring stiffly through the rain-flecked windshield, 'the one with the friend – I went through something like that when I was, oh, maybe a couple of years older than you are now.'

'No kidding?' Wayne said.

'I had a friend, a good friend. Or I thought he was. I really proved my friendship, and I thought we were going to be close forever. I didn't know then what I just told you, about people changing. Well, my friend changed. I didn't, but he did. And he just drifted away, out of my life. It didn't seem to bother him, but I felt lousy. It really hurt. For a long time. But then I found new friends, and gradually I forgot. That's probably what will happen to the guy you told me about. He'll make new friends, and he'll forget.'

'I don't think so,' Wayne Bending said dully.

William Holloway wondered what more he could say or do.

It suddenly occurred to him that this youth's pain might offer the moral choice he had been seeking. It was an opportunity to act as a virtuous man, succor one in need with no expectation of reward other than his own know-

284

ledge that he had acted unselfishly in a good cause.

'Wayne,' he said, 'I've lived almost four times as long as you have. That doesn't necessarily make me any smarter. But it does mean I've had certain experiences and have lived through situations that you may be facing. What I'm trying to say is that if you're ever in need of help or just want to talk about, uh, things, I'm a good listener. I won't volunteer any advice unless you ask for it. And you can be certain that anything you tell me will be private; no one will heard a word about it from me.'

' 'Preciate that,' the boy mumbled.

After a while, the obstruction up ahead was cleared, traffic began moving again. It was still pouring, and Holloway drove the youth to his home, letting him out under the carport.

Just before he slammed the door, Wayne turned back, grinned, and said, 'Thanks, Mr Holloway.'

Those eyes!

6

It was still raining on Thursday morning when Ronald Bending came dancing into the office.

'I feel great, Ted,' he said for openers. 'Everything's coming up roses.'

'Glad to hear it, Turk,' Dr Theodore Levin said with a somewhat sour smile. 'This weather doesn't depress you?'

'Nah. Into every life a little rain must fall. Just makes you appreciate the sunshiny days all the more.'

He looked like sunshine himself, in a three-piece suit of khaki poplin, a golden-yellow shirt with a wide, flowered tie, a silk pocket handkerchief that was a palette of primary colors. Ox-blood moccasins with tassels.

Levin watched without expression as Bending arranged himself in the armchair. He hiked his trousers carefully to preserve the crease, crossed his knees, then lounged back comfortably and lighted one of his filter-tips.

'What's the reason for the good mood?' the doctor asked casually, stripping the cellophane from a cigar. 'Business booming?'

'Couldn't be better,' Bending said cheerfully. 'For once in my life, things are coming my way.'

'Good,' Levin said, puffing away. 'It's a welcome change to have someone in this office without problems.'

'Oh, I've got problems. But nothing I can't handle. And talking about problems, how're you coming along with Lucy?'

'Making progress. Slowly. But I warned you not to expect quick results.'

'As long as you get her straightened out,' Bending said briskly. 'That's all I ask. Well, what do you want to talk about today? If I wet the bed at the age of eighteen or wanted to screw my mother?'

'Did you?' the doctor asked. 'Either of those things? Or both?'

Bending laughed. 'You don't have much sense of humor, do you, Ted?'

'No, I don't. I find that people, especially men, frequently use humor to conceal their true feelings.'

'Do you think I do that?'

'Do *you* think you do?'

'Well, what the hell, you can't go around with your feelings hanging out all the time, can you? Jokes are just the grease to make the world move a little smoother. You know what I'm getting at?'

'I know, Turk. But it's trying to make things move smoothly, and refusing to face the underlying reality, that bring so many people to this office.'

'So you want me to cut the crap. Is that what you're saying?'

'Yes, that's what I'm saying.'

They smiled genially at each other and let the silence grow.

Levin was wearing one of his shiny, rumpled black suits, the jacket lapels dusted with cigar ashes. There were even flakes of ash caught in his beard. He had pushed his heavy spectacles atop his thick, salt-and-pepper hair.

'Turk,' he said finally in his throaty rumble, 'let's understand each other. Your daughter is in therapy, and that's the only reason I'm talking to you – to help her. The longer you hold out on me, the longer you tell me lies or half-lies, the longer it's going to take to help Lucy.'

'I know that, doc – Ted.'

'I hope you do. I'm not treating you. I have no personal or professional interest in your life, except as it may affect Lucy.'

'I've got this creepy feeling that you're leading up to something.'

'The only thing that I'm leading up to is a request that you be more honest with me, more forthcoming.'

Bending frowned. 'You think I've been holding out on you?'

'Have you?'

'Well . . . maybe. But just on stuff that couldn't possibly affect Lucy.'

Levin slammed a meaty palm onto the desk. The crack startled Bending; he looked worried.

'Everything you do affects Lucy,' the doctor said. '*Everything*. And especially your relations with your wife.'

'Oh,' Bending said, 'that. Well, like I told you, we get along. The sex thing is practically nil, but we put up appearances. The happily married couple. I told you all that; I was honest.'

'I remember. I think "indifference" was the word we agreed on. Rather than "hostility." '

'Yeah,' Bending said. 'Indifference.'

Levin had several choices here. He could follow up on Bending's relationship with Grace, he could delve a little deeper into his past, or he could seek to find other clues in the man's activities away from his wife, children, home.

Looking at that debonair figure slumped in the armchair, noting the ironic smile – not quite a smirk – Levin had, he admitted, a totally irrational desire to dent the man. No one should be that cool and scornful.

'Let's talk about your, ah, extramarital affairs, Turk. From what you told me, I gather they have been fairly frequent.'

'Fairly.'

'Is there one type of woman you prefer?'

'That's a crazy question. The answer is No. But I'm curious about why you asked it.'

'You would be surprised at how many married men who

seek sexual gratification outside their home unconsciously select a woman who resembles their wife. Sometimes remarkably so.'

'Is that right? Well, it doesn't hold for me. None of the ladies who have granted me favors look like Grace at all, or act like her.'

'Prostitutes?'

Bending shifted irritably in his chair. 'Absolutely not! I don't have to pay for it, Ted.'

'You feel there's something shameful in paying for sexual pleasure?'

'I just don't have to do it, that's all. I'll never do it. It would spoil the whole thing.'

Levin flipped down his spectacles to his eyes. He leaned forward, regarded Bending narrowly.

'Spoil what?' he asked.

'The whole thing,' Bending repeated.

'If all you're seeking is sexual release, an orgasm, I fail to see how paying could spoil that.'

'You don't understand, Ted. You haven't got a clue.'

'Tell me,' Levin said gently. 'I'll try to understand.'

Bending took a deep breath. 'Well, I told you I wanted to be an artist. My whole training was in fine arts. Composition, harmony, proportion, color – like that. Well, I'm not an artist now, I admit it, but I think like one.'

He paused, his features suddenly slack. Dr Levin waited a moment, and then said, 'And . . . ?'

Ronald Bending rose to his feet. He thrust his hands into his trouser pockets. He began to pace back and forth before Levin's desk, head lowered, his voice earnest.

'It's not just sexual release,' he said. 'It's not just coming. For God's sake, if that was all I wanted, I could jack off, couldn't I? See, I'm being honest now. No, it's more than just getting my ashes hauled. The women I pick, the women I go after, are all beautiful. To me they are. My artist's eye. I mean, maybe it could be the texture of their skin. Or the curve of a hip. Maybe just one tit. Maybe the line of a bent leg. It could be a hundred things. But it's more, uh, sensual than sexual.'

He stopped. He took his hands from his pockets. He folded his arms across his chest. He gazed down sternly at Levin. 'You don't believe me, do you?'

'Is it important to you that I believe you?'

'Well, I'm just telling you the truth. Like I said, it's not sexual at all. It's sensual. The artist's eye. What it is, is a search for beauty. A love of beauty. Line, proportion, harmony, and composition. Like that.'

Dr Theodore Levin set his cigar carefully aside in the ashtray. He leaned back in the swivel chair, clasped his hands across his ash-flecked vest. He stared at the other man with a smile of soft benignity.

'Mr Ronald Bending,' he said, 'you're full of shit.'

Bending gave one hard bark of laughter. Then he threw himself back into the chair. He sat sideways, one knee hooked over the chair's arm. He fished into his jacket pocket for cigarettes. Levin watched him light up with fingers that trembled slightly.

'You're right,' he said, showing his teeth. 'I can't fool you and I can't fool myself.'

'Then what is it?' Levin asked.

'What is it?' Bending demanded loudly. 'What is it?' He took his leg from the chair arm, jerked forward. 'It's that goddamned tube of meat between my legs. It makes me do things I don't want to do. It controls me, for God's sake.' He began to gesticulate wildly. 'What can it weigh? A few ounces? Not more than a quarter of a pound – right? And it's ruined my life. Listen, it's all I can do sometimes to keep from raping some of those creamers I see on the beach. Yes, right there on the sand. Just grab them, you know. All because of that lousy tube of meat. I want to hump every woman I see. Why do you think they call me Turk? I got that name in college, and it's stuck with me all my life. Turk for a Turkish sultan with a harem. There's not one of them I can't love. They're so beautiful. Even the ugly ones.

290

There's always *something* there. I can't help myself. It's that lousy tube of meat. All right, you wanted me to be honest. Now I've been honest. Happy?'

Levin wanted to keep the confessional going. He didn't want to give the man a chance to cool off.

'So there have been many women?'

'Yes,' Bending said, nodding wildly. 'Many. Many.'

'Since your marriage?'

'Yes.'

'In motels?'

'Motels, hotels, her apartment, my car, the office.'

'And in your own home? When your wife was out?'

Bending gave him a hurt glance. 'Never. I'd never do anything like that.'

'Uh-huh. But you'd rape one on the beach? Right there on the sand?'

'Come on, Ted, that was just Loony Tunes time; you know that. I just said that to show you how I feel. But I'd never *do* it.'

'So you do have control over that tube of meat?'

'Not enough. I still make a fool of myself. Waste time. Neglect my wife and kids. I know it.'

'Is Grace aware of this, uh, predilection of yours?'

'Some. She doesn't know everything.'

'Your children? Do you think they're aware of your activities?'

'Nah. How could they know? The neighbors maybe. Bill Holloway and Luther Empt – a couple of drinking buddies of mine – maybe they know, or guess.'

Levin looked at the man, now slumped once again in the armchair on the other side of the desk.

'Turk, you seem to have regrets for the way you live. You've been very forthcoming so far; now let me ask you this: Are you sure you want to change? If you could?'

Bending tilted back his head, stared at the glittering stars pasted on the office ceiling.

'No,' he said softly, 'I guess not. First of all, I couldn't change even if I wanted to. And I don't think I want to.'

'In other words, you're more or less satisfied with the way you live? You recognize that what you do is deceitful, wasteful, perhaps foolish and self-destructive, but you're willing to continue?'

'Ted,' Bending said with a mocking smile, 'you really have a beautiful way with words. But I guess the answer is Yes. I'm going to continue. Until I'm six feet under. And then they'll have trouble getting the lid on the coffin.'

Dr Levin smiled briefly. 'In its most virulent form, your condition might be called satyriasis. But I prefer to think it's merely hypersexuality. The same thing that's troubling your daughter.'

Bending stared at him. 'You mean Lucy got it from me?'

Levin laughed. 'Oh no. No, no, no. I've never seen any evidence that the condition is inheritable. Not genetically. But if Lucy is aware of the way you live . . .'

'She isn't,' the other man said crossly. 'I told you that.'

The doctor settled back. He took up his cold cigar, used a wooden kitchen match to relight it. He puffed contentedly, then glanced at his desk clock.

'Turk, we have a few minutes left. With your permission, I'd like to forget Lucy for a moment and talk about you. A few minutes ago, I said I had no personal or professional interest in your life except as it affects Lucy. Perhaps that was an exaggeration. Because now I find myself curious about you, the way you live. Call it nosiness, if you like. What I'd really like to know is the reason for your womanizing. You seem to ascribe it to an insatiable sexual drive. Is that all it is?'

Bending lighted another cigarette. He uncrossed his knees, crossed them again. He began to drum on one knee with the fingers of his free hand. He examined his burning cigarette intently, then looked up.

'Ted,' he said, 'I honestly don't know. I know the sex part is very important. Who doesn't enjoy a good bang? But maybe there's more to it than that. That bullshit I gave you

292

about the artist's eye – well, that wasn't *all* bullshit. And also, we all have to eat so much dirt in this world, just to get along, that giving a woman pleasure and getting pleasure from her, I figure that's a kind of revenge. You know? And also the way it makes you feel. Like singing. Like you're going to live forever. Life is complicated.'

'Yes,' Dr Theodore Levin said faintly, 'that's true.'

7

Former Senator Randolph Diedrickson loved intrigue. *Loved* it! It was not a folly of old age, as a gaffer might turn to tatting or Trollope. No, it was a life-long study, habit, and practice that had served him well in his political career and his bewilderingly complex private life.

Diedrickson saw intrigue as an advanced form of chess, played with human pieces. But whereas chess had rules, intrigue was a ruleless game of instinct, imagination, and invention. All the great players – Machiavelli, Richelieu, Meyer Lansky – were essentially *creative* men.

So when Jane Holloway phoned to recount the latest progress of EBH Enterprises, Inc., and to ask for the senator's advice, he listened carefully. He interrupted her recital only once:

'This Ernie Goldman – he's a Jew?'

'Yes, I suppose so.'

The senator then heard her out, and promised to give the matter his careful consideration. He hung up the phone with a smile of pleased anticipation – the cat crouched at the rat hole.

Occasionally, of course, intrigue was played *pour le sport*. But generally, self-interest was the guiding principle. In this case, Diedrickson wished to retain the affection and ministrations of Jane Holloway. But surely, he reasoned, there might be other ways he could profit from moving and shaping this minor imbroglio.

He sat alone in the shade of the sundeck awning, a bottle of Mumm's Cordon Rouge chilling in a bucket alongside.

He pondered the problem, pulling gently at his rubbery lower lip. He worked out his opening moves. To others they might seem impractical, even farcical. To Diedrickson, they had an elegant logic.

Political cronies had alerted him to the existence of a talented assistant district attorney in Okeechobee County. This young man had recently prosecuted a case of homicide – a wealthy orange grower had hired a professional killer to dispose of his mistress's boyfriend – and had secured a conviction.

The case received statewide media attention, and the young prosecutor was termed a 'comer' in several Florida newspapers. Diedrickson contrived to meet him and liked what he saw. He was idealistic but not too idealistic, honest but not too honest, ambitious but not too ambitious, greedy but not too greedy.

Diedrickson was convinced the young man had enormous potential. Unfortunately, he was not a wealthy man and had not yet succeeded in building a money base to finance a significant political career.

The former senator had several discussions with members of his party in Florida, and ways were sought to move this young paragon along: mayor, perhaps, or state senator, and then House of Representatives, or state governor, and then – who knew? But strong funding was required.

Now, Diedrickson thought, he might very well have happened upon a money tree in this business of Jane Holloway's. Satisfied with his preliminary plans, he opened his iced Mumm's, delighted to find he still had the strength to twist the cork.

He sampled half a glass, smacked his thick lips, belched gently, and reached for the telephone.

The meeting with Rocco Santangelo and Jimmy Stone was arranged for the following Thursday afternoon, three days before the commemoration of Christ's birth. The former senator greeted his guests in his second-floor study, a gloomy, overstuffed chamber from which his secretary had been temporarily banished.

For the occasion, Diedrickson had donned a rumpled seersucker suit that looked like mattress ticking, a white shirt with a frayed collar and black string tie clasped with a silver and turquoise ring. His bloated, purplish ankles were bare, and he wore beaded carpet slippers, the gift of a grateful constituent twenty years ago.

His two visitors were carefully, even nattily dressed. Santangelo was a watercolor of pearl grays and light blues, everything monogrammed. He was the tall, carefully groomed one. Diedrickson wondered how long it had been since he had seen clocks on men's hose.

The other, Jimmy Stone, was the short, heavy one and, the host guessed, the leader. He didn't have Santangelo's gloss, but his presence dominated. He wore a dulled black worsted suit, vested, with white shirt and black tie, socks, and shoes. An undertaker's costume, Diedrickson thought, and probably fitting.

The senator got them seated and had Renfrew serve them drinks before he left. Since both his guests asked for bourbon, Diedrickson also drank it, to suggest to them that he admired their taste. He happened to detest bourbon, but business was business.

The two men were seated in heavy Victorian armchairs, upholstered in lavender velvet, now worn and greasy.

Diedrickson rolled his wheelchair out from behind the desk so he was closer to his guests. He wanted this to be an intimate meeting.

'Tell me,' he said, smiling benignly, 'how is my very good friend Uncle Dom?'

'He's okay, senator,' Santangelo said. 'His ulcer acts up sometimes, but considering his age, he's doing fine. He sends his regards.'

'Well, give my best to the dear man,' Diedrickson said warmly. 'I was hopeful that we might get together during the joyous holiday season, but neither of us finds the rigors of travel, ah, convenient. But I intend to telephone him to wish him the very best for the new year, I do assure you.'

'The present,' Jimmy Stone said in his low, growly voice.

'Oh, yeah,' Santangelo said, snapping his fingers. 'Uncle Dom wants us to thank you for that nice present you sent his nephew Nick when he graduated.'

'My pleasure,' the senator said, beaming. 'And what are the boy's plans for the future?'

'Wall Street,' Stone said. 'Bonds.'

'Excellent. Glad to hear it. If you should see the lad, you might remind him that I have many true and wonderful friends in the banking community down here, and if there is any way I may be of service, he has only to ask.'

His guests nodded politely, sipped their drinks, looked at him blankly, waiting . . .

'Well, gentlemen, I don't want to waste your time. I'll get right to the reason I asked you to join me today. Certain information has come to my attention which, because of my long association with and affection for Uncle Dom, I feel you should be made aware of. It concerns your plans to establish a processing facility in south Florida to convert your movie films into television cassettes.

Either they had been warned of his omniscience or trained in the art of imperturbability. They looked at him steadily, expressionless. But if they thought to daunt him by their coldness, they underestimated his mettle. He had dealt with men of their ilk before, many times, and understood that a display, even an indication, of anxiety would be fatal.

He told them of Ronald Bending's machinations to oust Luther Empt and, with the aid of William Holloway, gain control of EBH Enterprises, Inc. Then he paused in his recital, looking brightly at the two men, back and forth.

'Another drink?' he suggested smoothly. 'Please help yourself at the sideboard as I am incarcerated in this ridiculous conveyance.'

Santangelo rose to pour himself more bourbon, though

297

his glass was still half-full. A sign of disquiet, Diedrickson thought. But Jimmy Stone remained seated, staring at the senator thoughtfully.

'Where did you hear all this?' he asked.

'From Holloway's wife, Jane. I understand you met her.'

'Yeah,' Stone said. 'A bright broad.'

'She is indeed,' Diedrickson said. 'And understandably upset at the turn things have taken. Quite naturally, she feels Bending's plans may jeopardize her husband's investment. A quarter of a million, I believe.'

Rocco Santangelo had regained his seat after taking two quick swallows from his filled glass. Now he leaned forward, almost glaring.

'What has all this bullshit got to do with us?' he demanded.

'Please correct me if I am wrong,' the senator said affably, 'but I really can't see this Luther Empt meekly allowing himself to be fucked by his partners without uttering a word of protest. I would venture a guess that would mean a messy lawsuit and –'

'It's got nothing to do with us,' Santangelo said.

'Shut up, Rock,' Jimmy Stone said sharply. 'Go on, senator.'

'A messy lawsuit during which the purpose and business dealings of EBH Enterprises, Inc., would become a matter of public record. I would imagine that is the last thing in the world you gentlemen desire.'

'Yeah,' Stone said. 'You're right. Those assholes! They're going to bollix up the whole goddamn deal.'

'Precisely,' Diedrickson said, nodding. 'And that, of course, is the reason for Mrs Holloway's concern. She is, as you said, a bright broad, and knows a profitable business arrangement when she sees one. She is against anything that might endanger the mutually profitable relationship between you gentlemen and EBH.'

'Shit,' Santangelo said disgustedly. 'And everything was going so nice and quiet.'

'May I prevail upon one of you to pour me a little more of this excellent libation?' Diedrickson asked, holding out his glass. 'Amazing what a splendid medicine it is for the pains that afflict these old joints.'

His mild humor had the desired effect; his guests visibly calmed. Stone rose to fill the senator's glass and top off his own as well.

'Actually,' Diedrickson went on seriously, 'I do not believe matters have progressed to the point where action is required. But it is a situation I thought you gentlemen should be aware of. The potential is there for serious injury to your endeavors and plans for the future.'

'You can say that again,' Santangelo said mournfully. 'We got big plans for the future.'

'I am sure you have,' the senator said sympathetically. He addressed Stone directly: 'I assume you'll repeat to Uncle Dom the details of this conversation?'

'Yeah,' Stone said, 'we gotta tell him.'

'Of course. And please inform him that I am being kept abreast of the situation, on almost a daily basis, and will certainly contact you if any significant developments occur. Mrs Holloway visits here and telephones me frequently. I am sure she sees me as a wise father to whom she can come for advice and counsel. She is a very intelligent lady, shrewd and ambitious.'

'She's got some good ideas,' Jimmy Stone said.

'Of course she does', Diedrickson said heartily. 'In addition, she is very knowledgeable about financial affairs and business administration. In any event, she is keeping me fully informed as to what transpires with EBH Enterprises. And I, in turn, will keep you informed.'

'We appreciate what you're doing,' Stone said, looking at the senator curiously. 'And I know Uncle Dom will appreciate it, too. Speaking for myself, let me ask you this: What's in it for you?'

Randolph Diedrickson laughed, a deep, booming, resonating laugh that filled the room.

'Of course,' he said finally, 'and I am sure Uncle Dom will ask the same thing. *Quid pro quo*. Something for something. Well, I could tell you gentlemen that I am providing my services out of the goodness of my heart, and out of my deep, enduring friendship for Uncle Dom. But if I claimed that, I fear you would think me a fool or a liar or both.'

Santangelo grinned at that, and even stolid Jimmy Stone managed to twist his lips.

'Actually, there *is* something,' the senator continued. 'Not a demand, but merely a humble request that I would appreciate your bringing to Uncle Dom's attention. It will not, I assure you, result in any great profit tomorrow for you or for myself. But within several years, it may prove to be the best investment Uncle Dom ever made.'

Diedrickson then told them about the young, talented assistant district attorney in Okeechobee County.

'Contributions can be handled a hundred different ways,' he reminded them, 'to keep within the law. But I prefer to use the word "investment."'

'This guy is practical?' Stone demanded.

'I have had only one meeting with him, but my impression – based on many years of association with public servants – is that he is an eminently practical man. All I am suggesting to Uncle Dom is that he conduct his own investigation into this man's trustworthiness. If Uncle Dom wishes, I might arrange a discreet personal meeting. May I ask you to convey my sentiments?'

'Sure,' Stone said, 'we'll tell him.'

'Excellent,' Diedrickson said, smiling broadly. 'I think that with the assistance of my party and your, ah, organization, this man could have a very successful career, to the benefit of our great nation.'

They all relaxed then and had another drink.

When his guests rose to leave, Diedrickson rolled his wheelchair to the door, then held up a hand to restrain them for a moment.

'I just want to make clear,' he said, 'that all the information I shall be able to furnish you will be due to the perspicacity and alertness of Jane Holloway. She is indeed a remarkable young lady, and it might be worthwhile to consider how her ambition, intelligence, and executive ability could be put to more profitable use.'

They nodded, shook hands, and said they'd be in touch. Stone and Santangelo walked down through the shadowed, empty mansion. They exited into bright, searing sunlight. The uniformed chauffeur of their limousine scrambled out of the air conditioning to hold the rear door open for them.

Just before they entered the car, Jimmy Stone caught Santangelo's arm.

'She's blowing him,' he said.

8

The offices of Dr Theodore Levin were closed on Saturdays; neither he nor Dr Mary Scotsby saw patients on weekends, except in cases of direst necessity. However, both psychiatrists spent many weekend hours listening to tapes, reviewing cases, and bringing their personal journals up to date.

That year, New Year's Eve fell on a Saturday. The doctors planned to spend the evening together in restrained celebration: dinner at Down Under, an honored Fort Lauderdale restaurant, and then perhaps a bottle of wine at Pier 66 or a drive up to the Bridge in Boca Raton.

Levin had a set routine for Saturday mornings. His cleaning lady, Mrs Lopez, arrived at 9:00 A.M. and departed at noon. The doctor used this period for weekly chores: taking in and picking up laundry and drycleaning, shopping for food, liquor, and sundries, buying magazines and books, etc.

Since he didn't own a car (he didn't know how to drive and had no desire to learn), he went shopping on foot, trundling a two-wheeled cart. When this was insufficient for his purchases, he also carried a string-handled, brown paper shopping bag.

On that morning he spent some time in the gourmet section of the Publix supermarket he patronized. The reservation for dinner at Down Under had been made for 8:00 P.M., but Mary Scotsby had promised to come for him at seven o'clock, so he planned to serve a few hors d'oeuvres to whet their appetites.

He wasn't very good at entertaining – or at anything domestic, for that matter – and the enormous selection of delicacies bewildered him. He finally settled on rye-flavored melba toast, smoked oysters, chocolate maca-roons, black Icelandic lumpfish, tiny ears of pickled corn, a can of Swedish meatballs, cocktail sausages, herring in dill sauce, a large jar of baba rhum, boneless Portuguese sardines, garlic pickles, baby shrimp, a small loaf of black bread, capers, a container of sour cream, a can of macada-mia nuts, and blocks of Swiss cheese, sharp cheddar, and Muenster. Also, a small jar of Louisiana mustard that was labeled 'X-Rated.'

On the way home, he bought a box of cigars (Cuesta-Rey #95), and then stopped at the liquor store. Here he pur-chased a half-gallon of the rough jug burgundy he liked, and asked the clerk to recommend a dry white wine and a champagne. These last two were for Dr Mary Scotsby.

Upstairs, his apartment looked as littered as ever. Mrs Lopez dusted and vacuumed, and did a good job in the kitchen and bathroom. She also changed all the linen. But she was under orders not to touch the stacks of books, magazines, and papers, so the rooms never looked neat.

On the kitchen counter she had left him a small, home-baked lemon meringue pie and a New Year's card in Spanish, which pleased him. He sampled a sliver of the pie before putting it in the refrigerator. The flavor was so tart it puckered his mouth.

After his purchases were stored away, he lighted a cigar and took a bag of cookies and a waterglass of the jug wine to his living room desk. He took off his nylon jacket, loosened his belt, and unlaced the soft jogging shoes he wore when relaxing on weekends. He had never jogged in his life and didn't intend to.

He had a portable audio cassette recorder in addition to a large, expensive hi-fi system that could handle cassettes, LPs, open-end tapes, and eight-track cartridges. He used the small portable to play back the cassettes recorded in his office: the case of Lucy B.

He now had more than twelve hours of taped recordings, beginning with the initial interview with Mr and Mrs Bending, and ending with his most recent session with Ronald. Dr Levin figured he could listen to about half of this material before it would be necessary to start preparing for Mary Scotsby's arrival.

He was searching for – what? He didn't know exactly. A clue, an indication, a signal, an intimation – something he might have missed at first hearing. And he knew how valuable it was for the therapist to listen only to words without being distracted by the appearance, gestures, expressions, body movements of the analysand.

He had no great hopes of finding anything of value until he had run through all twelve hours of tape. And perhaps not once, but twice or three times.

But he was on his third hour of listening and finishing his second glass of wine (the cigar and cookies were long gone), when he found it. He slapped his forehead with an open palm, so chagrined was he that he had not recognized it before.

He jerked to his feet, glanced at his watch. He had about four hours before Dr Scotsby arrived. He thought he could have the job finished by then.

He put a blank tape on the big deck and began recording sections of the office cassettes. He worked frantically, sometimes running the portable player at double speed to find the parts he wanted. As he recorded, he prefaced each section with his own voice identifying the speaker and the number of the tape.

He finished a few minutes after 6:00 P.M., and, in his unlaced shoes, flapped into the kitchen to start opening jars, cans, bottles, packages. He spread a paper tablecloth on his walnut dining table. He put out everything in their containers, adding some cutlery and paper plates, and stood back to admire the effect. A feast!

He showered hurriedly, rubbed some cologne into his beard, and was half-dressed when his doorbell chimed. He went rushing to answer in his bare feet, shirt unbuttoned, wiry chest hair sprouting wildly.

Dr Mary Scotsby, looking tall, thin, angularly elegant, wore an ankle-length gown of wine-colored velvet. From one arm, on a linked chain, hung a beaded, fringed reticule, circa 1912. She also carried a box wrapped in holiday paper. High heels towered her.

'Happy New Year, Ted,' she said, smiling.

'Thank you, thank you!' he cried, going up on his toes to kiss her cheek. 'Come in, come in!'

'My,' she said, looking at him curiously, 'we are hyper tonight.'

'You'll see,' he said, grinning crazily. 'Or rather, you'll hear. Later.'

'What on earth *are* you talking about? You're not drunk, are you?'

He got her inside, door closed, and relieved her of cashmere shawl, heavy purse, and the package – which turned out to be a bottle of champagne. Then he led her into the dining room.

'Look,' he said proudly, making a grand, sweeping gesture at the laden table. The opened cans, jars, packages, bottles. How she laughed!

'Oh Ted,' she said, 'it's beautiful. We don't have to go to dinner.'

'Nonsense,' he said gruffly. 'Just a nosh. Now I have some white wine for you. All right? And I have a bottle of champagne, too, but we'll have that and yours later. All right? I'll put yours in to chill. And I'll pour you a glass of white wine now – the man said it's very good, very dry – and I'll go in and finish dressing. Just a few minutes. All right?'

'Ted,' she said, touching his cheek, 'will you please calm down? The evening is just starting.'

'Be right out,' he called over his shoulder, rushing toward the bedroom. 'Try the oysters.'

305

He wore his best black suit, the newest one, with a puce shirt and black knitted tie. He dressed hastily and came flying back to the dining room, crying, 'I forgot to get your wine!'

But Mary had already found the bottle, opened it, and poured herself a glass.

'All right?' he asked anxiously.

'Excellent,' she assured him. 'Very flinty. And I've sampled *everything*. Ted, you've got to try those baby shrimp.'

'Oh yes,' he said greedily, and plunged in.

They ate demoniacally, not a great deal of any one thing, but little snippets of this and that. They didn't try to converse, just going 'Ooh' and 'Umm' and 'Ahh,' and taking perverse pleasure from the raw clash of tastes.

'Enough,' Mary Scotsby said firmly, finally. 'We've got to get to dinner.'

'Yes, yes, of course,' he said. 'We can't be late.'

He was never late, not even for a restaurant reservation. Punctuality was a fetish. When he had to travel, he arrived at the airport two hours before takeoff. And when he had a personal appointment, he frequently showed up a half-hour early and walked around the block until it was time.

He popped a final meatball into his mouth, scrubbed his beard with a paper napkin, and – 'Let's go!'

'Aren't you going to put all this away?' she asked. 'You'll get roaches,' she warned.

'I already have them,' he said, giggling. 'It's New Year's Eve; let them enjoy.'

She had never before seen him in such an antic mood.

Dr Scotsby owned a brownish Ford Mustang coupe. She drove as she did everything else: coldly, efficiently, precisely.

'All right, Ted,' she said, swinging expertly into the fast lane on Federal Highway, 'what's this all about?'

'What's what all about?'

'Your mania. You haven't stopped bubbling for a minute.'

'Why shouldn't I bubble? I'm with a beautiful woman – that's a lovely gown, by the way – and it's New Year's Eve, and we're going out to celebrate.'

She thawed a little. 'You're sweet to say so, but you're a dreadful liar, Ted. Really incompetent. It's got something to do with work, hasn't it?'

'Well . . . maybe.'

She was silent a few moments, thinking, and busy turning east onto Ocean Park Boulevard. Then . . .

'The case of Lucy B,' she said definitely.

'You're so smart,' he said. 'You're so damned smart, it scares me.'

'Tell me about it.'

'Later,' he said. 'Let's have a nice, relaxed dinner. We won't talk shop. Then, after, instead of going on to some other place, I'd like to go home, to my apartment. There's something I want you to hear. All right?'

'Fine,' she said agreeably. 'We've got all that wine and two bottles of champagne. That should see us into the new year.'

It was a cool night, but Levin wanted to sit outside, on the Waterway. Dr Scotsby, wrapping her cashmere shawl around her bony shoulders, assured him she wouldn't be cold. So that's where they sat, a few feet from the water, watching the boats go by and hearing the raucous cries and drunken laughter of the boaters.

Mary ordered, because she was so much better at it than he was. After all those appetizers, she decided to keep the dinner simple: a rack of lamb and a shared Caesar salad. And absolutely nothing else. Except a bottle of a tingly California Chardonnay and, with their espresso, a dark, heavy, thick rum on the rocks.

During their leisurely meal, never once did they talk of their work. But the conversation never flagged. Mostly they discussed marriage. Levin had proposed, not several

307

times, but continually. Scotsby believed that he'd be better off with a full-time housekeeper.

This was an argument that had been going on almost since they met. Neither tired of it; both enjoyed it. They knew it was an intimate link between them. It brought them closer than most married couples they knew – this ceaseless, loving, chivying.

'You'd tire of me,' she told him. 'Eventually.'

'Never,' he vowed.

'Oh yes. And then you'd want a creamer in a string bikini. The kind Al Wollman goes for.'

'God forbid!'

'I don't know what you see in me,' she said honestly.

'I do,' he said.

And in the flickering candlelight, she was not an unattractive woman. Quirkily appealing. The kind glow eased her angles and corners and edges. The mousy brown hair took on a sheen; the pale, freckled skin a gloss.

In that soft illumination, all the sharpness of her face and figure was dulled. She seemed very desirable to him at that moment. He wanted her to sleep over that night, and he told her so.

'We'll see,' she said, giving him a dozy smile.

They got back to his apartment without misadventure, which surprised them. They were both conscious of functioning in a not totally rational manner or mood. The wine, no doubt.

All the appetizers on the dining table were congealing and browning.

'See?' Levin said. 'No roaches.'

They capped everything and jammed it all into the refrigerator. They decided a glass of cold champagne would be proper. Mary Scotsby opened the bottle – Levin was hopeless with anything more complicated than a screw-top – and poured into two handsome crystal flutes she had given him for his birthday.

She raised her glass. 'Happy New Year, Ted.'

'Happy New Year, Mary,' he responded, gulping, not sipping.

'Now then,' she said briskly, all business. 'What is it you want me to hear?'

Suddenly his confidence and enthusiasm were gone. Doubt flooded in. He thought miserably that it was a very frail reed indeed that he had clung to. It was really ridiculous. Dr Mary Scotsby would give him one of her twisted, ironic glances and think him an idiot.

'It's probably nothing,' he mumbled.

'If I think so,' she said, 'I'll tell you. But at least give me the chance to judge.'

'Well . . . all right,' he said. 'It's just a tape I put together. Excerpts from several of the Lucy B interviews.'

'Let's hear it.'

'You sit here, in the armchair. I'll put the champagne on the floor . . . here. You help yourself whenever you like.'

'Fine.'

'Would you like to take your shoes off? If you'd –'

'Ted!' she exploded. 'Will you please stop fucking around and play the goddamned tape?'

'What? Yes. Of course. Right now. I'll play it this minute. Here we go . . .'

His voice was the first to come on. Pontifical. The self-important tones of a television newscaster.

'The first excerpt,' he said, 'is from the initial interview with Mr and Mrs B. Tape LB-One.'

Grace: 'Well, for the past three years, about, since she was five, she – Ronnie, wouldn't you say it's been for the past three years?'

Ronald: 'Maybe longer. Maybe since she was four.'

Grace: 'Doctor, she has become increasingly, uh, affectionate. Hugging and kissing all the time. Hanging on to people. She's become very, uh, physical, and is always touching and stroking. Sometimes in a vulgar way.'

Then Dr Levin came on again, in his announcer's voice:

309

'The second excerpt is from tape LB-Three: an interview with Grace B.'

Levin: 'Does she wet the bed?'

Grace: 'No. Not now. She did in the past.'

Levin: 'When was this? At what age?'

Grace: 'Up to about three or four years ago. Then she wet the bed regularly.'

Levin: 'How often?'

Grace: 'Perhaps two or three times a week.'

Levin: 'But not recently?'

Grace: 'No.'

Levin: 'Not at all?'

Grace: 'No.'

Levin: 'It simply stopped?'

Grace: 'Yes.'

'The following,' Dr Levin's voice announced hollowly, 'is from tape LB-Four. Subject: Ronald B.'

Levin: 'Has your wife always had a lack of interest in sexual relations?'

Ronald: 'God, no! She used to be too much for me.'

Levin: 'So her, uh, coolness is a recent development?'

Ronald: 'Fairly recent.'

Levin: 'How recent?'

Ronald: 'Say about, oh, three or four years.'

Dr Levin introduced the next segment: 'From tape LB-Six, an interview with Lucy B.'

Lucy: 'Well . . . you see . . . my mother isn't my real mother. My real mother is dead. She was killed dead in a tragic car accident.'

Levin: 'When did this happen, Lucy?'

Lucy: 'A long time ago.'

Levin: 'How long?'

Lucy: 'Oh, maybe five years ago.'

'And now,' Dr Theodore Levin said, 'one short speech from tape LB-Seven. The subject, Wayne B, twelve years old.'

Wayne: 'Son of a bitch. You miserable shit. I haven't cried since I was eight. You lousy bastard.'

'The final excerpt,' Dr Levin said, 'is from tape LB-Eight, a session with Grace B.'

Levin: '. . . to which church do you belong?'

Grace: 'Officially, I am a Presbyterian.'

Levin: 'Officially?'

Grace: 'That was my parents' church. I am a registered member, and still attend faithfully. However, I have become interested in other beliefs and faiths, and sometimes attend their meetings as well.'

Levin: 'I see. And you have been doing this for how long?'

Grace: 'Doing what?'

Levin: 'Your interest in other beliefs and faiths outside the Presbyterian Church – when did this begin?'

Grace: 'Oh . . . perhaps four or five years ago.'

Then Dr Levin reached over and switched off the tape deck. He sat back, made a tent of his hands, stared at Dr Mary Scotsby over his fingertips.

'That's it,' he said, 'for the moment. What do you think?'

She rose suddenly. 'I've got to go to the bathroom. Be right back.'

While she was gone, he relighted his dead cigar and filled their glasses with more champagne. She returned by way of the dining room, picking up her beaded purse. She fished for a cigarette, lighted it. Then she donned her wire-rimmed glasses and looked closely at Levin.

'Ted, let me make certain we're on the same wavelength. You're predicating some family cataclysm, a traumatic experience, that affected parents and children alike – something that happened about four years ago?'

'Has to be,' he said, nodding. 'Four or five years ago. Everyone is very vague about the exact date. The event has been pushed away; no one wants to remember it. But it happened.'

'It couldn't be coincidence,' she said, half-statement, half-question.

'No,' he said, 'I don't think so. Not with six references to the same time frame. That strains the limits of coincidence.'

Dr Mary Scotsby sipped her champagne, regarding Levin thoughtfully over the rim of the glass.

'Very clever, Ted,' she said, 'to pick that up.'

'I concur,' he said, smiling.

'A sexual episode?' she suggested. 'Witnessed by Lucy?'

'I believe so,' he said. 'Possibly, probably in her own home, in her parents' bedroom. But not, I would guess, between her parents. Did you listen to the tape with Lucy on which she spins a fantasy of what she'd like to do with me if her father was absent?'

'I heard it.'

'That was adult dialogue she used. Very realistic. Very believable. I think she was repeating speeches she overheard, an event she actually witnessed.'

'Between whom?'

'Did you listen to the tape of my last session with the father?'

'No, I haven't gotten to that one yet.'

'I want to run one section for you now. It'll just take a few minutes.'

He found tape LB-Eleven, raced it through his portable recorder at double speed, then found the section he wanted. He played back to Dr Mary Scotsby the 'tube of meat' speech by Ronald Bending.

When it was over, she laughed softly.

'An honest man,' she said. 'Apparently an habitual womanizer.'

'Yes,' Levin agreed. 'Elsewhere on that tape he denies indignantly that he ever had an extracurricular affair in his own home. But I think we can take that with a grain of salt. He's a man who admits to lusting after young creamers on the beach, wanting to screw them right there on the sand.'

She thought a moment, frowning. 'So Ronald brings one of his creamers home?'

'Or it's a party,' Levin suggested. 'Everyone a little drunk. Inhibitions relaxed. Ronald takes one of the female guests up to the master bedroom. Lucy's bedroom is next to it. Grace told me that; it's on tape. And Ronald and the female guest get it off while Lucy listens at the adjoining wall or watches through a keyhole. Whatever.'

'And hears or sees the woman doing to her father what she, Lucy, has been doing ever since?'

'What she *wants* to do. To her father. All the other men have been father-surrogates.'

Mary Scotsby was troubled. 'It's awfully neat, Ted.'

'It covers all bases,' he argued. 'Assuming the entire family became aware of what had happened: the father involved in a sexual experience with a strange woman in mommy and daddy's bedroom. It would account for Lucy's subsequent behavior, for Grace seeking alternative forms of spiritual help, for Wayne's never crying and becoming a juvenile misanthrope. Harry, the younger son, was only one year old at the time, and probably has no subconscious recall. Still, I believe it possible that he, too, has been affected by the cold climate of indifference between his parents that resulted from that episode.'

'An elegant solution,' she admitted.

'Then what bothers you?' he demanded.

'Surely Ronald had been guilty of adultery before? I mean, it didn't start with that single event four years ago.'

'That's correct. He admits he has been unfaithful since the day he was married. But the special psychic injury to wife and children was caused by the place he selected for this particular seduction: the home, the sacred place.'

'Mmm,' she said. 'You may be right.'

He rose to empty the bottle of champagne into her glass. He was on his way to the kitchen to get the second bottle when they heard the sudden honking of horns, a tooting of boat whistles. A string of firecrackers popped somewhere outside. They turned to look at each other.

'It's midnight,' she said. 'Happy New Year, Ted.'

Still clasping the empty bottle, he strode to her. She rose from her chair to embrace him.

'Happy New Year, dear,' he said. 'Marry me?'

'No,' she said, 'but I would like to fuck.'

They took the new bottle into the bedroom. The wine wasn't cold enough, so they poured it over ice cubes; they didn't care.

They undressed slowly, jabbering about what they might do on New Year's Day: a picnic, a drive to the Keys, or just a lazy, domestic day with the Sunday papers, nibbling on all those leftover appetizers.

Their lovemaking always started with theatre: simulated protests and cries of affright from both. What a couple! He so plump and hairy, she so spare and freckled. Their disparity amused them both. They really couldn't take themselves together seriously. But there they were. They shared raunchy laughter.

'Do you know,' she said, 'I've never told anyone but my analyst this, but one of the reasons, the *real* reason, I wanted to be a psychiatrist was because I was so sexually frustrated and inexperienced. I wanted to know all about it, and I thought that by listening to sex fiends confess, I could pick up some good tips.'

'And did you?' he asked.

'Oh yes. How to masturbate while burning down a warehouse. How to pack a woman's vagina with Hershey Kisses.'

'You remove the foil first?'

'It's better that way,' she said solemnly, and they groaned and hugged.

In bed, her cold, precise, masterful manner dissolved, and she flung her bony, awkward body about like a wanton. The pale, shiny skin became feverish, hard breasts melted. She just opened up.

314

'I become a puddle,' she once admitted.

He liked to watch her during orgasm. Something wonderful and frightening happened. Her flesh seemed to become translucent, a skeleton shone through. He imagined she became an essence, teeth bared, eyes glittering. She spoke in tongues. He thought it was almost a religious excitation.

Afterward, she had another glass of champagne and announced grumpily that she wished to sleep awhile. He turned obediently onto his side, and she clove to his back, fitting like a spoon. Her free hand held his testicles in long, cool, splintery fingers.

After a while he heard her breathing steady and deepen, and knew she slept. But he was awake, thinking back on the case of Lucy B, testing his hypothesis, pondering what he might do to prove it out.

Perhaps it was all that rich food, all that good wine, but postcoital depression engulfed him. He felt like weeping for himself, for Mary Scotsby, and especially for little Lucy B, that poor, wild child.

So all of us, he thought dumbly, creatures of chance and accident, victims of fears we cannot name, driven by needs we cannot understand, go running and falling through life, crying with pain and hooting with laughter. We are all children of the dark, making up the stories of our lives.

PART V

1

Early in January, there was a week when clouds dissolved, the sky seemed chiseled, and the sun was a perfect round sliced from lemon paper and stuck up there. It looked like a Matisse cutout, Turk Bending said.

The air was so pure and lucid that Lighthouse Point never shimmered, and hovering gulls were painted on the blue. The days were warm enough for beaching, and people spoke of 'one-blanket nights.' Everyone knew it wouldn't last, but it was glorious while it did.

There were some small Portuguese men-o'-war on the sand, and a lot of tar gobbets. But swimmers went in anyway, the skin divers, too, and, when a swell was running, the surfers. The Goodyear blimp was up almost every day, yawing against the wind.

The new year brought a new sport: 'baling.' Drug-running 'mother ships' came up that stretch of coast from Central America. At a designated drop-off point (or when pursued by the Coast Guard), they threw overboard their waterproofed bales of contraband.

Most of the marijuana was picked up by drugrunners in power boats, coming out from Florida inlets. But some of the bales were missed and came bobbing in on the tide. Hence 'baling.' Kids went out in Hobie Cats and small outboards, armed with boathooks, eager for salvage. Sometimes they succeeded.

During that week when the weather was exactly as advertised in travel brochures, Teresa Empt and Edward Holloway had only a single tryst in the gazebo. This was not

319

due to lack of interest on his part, but Teresa was cruising.

She had discovered a whole new world in south Florida, a world of wealthy, mature women and impecunious and virile young men. Some of the latter worked as lifeguards, dance instructors, hairdressers, or bartenders. But many were simply beach bums, waiting for the next patroness to appear.

Teresa had her hard eye on a bagboy at a local supermarket. He was about five years older than Eddie Holloway but had many of the same physical attributes: long, golden hair, soft, bronzed skin, a tall and willowy body. But he had more presence and wit than Eddie.

The bagboy's name was Mike. He frequently helped Teresa out to the parking lot with her shopping cart. He accepted her generous tips with gratitude, a brilliant smile (like sugar cubes, those teeth), and a fervent wish that she might have a nice day. She was certain there was something doing there.

But she was not yet ready to make her move. So she agreed to meet Eddie in the gazebo, though his greed was becoming increasingly overt. They met, as usual, shortly after 9:00 P.M., both of them still unaware of the silent watcher.

Eddie lost no time in making his pitch. He said that Tony Sanchez had several potential buyers for the Hobie Cat. He figured Tony might take eight hundred cash if the deal could be closed immediately.

'And baling!' Eddie said enthusiastically. 'If I had that ol' cat right now, I could go baling. I know a guy, he picked up fifty pounds of the stuff last week. He's making a fortune peddling it all over school.'

'Uh-huh,' Teresa Empt said.

'Look,' Eddie said, hurt, 'I'm not trying to con you. If you're not interested, just tell me. I'll find the money somewhere else.'

'Of course I'm interested,' she said, stroking his cheek tenderly. 'I want you to be happy, Eddie. You know that.'

'Well, yeah, sure,' he said grudgingly. 'But, boy, some-times you sure don't act like it. I mean, the money's not all that important to you – is it?'

'Money is always important,' she said, laughing lightly. 'You don't just throw it away. You try to make a wise investment.'

'Well, this would be. You said you loved me. I mean, I heard you say it – right? So eight hundred doesn't seem such a big deal to me if you really love me.'

'Oh Eddie,' she said softly, 'there are so many kinds of love.'

She was wearing a wraparound skirt, nothing under-neath, and she wanted him to play with her. She took his hand and placed it in position.

'You be nice to me,' she said, giggling, 'and I'll be nice to you.'

He wasn't entirely happy with that vague bargain, she could tell, but he wasn't ready to climb to his feet and stalk indignantly away.

'You know,' she said thoughtfully, 'I met a woman the other day who's had several lovers. She claims she says to all of them: "Get it up or get out." Isn't that funny, Eddie?'

'Yeah,' he said mournfully, 'funny.' And he redoubled his efforts.

After a while, when they were both naked from the waist down, she became curious at just how far his avarice would take him. So she gave him orders and found that it took him very far indeed.

Do this, Eddie, she told him, or do that. And, after an initial hesitation, he complied. This complete sexual mas-tery was a new experience. Part of her could observe the process objectively, intrigued, and part was excited and went winging. Do this, Eddie. Do that.

Eventually, she admitted, it was not totally satisfying. She really did not want to suggest or command. She longed for a demon lover who might play her cello-shaped body like a maestro.

Meanwhile, she drove Eddie Holloway through his paces, deriving a distant, once-removed pleasure, but not really involved. So when she threaded him into her, and lurched to meet his frantic humping, she thought fondly of Mike, the bagboy, and was reasonably content.

After, when they were lying side by side, temporarily slaked, they lighted a joint and smoked in silence for a while. Then he started maundering about that stupid boat again, and she decided she was bored. She began to dress.

'Got to run,' she said breezily. 'My dear hubby will be coming home soon, wondering where I am.'

'There's almost half a joint left,' he said, almost angrily.

'You finish it, Eddie.'

'Will I see you again?'

'Of course,' she said, patting his shoulder. 'We'll get together and talk about that wonderful boat of yours.'

'Listen,' he said hoarsely, 'you really think you can come up with the loot? I mean, if not, tell me now so I can make, uh, other arrangements.'

'We'll talk about it, Eddie. Next time.'

He propped himself on his elbow, watched her stride away from him, into the darkness. Bitch! Still, he had to admit, she was a lot of woman. A great body for an old lady.

He was lying there, pulling in what was left of the joint, when Wayne Bending came out of the night and stood there, looking down at him.

'Where the hell did you come from?' Eddie demanded.

'Just taking a walk,' Wayne said in a low voice.

'Bull-*shit*!' Eddie said. 'You were watching us, I bet.'

Wayne sat down alongside him, took the roach from his fingers, and dragged on it.

'Give it up, my main man,' he said to Eddie. 'She's never going to come up with the bucks for the boat.'

'Sure she will,' Eddie said confidently. 'Just a question of time. I'm working on her. I've got her hooked.'

Wayne passed the roach back to Eddie. He sat there, hugging his knees.

'You're the one who's hooked,' he said. 'She's playing you.'

'You *have* been watching us,' Eddie Holloway said. 'Jesus Christ!'

'Please,' Wayne said, 'forget about her.'

'It was your idea, dumbo.'

'I know,' Wayne said miserably. 'I was wrong. It didn't work out. Let's forget it.'

'No way,' Eddie Holloway said. 'She's good for some bucks; I know it.'

Wayne bent over him. 'She's getting what she wants, but you're not. Can't you see that? What about us?'

'Well . . .' Eddie said lazily, 'what about us?'

'I thought we, uh, had something going.'

'Shit, that was just for kicks.'

Wayne looked at him. 'That's all?'

'Sure. You know. We were both stoned and didn't know what we were doing. Right? You tell anyone and I'll kick your ass.'

'You bastard!' Wayne cried, and tried to punch the other boy in the groin.

Eddie turned in time to take the fist onto his hip. Both scrambled to their feet. Faced. Trembling.

'Cocksucker!'

'Motherfucker!'

They came together in a flurry. Arms swinging. Legs pumping. They struck. Pulled away. Kicked. Embraced. Teeth shining. Eyes gleaming. Breath snorted. They danced about. Punching. Punching.

'Shiteater!'

'Pussylicker!'

Fury took them. They steamed, ready to kill. They grappled close, reaching for eyes and gonads. Grunting. Straining. Jerking out with elbows and knees.

Edward Holloway, taller, heavier, older, prevailed. He

323

bore the younger boy down, butted his nose with his forehead. He hammered Wayne's head into the hard-packed sand. He slammed fist after fist.

'Asshole,' he kept grunting. 'Fucking asshole.'

When, finally, Wayne Bending lay still, Eddie Holloway climbed groggily to his feet. He stood swaying, looking down at his crumpled foe. He kicked him in the ribs.

'Fucking asshole,' he muttered again, and staggered away.

The moon was there, hanging, and when Wayne Bending opened his puffed eyes, he thought he was looking at a window, a lamp in a window. Then he focused, saw the latticed roof of the gazebo. He felt his pain.

He lay absolutely still, wondering if it was possible to will yourself to die. It never occurred to him that he might be of finer stuff than the boy who had hammered him down. All he knew was that he had been defeated. Not him, physically, but his noble love.

What a splendid thing to die. Get out of it. Just dissolve into nothingness. An end to all the finkery and betrayal. Drift away and be gone. People would weep. His parents. Brother and sister. For a while. Then the world would be as if he had never been. No care or attention.

A snake crawled down his lip; he became aware that his nose was leaking. He sat up shakily, drew the back of his hand across his face. Stared at the bloody smear. So much for love and fidelity. It all ended in a bloody smear.

He would have wept if he let himself go. But he would not. He bit into his tongue, clenched his fists, tightened muscles, and did not cry. It was a small win, but important.

After a while he crawled to his feet, rose cautiously, tried to stretch his stinging body. He looked up and around. Nothing had changed. The moon still sailed. The sky wen on forever. A wind blew from nowhere to nowhere.

He shambled homeward, trying to brush himself off. His nose had stopped dripping blood, but there were tender patches on his cheekbones, jaw, ribs. His balls ached dully, but he supposed that would go away. It didn't matter.

Nothing mattered.

2

On a drizzly day, the sky as colorless as an elephant hide, Lloyd Craner picked up Gertrude Empt and proposed they take a ride in his ancient Buick.

'Why not?' she said chirpily. 'Maybe we can take a closer look at those motel units where you're planning to get in my bloomers.'

It was the first time she had displayed any real interest, and he was careful not to show surprise or delight.

, 'Fine,' he said casually. 'We'll look the place over, and then perhaps we'll drive down A1A and have lunch at the Sea Watch.'

'As long as you're paying,' she said.

They drove slowly south, windshield wipers going and headlights on because it was a gloomy, misty day, the grainy sky pressing down.

'Remember the other day?' she said. 'We were talking about the kids?'

'I remember,' he said.

'They got their own lives to live,' she said, 'and they can go their own way; I don't care. But sometimes I feel sorry for them.'

'Oh? Why is that?'

'Look at your grandchildren. And the Bendings' kids. They don't seem to be getting a hell of a lot out of life. Oh shit, I know all kids feel miserable at times. I did. But these kids seem to be missing a whole part of life.'

'Innocence,' he said. 'They have no innocence, the best part of being young. They seem to have been born old.'

'If you say so,' she said. 'You're the perfesser. All I know is that they run around half-naked, smoking their muggles, and if they haven't made out by the time they're ten, they figure something's wrong with them. You know something? I'm glad I'm old. I wouldn't want to be a kid today. Too much of a hassle.'

The motel unit they inspected was the one-bedroom apartment with a kitchen large enough for a dinette set. The ex-New Jersey cop, or his wife, obviously had a passion for pink.

'You could lose a flamingo in here,' Gertrude Empt observed.

The potbellied owner showed them around with pride.

'All your modern conveniences,' he said. 'Your toaster, your mixer. Your vacuum cleaner. Your twin beds with Sealy Posturepedic mattresses and box springs. Your television set with remote control. Your radio in the bedroom. Alarm, naturally, with Snooz-Control.'

'And how much is this palace?' Gertrude asked.

'Four-fifty a month,' potbelly said, 'on an annual basis. A two-year lease. That includes use of the pool, shuffleboard court, patio, outside shower, and so forth. You pay Florida Power and Light, and Southern Bell. Take your time, folks. Look around. I gotta run now. Just slam the door when you leave. You won't find a better buy in south Florida, that's for sure.'

They wandered about, opening cupboard drawers, inspecting kitchen cabinets. The apartment was completely furnished with linens and cooking equipment and implements.

'All we'd have to bring are our toothbrushes,' Craner said.

'Not much closet space,' Gertrude said.

'I don't have all that many clothes. Do you?'

'No,' she said shortly.

She bounced up and down on one of the beds.

'Not bad,' she admitted. 'Firm. The way I like it.'

327

'Nice bathroom,' he offered. 'At least it's got a tub.

'You think he'd let us redecorate?' she said. 'Get rid of this pukey pink? Do this place in white, and it'd look twice as big.'

'I'm sure he would,' the professor said, 'if we paid for the painting.'

He sat down on the bed alongside her. He picked up her worn hand. She let him hold it.

'Well?' he said.

She sighed. 'It's a big decision.'

'Not so big,' he said gently. 'What's the worst thing that could happen? It doesn't work out. You could always go back to your son's home.'

'Not me,' she said. 'Once I cut loose, I'm *loose*.'

'I'd try to make it work,' he said. 'I promise you that. I suppose we're both a little old to be talking about love and undying passion. But I do have a real affection for you, Gertrude, and I hope you feel the same way about me. Do you?'

'I guess,' she said.

'Well then,' he said. 'With a little effort and a few laughs, I think we could make it work.'

'Ah shit,' she said, troubled. 'I just don't know.'

'Let's go have some lunch,' he suggested.

Outside, they took a closer look at the grounds. In that mournful drizzle, everything seemed a bit bedraggled. But there was no denying that the pool was clean, shuffleboard court freshly painted, lawn trimmed, palm trees cropped.

'It's nice,' she allowed. 'Small but nice.'

'Like us,' he said.

'Yeah,' she said, laughing wryly. 'Just like us.'

In the restaurant, they sat close to big picture windows, looking out onto a deserted beach, smoky sea beyond. The sky had brightened a little; there was a sun up there somewhere. But still the mist fell.

' ". . . droppeth as the gentle rain from heaven," ' Lloyd Craner said.

Gertrude said: 'I'll bet that's from Shakespeare.'

'You're exactly right,' he said, smiling. '*The Merchant of Venice*. How would you like a Gibson straight up?'

'Is that from Shakespeare, too?'

'No,' he said, laughing, 'that's from me.'

'Grand,' she said, 'but make it on the rocks.'

They had a second drink, and ordered hamburgers and a salad. Meanwhile, they looked out at the scrimmed scene. It was elegiac, the professor thought. That sad, dripping curtain. And on the wet sand, the restaurant's props: splintered dinghy, anchor, bleached this and that. All rust, wear, age.

They ate their meal in silence, smiling. Finally, when it came time for black coffee and fresh strawberries, he looked at her closely and said, 'You want to tell me something?'

'I don't know . . . It's been so long since I've felt anything for a man, it's like I've got to learn all over again how to do it. I just wondered if you thought it was possible. Between us, I mean.'

He leaned stiffly across the table to stare into her eyes. 'Yes, I think it's possible. No guarantee, but I think it's possible.'

Then he straightened back into his chair. 'And now,' he said, 'how about a brandy?'

'You sure know the way to a girl's heart,' she said.

3

Dr Theodore Levin, looking over his appointments for the day, saw he had Mrs Grace Bending scheduled for 3:00 P.M. He paused, stared upward at the paper stars pasted on his office ceiling.

It was amazing how often familiarity bred respect. At first meeting, he had thought her a stiffish woman. Subsequent sessions had mellowed that judgment. He saw her now as softer, more vulnerable. Her search for spiritual guidance had become touching.

What *does* a wife do who is linked to a sexual profligate? Burdened by children disturbed by their parents' hostility? Ape her husband, Levin thought: become as lickerish as he. Or seek divorce. Or the path Grace Bending had apparently taken: the comfort of Jesus and hope of redemption.

Or, he thought with some bemusement, take a hatchet to her husband's skull.

He warned himself, not for the first time, of the dangers of labeling. His discipline, like all others, had its special vocabulary. That was necessary. But a hazard lay in categorizing. In his field, the variations were infinite; there was no neat filing system. Each case different, each case unique.

He put his cigar aside and was brushing ashes from his lapels when he rose to greet Mrs Bending promptly at 3:00 P.M.

He had little awareness of fashion (male or female), but it seemed to him there had been a 'feminization' in Mrs

Bending's dress since the initial interview. Just as her manner and response to him had thawed, so had her costumes become gentler and softer.

Today she was wearing a flowered shirtwaist dress of some gossamer stuff that flowed. Her good legs were bare, feet in a cobweb of straps. Her long hair flung free, and there was makeup and vitality he had never noted before. She seemed especially alive to him, alert and eager.

'Well, now,' he said with his smile of heavy benignity, 'have there been any developments? Any new incidents involving Lucy?'

'None at all, doctor,' she said. 'I really think her, uh, talks with you have done her the world of good.'

He shifted in his swivel chair uncomfortably. 'I would like to take credit for it, Mrs Bending, but in all honesty I cannot.'

'Well, my goodness, she hasn't misbehaved since she started seeing you.'

He sighed. 'She will. Eventually. I have not yet been able to establish the cause of her, ah, aberrance. Until we do that, I cannot promise any improvement. You must not be too shocked if more incidents do occur. Lucy is a very disturbed child, and a long way from adjustment.'

And that, he thought morosely, was the bullshit double-talk you gave the parents of nutty kids. What did 'disturbed' mean? Or 'adjustment'? It sounded calm and authoritative. What it came down to was a poor, possessed child driven by furies she (and he) could not understand.

'But surely, doctor,' Grace Bending said, twisting her wedding band nervously, 'you've made *some* progress?'

'Perhaps,' he said noncommittally. 'Mrs Bending, what happened to your family four or five years ago?'

He threw it at her that fast, hoping to elicit a spontaneous reaction. He thought he saw her stiffen, but he could not be sure.

'Four or five years ago?' she said. 'I don't understand.'

Then he was certain she was stalling, framing her reply.

'Four or five years ago,' he repeated patiently. 'Probably in your own home. An incident which Lucy witnessed, or of which she was aware, that may have triggered her deviant behavior.'

She gazed fixedly at a point over his head. She went through all the expressions of thoughtful consideration: head cocked, features composed in frowning intensity.

'I don't remember any incident like that,' she said. 'My goodness, Lucy couldn't have been more than three or four at that time. She wouldn't remember anything.'

'Uh-huh,' he said.

He thought about the vagaries of memory. His own earliest recollection was of being given a cup of warmed milk with a blob of butter in it. He could not recall where that happened, or how old he was – four or five he guessed – but he could still see that cup of golden milk clearly, and taste it.

Most people, he knew, could not consciously recollect anything that had happened prior to their fifth year of life. That did not mean the memories were not there, hidden, encrusted. Ask Papa Freud.

But now, faced with Mrs Bending's obduracy, he decided on another approach.

'You told me,' he said, 'that you are aware that your husband has been unfaithful to you on several occasions.'

Her relaxation at this change of subject was obvious.

'Many,' she said. 'Many occasions.'

'I don't wish to probe into matters that give you pain, but there are things I need to know. You are certain of your husband's infidelity?'

'Yes.'

'Have you any idea where these incidents have occurred?'

'Where?' she said wildly. 'Where? Why, all over, I

suppose. Hotels, motels. In his car. In his office. Any-place.'

He paused a moment, staring at her.

'In your own home?' he asked.

Her reaction was more than he expected. She started, flushed, glanced about frantically as if seeking an escape.

'Uh . . .' she said. 'Uh . . . Why do you ask that?'

'Was your husband unfaithful to you in your own home?' he persisted.

'No,' she said in a low voice, hanging her head. 'No. Not to my knowledge.'

He wondered why she insisted on defending her husband, and decided to come at her from a third direction, trying to pry from her an acknowledgment of her spouse's guilt.

'Mrs Bending, during our first interview, your husband told me of an incident that occurred during a party in your home. He caught Lucy in the kitchen with one of your friends. A male friend. He described in graphic detail exactly what Lucy was doing to this man. Do you recall that?'

'I remember Ronnie telling you, yes. But I told you, I didn't actually witness it.'

'But you believe such an incident occurred?'

'Yes.'

'And when, exactly, did this happen?'

'Last Labor Day. We had a cookout.'

'But surely there had been similar incidents before that?'

'Yes, but none so – so – so ugly.'

Levin pondered a moment. He remembered what a professor had once told him. 'There are no wrong answers; just wrong questions.'

'Mrs Bending, this man involved with Lucy in the kitchen incident, is he still considered a friend by you and your husband?'

'Well, he was drunk, you see. He didn't know what was –'

'Is he still considered a friend, Mrs Bending?'

'He still visits at our house, yes.'

'Do you know of any other incidents between Lucy and this particular man?'

'No.'

'Now I want you to think carefully and try to remember: When did you first become aware that Lucy's behavior was abnormal?'

'Oh,' she said vaguely, 'maybe four years ago. Around then.'

'And was there one particular episode that convinced you that she might need help?'

'Well . . . Ronnie had some men over, and they were sitting on the terrace having a few drinks. I was in the kitchen making sandwiches. Lucy was supposed to be in bed hours ago. But she suddenly walked out onto the terrace. She had taken all her clothes off.'

'I see. She was about four years old at the time?'

'About. Maybe a little older.'

'And what happened then?'

'All the men laughed. And my husband came back to the kitchen to get me to put Lucy back to bed.'

'You spanked her?'

'No, but I tried to explain to her that young ladies didn't do things like that.'

'But the incident obviously upset you?'

'Yes. It was the first time she had done anything like that.'

'Tell me, Mrs Bending,' Levin said idly, not really knowing where he was going, but wanting to keep her talking, 'was one of the men on the terrace the man with whom Lucy was, ah, involved with last Labor Day in your kitchen?'

She paused.

'Mrs Bending?'

'Yes,' she said finally. 'He was there.'

'If this happened four years ago – Lucy walking naked

into a party of men – why did you wait so long before seeking professional help for the child?'

She looked down at her hands, gripped so tightly that knuckles jutted. 'We thought she'd outgrow it. That it was just a phase.'

She looked at him helplessly, and he nodded in what he hoped was a sympathetic manner. That part of her story he could believe. What parents wanted to acknowledge they were incapable of curing their children's woes?

'I gather,' he said, 'that it was your decision to seek help.'

She lifted her chin, looked at him defiantly. 'Yes, I made up my mind and talked Ronnie into it. We should have done it years ago.'

The child was ready, Levin reflected sadly, but you weren't.

'I asked you, Mrs Bending, if Lucy has a crush on one particular man or woman. You denied it. From what Lucy has told me, it seems that you're correct. But I'd like to talk about this man, the family friend, who was on the terrace when Lucy appeared naked and who later was the object of her –'

'Why do you keep coming back to him?' she said testily. 'My goodness, he's got nothing to do with it. He's just a man.'

Dr Levin was surprised by the heat of her response. He did not think his query merited that much spleen.

'Mrs Bending, I'm just trying to determine if there may be a special relationship between Lucy and this man.'

'Well, there isn't,' she said sharply. 'He isn't the only one. She makes up to other men, too. It's not just him.'

Levin let it go for the moment. Sometimes it paid to tell the interviewee baldly that he or she was lying. He didn't feel that such a ploy would be productive in this case.

He came at her from still another direction, determined to prove his hypothesis of the traumatic incident, the psychic wound that had generated Lucy's deviance.

335

'Mrs Bending, about the same time as the initial happening – Lucy exhibiting herself naked to the men on the terrace – you began to investigate other religious beliefs and faiths. Isn't that true?'

She looked genuinely bewildered. But Levin could not believe that she had not, consciously, made the connection.

'About the same time,' she admitted. 'But I don't see what one thing has to do with the other.'

'Let's talk about it,' he said gently. 'Your daughter behaves in a manner that upsets you. In a manner you consider, ah, immoral. Did you feel that her conduct was a reflection on your worth as a mother? Did you think that her failure was *your* failure?'

'I was worried,' she said.

'Of course you were worried. A very normal, understandable reaction. But instead of seeking help for Lucy, you sought help for yourself. Spiritual solace to see you through this difficult time. You think that an accurate assessment of how you felt?'

'I don't know,' she said confusedly. 'I just wanted to . . .'

Her voice trailed away.

'Seek forgiveness?' he suggested. 'For not being a proper mother? You were aware that something had happened, was happening, to your daughter. Something that you considered – well, I don't think "evil" is too strong a word. That is the way you felt. And because you believed you had failed to protect your daughter from this evil, you were guilty. And the only way to expiate your guilt was to devote yourself to a strong faith that demanded confession and allegiance to a new spiritual life. Is that close to the truth, Mrs Bending?'

She hung her head.

'Yes,' she said. 'Yes.'

He thought he was almost home now.

'An incident,' he said. 'In the sanctuary of your own home. Involving someone very close, very dear to Lucy. We need not go into details at this time. But your daughter either witnesses it or is aware of it. A trauma that turns her around. She cannot cope with it. She is, after all, a child. And this, uh, accident is a cataclysm to her. It upsets her world. And she begins to act in a manner she may know is wrong, but which she cannot resist. A sexual incident, Mrs Bending? Could it have been that?'

She did not answer.

'Yes!' he said, slapping the desk top with a heavy palm. 'A sexual incident! It reveals to Lucy a whole new world she never guessed existed. New relationships, new sensations. Could such a thing have happened, Mrs Bending?'

She raised her head slowly to stare at him blankly, no expression in her features, no light in her eyes.

'I don't know what you're talking about, doctor. There was no such accident or incident in my home. Something may have happened to Lucy in school or on the beach. Something like what you're suggesting. But she never mentioned anything like that to me.' Then, sharply, eyes suddenly glittering, 'Did Lucy tell you anything like that?'

He looked at her a long moment. 'No,' he said.

'Then you're imagining. All this is just your theory.'

'Yes,' he said softly, 'just my theory.'

He watched as will and resolution flowed back into her. She straightened in the chair. Pushed long hair back from her temples. She pulled her skirt lower over her bare legs.

'I don't believe anything like that happened,' she said severely. 'My husband did not have an affair in our home – if that's what you're thinking. At least, to my knowledge he didn't. Nothing happened that suddenly made Lucy start acting the way she does. I'm afraid you're wrong, doctor.'

'I may be,' he said placidly. 'But we're only at the beginning of Lucy's therapy, are we not, Mrs Bending? We'll have ample opportunity to look into this matter further.'

'If you wish,' she said, once more composed and in control.

'And now,' he said, glancing at his desk clock, 'I see our time is up. Thank you for your cooperation, Mrs Bending.'

4

Empt sat at a scrambled desk in his air-conditioned office. With Ernie Goldman looking over his shoulder, Luther was inspecting a mock-up of the sales carton for the video cassette of *Teenage Honeypots*.

'You checked the size?' he demanded.

'The dimensions are okay,' Goldman said, blinking nervously. 'About an eight-inch leeway all around. But it's a kinda cheesy package, don't you think?'

'Yeah,' Empt said heavily. 'Real schlock. Do they want this one back?'

'The messenger said no. He said Mr Santangelo would call at five o'clock to get your reactions.'

Luther sat staring at the empty cardboard box. It was thin, grayish in hue, with four-color labels pasted top and bottom. The labels had 'X-Rated' in big type, then the title of the cassette, running time, and an illustration of a young girl in a topless bikini eating a banana.

Nowhere on the carton were the names or addresses of performers, director, producer, manufacturer, or distributor.

'Real schlock,' Empt repeated. 'We worked our ass off on that lousy film, and it's going to be marketed in this lousy package? I wish I could show it to Jane Holloway; she'd have some idea on how to dress it up.'

'Why don't you?'

'Yeah, I will. When that bum calls tonight, I'll tell him to hold off until Jane has a chance to see it. You know, Ernie, we could do a better job of packaging than this. Scoville over in Margate could do the box, and What's-his-name in Boca – the printer?'

'Thomas Associates?'

'Yeah, that's the outfit. They do great four-color work on labels. Maybe I'll talk to Santangelo and see if we can get a contract on the packaging. Not only could we do a better job, but we could make a nice coupla bucks – right?'

'Right,' Goldman said.

'Okay,' Luther said. 'I'll take it from here. Anything else, Ernie?'

'Well, uh, yes,' the other man said in his breathless, quavery voice. 'I was wondering if –'

'Jesus Christ!' Empt cried. 'Not another advance?'

'Not a full week,' Goldman said hastily. 'A hundred would help.'

Luther wheeled his swivel chair back and looked up at the man. Ernie was blinking frantically. His complexion was yellower than ever. His shoulders seemed bent lower; his stick body looked ready to snap.

'The sharks again?' Luther asked.

'Uh . . . yeah,' Goldman said. 'Kinda.'

'You're never going to get even,' Empt told him, his raspy voice almost sympathetic. 'You know that, don't you?'

'Sure I will,' Goldman said hopefully. 'One big win.'

'How much you in for?'

'Almost ten. Ten thousand.'

'Good God!' Empt said. 'How come they let you in for so much?'

'Well . . . uh . . . you know . . . I own a car and a house.'

'Yeah,' Empt said with a cruel grin, 'and a wife and three kids. Ever think of them?'

Suddenly Ernie Goldman was weeping, slow tears oozing down his sallow cheeks.

'I don't know what to do,' he said, choking.

'Okay, okay,' Luther Empt said hastily. 'I'll tell Sylvia you can draw a hundred. What's it for? The juice – or a hot tip?'

340

'Groceries,' Goldman said, sniffling. 'It'll all go for groceries.'

'Sure it will,' Empt said, and watched the man shamble from his office. He figured it would take Ernie about two minutes to get on the phone to his bookie and lose the hundred.

He stood, thrust hands into his pockets, wandered to a picture window overlooking a crowded parking lot. He stood staring down at neat rows of brightly colored cars reflecting the noonday sun.

Weaknesses like Ernie's disgusted him. He could not understand how a man could get hooked to the point where he endangered his wife, children, his job, car, home, everything. Maybe even his own life.

It must be a sickness, Empt decided. As fatal as cancer or syphilis. You caught it and that was the end of you. He shivered and crossed his fingers. It was all luck; he knew that. Everything, when you came down to the nitty-gritty, was luck.

He poured himself a belt of scotch at the office bar. He felt depressed, restless, fretful. That lousy package for the cassette. Ernie Goldman's addiction and the thoughts it engendered. He needed a lift.

He went back to his desk, pawed through papers, glanced at his appointment calendar. There was nothing that couldn't wait. Just that call from Rocco Santangelo. But that was five hours away.

He dialed on his outside line. The one that didn't go through the switchboard. He had never visited May during the daylight hours, but suddenly he wanted to see her. He had to see her.

She lifted the phone after the second ring.

'Hello?' A frail voice. So like her. Tentative and hopeful.

'Hi,' he said throatily. 'It's me.'

'Oh daddy!' she said, laughing happily. 'I was just thinking of you and hoping you'd call. I willed it. I concentrated:

341

"Make daddy call, make daddy call." And here you are!'

'Yeah,' he said, thinking what a whacko she was. 'Listen, I can take a few hours off. I got to get back here later this afternoon. For an important call. But I got a few hours. How's about I pick up a pizza and a cold pack and come over for lunch? Okay?'

'Oh yes! Yes, yes, yes!'

'All right. Be there in half an hour or so. Maybe a little longer. What kind of pizza you like?'

'Whatever you say.'

It was almost an hour before he got to May's apartment. It was stifling. She had no air conditioner ('The plants wouldn't like it,' she explained), but he had bought her an enormous electric fan, and that helped a little. But still he took off jacket, tie, and shirt.

He sat in the worn armchair, eating pizza from the big box on the floor. She sat alongside, rising occasionally to fetch him a cold beer. He didn't like the idea of her, with that gimpy leg, getting up and then sitting again on the floor, obviously with difficulty. But she insisted on doing it, so he let her.

While they wolfed the pizza and swilled the beer, she chattered about what she had been doing since he saw her last. He let her run, smiling and nodding, and gradually the knot of unease loosened; once again he felt comfortable and at home.

'I've got to show you a new bikini I bought,' she said breathlessly. 'I'll model it for you. I went all over to find something I liked and that fit just so. You've got to like it, daddy. It's very hard, you know, to get a good fit. I've been going to the beach in the morning for a few hours. Don't you think I'm tan? Well, not tan exactly, but I do have color now, don't I? How long can you stay, daddy?'

'A few hours. Two.'

'Well, then, you'll see. And I take a thermos of iced tea with me, and maybe some seedless grapes, and in the morning tne public beach isn't crowded at all. And yesterday morning, when I was out there, just sunning and swimming, do you know what I thought, daddy?'

He was slopping a wedge of pepperoni pizza, gulping a beer. It took him a moment to ask, 'What? What were you thinking, May?'

'I was thinking that the only reason I could live like that and be so happy was because of my daddy. My own sweet daddy. Because he's so good to me.'

He smiled at her fondly, reflecting that she might have faults, but ingratitude wasn't one of them. And following hard on the heels of that judgment came the thought that hers was whore's talk. But he put that nastiness from his mind.

'Another slice, daddy?' she asked.

'Oh God, no,' he said. 'I've had it. Put the rest in the refrigerator. Maybe you'll want to heat it up later.'

'Will you be able to come over tonight?'

'No.'

'All right,' she said equably. 'Then maybe I'll just freeze what's left and have it for lunch someday.'

'Good idea,' he said heavily. 'Lemme have another beer.'

She popped another beer. She brought it to him. She wiped his lips with a paper napkin. She stroked lightly, lovingly over his stiff, brushy hair. She touched his cheek. She let her palm fall onto his naked shoulders.

She played with the hair on his chest. She pinched gently at the rolls of fat about his waist. She smoothed the heavy muscles of his neck, his back.

And all the time she stared into his eyes with a look that was soft, tender, giving. He didn't know; he just didn't know.

'And now,' she said formally, 'I would like to model my new bikini for you. I hope you'll like it.'

'I'll like it,' he assured her.

She limped into the bathroom, closed the door. He sat lumpishly in front of the electric fan, working on his third beer. Slowly he cooled and dried. The morning's fears and frustrations faded. He felt sparky again and could look around at that jungly apartment with a smile.

She came out of the bathroom, giggling nervously. The new bikini was a little white thing, straps and patches. Hardly more than a G-string and two quarter-moons cupping her small breasts.

She would never be a creamer, no way, and the slivers of cloth made her body seem even younger, more fragile. A delicate plant. A new stem. She turned to show him, the sleek hair swinging across her ribbed, sun-flushed back.

'Baby, it's beautiful,' he said.

'Really? Do you *really* think so?'

'I really do. It's lovely.'

'Look,' she said, reached behind her, unhooked the bra, swung it away. She came close to him, standing between his spread knees. 'See? Here above my titties. See the line? I'm getting a burn. It's just pink now, but I'll be all tan pretty soon.'

'Sure you will,' he said. 'Just take it easy. Don't try to do it all at once.'

He put his beer aside. He put his hands on her hips, where bones lifted the skin. She pressed to him. He stared at those feathery white breasts. Pink eyes. She felt so frail that he thought if he clenched his big hands, he might crumple her.

He leaned forward to lay his cheek onto her cool softness. He felt her stroking his hair. She was murmuring something, but he couldn't hear. She moved away. She took his hand, pulled him. He rose clumsily, followed her to the sofa.

She climbed up, bent onto knees and forearms. Her head was down between her flat palms. He stared at that thin, suppliant back. He reached to comb the glossy hair so it ran like black water along the channel of her spine.

'Please, daddy,' she said in a dozy voice, 'be nice to me.'

She knelt before him, bowed, presenting her buttocks

thrust high. But still it was obeisance. Abject surrender. An offering. He pulled the bottom of her bikini away, worked it off her legs, knees, feet, then tossed it aside. He reached beneath her, felt her.

'Thank you,' she breathed. 'Oh, thank you.'

He played with her slowly, not listening to her baby talk. His satisfaction was so intense he could not comprehend it.

He had a sturdy, practical business mind. He could work a sweet deal or rig a contract. But his brain was not a subtle one; it could not encompass the interchangeability of master and slave.

He only knew that he was experiencing a fervid happiness and, because he was not a creative man, could not bear the ambiguity of his role. So he had to assert what he believed to be his 'real' character.

But when he unbuckled his belt, unzipped, let trousers and undershorts fall to his ankles, he found to his chagrin that his member was as flaccid as uncooked dough. He stared at it with mortification and fear.

May must have sensed his hesitation, for she lifted her head, looked at him over her shoulder. Then she pushed herself up, turned, sat on the edge of the sofa, facing him.

'Let me do it, daddy,' she said gently.

He let her do it. He watched her clever fingers at work, and then her bobbing head. Manhood returned, and with it came a surge of love and gratefulness toward this girl-woman-whore who was making him whole.

When he could no longer endure, he pulled away and spent on her breasts, insensate, following instinct, want, need that he had never felt before and could not understand.

He collapsed alongside her on the couch. When he kissed her, lips glued, he began to sense the depth of his commitment to this maimed child who looked at him with trusting eyes and called him 'Daddy.'

5

William Holloway called his revolver Eric, for reasons he could not determine since, to the best of his memory, he had never known anyone in his life named Eric. But it made it easier when talking to his gun, or talking to himself about his gun.

He recognized well the dangers of a man who drank as much as he did fooling around with a loaded weapon. So he exercised extreme caution when handling the gun, planning his moves carefully in advance and warning himself . . .

'Now you are going to take Eric slowly from the holster.'

'Hold Eric by the grip, keeping your finger out of the trigger guard.'

'Point the muzzle away from you and swing the cylinder out.'

'Unload Eric completely and do not begin cleaning until you are perfectly certain he is clear.'

Then he could begin his weekly chore of dusting, wiping, oiling and, finally, reloading the revolver. It was a job he anticipated, enjoyed, and performed with the same sweet comfort that, as a boy, he had brought to his piano lessons.

He was aware that Jane knew he owned a handgun, and kept it holstered in the drawer of the bedside table. Maria, the Cuban maid, had probably seen it there. Holloway didn't think his daughter, Gloria, knew of it, and he hoped to hell his son didn't.

Friday night dinner was a hurried affair. The children ate and scattered to their friends on the beach. Jane went into the study to sit at the leather-topped desk, inspect a sample carton for the video cassette of *Teenage Honeypots*, and make notes for improvements.

Maria cleaned up, started the dishwasher, and went to her room where she would listen to a Spanish-language radio station and make innumerable phone calls. William Holloway went upstairs to clean Eric, oil it, polish it lovingly, and return it to its soft leather nest.

Then he changed to Bermuda shorts (no undershorts), loafers (no socks), and a bright red Izod shirt (no undershirt). He went slowly downstairs, humming a theme from *The Well-Tempered Clavier*. Jane was on the phone to Luther Empt, telling him what was wrong with the cassette carton. Holloway reflected that his wife never conversed; she told.

He mixed himself a tall beaker of vodka and water with a squeezed lime wedge. He sampled it and added more vodka. Then he wandered onto the terrace, dimly illumined by the muted lamplight coming through the picture window. He stood at the railing, looked up at the night.

It was a jigsaw: black sky and nacreous clouds. Everything was jagged, but everything fitted. Holloway thought his own life was something like that: ridiculously disparate elements that all came together and added up to . . . what?

His entire life had been a series of incongruous incidents and events, over most of which he had no control. He had been pushed and pulled, hauled and shoved. And here he was in south Florida, wearing silly clothes, with a family he didn't know and really, he admitted, didn't want to.

'What a waste!'

'Yes, a waste,' he replied. 'Because you know, in your heart of hearts, that you started out with a great capacity.'

'For what?'

'Love, for starters.'

'Oh-ho! A few weeks ago, drinking in this same spot, you declared you had a great capacity for virtue. Now it's love.'

'Are the two so different?'

'Wise-ass!'

347

Thankfully, he was not speaking aloud to himself when Jane came out onto the terrace and told him she was taking the cassette carton back to Luther Empt and would be gone for a while. He nodded and let her go. Idiocy was engulfing him.

He drank awhile, dreamed awhile, went back inside to mix himself a fresh drink. He kissed the bottle of vodka. 'God bless you,' he said.

The sky seemed lighter when he came back out. The air was warmer, more caressing. It stroked, that air; it whispered. He kicked off his loafers and straggled down to the beach, carrying his slopping beaker. He sat down in the sand, about twenty feet from the surf.

He saw a meandering figure, a boy zigzagging along the strand, kicking at shells, coral rocks, seaweed.

'Wayne?' Holloway called. 'Wayne Bending? Over here.'

Wayne stopped, peered. Then he came slowly. He sat down on the sand alongside.

'Hi, Mr Holloway,' he said in a grumpy voice.

'Hi,' Holloway said. 'Nice night.'

'Yeah, it's okay.'

Holloway looked closer at the lad. 'What happened to your face? A black eye?'

'Nah. Just a bruise. I fell. At school. It's better now.'

'Uh-huh. How you doing, Wayne?'

'At school? Okay.'

'No, I meant what you told me about. You know – this guy and his friend. When I drove you home in the rain . . .'

'Oh,' the youth said. 'That. Well, that's all over, all finished.'

'Sorry to hear it.'

They sat in silence then, Holloway drinking slowly, the lad picking up fists of sand and letting the grains dribble through his fingers.

'Mr Holloway, can I ask you something?'

'Sure.'

348

'Can you lend me some money? Not a lot. Just some. I'll pay you back, really I will.'

'Money for what, Wayne?'

'I want to go away. I want to get out of here.'

Holloway drew a deep breath. The kid was an open heart, doomed to feel. The kid was him, William Jasper Holloway. When he was Wayne's age, he had the same furies and restraints, the same pains and longings.

'You're putting me on the spot,' he told the boy. 'I give you the money and you run away. Maybe the police find you, bring you back, and it comes out that I gave you the money to go. I like your parents; they're my friends. They find out I gave you the money to take off, and that's the end of that friendship.'

'I'd never tell,' Wayne said.

'I know you wouldn't, but sooner or later these things come out – you know that. Look, right now I won't say yes and I won't say no. I just want you to think about it. All right? If you finally decide you want to go, then come to me and I'll give you what you want.'

'I have thought about it,' the youth said. 'I decided I got to get out of here.'

'Oh? Why?'

'Because it's all shit.'

'Sure it is,' William Holloway said cheerfully. 'And where do you think you're going to go where it's not all shit?'

'I don't care,' the boy mumbled. 'Anywhere different.'

'What about your family? Your mother and father? Have you thought about how they'll feel if you just take off?'

'They wouldn't care.'

'What about your friends?'

'I got no friends.'

Holloway felt a throb so intense it gave him a headache. But despite his pain, he wanted to take on the boy's grief, too. He could handle it; he had the experience. It wasn't right for one so young to take that kind of punishment.

'I thought I was your friend, Wayne,' he said.

'Well . . . yeah . . . but you're old. You know?'

'Sure,' Holloway said with a slanty smile. 'I know.'

He turned, leaned, stared closely at the poor, gnarled lad. He slid an arm lightly across Wayne's shoulders. He wanted to hug him close, kiss his bruises. But he staunchly resisted that temptation. Virtue, he told himself. Love.

'Wayne,' he said, 'I'm not going to give you a lot of bullshit about going through a phase, and everything will look better to you in a few weeks. Maybe it will, maybe it won't; I don't know. But I do want to tell you that you're not alone. A lot of other boys your age have felt the way you feel and have come out of it. I know you think it's the end of the world for you, but it doesn't have to be. Crazy things happen in life. Some good, some bad, I admit. But at your age, don't make up your mind that the way you feel now is the way you're going to feel for the rest of your life. You'll change. Everyone changes. Just leave yourself open to it; that's all I'm saying.'

'I'm still going,' the boy said in a low voice. 'I'm getting out of here. There's nothing for me here.'

'Where will you go?'

'I don't know.'

'How will you live?'

'I don't care.'

Holloway's arm trembled about the boy's shoulders. He restrained himself from gripping tighter.

'Look,' he said earnestly, 'I'm going to ask you something as a personal favor. Give it another month. Will you? Just a little more time to think about it. What difference can a month make? If you still feel the same way a month from now, then you take off.'

'Well . . .' Wayne said hesitantly. 'You won't tell my father, will you?'

'Of course not. This is just between you and me.'

'And if I decide to split, you'll give me some money?'

'Yes.'

350

'A loan, like. I'll pay it back.'

'Sure.'

'Well, okay then.' The boy scrambled to his feet. 'But I still say it's all shit.'

He went slouching away. Holloway watched him go, his empty arm lax, fingers digging into warm sand.

He drained his beaker of vodka and water, crunching the soft chips of ice between his teeth. If he could only keep stalling for time. Time to get to know the boy better. To advise him. Guide him.

That would be a virtuous, loving act – to rescue this sad, wounded boy and teach him how to live. How to recognize the glories and the flunks of this world. What had value and what was dross. How to reject today's delights for the sake of tomorrow's happiness.

All the things William Jasper Holloway had learned – too late.

He climbed briskly to his feet, went trotting back to his home for another drink. He was filled with sturdy resolution; he would save Wayne Bending. And he never, for a moment, doubted that the boy was worth saving.

He stood at the terrace railing, looking out at the black, trembling sea. He wondered where Wayne Bending was at that moment.

At home in bed, Holloway supposed. But awake. Perhaps lying naked with the sheet thrown back. Hands clasped behind his head. Staring sightlessly at the ceiling. He wished he could be with the boy. To comfort him.

No comfort from his father, that was for sure. Turk Bending went tap-dancing through life. His son's problems would amuse him. He would pay to get the kid laid, thinking that would solve everything. It did for Turk.

Look at the way Bending had immediately agreed when Jane had suggested skinny-dipping the night of the Empts' party. The man had no hang-ups. He didn't care; he just didn't care.

'And why didn't you join in?'

'The whole thing was infra dig. Disgusting.'

'You've seen naked women and men before.'

'Exhibitionism holds no particular delights for me.'

'Don't be such a prig. It was just innocent fun after a drunken party. What's so awful about swimming naked in the sea?'

'Nothing. But, uh, married couples . . . That's just not, not, not *right*.'

'You think they fucked each other on the beach? Or in the water?'

'No, I don't think that. They just fooled around and had, ah, fun.'

'So what was wrong with it?'

'Nothing!' William Jasper Holloway cried. 'Nothing!'

He flung his empty glass over the railing onto the sand. With frantic fingers he unbelted, unzipped, and pulled down his shorts. Kicked them away. Yanked his shirt over his head. Naked, he leaped down the steps to the beach, went dashing to the Atlantic Ocean.

He went like the wind, feeling that he was swimming through cool air. Skin tingling. Belly jouncing. Testicles flopping. Bravely he plunged into the water, gasping. He waded, then dived, came up, swam out with thrashing strokes.

'Hoo-hah!' he shouted.

He flung himself onward until he tired. Turned onto his back. Floated. It was a wonder. The sea bore him up, fondled him. He rolled over and over, spluttering and coughing. He surface-dived, reared up, roaring with laughter.

He took in mouthfuls of the ocean and immediately spat them out. He urinated, leaving a warm patch, and swam away from it. He danced on the soft waves, cavorting. Oh! Oh! He writhed in this cuddling medium, luxuriating in its embrace.

Then he swam back to the deserted shore. He looked for the moon, wanting to howl at it, but it was gone. He began to run up and down the beach to dry, slapping shoulders and thighs, whooping deliriously. He was free. Free! The world belonged to him.

He had dashed past the Empts' place when he saw, in the gloom, a flashlight beam, a white puddle, jerking across the sand toward him. And behind, dimly, two hulking figures.

Muggers! Muggers!

Alarmed, the naked William Jasper Holloway, bank president, turned and began sprinting desperately for his own home. But he was plump, winded, the sand was soft. He floundered, stumbled, his breath coming now in great heaving sobs.

He looked over his shoulder. The assassins were closer, running faster than he. There was a pain in his side that threatened to split him wide open. He choked, faltered, and then they were on him, reaching with clawing hands.

He fought hysterically, punching out, kicking. And when they swarmed over him, he tried to knee them, screaming, biting anything that came close, yelling for help, kicking, fighting for his life.

When the phone rang on Ronald Bending's bedside table, it awakened him from a glorious dream. He could not remember the details, but he knew it had been glorious.

He fumbled for the lamp switch, got some light. Grace was turned onto her side in the other bed, sleeping soundly. Ronald picked up the phone.

''Lo?'

'Turk?'

'Yeah. Who's this?'

'Uh, Bill Holloway. Listen, Turk, you've got to help me. I've been arrested.'

'Arrested? Jesus Christ! For what?'

'I bit a policeman.'

6

Levin imagined that most laymen thought of psychiatrists, psychologists, and psychoanalysts (even marriage counselors!) as wise, kindly, sympathetic, understanding folks, a little like Lionel Barrymore at his disarming grumpiest. There may have been therapists like that, but Levin had never met any.

Sympathy and understanding were fine qualities, no doubt of that, but they were of little value when treating a grown man who insisted on exhibiting himself in the meat sections of supermarkets, or a ten-year-old boy who delighted in setting fire to cats.

Levin believed his work required an adversary relationship with his patients. There was an element of priestliness in his role. He did not think he was wrestling with the Devil for a sinner's immortal soul, but his job usually made a struggle with the patient inevitable.

This struggle was to illume the dark side of the moon (psyche) and hope that light might be the first step toward mental and emotional health. The patient resisted this revealment of his innermost secrets, since it would leave him open, raw, vulnerable. In this sense, every patient was an opponent.

In the case of Lucy B, Levin remained convinced that her aberrant behavior resulted from a psychic trauma not of her making. She was concealing the wound, and her parents (one or both) were similarly burying it. It would take more than sympathy and understanding to dig it out.

'Good afternoon, Lucy,' he said, unable, as always, to refrain from smiling at her radiant beauty.

'Hello, Doctor Ted,' she said pertly, twirling for his inspection. 'Do you like my dress? It's new.'

'Very pretty,' he said, nodding approvingly. 'It makes you look grown up.'

'That's what I thought,' she said, looking down at herself. 'I'm getting too old for white things with sashes. I wanted black, but mother insisted on this blue. But I do think it makes me look more, uh, sophisticated – don't you?'

'No doubt about it.'

'Well . . .' she said, lifting herself into the armchair. 'What are we going to talk about today?' She smiled at him brightly.

'What would *you* like to talk about?'

'Umm . . . I think I'd like to talk about when a man and a woman get married, well, they have babies – you know? But they don't *have* to be married, do they? To have kids?'

'No.'

'That's what I thought. But I was talking to Elizabeth McCarthy, she's a friend of mine, and she thinks people have to be married before they can have children. My goodness, I told her, that's silly. So I'm glad to find out from a doctor that I was right. Could I have a baby, Doctor Ted?'

'Not now, no. You're not old enough.'

'How old do I have to be?'

'It depends,' he said cautiously. 'But you don't want to have children until you finish school and graduate from college. And maybe by that time you'll feel differently about it.'

'I might and I might not,' she said airily. 'Sometimes I think I would like to have a baby all my own right now.'

He peered at her owlishly. 'A boy or a girl baby?'

'A girl,' she said promptly. 'All my very own. I'd bathe her and powder her, like they do, you know. And I'd dress her up so pretty.'

'Like a living doll?'

'Yes, just like a living doll. And I'd love her so much. I'd

355

just love her to death. I'd kiss her all the time and hug her, and I'd spank her when she was bad. But she'd never be bad because I'd love her so much.'

'Like your mother loves you?'

Pause. 'Yes. But better.'

'Better how?'

'Oh . . . you know.'

'No, I don't, Lucy. Why don't you tell me. How would you love your baby better than your mother loves you?'

'Just more,' she said. 'Just all the time. Every second of every minute of every hour of every day!' She finished this declaration triumphantly.

But Levin thought she was deliberately beguiling him. He had, constantly, to remind himself of her slyness. It was her physical beauty that made him forget her cunning.

'Your mother loves you every second,' he said. 'Doesn't she?'

'Sometimes,' Lucy said. 'But she's awfully busy.'

'She's never been mean to you, has she?'

'You mean like whip me? Of course not.'

'Or your father either?'

'Oh, he'd never do that,' she said, laughing. 'He's so funny.'

'Funny?'

'You know. He's always making jokes and just fooling around. Once he pretended he had forgotten my birthday, and I was ready to cry, but he hadn't, of course, and he hid my present under my pillow. This really beautiful bracelet with all kinds of shells on it.'

'It sounds to me like both your parents love you very much.'

'I guess.'

'Then why did you say you would love your own little baby girl better than your mother loves you?'

But he could not pin her down; she slid away from him again.

'Well . . . maybe not better. But, you know, *different*.'

He had endless patience. He could fence as long as she.

'You'd love your baby differently from the way your mother loves you?'

'Yes.'

'Tell me about it. How would you love your baby differently?'

'Well, for one, I'd never do anything to hurt her.'

Levin didn't reveal his surge of interest in that answer. As casually as he could . . .

'But you just told me that your parents never hurt you.'

'Well, that's true. They never whip me, if that's what you mean.'

He looked at her narrowly. He thought there was something significant in her evasions. And even more meaningful might be her choice of words. He had a vague feeling that she was trying to tell him something without saying it.

'There are lots of ways of hurting people, Lucy,' he said softly. 'One way is to hit them, spank them, whip them. But we know your parents don't do that, don't we?'

She was silent.

'Another way to hurt people,' he went on, 'is to hurt their feelings. Disappoint them. Make them feel foolish.'

'I don't know what you mean.'

'Sure you do, Lucy. You know very well. If your father kissed another woman, for instance, you'd be disappointed in him and feel hurt, wouldn't you?'

'My father kisses other women all the time,' she said defiantly. 'All the grown-ups are always kissing, at parties and things. It's just fun. My goodness, that wouldn't hurt me.'

'What if your father did something that proved he didn't love your mother. That would certainly hurt you, wouldn't it?'

'My father would never do anything like that.'

'But *if* he did, you'd be hurt, wouldn't you?'

'I suppose.'

'You might even cry.'

'Maybe.'

'Well, then, you agree that you can be hurt in other ways than spanking or whipping. Your feelings can be hurt.'

'Oh, I know what you mean!' she cried, bouncing up and down. 'Like once, on the beach, I saw Miss Carpenter, she's my homeroom teacher, well, she was on the beach, and I waved to her, and she didn't wave back. And I thought she was mad at me or something, you know, and I felt real bad. But then it turned out she wasn't wearing her contact lenses, and didn't even see me. So that was all right. But it hurt my feelings when I thought she was mad at me and wouldn't even wave. That's what you mean, isn't it?'

Dr Levin looked at her with wonder, convinced she was trying to hoodwink him again, and cleverly at that. Her slippery skill amazed him. But he was determined not to let her completely escape.

'All right, Lucy,' he said quietly. 'You know what hurt feelings are. Now let's get back to what we were talking about. Has your father or your mother ever hurt your feelings?'

She thought a moment. 'You mean like not letting me watch TV when I want to?'

'No, I mean something more important than that. I mean something that really hurt you, that made you wonder if they really loved you as much as you thought they did.'

She stared at him, eyes widening. As he watched, tears appeared, brimmed, began to course down her cheeks. She made no effort to wipe them away, but her soft lips trembled.

'I think you're mean and spiteful,' she said.

He sat stonily and let her weep. There seemed to be no end to those tears; they poured down, dripped off her chin, onto the bodice of her new frock.

'I didn't think you were,' she said, 'but now I do.'

'Why am I mean and spiteful, Lucy?'

'Because of what you said about mommy and daddy not loving me.'

358

He caught that 'mommy and daddy.' He thought it might have been the first time she used the words. Heretofore it had been 'mother and father' or 'parents.' The 'mommy and daddy' sounded like a regression, the usage of a younger child.

'I didn't say your parents didn't love you, Lucy, and you know it. I just asked you if they had ever hurt your feelings, if they had ever made you wonder if they loved you as much as you thought.'

'Well, they never did. They never hurt my feelings. So there.'

'Then why are you crying?'

'I guess I didn't understand what you meant, Doctor Ted,' she said blithely. She opened her plastic purse, took out a little hanky, dabbed at her wet eyes and cheeks. 'My goodness, I must look a mess.'

But he was in no mood for compliments, or even reassurance.

'Lucy,' he said, 'let's play a little game. All right?'

'What kind of a game?' she said suspiciously.

'I want you to tell me the first things you remember happening to you.'

She puzzled that out. 'You mean when I was just a little kid?'

'Correct. How far back can you remember?'

'Well . . .' she said, happy again with this game, 'once I fell down the stairs; I remember that.'

'How long ago was that?'

'Oh, a long, long time ago. I was just a baby.'

'How old do you think you were when you fell down the stairs?'

'My goodness, I'll bet I was like three years old. Maybe two.'

'Can you remember anything else?'

She pondered. 'I can remember when Harry was a little baby. He was so chubby and pink and cute. He's five now, so that was over four years ago. I can remember my father tossing me up to the ceiling. He'd throw me up high and then catch me. I loved that. But then I guess I got too heavy for him to throw because he stopped it. And I . . .' Her voice faded.

'Yes?' Levin prompted.

'I think once, when I was very little, I had a bad dream or something, and my mother let me come into her bed. I'm not sure about that, but I seem to remember it. I remember how nice she smelled.'

'That's fine, Lucy. You're remembering way back. Now, Harry was born five years ago; you remembered how he looked as a baby. What do you remember happening after Harry was, say, a year old? Do you remember things that happened four years ago?'

'I was in nursery school; I remember that.'

'Do you remember anything that happened at home?'

'When I was four? Well, there were parties and stuff. It's all mixed up.'

'Memories usually are,' he said encouragingly. 'Do you remember any special party?'

'There was one,' she said vaguely, 'with a lot of people.'

'In your home?'

'Yes.'

'What was special about it?'

'Well, it was the first party where they let me stay up past my bedtime. I could come downstairs and eat from the same table as the grown-ups.'

'That sounds like fun.'

'Yes, and I had a new dress. Not like this one,' she added, plucking at her skirt, 'but a little girl's dress – you know? And there was music. I remember now! And my father danced with me.'

'See?' he said. 'You do remember.'

'Just everyone was there,' she said dreamily. 'A big, *big* party, and I had a new dress. A white dress. With pink ribbons. And my father danced with me for the first time.'

'And they let you stay up late,' he added gently.

'Well, you know, just an hour, like, past my bedtime. Then I had to go around and say goodnight to everyone.'

'And then you went up to your room?'

'Yes.'

'I'll bet you were so excited,' he said, 'with the party, the new dress, dancing with your father, I'll bet you didn't go to sleep for a long time.'

'Yes,' she said in a troubled voice, 'that's right. I remember now.'

Levin was aware that he was telling the story. No, he was *creating* a story from Lucy's hazy memories and from Lucy's lips. And this story, he acknowledged, might be as fantastical as any of the yarns she had spun for him.

'I suppose,' he said with a tinny laugh, 'your mother or father came upstairs to undress you.'

'I can undress myself,' she said crossly.

'Then? When you were four years old?'

'Of course.'

'Oh,' he said. 'Well then, your mother or father came upstairs to tuck you in?'

'I danced with my father,' she said in a faraway voice. 'Everyone said I looked so pretty.'

'Yes, yes,' he said, somewhat testily. 'You were pretty, you danced with your father, and –'

'For the first time,' she reminded him.

'You danced with your father for the first time. Then you went up to bed. In your own bedroom. Harry was asleep by then?'

'I guess.'

'And Wayne?'

'I don't remember where he was. Maybe out somewhere. Like on the beach. Maybe down in the party.'

'Oh my,' he said heartily. 'See how much you remember when you try? And then your mother or father came up to tuck you in?'

'I suppose.'

'But you didn't go to sleep for a long time. You told me that.'

'Did I?' she said. 'I guess I didn't. Maybe I was all excited. The party and all.'

'Of course. That's understandable. It was a while before you could get to sleep.' Then, imagining it: 'The music and voices and laughter from downstairs. All the grown-ups having a good time. It was hard to get to sleep.'

'Yes, it was.'

'And then what happened?' he asked, leaning toward her. 'While you were lying in bed, in your own room, trying to sleep – what happened then, Lucy?'

He thought a film came over her eyes. He could almost see her dwindling away from him.

'I don't remember,' she said in an echoing voice. 'I guess I just fell asleep.'

He stared at her, convinced that now she was not consciously deceiving him. If the incident he imagined had occurred, she did not remember it. The fragile tendrils of recall were cut. She had washed the happening from her mind. Why? Easy. The experience was too painful for her, inexplicable, frightening. Something to be interred.

It was at moments like this that Levin wished his ego were monumental. He wanted a granite surety that would enable him to press her, badger, bully, until he had torn the memory out by the roots, bloody and dripping.

But, being the kind of man he was, he could not do that. He thought wildly of hypnosis, drugs – anything to get inside her closed mind and open it up. He rejected such artifices. There was no way for him but to keep digging, peeling the layers away.

'Well!' he said, smiling as brightly as he could. 'That must have been quite a party for you to remember it so well. Your dress and dancing with your father and all that . . .'

She looked at him, perplexed. 'I didn't remember it at all, Doctor Ted, until you asked me about it.'

It was the finest compliment she could have paid him.

'Lucy, do you remember that night, that party, as being happy? I mean, is it a happy memory for you?'

'Oh yes!'

'It gives you pleasure to recall it – correct! Your dress. Dancing with your father for the first time. Everyone saying how pretty you looked. That must be a happy memory.'

'It certainly is.'

He sprang the trap. 'Such a happy memory. And how odd that you didn't recall it until I asked you about it. Don't you think that's odd, Lucy?'

He had her and she knew it. He watched her reactions with professional interest.

Ignorance:

'I don't know what you mean.'

'Of course you do, Lucy. This was a joyous experience, wasn't it? But you didn't remember it until I dredged it out.'

Bluster:

'Well, my goodness, I've had a lot of good times. You can't expect me to remember *all* of them.'

'But this was a special time. That's what you called it: "special."'

Confession:

'Oh, I just forgot about it, Doctor Ted. It just slipped my mind. What's so important about it anyway?'

He smiled at her.

'Well, if it's not important,' she went on, twisting her body nervously, 'I don't see why you keep talking about that silly party.'

It was close to the end of her session. He wondered if he should keep her over for a few minutes, but doubted if moments, at this juncture, would yield any more than he had already learned.

He felt that from the 'four or five years' mentioned in all those tape recordings, he had zeroed in on one particular night, one particular party. That was no small accomplishment.

The therapist and the patient were a living hourglass.

363

The sand streamed from one to the other. Dr Theodore Levin really believed the grains were finally coming his way.

He ushered her out, letting his hand brush lightly over her hair, as fine and fragile as spun cotton candy.

'Thank you, Lucy,' he said.

7

Ronald Bending needed women as much as another man might need alcohol, golf, or the Cross. Women were the crutch that supported, the only justification for enduring. Bending was incapable of expressing such sentiments; he only knew that he was a willing slave to his need.

He came from his office to the parking lot and slid into the driver's seat of his silver-gray Porsche 924 Turbo. (His wife's car was a black Volkswagen Rabbit – but that was her choice.) Bending loved this beautiful car, his greatest sorrow being that he couldn't get it into bed.

He sat in the bucket seat of soft glove leather and inhaled deeply. He had owned the Porsche for two years, but it still had a new-car smell, a perfume of money and power. He sat there for almost five minutes, just enjoying. He had no intention of going home; this was the best part of the day.

He finally decided on the Chez When on Commercial Boulevard. The food was so-so, but the bar was the best make-out joint in Fort Lauderdale. Lots of secretaries, schoolteachers, young widows, divorcees. If you couldn't score at the Chez When, Bending figured, you might as well hang up your nuts.

He drove south on Federal, resisting the temptation to let the Porsche run so he could hear the burbling roar. He had never pushed the car to its limit, but he kept vowing: One of these days!

He turned the keys over to Jimbo, the parking valet, who knew him well.

'Any action?' Bending asked.

'Looks good,' Jimbo said. 'A blonde came in about ten minutes ago. Driving a white LTD. Hair down to her sweet little fanetta. You'll want to catch that.'

'I will,' Bending assured him. 'Don't scratch the paint.'

'Have I ever?' Jimbo said, aggrieved.

The barroom was narrow and dark, lined with lighted aquaria of tropical fish. The bar itself was oval-shaped, with three bartenders who always seemed busy at blenders, pureeing banana daiquiris and strawberry margaritas.

Bending waited a moment until his eyes became accustomed to the gloom. Then he inspected the prospects. It looked good; women outnumbered the men by almost two to one, and not a dog in the lot. Turk took a bar stool with empties on both sides; he was in no hurry.

He treated himself to a double Jack Daniel's on the rocks, lighted one of his filter-tips, and looked around casually. He spotted the blonde Jimbo had mentioned. She was a creamer all right, but a guy had already moved in. A guy fifty pounds heavier than Turk and ten years younger. He wasn't about to challenge *that*.

Fortunately, there was a lot of movement in the bar. New arrivals. Pickups taking off. People going into the back room for dinner. Bending sipped his drink slowly and relaxed. This was his world. He knew it like a pygmy knew the jungle. He was at home here.

He had just ordered a second drink, was leaning forward, inspecting the display of liqueur bottles on the back bar, when he became conscious of someone sliding onto the stool on his right. He caught a whiff of perfume. *Joy*, he thought. He was a man who could identify women's scents.

He didn't turn to look, but he saw the hands: chubby but beautifully manicured. He waited while those hands flipped a cigarette from a pack. Then Bending was there with his gold lighter.

'Thank you,' she said in a low, laughing voice.

Then he looked at her.

Not fat, exactly, but plumpish. Young. About twenty, he

366

estimated. Cute more than pretty. Pug nose. Eyes with a ton of green shadow. And skin so fine and flawless, it looked like a special honey shade of Ultrasuede. Her features were just a wee bit piggy. Hair cut in a Dutchboy bob: bangs and straight around. A nice, glossy chestnut.

She was wearing a white nylon blouse, no bra, and designer jeans. The body was bountiful. Rubens would have loved that body. It didn't dismay Ronald Bending either.

'I beg your pardon,' he said to her, 'but I couldn't help admiring your bracelet.'

It was his standard opening; if they weren't swift enough to pick up on his tomfoolery, he wanted nothing to do with them.

She looked down at her bare wrist. 'Oh, this old thing,' she said. 'An heirloom. Been in the family for at least a year. I don't even think it's real brass.'

He thought she'd do.

'My name is Franklin Pierce,' he said.

'Weren't you president?'

'Vice president, actually. I was in charge of vice. What's your name?'

'Florence Nightingale.'

'No kidding? Weren't you burned at the stake?'

'No,' she said, 'but once I was scorched by a hamburger.'

They both burst out laughing, then sobered and started in again.

'What do you do for a living?' she asked him.

'I'm a brain surgeon for gerbils. And you?'

'I give high colonics to piranha.'

'Ticklish work.'

'Oh yes; they're always laughing. Do you live near here?'

'I live *in* here. Men's room. Third stall on your left.'

'That's odd,' she said. 'I've never seen you there.'

A half-hour later they were having dinner in the back room. He watched, fascinated, as she demolished a double shrimp cocktail, a one-pound sirloin with side orders of spaghetti and french fried zucchini, a dessert of Bavarian cream pie, and a Brandy Stinger. She had also made three trips to the salad bar.

'What refugee camp are you from?' he asked her.

'I just escaped from Dr Slotkin's Magic Thirty-Day Diet. Are you going to finish your sherbet?'

'Finish,' he said, pushing it across to her. 'God forbid that you should faint from malnutrition.'

'Do you think I'm too fat?' she said, licking her dessert spoon while staring into his eyes.

'Absolutely not,' he said honestly. 'I would term your body, ah, generous. But fat? No. I see you as all luscious hillocks and tender, shadowed valleys.'

'That's beautiful,' she said. 'Are you older than forty-five?'

'Of course I'm not older than forty-five,' he said indignantly.

'Good,' she said. 'I never screw anyone over forty-five until I've checked his EKG.'

So that was all right; he paid the bill happily.

When Jimbo brought the Porsche around, she looked at it and said, 'Gol-*lee*! Is this your car?'

'Mine and the bank's. We're partners.'

'I think I'll have my hair done that shade.'

'Good idea,' he said. 'And while you're at it, get power windows.'

She lived in the same condo as Dr Levin, but Bending didn't know that. Her apartment was the usual Florida Renaissance: vaguely Louis XIV with a lot of gilt, scrolled table legs, and satyrs chasing nymphs all over the wallpaper.

The place looked too big and expensive for just one occupant. He wondered if she was a pro.

'Got a roommate?' he asked casually.

'I do now,' she said, and poured him something green.

'What's this?'

'Melon liqueur.'.

'Oh God,' he said, and tried a sip.

'Like it?'

'Well . . .' he said.

The air conditioning in the bedroom was going full blast. You could have hung sides of beef in that room.

'What do you like to do?' she inquired as they undressed.

'Everything.'

'Me, too,' she said. 'Except standing up in a hammock.' When he was naked, she examined him critically. 'Not bad.'

'It's not the size that counts,' he told her, 'it's the ferocity.'

He looked at her admiringly, delighted with what he saw. He had been right; she was a superbutterball. All rose and cream. Pastel. Not a blemish on that perfect hide. Full, jouncy curves. She was bursting with juice.

'Prick you,' he said, 'and you'd squirt.'

'Prick me,' she said.

She was not one of the silent ones. She moaned, yelped, raved, bleated. Nor did she go gentle into that good night, but bucked, reared, rolled, thrashed. Bending hung on and gave it his best shot. It must have been sufficient because when they were finished, she kissed his cheek and said, 'There goes four hundred calories.'

She padded naked into the kitchen and came back with two cans of icy Michelob.

'Plasma,' Bending said gratefully.

'How long do I have to wait for an encore?' she demanded.

'After what we just did? About four years.'

She laughed and went to work on him with a right good will.

She might not have been as skilled as Jane Holloway, but what she lacked in expertise she made up in youth and enthusiasm. Her ministrations succeeded. Twenty minutes.

'I want to sit on you,' she announced.

'Be my guest,' he said, thinking of it as the Ms-sionary Position.

This one took longer and lacked the frantic acrobatics of their first combat. It was slow, thoughtful, deliberate, more of a dance than a struggle.

Finally, she slumped over, drowning him in her fragrant flesh. He felt her heart pound against his chest. Her skin was as fevered as his, as moist. He was still rigid within her.

They were lying thus when he heard the unmistakable sounds of the front door being unlocked and opened. The superbutterball raised her head.

'My God,' she said, unwittingly quoting from a Feydeau farce Bending had seen on Broadway twenty years ago, 'it's my husband.'

His physiological reaction was immediate; he shriveled within her.

I'm dead, he thought.

He rolled her off him, then rolled out of bed himself, landing on hands and knees. He scrambled for his nylon briefs. He got them on, had one trouser leg pulled up when he raised his eyes and there, in the bedroom doorway, was one of the most beautiful women he had ever seen.

She was staring at the naked girl on the rumpled bed.

'You bitch!' she said savagely. 'You're at it again.'

Superbutterball wailed. 'You weren't supposed to be home till tomorrow.'

Bending grabbed his clothes. Hopping, holding up his pants on one leg, he tried to slink past the furious woman who was now inside the room.

She twisted from the waist, then came around with the back of her hand against his face. It made his ears ring. He dropped his clothes.

'Hey,' he said. 'Now just wait one –'

Then she was all over him, claws and knees. He pushed her and she sat down hard on the floor.

'You cocksucker!' the naked girl cried, bouncing out of bed. 'Don't you dare touch her!'

Then they both swarmed over him, scratching, pounding on his head, trying to kick his family jewels to dust. He defended himself as best he could, shoving, pulling. He knew his face was bleeding, and a punch on his Adam's apple made it difficult to swallow.

He finally took them on one at a time. He flung the naked girl toward the bed. She went windmilling, then sprawled on her back, legs spread wide.

The 'husband' he tripped with a heel behind her ankle. She went down in a bundle of brilliant couturier fashion. In the brief moment both women lay dazed, Bending scooped up his clothing and shoes and went hobbling for the front door, still wrestling up his pants.

He slammed the door behind him, ignored the elevator, and stumbled to the fire exit. He almost fell down two flights of concrete steps before he paused to listen for sounds of pursuit. Nothing.

He dressed hurriedly with trembling fingers. He realized he had left his Countess Mara tie behind. Screw the tie. He pounded the rest of the way down and came out a steel fire door into the parking lot. He found his Porsche and gunned the hell out of there.

By the time he hit Federal Highway, he had stopped hyperventilating and his sweaty hands were relaxing on the wheel. At the first red light he inspected his face in the rearview mirror. A mess. Scratches. Dried blood and one deeper gouge still oozing. A bruise on his cheekbone, already purpling.

Sighing, he took out his handkerchief, spat on it, and, as he drove with one hand, tried to wipe his face clean. He hoped to God that Grace was already in bed and asleep. But in case she wasn't, he began to frame a cover story to account for his appearance.

He drove home slowly and carefully. All he needed right now was to be stopped by the police and asked to explain the booze on his breath and the scratches on his face. Then he'd have to do for himself what he had done for Bill

Holloway: lie like hell and pass out enough cash to placate the cops and get the charges dropped.

After a while he was able to laugh. A sour laugh. He wondered if he might not be getting too old for this game. He had his hair styled and blow-dried at a unisex barbershop. Occasionally he wore chest medallions on heavy chains. He tried to keep up with all the new rock groups. But still . . .

When he got home, the light was on in the master bedroom upstairs. He went directly into the downstairs lavatory, washed up quietly, and examined the damage. Nothing fatal, but there was no doubt he had been in a fight.

He tiptoed to the living room bar and, in the dim illumination of a night-light, poured himself a big brandy. He swallowed half of it in one gulp, then clutched his stomach when it hit. Jesus! What a way to live.

He took the remainder of his drink out onto the terrace. And there was Grace, sitting quietly in the darkness, staring at the froth-flecked sea.

'Hi there, dear,' Ronald Bending croaked.

She didn't look up and said nothing. Which made him wary. He sat in a sling chair a little behind her where she might not see his ravaged face.

'Get you a drink?' he said hopefully.

'No,' she said. 'I've got to talk to you, Ronnie.'

'Sure,' he said bravely. 'About what?'

'Lucy.'

'What about Lucy?' he asked, feeling a surge of relief that this wasn't to be another jeremiad about his delinquencies.

'I think she should stop seeing Doctor Levin now.'

'Oh? Why do you think that?'

'Well, she hasn't, uh, misbehaved for more than six months. So maybe just talking to him has done her good. I don't see any point in keeping on with the therapy. It's costing so much money.'

'Uh-huh,' he said, leaning forward awkwardly in his sling

chair. 'Look, babe, you were the one who talked me into taking Lucy to Levin. We knew how much it would cost, and we agreed to go through with it. The money doesn't matter. The important thing is what's right for Lucy.'

'Well, she's better,' his wife said sharply.

'She is? You think she's cured?'

'She hasn't, ah, done anything since she started seeing him, so I think we can stop.'

He sat back, took a pull at his brandy. 'Have you talked to Levin about taking Lucy out?'

'No. I wanted to discuss it with you first.'

'Don't you like Levin?'

'What a question! I don't like him or dislike him. He's probably very competent. I just don't think Lucy needs him anymore, that's all.'

'Do you think you're as competent as Levin? Or more competent?'

'Oh Ronnie, I know my daughter. She's better; I know she is. I just think we're throwing money away.'

'Be right back,' he said. He heaved himself out of the deep chair, went back to the living room bar. He poured himself another brandy, but added some mineral water to this one.

When he came back onto the terrace, he stood at the railing, his shoulder to Grace. She couldn't see his face, and he hoped to God she wouldn't notice that he had come from work without a tie.

He stared up into the night sky, swirling his drink slowly. He tried to figure what was going on here.

'I think Levin is a good man,' he offered.

'I suppose,' his wife said faintly.

'He asks embarrassing questions sometimes, but that's his job. At least he asks me embarrassing questions, and I imagine he does you, too.'

'Not so much embarrassing,' she said, 'as *private*. Things that have nothing to do with Lucy. He has no right to ask such things.'

'Is that why you want to drop him?' he said quietly.

She didn't answer.

'Look,' he said, 'I've told him a lot of things I didn't want to tell, but if it's going to help Lucy – what the hell. Don't you feel that way?'

'It's all so ugly,' she burst out.

'Ugly? Well . . . maybe. But I imagine he's heard worse. Everyone's got secrets. Sure, sometimes it's, ah, painful to talk to him, but I always feel better later. Just getting it off my chest. Don't you feel relieved after you've talked to him?'

'No,' she said.

He sighed, took a sip of his drink. 'He told us it would take at least a year. To get Lucy straightened out. Maybe longer. If we quit now, it's all wasted. Not the money. Screw that. But all the time we've put in. With the danger that Lucy will go right back to acting the way she did. Did Levin tell you he thought she was all straightened out?'

'I didn't ask him.'

'Well, he'd have told you if that's what he thought. He strikes me as an honest man. Do you really want to run the risk of Lucy acting up again?'

'You do what you want to do!' she cried. 'You always do anyway.'

She wrenched herself from the chair. She flung the sliding door back, rushed into the darkened house. Bending watched her go, startled. Then he slowly slid the door closed behind her. He pulled the sling chair forward, slumped into it, put his feet up on the terrace railing.

He tried to figure out the reason for her agitation. Old Levin must have been cutting pretty close to the bone.

In the last few years, he acknowledged, Grace had become increasingly reserved. She spoke to him about religion, his transgressions, the children, their home. But never, or very rarely, did she now speak to him about herself.

It hadn't always been like that. In the first passionate

374

years of their marriage, they had traded secrets and yearn-
ings, fantasies and wishes. That's what marriage was all
about, wasn't it?

He wished – oh, how he wished! – that he had the balls to
go upstairs right now, take Grace in his arms, and ask what
was troubling her. He would be kind and sweet and understanding, and he would listen and nod, and nothing she
might tell him would shock him or make him love her less.

But then, of course, she'd see his beaten face, and he'd
have to start lying again. He groaned.

Life was a pisser, he reflected sadly. You could start out
with the best intentions in the world, but sooner or later
they all turned to shit. Then you ended up with a couple of
freaky dames pounding on your skull while you ran for your
life, trying to hold up your pants.

He had to laugh at that image. It was all madness.
Everything was. Burlesque. And the only way to hang on to
some semblance of sanity was to go along with it, roll with
it, and not make yourself miserable by trying to be something you could not be.

He had another drink, a small one. And then, when he
judged his wife would be asleep, he went up to bed.

8

'Amateurs,' Jimmy Stone said disgustedly in his low voice. 'They're all fucking amateurs.'

'You're right, Jimmy,' Rocco Santangelo chimed in. 'Every time we try to deal with amateurs, we get it in the kishkas.'

'"The best-laid schemes . . ."' former Senator Randolph Diedrickson quoted sonorously.

Jane Holloway said nothing, but watched the three men closely. She had come to this meeting with some trepidation, impressed by the wealth, power, and experience of the others. Now she concluded she had little to fear; she could handle them.

They were in Diedrickson's study. Renfrew, the black houseman, had conducted the visitors upstairs and served the first round of drinks. Then, leaving a tub of ice cubes, he discreetly withdrew. The men were drinking bourbon. Jane Holloway sipped a glass of Perrier with a lime wedge.

'You better tell us something about these guys,' Santangelo said, addressing Jane. 'Not your husband. The other two. We know their business and bank records. But what about the personal stuff? Are they lushes, on drugs, or what?'

Speaking in a steady, steely voice, Jane told them what she knew about Luther Empt and Ronald Bending: their families, personal habits, frailties, ambitions. Her report was brief, concise, complete.

The two mob representatives looked at each other.

'Put Sam on them, Rock,' Jimmy Stone ordered. 'I want

to know everything: where they go, who they see, where they hang – everything.'

'Right, Jimmy.'

Stone turned back to Jane. 'This Ernie Goldman, the tech . . . What's his problem?'

'He's a very heavy gambler,' she said. 'The tracks. Horses and dogs. He uses a local bookie.'

'All right,' Stone said, 'that helps. Rock, have Sam find out who's holding his markers, what he's in for.'

There was silence then. Diedrickson, beaming benignly, let it grow. He had briefed Jane carefully before this meeting. One of his suggestions to her had been to answer all questions honestly, but to volunteer nothing.

'Rock,' Jimmy Stone said, holding out his glass, 'get me another blast, will you? Easy on the ice.'

The impeccably clad Santangelo rose immediately, filled Stone's glass and his own. While he was at the sideboard, he spoke over his shoulder to Jane:

'This Bending, he wants to go ahead with the cross?'

'He did,' she said, 'the last time I spoke to him. He's already sounded out Ernie Goldman. He says Goldman will come with us if we dump Empt.'

Santangelo brought Stone his drink, then sat down again, adjusting the sharp creases in his creamy raw silk suit.

'Jimmy,' he said, 'I think we gotta move on this.'

'Yeah,' Stone said. 'I talked to Uncle Dom. He says take over.'

Silence again. The two shtarkers sat morosely, nursing their drinks. The senator, behind his desk in his wheelchair, smiled like a decrepit Buddha. Jane Holloway, cool and crisp in a modest white linen suit, sat immobile, waiting patiently for action.

'Rock and me haven't got the time,' Jimmy Stone complained, as if speaking to himself. 'This is just one thing. We got a lot of stuff going down. There's this big condo near Sarasota. Maybe jai alai in Jacksonville. There's this guy, he's got the hots for a chain of nursing homes. Not for the old bums, you understand, but for the rich old drunks and loonies. It could be big. So what with one thing and another, we're spread thin.'

'Ah yes,' the senator said, nodding understandingly. 'What you're looking for are individual managers for each of your several enterprises. Am I correct in that assumption? Efficient, trustworthy, and discreet executives to take the day-to-day chores of management from your shoulders?'

'Yeah,' Jimmy Stone said, 'something like that.' He looked directly at Jane. 'I like your style,' he told her. 'You got class. And you're a bright lady. You got some good ideas – about better films and packaging. You think you could handle this porn setup?'

'Yes,' she said.

'Here's what it would mean,' he said. 'At first, you get the processing of the cassettes organized. Then when that's running smooth, you do the packaging. Eventually, if things work out, you take over the production of the films. It's a full-time job.'

'What about distribution and sales?' she asked.

'No,' Stone said.

'We got an organization for that,' Santangelo explained. 'It's complicated – you know?'

She nodded. 'How do you propose to gain control of EBH Enterprises?' she asked them.

'Look,' Jimmy Stone said earnestly, 'we're not thieves. We work legal. We'll buy them out. No one's going to lose a penny.'

'I don't think Empt or Bending will go for that,' she said.

'As I comprehend the situation,' Randolph Diedrickson said smoothly, 'there are no written and signed contracts in existence. It was an oral agreement which, I judge, would have little force in a court of law if Empt and Bending were foolish enough to seek recourse.'

'I still think they'll, ah, cause trouble,' Jane said.

Rocco Santangelo laughed harshly, then cut it off when Jimmy Stone glanced at him.

'We'll go over that bridge when we come to it,' Stone said. 'I think we can persuade Empt and Bending to sell out. Like I said, they're not going to lose a penny. They get their money back, with maybe a little sweetener to keep them happy, and we get the new factory and machines. Senator?'

'A very equitable arrangement,' Diedrickson boomed.

'Sure it is,' Jimmy Stone said. 'No one gets hurt. Now we come to your husband, Mrs Holloway. Will he sell out?'

'I talked him into it,' she said, 'I can talk him out of it.'

'Yeah,' Stone said, 'that's what I figured. But what about you taking over the whole megillah? Like I told you, it's a full-time job. Is he going to go for that? His wife heading a porn operation, with him being a bank president and all?'

The senator had warned Jane about this question, and she had given the matter a great deal of thought.

Her husband was a weakling and her father dithered, so she had no one to consult but herself. But as she pondered what she first thought was a simple business decision, she began to see the necessity of discovering what she really felt as an individual, in contradistinction to what she was supposed to feel as wife, daughter, mother.

It was not an easy process – painful, in fact – and it revealed to her how many of her judgments were dictated, how many opinions were borrowed. She had to slough off a lifetime of mental baggage she now found irksome and disadvantageous. 'Propaganda,' she called it.

Like a surgeon, she sliced away all that was extraneous in her life, all that had swaddled and smothered her. She came to self-recognition, the essence. She examined herself, stripped bare, and was not daunted by what she saw.

Finally she knew who she was and what she wanted. Everything else was bullshit.

'If there's any trouble with my husband,' she said firmly to Jimmy Stone, 'I can deal with it.'

'Yeah,' he said, looking at her admiringly, 'I bet you can.'

'What are you offering?' she asked him.

'Thirty-five K a year,' he said. 'For starters. Then, as you take over more and more of the operation, we can talk more bucks.'

'No,' she said definitely. 'Fifty thousand the first year. That's what Empt is taking down right now to honcho the whole thing, and I'm smarter than Luther.'

'Jane,' Diedrickson started, 'don't you think –'

'Pardon me, senator,' she said sharply, 'but let me handle this. I want fifty thousand for the first year. Then, after you see what I can do, I want a hundred thousand against five percent of the profits.'

'Five points!' Rocco Santangelo burst out. 'Lady, are you crazy? Uncle Dom will never go for that!'

She whirled on him. 'You'll never know until you ask, will you? And what have you got to lose? You can dump me anytime you like – you know that. Look, taking on this job will represent a big personal sacrifice on my part. I don't expect that to influence your decision. But I have to feel I'm getting something for what I'm giving up.'

'We'll talk to Uncle Dom,' Jimmy Stone said slowly.

'Do that,' she told him. 'And if he wishes, I'd be happy to meet with the gentleman personally and, ah, explain my position. But you can tell him that if he agrees to what I'm asking, I'll work my ass off for him and make a classy, profitable business out of this schlocky operation.'

Stone looked at her, brooding. 'Yeah. I'll tell him what you said. You'll be hearing from us.'

He stood up. Santangelo immediately leaped to his feet. The two men shook hands with Jane, then leaned across the desk to shake Diedrickson's big mitt.

'Thanks, senator,' Stone said. 'We'll be in touch.' He paused at the door, then turned back. 'About that young guy in Okeechobee County. The assistant DA . . .'

'Yes?' Diedrickson said, not hiding his eagerness.

'We sent a man up there to check him out. It looks good. Uncle Dom will contact you.'

'Excellent!' the senator cried. 'Delighted to hear it! Give my very best to the dear man.'

When the door closed behind the two guests, Diedrickson wheeled his chair around until he was facing Jane Holloway.

He looked at her thoughtfully. 'You know, my dear, if you were a man, I'd say you have balls.'

'Do you think I'll get what I asked for?'

'No,' he said promptly. 'To give you everything would signal weakness on their part, that they need you desperately. They don't want you to get that idea. In my judgment, they'll agree to fifty thousand for the first year, but hold off on any future commitments until they can ascertain just how well you handle your responsibilities.'

She thought about that. 'All right. If they offer the fifty, I'll take it. But I'll make myself so indispensable that eventually I'll get what I want.'

He boomed a laugh. 'Ah, the optimism of youth! Not, I am sure, misplaced in this case. Jane, when you alluded to a personal sacrifice on your part to accept this position, were you, perhaps, thinking of divorce?'

She nodded. 'I think it will come to that, senator. Bill is a very *proper* man. He's in this business only because I nagged him into it. But it sticks in his craw, I know. He'll never go along with my taking over the whole thing.'

'And then you'll leave him?'

'Yes.'

'And the children?'

'He can have the monsters,' she said.

He drew in a deep breath, then blew it out noisily with a burbling of thick lips. He toyed with his untasted tumbler of bourbon, turning the glass in his puffy fingers. Then he pushed it away from him. He gave Jane one of his benign smiles.

'Would you, my dear, refurbish me with a vodka in a tall

glass with a great deal of ice, a wedge of lime, and just a splash of water? I thank you.'

She went to the sideboard and fixed his drink. She was surprised to see that her hands were trembling slightly, so she poured a vodka over ice for herself. She brought the drinks back to the desk.

The senator hoisted his glass. 'To your new career,' he toasted. 'I wish you every success.'

'Thank you,' she said faintly. 'But it's not certain yet that they'll want me.'

'They will,' he assured her. 'I can practically guarantee it.'

'But I've had very little business experience, and none in this, uh, field. How can you be so sure?'

He didn't answer her question. But his beamy smile faded, eyes narrowed. When he stared at her, all glower and menace, she felt a vague unease and wondered if that was the look he gave his enemies just before their heads rolled.

But when he spoke, his voice was gentle enough. Cajoling, in fact . . .

'Let's talk about us,' he said softly. 'You and me. It would be quite natural that, with your new responsibilities and independent income, you should begin to question if our, ah, unique relationship is advantageous to you.'

'Senator,' she began, 'I swear I –'

But he held up a meaty palm to interrupt her. 'Perhaps not yet, but eventually you will ask yourself what on earth you are doing providing pleasure for a dilapidated old man who, unfortunately, cannot extend to you the same courtesy. That would be a very normal question for you to ask yourself. Having achieved your objectives, why waste time on an occasional activity that would seem to have no discernible profit?'

'I never thought –'

'However,' he continued inexorably, 'since you are about to dip your toes, so to speak, into the world of money and power, I think it only kindly on my part to warn you in regard to those customs by which that world endures. Briefly, my dear, your success, or lack of it, depends to a great extent on your financial or political clout. Since, at the moment, you have neither, nor can you reasonably expect to accumulate a great deal for some time to come, you are still in need of, ah, a protector.'

'I understand, senator.'

'Of course you do,' he said heartily, then took a deep swallow of his vodka and smacked his lips. 'As Mr Stone remarked at a previous meeting, you are a smart broad. And being smart, you will endure the ignominy of being the protégée of a ruined gaffer with good grace as long as you feel you may benefit from such a relationship.'

'I entered into our relationship of my own free will, senator.'

'Of course, of course,' he rumbled. 'I understand that, and cherish you for it. And you may end it of your own free will, may you not? But before you do that, I suggest you consider carefully my comments about the need of clout in a world that worships money and power. And that, in my circumlocutory manner, brings me back to your original question: How can I be so sure that Uncle Dom will offer you employment?'

'Yes,' she said, 'how do you know?'

'These men are not stupid,' he intoned. 'Crass, perhaps. Maybe uneducated. But they are shrewd. I am certain they have perceived that you and I enjoy a personal relationship, and this fact has been brought to Uncle Dom's attention. It is true the dear man has done me many favors. It is also true that I am not yet so toothless that I cannot assist him, in varied ways, when the need arises.'

'Are you saying that I will get the job only because Uncle Dom wants to do you a favor?'

'Oh no,' he protested. 'No, no, no. That is but *one* factor. I am sure Mr Stone has reported on your interesting ideas to improve their, ah, product. And you are a personable young lady with obvious ambition and drive. You are tough-minded; they can see that. All these things will go into Uncle Dom's final decision. His desire to please me will be only one of his considerations. But, without wishing to boast, I believe it will be the deciding factor.'

'I see,' she said.

He gave her a bleak smile. 'I knew you would. I wanted to bring all this to your attention merely to make you aware of the way things get accomplished in this brave new world you are about to enter.'

'Something to think about,' she said, staring at him, 'in case I get ideas about ending our relationship?'

'Precisely,' he said, showing his tarnished teeth. 'Since you have little or no clout of your own at this moment, I think it would be most unwise to reject that of a good friend.'

'I think you're right,' she said thoughtfully. 'As always, your advice is very practical.'

'You are kind,' he said with a wave of his hand. 'I merely try to assist my friends. My entire career in the Senate of the United States of America was based on that belief. Help your friends and, if they are worthy of your assistance, they will help you.'

'A noble sentiment,' Jane Holloway said, no irony in her voice, and she reached out and pulled Randolph Diedrickson's wheelchair closer until their knees were touching. 'Now, senator,' she said, 'tell me how I may assist you.'

He told her.

9

In the case of Lucy B, Dr Levin was suffering a preoccupation that, he admitted, came perilously close to an obsession. He feared he might be neglecting his other cases, so intense was his fascination with the puzzle of this hyper-sexual child.

When he expressed his fears to Dr Mary Scotsby, she attempted to reassure him, with little success.

'Ted, has it occurred to you that your interest in this girl may be sexually oriented?'

'Come on!'

'Ted, I've seen her. She's gorgeous. Is it so far from normal for any man to be attracted to such physical beauty?'

'That's nonsense,' he said angrily. 'It's a professional problem; I don't want to bed the girl. I'm convinced I'm on the right track – the psychic trauma. But it's not working out the way I thought it would.'

'You'll get it,' she told him.

'I wish I had your confidence,' he said gloomily. 'I keep thinking I'm close to it, but I need more time. Did you ever dream that you'd be able to devote your entire professional career to one case? Your whole life spent in studying just one human being. Wouldn't that be grand?'

'We all do that,' Dr Scotsby remarked. 'Ourselves.'

Levin went back to his brooding, convinced his premise was correct, but frustrated in his desire to nail down exactly what had driven Lucy to such deviant behavior.

Now he saw his world as not unlike that of a detective. A crime had been committed. For was it not criminal to bend a child's psyche? All clues pointed to the guilt of the father. Not premeditated, of course. Unintentional. An accident. Not homicide but manslaughter. The result was the same.

A party at the Bendings' home. Everyone drinking, happy, laughing. A little girl dancing with her father for the first time. Then going up to bed. And later, a befuddled father coupling with a strange woman in the bedroom alongside that in which the child lay wide-eyed in the darkness, listening. Then running out to find the source of those frightening cries and moans.

Levin could see the entire incident so clearly. It was a porn film that played over and over in his mind's eye. He knew the players, heard their speeches. It was a believable plot; all the actors played their parts. It was so *complete* he could not doubt it.

But its very perfection worried him. He had learned long ago that human troubles did not lend themselves to neat solutions. There were always loose ends, slubs. In fact, there were no solutions to human ills; there were arrangements, deals, that no one could label victory or defeat.

When Ronald Bending came lounging into Levin's office, the doctor inspected him closely, as if physical examination might reveal the man's guilt. But Bending was his usual ebullient self, nattily dressed, his wry, ironic smile set firmly in place.

'Ted,' he said, 'how're you doing?'

'Fine, Turk,' Levin said, motioning him to the armchair. He started the tape running, then noticed a fading bruise on Bending's face. Leaning forward, peering, he saw half-healed scratches. 'What happened to you?' he asked.

'A slight altercation,' Bending said, grinning. 'A dingo jumped me in a parking lot. He marked me up some before I could break free and run like hell.'

'Did they catch him?'

'Nah. He was long gone by the time the cops got there.'

Levin knew the man was lying; he was too glib. The

doctor wondered if there had been a fracas between husband and wife. He doubted it; he didn't believe Grace was capable of physical violence. Still . . .

'Ted,' Bending said, looking toward the windows, 'did my wife say anything to you about taking Lucy out of therapy?'

Levin hesitated a moment. 'No,' he said finally.

'She wants to,' Bending said. 'Told me so.'

'Oh? Did she give any reasons?'

'She thinks Lucy is better. The kid hasn't acted up since she's been seeing you. So Grace wants to pull her out.'

'How do you feel about that?'

'I don't want to. I told her so. Unless you tell me that Lucy is completely cured and doesn't need to see you anymore.'

'No, I can't tell you that. But I don't wish to be the subject of dissension between parents. Perhaps you'd prefer another therapist?'

'I want to stick with you. When you say Lucy can stop, then we'll stop. Besides, I don't think Grace was giving me the real reason why she wants to end it.'

'Ah? What do you think the real reason is?'

'I think you've been digging a little too deep for her comfort. My wife is a very private woman, Ted. It must be tough for her to answer some of your questions. Me, I can take it; I don't give a damn. But I think it's upsetting her. She didn't tell me that; it's my own idea.'

Levin sighed. 'Your wife has been very cooperative. As you have too, of course. You must have known this would not be easy.'

'Oh sure. We talked about it, Grace and I. We know that whatever you ask, it's for Lucy's sake – right?'

'Right. Then you wish to continue?'

'Why not?' Bending said offhandedly. 'If it helps Lucy.'

There was something disquieting here, and Levin decided to probe deeper.

'Correct me if I'm wrong, Turk, but during our initial

interview I got the distinct impression that bringing Lucy to see me was your wife's idea, and you weren't too enthusiastic about it. In fact, I felt that she had bullied you into it.'

'Right on,' Bending said sardonically. 'That's the way it was. It was the money that was bothering me.'

'But the money is no longer a consideration?'

'Not with me it isn't. Grace mentioned it, but that's not the reason she wants to stop seeing you.'

'So we have a role reversal here – correct? Now you are the one seeking help for Lucy, and Grace is the recalcitrant one?'

'Yes – if recalcitrant means what I think it does.'

'And you believe Grace's change of attitude has come about because I have asked questions which she believes invade her privacy?'

'I'd almost swear to it.'

Levin felt the tickling of an idea, so faint it still existed in an amorphous state. He could not grasp it nor give it form. It floated, a vagary, and after a moment, unable to define it, he let it temporarily drift.

'Turk,' he said, hunching forward over his desk, 'I am now going to ask you a series of questions that I suspect you will consider extraneous to Lucy's problems. But I assure you, I believe them to be important, and I hope you will answer as honestly as you can.'

'Sure. Go ahead.'

'In the neighborhood in which you live, do you have a lot of parties?'

'Parties? Oh hell, yes. South Florida is a partying place. Dances, barbecues, formal dinners, cookouts, drinking bashes. We're partying all the time.'

'How often?'

'Oh my God, I never stopped to figure. At least once a week, I'd guess. Probably more. I mean, we're *always* partying.'

'Are there some you particularly remember? Some that

388

stick in your memory for whatever reason?'

Ronald Bending pondered. 'Yeah, I guess so. Like maybe there was a fight. Or someone got pissy-assed drunk and made a fool of himself. Or herself. Or everyone went skinny-dipping. Parties like that you remember. Mostly because people still talk about them years after they happened.'

'Of course,' Levin said. 'Very understandable. Now I am going to ask if you recall a party in your home about four years ago. It was probably a sit-down dinner. A lot of people. Music. Dancing later.'

'Music?' Bending said. 'You mean a band or a tape or what?'

'I don't know,' Levin confessed, 'but there was music. A dress-up party.'

'About four years ago?' Bending said, frowning. 'I don't recall anything like that.'

Levin played his final card.

'It was the first party where Lucy was allowed to come downstairs and eat at the same table with the grown-ups. And then, later, you danced with her. She was all dressed up. A white dress. With pink ribbons. It was the first time you had danced with her.'

Bending's face cleared, and he laughed. 'Oh hell, yes. I remember. Who told you about it? Grace?'

Levin didn't answer.

'Oh yes,' Bending said, smiling, 'that was a great party. Twenty people to a sit-down dinner. Maybe more. We had it catered. It cost a bundle, but I had just landed a big contract and we decided to celebrate. You're right; we had music. Some kind of a cockamamie trio. And I danced with Lucy. That was a big thrill for that little girl. My God, that was like four, five years ago. Now she wants to go to discos. Where does the time go?'

'Yes, yes,' Dr Levin said impatiently. 'But about this party . . . After a while Lucy went up to bed. Then what happened?'

'What happened? Why, the party went on. Drinking, dancing, joints being passed around.'

'Try to recall,' Levin urged. 'Try to remember exactly what happened.'

Turk lighted another cigarette slowly. He leaned back, crossed his knees. He stared at the paper stars pasted on the ceiling. When he spoke, his voice was low, reminiscent . . .

· 'Funny you should mention that particular party, Ted. It all comes back to me now. It turned out to be a very wet party. Everyone got whacked out of their skulls.'

'Grace, too?'

'Oh sure. She was drinking then. A few people left. The trio took off at midnight, I guess. But I put on some tapes and we kept dancing. People started pairing off. Not husbands and wives, you understand. A lot of trading going on. I mean they'd drift outside. Onto the beach or into the bushes. Then they'd come back in, laughing like maniacs. It was that kind of a party. Jesus, it was fun.'

At last, Levin thought. I've got him.

'And you, Turk?' he asked softly. 'What did you do?'

'Me?' Bending said with a little chuff of mirth. 'I guess I behaved as usual. I drank up a storm, danced my legs off, acted the fool. Par for the course.'

'And did you pair off with someone?'

Bending suddenly sobered. He uncrossed his knees, straightened. Then he leaned forward in the armchair, staring intently at Dr Levin.

'No names?' he asked.

'No names,' Levin assured him.

'Yes, I paired off. Maybe that's how come I remember that party so well. It was the start of a long and beautiful friendship. Jesus, it's still going on – can you beat that?'

'Someone you knew?'

'A neighbor. The wife of a friend of mine. They got a couple of kids, but that makes no difference. Anyway, I had the hots for her since the day we met. And that night, at the party, we made out. First time.'

390

He giggled in a way that Levin found offensive. But he was careful not to let his reaction show.

'You paired off with your friend's wife,' he stated in a monotone. 'And this affair has lasted four years?'

'That's right,' Bending said complacently. 'It's no big deal. For her or for me. I mean, it's not one of your great love stories. We just have a little fun, that's all.'

'How often?'

'Oh . . . maybe once or twice a month. I've got others, and I guess she's got others. We're not exactly what you might call faithful to each other.'

'Then the attraction is purely physical?'

'Well . . . that's most of it. She's a tiger in the sack. Also, we can let our hair down with each other. And right now we've got a business deal cooking that we're both involved in. But yes, I'd say it's mostly physical. She's got this great bod . . .'

'All right, all right,' Dr Levin said somewhat testily. 'Let's get back to the party. You paired up with this woman for the first time. Did you just come right out and ask her?'

Bending's lips twisted in a smarmy grin. 'As a matter of fact, I did. I told you I had eyes for her for a long time. I knew there was something doing there but, what the hell, she was my friend's wife, so I played it cool – you know? But that night, with the drinking and dancing and joints, I just didn't care. So I said to her, "Let's fuck." And she said, "Why not?" '

'So you left the party together?'

'Nah, that's not the way it's done. She just sort of drifted away – no one noticed her leave – and a few minutes later I went to the downstairs john, and then I ducked outside and met her on the beach.'

Levin blinked. 'On the beach?'

'Sure. A few doors down from my place.'

The doctor drew a deep breath. 'This, ah, sexual encounter – where did it take place?'

'Where? Oh, down the beach a way. A house that

belonged to a couple I knew were still at my party. We went around to their patio and used one of their pool lounges. Is it important?'

'Yes,' Levin said, 'it's important. You left your house, walked down the beach, went around to a pool patio, used one of the lounges?'

'That's right.'

'No one saw you?'

Bending looked at him curiously. 'Are you kidding? Of course no one saw us. It was like one, two in the morning. Who would see us?'

The nebulous idea that had previously occurred to Levin came into sharper focus. He sat silently, mulling it, letting it grow. It began to take on an order, a logic. He inspected it with a kind of awe, excited by its simplicity and elegance, amazed that he hadn't considered it before.

Bending was telling him the truth; he was absolutely convinced of that. The man claimed to have acted exactly as he might have been expected to act. There were no false notes in his account.

Levin was silent for so long, lost in the implications of what he had just heard, that finally Bending, with a nervous laugh, said, 'Hey Ted, I'm paying for this time.'

'What?' Levin said. 'Oh. Sorry. And after it was over, the incident on the pool lounge, what did you do then – go back to the party?'

'I did; she didn't. The lady went back to her home. I went back to my party. I remember her husband was still there, bombed out of his gourd.'

'You didn't have any other, ah, adventures that night, did you?'

Bending laughed. 'Imfuckingpossible. That lady wrung me dry. No, I just had a few more drinks, a few drags on a joint. Then the party broke up. I finally got everyone out of there and I went up to bed.'

Dr Levin swung back and forth in his swivel chair, hands clasped over his belly. He was frowning, staring over

Bending's head at the nursery rhyme characters painted on the opposing wall: moon-jumping cows and fiddle-playing cats.

Then he stopped swinging, sighed, dug a cigar from the desk drawer. He stripped the cellophane away, bit off the tip, lighted it with a wooden kitchen match. Puff, puff, puff.

'Turk, you said that when this party took place, your wife was drinking. Correct?'

'She was never what you'd call a heavy drinker, but yes, she had some at that party.'

'And did she smoke a joint?'

'I don't remember. I suppose she did. There were plenty available.'

'She doesn't drink now?'

'Very rarely. Maybe one or two at a party. Usually wine.'

'Smokes marijuana?'

'Now? No, she doesn't.'

'How long would you say you were absent from the party? With your friend's wife?'

'My God, Ted, that party's really on your mind, isn't it?'

'Yes, it is. How long were you absent? Thirty minutes? An hour?'

'Probably around an hour.'

'And when you returned to the party, was your wife still there, entertaining your guests?'

Bending thought a moment. 'I really don't remember.'

'When you went up to bed, was she there? In your bedroom? Asleep?'

'I don't recall, but she must have been because everyone had left. I locked up and turned off the lights. So I guess Grace was already in bed.'

'Did you have sex with her that night?'

'No way! I don't know if I went to sleep or passed out. Half of each, I guess. I was zonked. As I said, it was a grand party.'

'The next day, do you remember if Grace mentioned anything about your absence from the party?'

'Not a word. For which I was deeply grateful. I guess she didn't even notice I was gone.'

'Probably,' Levin said, nodding.

He believed he had extracted all he was going to get from this man's memory. But it was sufficient to turn his thinking around, to prove to him once again the danger of facile explanations of human behavior.

'I suppose you think I'm some kind of a crud,' Ronald Bending said, trying for a casual tone and not quite making it.

'A crud? I don't understand, Turk.'

'For screwing my friend's wife. For being unfaithful to mine every chance I get.'

'I don't judge people. That's not my job.'

'If I told you I still love my wife, would you believe me?'

Levin didn't answer.

'Well, I do,' Bending said. 'All these women – they've got nothing to do with Grace. I don't expect her to understand that, but it's true.'

Levin stared at him. 'What do you want from me, Turk – absolution? Pardon for your sins?'

'You think they're sins?'

'They are if you think they are.'

'No, I don't think they are. And I don't want your pardon. I just thought that you being a man, you'd understand.'

'Oh, I understand, I assure you.'

'Ted, I called you a snotty bastard once, and you are – in spades.'

'You are not my patient,' Levin said tonelessly. 'My only interest in you is how your behavior affects Lucy's problem. When that has been, uh, satisfactorily treated, you may wish to enter therapy yourself.'

A harsh bark of laughter from Bending. 'You think I need it?'

'That's for you to decide. But I must tell you that I detect in you a certain dissatisfaction, a weariness with the way you live. I think you are beginning to question the meaning of your life, and are perhaps frightened – well, maybe not frightened, but dismayed by what you see.'

'Not me, Ted. I'm on top of the world.'

'Glad to hear it,' Dr Theodore Levin said stonily. 'And now I see our time is up.'

After Bending had departed, the doctor glanced at his appointment calendar and saw that his next patient was a twelve-year-old boy, a chronic masturbator.

Levin very rarely drank in the office, but now he went to a file cabinet and from the bottom drawer withdrew a bottle of California brandy. He poured an inch or so into a water-glass. Then he sat at his desk, feet up. He sipped his drink and finished his cigar.

After a few moments he called Dr Mary Scotsby and asked if he might take her to dinner. She readily agreed, and he was pleased. He wanted to tell her his new theory in the case of Lucy B.

PART VI

1

The affair with Eddie Holloway had released Teresa Empt. She could not think of a better word than 'released,' for she felt unfettered, free. She was, she told herself, still a young woman; there was nothing she might not do with her newfound gumption.

She had seduced the boy – had she not? Managed a sexual liaison of months' duration without being discovered. And now she was ready to end the affair. She had confidence in her ability to handle it with dispatch and discretion.

She bathed, anointed herself, and dressed with particular care for her final meeting with Eddie in the gazebo. Experience had taught her the most efficient costume to wear: a blouse that opened down the front, a wraparound skirt that didn't soil too easily, and no pantyhose.

She carried a small coin purse into which she had tucked the payoff: a new, crisp hundred-dollar bill, neatly folded. She wondered if Eddie had ever seen a hundred-dollar bill.

She drifted across the dark lawn at the appointed hour, humming softly. He was waiting eagerly for her on the spread blanket. When she sat down beside him and stroked his long hair, she thought he really was a pretty boy. Stupid, but pretty.

'Listen,' he said hoarsely, 'about that boat . . . I think I can get it for –'

'Later, Eddie,' she interrupted gently, touching his cheek. 'First let's see if you remember what I taught you.'

With a little prompting, Eddie remembered. She led him

through his paces. The only things lacking were hoops through which he might leap, growling ferociously.

Lying on her back naked, fevered skin exposed to the night breeze and Eddie's frantic tongue, Teresa thought she had never been happier. To be loved and to be in control – was there another combination that offered such bliss?

The boy followed her instructions willingly and with the enthusiasm of youth. She had learned the secret of giving herself up, total surrender to the demands of her body. She felt herself awake inside, stir, convulse, and finally melt.

'About that boat . . .' Eddie said.

'Later,' she murmured again, and went to work on him with cool, deliberate fingers, ignoring his giggles and protestations. Lying on her side, manipulating his body intently and sometimes cruelly, it suddenly occurred to her that she owed a great deal to this youth.

Through him she had learned the hidden hungers of her own flesh and the subtleties of her desire. It transcended physical want. There were deep emotional needs there, some of a dark nature she didn't wish to name.

Edward Holloway – satiny skin, hard bone, blood-flushed muscle – had been her introduction to self-knowledge and a new world. She bent over him and gave him pleasure out of gratitude for what he had given her, and as a kind of benediction.

'Now then,' she said at last, sitting up and looking down at the gasping boy, 'I'm afraid I have bad news for you, Eddie.'

He struggled up to a sitting position and looked at her warily.

'Yeah? What's that?'

'I'm afraid we won't be able to see each other anymore.'

'Why not?' he cried.

'Shhh. My husband has been acting very suspicious. I

don't know how he found out. Maybe the old woman said something to him. Anyway, it's just too dangerous for us to continue.'

'We could go somewhere in your car,' he said hopefully. 'And park – you know? Or maybe a motel. Have you got a friend with an apartment we can use?'

'No, Eddie,' she said. 'My husband's liable to follow us. Or hire a private detective.'

The full meaning of what she was telling him sank in slowly. Teresa waited patiently. Eddie Holloway wasn't the swiftest lad in the world.

'Jeez,' he said finally, with a groan. 'You mean we gotta split up?'

'I'm afraid so,' she said gravely. 'This is the last time I can see you alone.'

'I thought you loved me,' he said, in such a piteous voice that she was touched.

'I do, I do. And I'll always remember the wonderful times we had together. Weren't they wonderful, Eddie?'

He was silent awhile, then . . .

'Shit,' he said disgustedly. 'You say it's over, and it's over. Just like that, huh?'

'Can't you see that it's best for both of us?' she said. 'You're so much younger than I am. It had to end, sooner or later. You'll find a nice girl, someone your own age, and you'll –'

'You're a real bitch!' he shouted at her.

'Oh Eddie,' she said sorrowfully.

'Well, screw you,' he said. 'I've got something to say about it. And I say we keep on just the same way. We can always find a safe place.'

'No, Eddie,' she said. 'It's over.'

He stood up and began dressing, pulling on underwear, shirt, pants, with trembling fingers.

'That's what *you* think,' he said wrathfully. 'How would you like it if I went to your old man and told him what we been doing?'

401

She had come prepared for this. She dressed slowly, calmly.

'I don't think my husband would believe you,' she said in a silky voice. 'A woman my age and you, a boy of – what is it? Sixteen? He'd never believe it. But he might believe it if I told him you raped me. Or tried to. If I went to him, crying, and told him what you tried to do to me while I was out for a walk. My husband owns a big revolver, Eddie.'

She saw his mouth drop open. In the faint starlight she thought his face paled.

'You wouldn't?' he gasped.

'Oh yes, I would,' she said, laughing lightly. 'If you insist on acting like a vindictive child instead of a man.'

She had said the right thing. He could not endure the thought of being considered less than mature. Sophisticated. Cool – you know? Smooth. A cool, smooth cat.

'Well, what about my boat?' he demanded.

'Oh Eddie,' she said. 'I couldn't take that much money from our account without my husband asking what it was for.'

'Ahh, shit,' he said despairingly, 'I really wanted that boat.'

'I know,' she said. 'And I want to help you get it. Here . . .'

She unsnapped the coin purse, handed him the hundred-dollar bill. She watched him closely as he unfolded it, inspected it, his eyes widening. Then he turned it over, examined the back.

'Wow,' he said with awe. 'A hundred.'

'It's for you, Eddie. To help you get your boat. And to help you remember what fun we had together.'

'Yeah,' he said, brightening, 'we did have fun, didn't we? A real gas.'

She knew he would brag about it for years to come.

'A goodbye kiss?' she asked.

'What? Oh. Yeah.'

His kiss was brisk and perfunctory. Then he grabbed up

the blanket, gave her one of his golden smiles, and trotted away, still looking at the hundred-dollar bill.

She watched him go, feeling an unexpected pang. But then, she assured herself, there was Mike, the supermarket bagboy. And hundreds, thousands of other Adonises in south Florida, all with long, sun-bleached locks, smooth skin, and the wild fervor of youth.

She wandered back to the house. Gertrude was watching a biblical drama on television. She looked up when Teresa entered.

'Have a nice walk, dearie?' she said brightly.

Teresa nodded absently. She mixed herself a tall rum and Coke at the living room bar. She took it out onto the terrace. She stood at the railing, sipping her drink slowly, staring at the darkling sea.

This land had changed her into someone quite different from the tight, frozen creature who had come down from the north seeking the sun. This was a place of growth. Plants and people sprouted and grew overnight. Life flourished, ripened quickly, decayed just as fast.

She supposed she was being paganized, and found the idea attractive. A hibiscus bloom behind one ear. Long, oiled hair falling free. Her naked body . . . Running down the strand . . . A naked lover awaiting her . . .

She laughed aloud at the fantasy. As the door behind her slid open and Luther came out onto the terrace, drink in hand.

'Hi babe,' he said in his raspy voice. 'What'cha doing?'

'Just dreaming,' she said with a secret smile.

2

The meeting was held in the same motel suite where the original deal had been made.

'I don't know what it's all about,' Empt told Turk Bending and Bill Holloway. 'They just called up and said we gotta meet. I suggested my office, but they said no. Maybe they're afraid the place is wired, for God's sake. Anyway, they want us all at the motel. Who knows what the hell they want?'

It didn't take long to find out.

'What's happened in this,' Rocco Santangelo started. 'We got this hotshot management consultant, he comes in and looks over our whole setup. Production, processing, packaging, distribution, sales – the works. Now what he says is this . . . We got to have a vertical organization. Like the big oil companies – you know? I mean, they get oil out of wells they own, they make it into gasoline in refineries they own, and they sell that gas in service stations they own. Right? So we got to do the same. Produce our stuff in our own studios, process it in our own factory, and sell it through our own outlets. This guy has the numbers to prove that we –'

'Hey, wait just a minute,' Luther said, beginning to bristle. 'Are you saying what I think you're saying?'

'It's dollars and cents,' Santangelo said earnestly. 'It's got nothing to do with the job you've done. You've done a great job. Am I right, Jimmy? But we got to reorganize like this hotshot business guy says. Which means we got to control the processing of the cassettes.'

Empt looked wonderingly at Bending and Holloway. 'This stinks,' he said.

'Look,' Santangelo said, 'you're not going to lose a penny on the deal. Not a penny. Whaddya think, we're bandits or something? The three of you get your original investment back. Every cent.'

'Screw that!' Empt said furiously. 'What about all the work we did? The time we put into this thing? All that's down the tube?'

'We recognize all that,' Santangelo said smoothly. 'Sure, you worked hard and all. That factory is up and ready to run. So maybe we can add a little sweetener for your time and trouble.'

'No, no, and no!' Empt cried, clenching a fist. 'Listen, you came to us; we didn't go to you. And you sang us a pretty song. You had the recommendations and all, so we *trusted* you, for God's sake. Now you want to cut us off at the knees. Turk, how do you feel about this?'

'It sucks,' Bending said, his face flushed. He turned to the silent Jimmy Stone. 'I don't know about the others, but I had to scramble to come up with my share. I sold some bonds and took a bath. I figured it was worth it because your numbers looked so good. Now you're telling us it was all a mistake because some wet-brained bookkeeper says you should be like Standard Oil or Exxon. That's crazy! Bill, what do you think?'

'Uh . . . a very unfortunate turn of events,' said Holloway.

'Let me get this straight,' Empt said furiously, his voice harsher than ever. 'You're going to buy us out, pay us what we put in, throw us a couple of extra bucks for our trouble, pat us on the head and send us on our way. Is that about it?'

'We're taking over the processing end of the business,' Rocco Santangelo said, face expressionless. 'Yes. That's it.'

'Bull-*shit* it is!' Empt said. 'You think we're just going to lay down and roll over? No *way*! What the hell kind of men

405

are you? You look us up, jerk us off, and now it's goodbye, Charlie? In a pig's ass it is! You made a commitment to us. An oral contract. And by God, you're going to stick to it.'

'Damned right,' Bending said. 'What kind of shit is this? You expect us to take it without making one hell of a ruckus? So maybe we've got nothing on paper. But we can sure cause a hell of a stink. Is that what you want? Big headlines: "Porn Kings Sued by Processors." Is that really what you want?'

Jimmy Stone leaned forward from the shadows. His voice was low, uninflected, difficult to hear.

'No,' he said, 'we don't want that. And I don't think you do either. All three of you are responsible businessmen. Good reputations in the community. Do you really want the courts and newspapers to know that you planned to make a lot of money by turning out copies of *Teenage Honeypots*?'

There was silence a moment. Broken when Luther Empt rose suddenly to his feet and began to stalk angrily about the room.

'I don't give a good goddamn!' he shouted. 'I've worked too long and too hard to let a bunch of creeps fuck me in the ass. Screw my reputation as a responsible businessman. I'm going to my lawyer first thing tomorrow morning. And if he says there's nothing I can do, I'll burn down the factory. I'll blow it up before I let you bums take over.'

'I'm with you, Luther,' Bending said.

Bill Holloway was silent.

'Are you threatening us?' Jimmy Stone asked quietly.

'Goddamned right I'm threatening you!' Empt yelled. 'You stick to your original agreement or we'll give it to you like you're trying to give it to us.'

'I don't think we're doing anything so bad,' Jimmy Stone said mildly. 'Plans sometimes change. I'm sure all you gentlemen have had to adjust when things didn't turn out the way you thought they would. You're getting your investment back. We can come to some friendly agreement on payment for your time and trouble. So what's the need to scream and call us creeps and bums and say you're going to do this and you're going to do that?'

'You talked big profits,' Bending accused him, 'just to get that factory built. To use our money and Luther's know-how. Now that it's built and ready to go, you decide you don't need us.'

'No,' Stone said, shaking his head, 'that's not true. When we started this with you gentlemen, we were honest and sincere. We really expected things to go smoothly. The numbers we gave you were right. But now things have changed and we've got to change along with them.' He shrugged.

'No way am I going to sit still for this,' Luther Empt told him. 'What do you think – we're a bunch of patsies? You keep calling us gentlemen. I'll show you what gentlemen can do when someone tries to fuck us up.'

'Think it over carefully,' Jimmy Stone urged in his monotone. 'Don't do anything stupid. You're all family men with lovely wives and beautiful children. Nice homes. Don't act like fools.'

They stared at him. The menace was there. Not defined. But there was no mistaking it.

'Listen to Jimmy,' Santangelo said. 'Don't do anything you might regret. What the hell, you're not losing any money. And life is short – am I right? Live, laugh, and love: that's my motto.'

There was a bout of glaring. Then the two mob representatives rose to leave. They didn't offer to shake hands. The three partners watched the door close.

'Bill,' Ronald Bending said, 'what's our legal position on this?'

'So thin,' Holloway said, 'it's practically nonexistent. I suggest we take our money and try to forget the whole thing.'

'Not me,' Empt said in a murderous voice. 'No one fucks Luther Empt and gets away with it.'

'What can we do?' Holloway asked in a hopeless voice. 'Sue? We haven't got a chance. Burn down the factory? What would that accomplish? They'd build another somewhere else, and we'd never get our money back.'

'I'll think of something,' Empt said darkly. 'I'll put it to those bums.'

They sat in silence then. After a while they stood up, still wordless, not looking at each other. They left separately, Holloway to his vodka, Bending to the Chez When, and Luther to May, his sweet little girl.

As he sped south on Federal Highway, Empt's rage did not cool. It wasn't the money involved. Screw the money. He'd have felt the same if some louse tried to beat him out of a five-buck bet. What fueled his anger was being treated as a fool, as a – as a *nothing*. Well, they'd learn that Luther Empt was not a nothing to be pushed around.

He hadn't phoned May, but she was there, waiting for him. Her face glowed when he tramped in. But then she must have seen something, because she caught his arm anxiously.

'What's wrong, daddy?'

'It's nothing,' he said gruffly. 'Business stuff. Get me a Cutty. Bring the bottle.'

He sat in the armchair, leaning over, hunched, the glass clasped in both hands. He gulped down the drink, poured another from the bottle on the floor at his feet.

May perched on the edge of the sofa, looking at him solicitously. 'Are you hungry?' she asked.

'No. I ate. How about you?'

'I had dinner. I made myself a nice hamburger with a baked potato and a salad with that creamy dressing.'

'That's good,' he said. 'Fix yourself a drink.'

'I don't really feel like a drink, daddy.'

'Well, have a beer then. Have something, for God's sake. Just don't sit there.'

Obediently, she went into the tiny kitchenette and

poured a small glass of beer, putting the half-emptied can back into the refrigerator.

'Those bastards!' he said savagely. 'I'll get them.' He drank. 'Think they can push me around.' He drank. 'I've taken on tougher nuts than those goons.' He drank.

'Daddy,' she said, 'why don't you take off your coat and vest and loosen your tie? Make yourself comfortable and relax.'

'Yeah,' he said. 'Good idea.'

He stood up and struggled out of his jacket and vest, ripped off his tie. May took them from him and hung them away. He flopped back heavily into the armchair and poured another drink. She knelt awkwardly on the floor, unlaced his shoes, eased them off.

'There,' she said. 'Isn't that better?'

He nodded, beginning to feel the tension lessening. The anger was still there, but that hot need to crush, to destroy, was ebbing.

'People are shits,' he said to her. 'You know that?'

She pulled herself up. She went behind him, began to massage the back of his neck and his shoulders. His head lolled.

'Yeah,' he said, 'that feels good.'

'You're all knotted up,' she said. 'You shouldn't let yourself get so upset.'

'I can't help it. When someone tries to do me dirt, I've got to get back at them. I've always been that way.'

'Shhh,' she said. 'Just relax. I'll take good care of you, daddy. I'll help you relax.'

Standing behind him, she unbuttoned his shirt, slid her palms over his bare chest.

'Isn't that nice?' she whispered. 'Don't you like that?'

He grunted, not wanting to admit he could feel pleasure while wrath consumed him. But gradually her stroking lulled him. At least here, in this apartment, he was safe. He was loved and respected.

He ordered her to undress. He commanded her to stand

naked before him. She complied willingly. And when she stood close, smiling hopefully, tilted a little because of her crippled leg, a thin, peeled wand of a creature, he suddenly reached up and struck her.

He may have been brutish in bed with whores. He may have slapped one of his wives occasionally, but that had been from irritation, not from any desire to inflict pain. But this was something different.

It was open-handed: half-crack, half-blow. It knocked May's head to one side, broke her smile into a lopsided grimace. She staggered back. Her hand flew up to her cheek. Tears began to well, more from shock than injury.

He stared at her, his mouth open. He could not believe what he had just done. He had acted from such a fragile amalgam of anger and desire that it was beyond his ken. He could not have said why he had done such a thing.

He leaped to her with a groan. He held her to him, kissed the reddening cheek, wet eyes, trembling lips. He apologized a hundred times, begged her forgiveness. He said he was out of his mind, business worries had driven him crazy, he was a filthy, rotten animal. He began to cry.

And so, eventually, she comforted him. She said the blow hadn't hurt her; she had known worse. She said she could tell he was terribly upset the moment he walked in, and if hitting her made him feel better, why then he could beat her up, he could whip her, and she would accept it gladly.

'Do you still love me?' she asked him.

He nodded dumbly, still stricken by what he had done and trying to find the why of it.

She led him to the couch, sat him down, brought him his glass. He gulped, coughed, spluttered. She sat beside him, running her palm over his short, bristly hair, murmuring in his ear.

'Oh Jesus,' he said, sighing. 'Jesus Christ Almighty.'

He put his drink aside and turned to her. She came into his arms eagerly, and he could feel how fragile she was. He

410

could feel the child's tender bones, thin skin, soft muscle. He held her timorously, fearing to bruise, not trusting himself.

She moved away from his grasp. She lay back on the couch. Her long black hair curled forward over one shoulder and feathered on her delicate breasts. She held her arms up to him suppliantly. He took her frail hands, kissed her fingertips. He stared down at that pale slip of a body.

She was his little girl, his virgin. What she had been, her 'May I accommodate you?' – all that was forgotten. He saw her now as his own sweet, loving maiden. Her breath was pure, flesh untainted.

There was something almost – almost – 'holy' was the only word he could think of to describe how he saw her. There was a luminosity to her skin, an adoring light in her dark eyes. She was his, totally, and not any other man's.

'Love me, daddy,' she said. 'Please.'

His tears threatened to start afresh. Not only from complete happiness, but from the gratitude he felt when he contrasted the trust of this unspoiled child with the disgusting chicanery and deceit of the thugs with whom he had just dealt.

This was clean, open, wholesome innocence. She was all love, asking nothing but love in return. Somehow her chastity strengthened him, gave him a hope he could not define. It was a quiet, lighted candle, while all about the darkness roared.

She undressed him with lazy fingers, and he let her. And all the while she spoke to him breathlessly of what they might do. She used certain words, and then giggled as a child would.

When she was naked beside him, she leaned over him, saying, 'Let me do it. Let me do it.' And it had somehow come about that only by her slow, clever ministrations could he find release; he could no longer play the rabid despoiler.

He did not wonder at this, but accepted it greedily. In

some puzzling way, their manner of love preserved her virginity and the unique relationship he found so satisfying. To act the stud would have demolished all that.

So they loved and dreamed on, actors in a play they had created. They had both turned inside out, and revealed to each other open viscera, hearts, gray lobes and beating souls.

Their dialogue was spoken in a language foreign to both. Yet now there was a communication of hungers, each finding an answering need in the other.

Crying out, insensate to the world about them, they were joined in their buried wants, and hugged and kissed and said they loved each other.

3

Dr Mary Scotsby counseled against it:

'Ted, it's still a theory, a hypothesis. And if you're wrong, you're going to lose a patient.'

'I am not wrong,' Levin said stubbornly, 'and I am not going to lose a patient. I've twiddled around with this thing long enough. What we're doing is an art, not a science; you know that. Well, I've got to follow my instincts on this.'

'Good luck,' she said.

He listened to the tape recording of his last session with Grace Bending. He listened to it again. It seemed to him that if he had been harder, more demanding, he might have uncovered the truth. She had been close to breaking, but he had let her off. This time he was determined not to let her escape.

He sensed her hostility the moment she strode into his office. Her shoulders were back, spine stiff. And she had reverted to her former mode of dress: man-tailored suit, blouse buttoned to the neck, hair drawn back tightly and wound into a chignon.

Her manner was definitely chilly. Her smile was a ghost. She answered his polite greetings with monosyllables. She assumed a ladylike position in the armchair: knees together and turned to one side, ankles crossed, her white-gloved hands clasped in her lap.

But, peering at her closely through his thick glasses, Dr Levin thought he detected signs of tension. Chin held rigidly lifted. A slight tremor in those clasped hands. She met his stare briefly, then her eyes slid away.

'Mrs Bending,' he began gently, 'I need your help.' He paused, but when she made no comment, he continued. 'We are now at a stage in Lucy's therapy where absolute honesty from all concerned is not only desirable but essential if we are to discover the cause of Lucy's behavior. And once having established the cause, her adjustment becomes surer and swifter.'

'I have always been honest with you, doctor,' she said in an iron voice.

He combed his beard with his fingers and looked down, surprised, as flakes of cigar ash fell onto his lapels.

'I think,' he said, 'that there are things you feel I have no need to know. Yes, I believe you have been honest – but only up to a point. You have not revealed to me certain information because you felt it was not germane to Lucy's problem.'

Again he waited, but again she made no reply.

'What you have done, Mrs Bending, is to follow your own judgment as to what is relevant, rather than trusting mine. As a result, I have not been given all the pertinent, uh, background that might enable me to help Lucy the way she should be helped.'

'I don't know what you mean,' she said, looking down at her white gloves.

'Oh, I think you do,' he said. 'You have withheld things from me, not from any conscious desire to prolong Lucy's therapy, but because they concerned matters too painful to reveal. Too painful to *you*.'

'I've answered all your questions,' she said defiantly.

'True,' he said, nodding. 'But I did not ask the right questions. You could have overcome my lapse by volunteering information, which you did not.'

'I don't know what you're getting at,' she said tensely.

'I shall inform you,' he said pontifically. 'But first I want to assure you that I am not here to judge. Still less to condemn. I ask you to be as open with me as you possibly can. I realize that I am asking a great deal. Confession can frequently be an agonizing, a traumatic experience. It can also be a catharsis that may aid you as much as it helps Lucy.'

'I don't know what you're talking about.'

He sighed. 'Mrs Bending, do you remember a party you and your husband had at your home about four years ago? A sit-down dinner for about twenty people?'

'My goodness, we've had a lot of parties over the years.'

'This was a special occasion. Your husband had just won a large contract and you decided to celebrate. You had the dinner catered, and even hired a trio to provide music for dancing.'

She mimed deep thought: brows knitted, forehead wrinkled. 'I seem to recall something like that, but it's very hazy.'

'Is it? Lucy remembers it very well. She wore a new dress. A white dress with pink ribbons. It was the first time she was allowed to come downstairs and dine at the same table with the grown-ups. The first time she danced with her father. And the first time she was allowed to stay up an hour past her usual bedtime.'

'Well, I suppose a child would remember things like that. It must have seemed very important and exciting to her.'

'Lucy remembers, but you do not – is that it?'

'That's correct.'

He sat back and regarded her gravely. There were three possibilities: (1) she actually didn't remember; (2) the memory was there but blocked by the self-protective mechanism of the psyche; (3) she was deliberately lying.

Actually, he realized, (2) and (3) were probably one: she was lying because she was blocking. Admission would be too devastating; it would tear her apart. So she thought. Dr Levin was willing to risk it.

'You don't remember,' he repeated. 'Odd. Your husband can recall that party as clearly as Lucy. A great deal of drinking going on. Dancing. The smoking of marijuana cigarettes.'

She shrugged. 'That could have been any party.'

'It happened four years ago. You were drinking at that time?'

'I suppose so.'

'You smoked a joint?'

'I may have.'

'Things got looser and looser, did they not? Couples began to pair off, to disappear into the darkness. Not husbands and wives, but –'

'Will you stop it?' Grace Bending said in a loud voice. 'Will you just stop it? I find this all very vulgar and, uh, disgusting.'

'No, I will not stop it,' Levin said stonily. 'I shall continue. At this party, men and women, swapping mates, left for periods of time for the beach, the bushes, parked cars. And they –'

'I'm leaving this office,' she declared, looking about wildly. 'I refuse to sit here and listen to –'

'Your husband amongst others,' he went on inexorably. 'Just disappeared. But you were aware of his absence. And, perhaps, looking around to see which women were gone, you could guess who it was he –'

'Stop it!' she screamed at him. 'Stop it this instant!'

'Was it revenge, Mrs Bending? Or just the drinking, the joints, the sexual excitement of that night? Maybe you didn't give a damn where your husband was; he had been unfaithful so often before. Maybe you just decided what was sauce for the goose . . . and so forth. Your motives aren't important. I don't care about your motives. But you –'

'I didn't!' she yelled. 'I swear I didn't!'

'You did!' he said, slamming a heavy palm onto his desk top. 'I know you did. Everyone else was doing it; why not you? Lucy had gone up to sleep a long time before. So you thought it was safe to take this man –'

'Oh, you bastard!' Mrs Bending spat at him. 'You fucking bastard!'

416

'Would you like me to repeat the dialogue?' he said cruelly. 'I can even do that. You said, "I don't care. I just don't care." And the man said, "Are you sure we're alone?" And then he touched you under your dress, and you said, "Hurry. Hurry." '

He saw Grace Bending begin to rock, bobbing back and forth in the armchair. Her arms hung limply, white gloves dangling. She seemed to be choking for breath, face suffused, eyes swollen and tongue protruding.

'I made the mistake of thinking Lucy saw your husband,' Levin went on. 'But now I see it can only have been you and another man. Your husband would never have said, "Are you sure we're alone?" to a woman he had brought up to your bedroom. But another man would say it, to you. And Lucy, next door, still awake after the excitement of the party, heard the voices. Did she come toddling out, Mrs Bending? Did you neglect to lock your bedroom door? Did Lucy open the door, stand there in her little white night-gown perhaps, rubbing her eyes and watching what –'

'Motherfucker!' Mrs Bending shrieked. 'You cocksucker! Oh, you piece of shit! You're like all the rest, you filthy, rotten man. I hate you, you slimy, crawling thing. Vile! You stinking . . . You call yourself a doctor. You lousy son of a bitch. I hate you, you goddamned . . . You disgusting . . . I'd like to cut off your prick and balls, you sickening monster. I'd like to kill you, yes, rip your filthy heart out by the roots and let you bleed to –'

He let her rave, watching her hysteria with clinical detachment. Noting the white spittle gathering in the corners of her lips. Bulging eyes. Distended cords in her neck. Complexion flushed. Limbs in uncontrollable quiver. He saw her head go back, mouth in ugly rictus.

'Oooh!' she howled. 'Yes! Yes, yes, yes! I did! I did! It's all my fault. The first time. Oh God! The first time. And he . . . But I . . . Jesus, forgive me. Jesus, I have sinned, I have sinned grievously. Oh, pardon my sins, Lord Jesus. Wash me clean, Lord Jesus. Give me your strength. Give

417

me your love. It's all my fault. Lord Jesus, I confess. Yes, yes, everything. Take this burden from my heart. Cleanse me of filth and wickedness. Oooh, oooh . . . It's all my fault.'

She slumped, eyes closed. Her body went slack, threatened to slide from the chair. There was sudden paleness. Her breathing seemed weak. Necklaces of sweat beaded her brow and upper lip. Her head flopped to one side.

Dr Theodore Levin had smelling salts in his desk, but he preferred to let her revive normally. The swoon lasted little more than a minute. She stirred, blinked, looked about dazedly. She slowly straightened in the chair.

He poured water from his desk carafe and pushed the glass across to her. She sipped gratefully.

'I'm sorry,' she said in a quavery voice.

He wanted to tell her that the only thing she had to be sorry for was not telling him sooner. She had prolonged Lucy's therapy by her silence. But, he supposed, she realized that.

'Breathe deeply,' he advised her. 'Take a few minutes. If you still feel faint, bend over and put your head between your knees. And above all, know that the world hasn't come to an end.' He gave her a crooked smile.

She breathed deeply. She plucked her clothing straight. She opened her purse to peer in the mirror. She poked at her hair. She dabbed at brow and neck with a tissue. Then she snapped her purse shut, resumed her ladylike posture. She looked everywhere except at Dr Levin.

'I apologize,' she said in a dead voice. 'For my language.'

He shrugged. 'You didn't use any words that I haven't heard before.'

'Lucy doesn't use language like that, does she?'

'No. Lucy, except for her aberrance, is a very well-behaved child.'

'Thank you,' she said faintly. Then: 'I suppose that what I did, uh, I suppose that's why Lucy acts the way she does.'

'Oh, Mrs Bending,' he said with a wave of his hand, 'human behavior is such a tangle. A can of worms. I wish I could give you a definite answer. I wish I could say Yes, Lucy saw you making love to a strange man in a bedroom used only by you and her father, and that experience triggered her deviant conduct. It would be wonderful if life was that simple, if A led inevitably to B. But we are not neat, simple, logical beings. There is always C and D and E, and on through and beyond the alphabet. All I can say now is that witnessing the, ah, incident was undoubtedly a contributing factor to Lucy's problem. It might help if you told me a little more about it.'

She looked at him, amazed. 'I thought you knew. You described it so well. I thought Lucy had told you.'

'Suppose *you* tell me.'

She inhaled deeply. 'Of course I remember that party. How can I ever forget it? It was like you said: drinking, dancing, smoking pot. I suppose things got a little out of hand. I don't know what it was. But some parties are like that. I know I was wild. I'm not going to blame it on the drinks or the grass; I knew what I was doing. It's all my fault.'

'You knew your husband had left?'

'I didn't see him leave, but I knew he was gone, yes. And I guessed who he was with. So I thought – why not me? Why should I be left out?'

'Mrs Bending, I don't want to know any names, but can you tell me this: Was the man you, ah, went upstairs with, was he the husband of the woman you suspected of being with your husband?'

'No. Do you mean did I do it to get back at Ronnie? Oh no, it was nothing like that. I just did it to – to – I guess I did it because I wanted to prove I was still attractive to other men. I really don't know why I did it.'

'And Lucy witnessed it?'

'Yes. Briefly. It happened pretty much as you said. We should have locked the door, I know, but we didn't. Too

419

excited, I guess. Then I looked up, and Lucy was standing there. By the way, she was wearing pajamas, not a night-gown.'

'Was the act, ah, consummated?'

She smiled wryly. 'In the process. After I saw Lucy watching us, it was never, as you say, consummated.'

'What happened after you saw her?'

'I think I screamed. I know I got off the bed. Lucy ran back to her own bedroom and slammed the door. I wanted to go to her, but the man I was with, he said maybe it would be best to leave her alone. He said maybe she'd fall asleep, and when she woke up in the morning, she wouldn't remember it. Or think it had been a bad dream. He said not to make a big deal out of it.'

Levin couldn't have told her whether or not that was the wisest course. Who could predict what the child might or might not remember? Who could have said whether it might or might not affect her future behavior? Undoubted-ly other young children had witnessed similar episodes with no lasting harm.

'Mrs Bending, you told me that the first manifestation of Lucy's deviant behavior was when she appeared naked on the terrace while your husband was entertaining male friends?'

'Yes, that's correct.'

'Did you immediately connect the two events – what had happened the night of the party and the terrace incident?'

'No, not immediately. I thought it was just one of those silly things that children do. Then, when she continued to misbehave, I began to think there was a connection.'

He looked at her sympathetically. 'And blamed yourself?'

She stared down at her white gloves. 'Yes.'

'You've been through a bad time.'

She raised her head to look at him. 'I've been through hell. Hell!'

'And turned to religion for rescue?'

'Yes,' she said, lifting her chin.

'But it took almost four years to seek help for Lucy.' A statement, not a question.

'Doctor, there's nothing you can accuse me of that I haven't accused myself of a hundred, a thousand times. I told you, it's all my fault.'

'Well, let's not waste time on recriminations. The important thing, the *only* thing, is to restore Lucy's mental and emotional health.'

'Well,' she said, sighing, 'my part of it's over. I thought it would kill me to tell you, but it didn't.'

'Confession is rarely fatal,' he said dryly.

'What will you do now, doctor?'

'I don't know,' he said frankly. 'I must think about it.'

'Does Lucy remember? What she saw?'

'Oh, I think the memory is there. She cannot yet verbalize it. She recalls the events leading up to it. Then the curtain comes down. I think she must dredge up the entire incident. Only then can we begin to talk about its meaning and how she feels about it.'

Grace Bending shuddered. 'She'll hate me. I know she will.'

Dr Levin began to swing slowly back and forth in his swivel chair. He longed for a cigar.

'That may be her initial reaction,' he admitted. 'Part of my job will be handling that hate. Do you hate her, Mrs Bending?'

She started as if he had struck her. 'How can you say such an awful thing?'

'It would be understandable if you did. After enduring such anguish on her account.'

'I love my daughter, doctor.'

'Do you? Almost inevitably, I find, successful therapy for a child involves therapy for the entire family. This is just a suggestion, Mrs Bending, but what would you think of a session, or several, at which you, your husband, and all your children would be present and involved?'

421

'Group therapy?'

'Something like that. I would serve – oh, as a kind of master of ceremonies. But it would be up to all of you to come to a better understanding of who and what you are, as a family. It is a procedure that quite possibly might yield positive results. But first we must help Lucy. At the moment, that's our first objective. I believe our time is up, Mrs Bending.'

He saw her to the door, hovering close, fearing she might be unsteady after her emotional outburst. But she seemed sturdy enough. Almost blithe, in fact.

She turned suddenly and kissed him lightly on the cheek.

'Thank you, doctor,' she said breathlessly.

He smiled and nodded. When the door closed behind her, he headed immediately for his desk to switch off the tape recorder and light a fresh cigar.

He thought her a remarkably attractive woman.

4

On Saturday morning, William Holloway cleaned and oiled his revolver. He crooned over Eric, handling it with excessive caution. As always, he spoke to himself (or the gun) aloud, detailing what he was about to do, was doing, had done.

Saturday morning was really the best time of the week. The kids were off somewhere, Craner was probably walking the beach with Gertrude Empt, and Jane was absent on one of those vague 'errands' that were taking her away from home with increasing frequency.

And Maria had the day off, gone to Miami for an anti-Castro rally. So Holloway had the house to himself, which was a pleasure. The whole day stretched ahead of him, filled with lonely promise.

After he finished with Eric, holstered and tucked it away, he wandered downstairs in bare feet, wearing white duck trousers and a white guayabera shirt. A costume which, he admitted, made him look like a paunchy barber.

It was about 10:45 A.M. But, like all heavy drinkers, Holloway told himself it was noon somewhere in the world. So he mixed a spicy Bloody Mary, taking almost as much pleasure in the preparation as he would in the consumption.

He swathed the glass in a paper napkin and carried his first drink of the day out onto the terrace. He walked into a pearly world.

A translucent haze filled the sky, hanging down close to the sea. This milky glow seemed thick and swirly, shot through with sparkles. It gave a shadowless light over water and land that softened everything it touched.

The ocean was rough and the surfers were out. They paddled resolutely until they were lost in the mist. And then suddenly they came shooting in, crouched, riding a high breaker. Their shouts came faintly, muffled but joyous.

Holloway settled comfortably onto a padded deck lounge, after adjusting the back to a half-reclining position. He looked about at the creamy day, wondering why the brisk breeze didn't drive the fog away.

He watched the surfers.

There were about twenty of them, boys and young men. A few girls sitting on the beach waited for them to finish. But the surfers were oblivious to their audience. They sat astride their short Florida boards, waiting for the right comber.

Then, finding one to their liking, they stood, bent and limber, and came rushing in. Keeping a precarious balance, steering by shifting weight, they rode the wave until it subsided or until it crashed, and they were spilled, lost in the creamy foam.

William Holloway took his second drink down to the beach, sat, and watched. He took his third drink down to the shore, sat, and watched. His son was not surfing, but Wayne Bending was out there, wearing cutoff jeans and a blue tanktop.

But for the moment, Holloway didn't concentrate on him; he was trying to absorb the whole scene. The milky haze, a charging sea, surfers exploding out of the mist, hissing speed, blond hair flying, wet skin gleaming, the violent spill . . .

They were all beautiful, Holloway thought. All of them. The daring and danger only accented their beauty and youth. What did it matter if they might be vulgar, stupid, or worse? At that moment, in that setting, he saw them as young gods taming the sea, and he loved them all.

424

Here they came! Arms outstretched. Grinning and exultant. Working their boards. Dipping, zigzagging. And then, as the wave died, standing erect. Proud. Triumphant. It was all so elegant, so innocent, that William Jasper Holloway felt like weeping. Theirs was a joy he could witness but could not share.

And he wanted to share – his hope of living a virtuous life, enduring a wound, sacrificing . . .

He wanted to tell all this to Wayne Bending, but the boy returned again and again to the sea, never tiring. Holloway marveled at the young strength in that blunt body: bunched shoulders, sturdy legs, the soft skin streaming with froth.

'Have you thought any more about what you told me, Wayne?'

'About leaving, Mr Holloway? Yeah, I just about decided. I'm going to split.'

'I wish you wouldn't.'

'There's nothing for me here.'

'I'm here, Wayne. I'd like to be your friend.'

'Yeah . . . well . . . 'preciate that. But . . . you know . . .'

'I'm much older than you; I know that. But there's so much I could teach you.'

'Yeah? Like what?'

'Not to make the mistakes I made. To go with your feelings, your instincts. Not to be ashamed of what you are. To learn to live with yourself and to soar –'

He sat there for the remainder of the afternoon, drinking slowly but steadily and hugging his knees. And all the time the beautiful boys faded into the mist and then came rushing toward him, tense and eager.

Young bodies shining. Hair flickering like flame. Arms stretching wide. Out of the haze they came, a glittering platoon, skimming the sea. They would live forever. They would never age, never die.

425

5

It was the last fuck Ronald Bending was going to get from her. She didn't think it wise to tell him that, but she was unusually affectionate and solicitous of his pleasure during their final tryst.

Jane Holloway thought of sex as – well, perhaps not as an art, but certainly as a skilled craft. Blessed with a whippy body that turned men lickerish, she had concluded at an early age that she would be a fool not to use it. Sex became her route to popularity and success.

It never meant a great deal to her – similar to scratching a mosquito bite, she reckoned – but she recognized its importance as a weapon in her war with men. And she had the determination to become proficient. Patience, practice, and a willingness to learn – from whatever source.

Turk Bending, no slouch in the mattress department himself, acknowledged her expertise.

'You could give Errol Flynn an erection,' he told her.

'Turk, he's been dead for years.'

'I know.'

They were in that grungy motel, air conditioner still whining, walls still blotched with maps of strange worlds. She had brought along a bottle of chilled champagne and they were drinking it out of plastic cups.

'What's the occasion?' he had asked when she unwrapped the bottle.

'Oh,' she said casually, 'I just felt like it.'

He had learned to accept her whims and thought no more of it. They polished off half the bottle and then had a grand toss in the hay during which she got them into a position which he was certain threatened his sacroiliac.

'Jesus!' he shouted. 'Take it easy.'

So she took it easy. So easy that his fears turned from spinal injury to cardiac arrest. After he had exploded, imploded, and decompressed, they sat up in bed, finished the champagne, and smoked his filter-tips.

'What are you going to do?' she asked him.

'At the moment? Recuperate.'

'You know what I mean. About the corporation.'

He turned to look at her. 'What's Bill going to do?'

'You know Bill,' she said, shrugging. 'He doesn't want any trouble. He just wants out. After all, he's a bank president.'

'What am I – chopped liver? Well, Bill can do what he likes. Luther and I are going to fight those slobs.'

'You haven't got a legal leg to stand on.'

'That's what our attorney told us. But we've got something better – the threat of publicity. We take them into court – even knowing we're going to lose – and their whole operation gets opened up in newspapers and on TV. Then the bible-thumpers start screaming – and who knows? Maybe they'll have to close up shop or at least get run out of the state. Luther and I figure they'll do just about anything to avoid that. We've got them over a barrel.'

She leaned across him to stub out her cigarette in a cracked ashtray that had *Casa Mañana* printed on the side.

'I wish you wouldn't,' she said. 'I think you're just asking for trouble.'

'What kind of trouble?' he said, laughing. 'You think they're going to send a limousine full of bent-noses to mow us down with tommy guns?'

'No, I don't think they'll do that. But they have money and power. I don't think you should take them lightly.'

'Hey,' he said, 'you're the lady who was all for this deal, with your cash fee for talking Bill into coming along, and wanting a percentage when we ease Luther out. How come you've changed your mind?'

'I just think they're too strong to buck,' she said. 'I think the three of you should take your money and run.'

'Bullshit to that,' he said. 'We'll threaten to drag them through the mud and they'll come around – you'll see.'

'If you say so,' she said, thinking Jimmy Stone had been right when he called them amateurs.

'When are you going to do all this?' she asked him.

'The lawyers are drawing up the papers now. We'll show copies to Stone and Santangelo before we actually file. Just seeing what we're going to do will make them sit up and beg.'

She turned toward him, onto her side. She moved close to him.

'Put your cigarette out,' she commanded.

He did.

She pulled him to her until their noses were almost touching.

'Now what?' he said.

'Stare into my eyes. Don't even blink. And don't say a word.'

Only their faces were close. Their naked bodies were apart, and her nailed fingers were busy.

'Where did –' he started.

'Shhh,' she said sharply. 'Not a word. Just keep looking into my eyes.'

She worked on him slowly, with cruel deliberation. His mouth fell open; his breathing quickened. But she would not let him move his body closer, but kept him pushed away while she searched his eyes.

'No,' she said, halting her services, 'not yet.'

Then, watching him for a moment, she began again: starting, stopping, starting, stopping, her expression vulpine. She was a marvelous tart. Only passion was lacking.

When he convulsed, she showed her sharp teeth in what might have been a grin. Only then did she cleave to his

428

sweated, sticky body. She kissed his closed eyes, temples, ears, lips. Chaste, fleeting kisses.

'My God,' he breathed finally, 'you're awfully loving today.'

She was silent, but held him tightly, would not let him go. He surrendered to her embrace, thinking himself the most fortunate of men, and gloating. After a while:

'Shower?' he asked her.

'Not yet,' she said, slowly disengaging, rolling away from him.

She lay upon her back, stared at that cracked ceiling. She went through the usual drill: feeling her own body, probing smooth thighs, flat abdomen, hard breasts. She slicked herself with her palms, fondling a valuable belonging. Bending watched, amused.

'I can never get enough of you,' he told her, 'and you can never get enough of you.'

She nodded agreement.

'Jane, I wish you'd talk Bill into coming in with Luther and me on the lawsuit. We can make those cruds beg for mercy.'

'No,' she said. 'Bill wants out, and this time I think he's right.'

'It'll change things,' he warned her. 'We'll win, and if Bill doesn't help, we'll dump him. You know that, don't you?'

'I know it,' she said, 'and I suppose Bill knows it. He just doesn't care.'

'Okay,' Bending said. 'As long as you and I can keep rubbing the pork . . .'

She took his head lightly between her palms and thrust up to meet his mouth.

'My hero,' she said.

6

Ernie Goldman was working late at the office. Everyone else had gone. The drapes were still drawn against the afternoon sun. The air conditioners still hummed. Overhead fluorescent tubes cast a pallid glow that turned Goldman's saffron complexion to mustard.

He was not sweating over Luther Empt's business affairs; Goldman was working on his personal finances. On the desk before him were a plastic bottle of Di-Gel and a shotglass.

He had assembled copies of all his gambling markers, current household bills, bank statements, and indignant letters from attorneys representing the savings and loan association that held his home mortgage, the company that had financed his car, and a personal loan service that, in effect, now owned his furniture, clothes and, for all he knew, his wife and children.

With quick, nervous stabs, Ernie Goldman ran up totals on a pocket calculator. When he finished and inspected the results, he sat back and rapidly slugged two shots of Di-Gel.

Suicide was one possibility. But the thought of self-inflicted pain made him blink faster than ever; he reached for more of the antacid. Another possibility was to declare personal bankruptcy. Take a bath. He could imagine how Sammy Brokar, the bookie who held his markers, would react to that. Crushed kneecaps for Ernie – at the very least.

He had stopped questioning how he had dug such a pit for himself. It had started with a slip and ended with a slide.

Now he was in so deep, he knew he could never claw his way up and out. Empt had cut him off from further salary advances that afternoon. Goldman's relatives hung up on him.

He swept all the bumf into a desk drawer and rose wearily, a young old man. He pulled on his jacket (five years old, that doubleknit polyester). He went through the offices, turning off lights and adjusting air conditioners to night temperatures. Ernie Goldman was always the last to leave; everyone knew that.

When he left the building, it was twilight, a dim violet glow in the western sky. Goldman shambled into the parking lot, mildly surprised to see that his six-year-old clunker had not yet been repossessed. He was fumbling for his keys when suddenly they were there, hemming him in, pressing him against the car.

Two burly young guys wearing T-shirts with the sleeves rolled up above their biceps, and faded jeans so tight you could count their balls. One had a scraggly blond mustache that covered his mouth. The other needed a shave and had a fresh tattoo on his left forearm: heart, dagger, and 'Mother.'

'Hi, Ernie,' mustache said genially.

Goldman didn't know them, but he knew who they were. No-necks, he called them.

'Listen,' he said quickly, licking his lips, 'tell Sammy I'm going to come up with some scratch. Tomorrow noon at the latest. Absolutely.'

'Nah,' tattoo said, smiling. 'Not to worry. Sammy's out, Ernie.'

'Out?'

'And we're in,' mustache said. 'Ain't that nice? You're owned by Jimmy now.'

'Jimmy?'

'That's right,' tattoo said. 'A guy named Jimmy got you out of hock. That make you happy, Ernie?'

'Well . . . uh . . . yes . . . sure.'

'Here,' mustache said, thrusting a business card at Gold-man. 'Aristocrat Productions. This is the number you call for action. Horses, dogs, football, baseball, basketball – whatever. Ask for Jimmy.'

'Thank you,' Ernie Goldman said faintly. 'This, uh, Jimmy bought my markers?'

'No sweat,' tattoo assured him. 'He's a reasonable man. You'll like Jimmy. You do something for him, he'll do something for you.'

Emboldened by the hope that he was not to have his kneecaps crushed, Goldman said, 'Well . . . sure. What-ever I can.'

'That's the boy, Ernie,' mustache said. 'Cooperation. It makes the world go 'round – right?'

Tattoo held a thick forefinger in bent tension on his thumb, then reached out and flicked the end of Goldman's bulbous nose. It hurt so much that tears came to Ernie's eyes.

'Hey,' he said in mild protest.

'You just behave,' tattoo said, flicking Ernie's nose again. 'We'll be in touch and let you know how you can help Jimmy.'

'Whatever you say,' Goldman said, holding a cupped hand over his throbbing nose.

Mustache pulled his hand away and tattoo flicked the nose again. The pain was so sharp, so intense, that Gold-man reeled and fell back against the car.

'Don't get any bright ideas,' mustache said. 'Like taking off for parts unknown or going to the cops. Nothing like that.'

'Oh no,' Ernie said, his voice a sob. 'I never would.'

'Good,' tattoo said, giving his nose a final flick. 'Just go about your business and act normal. You'll be hearing from us. And don't worry about your markers.'

'Thank you very much,' Ernie Goldman said humbly, touching his nose.

*   *   *

432

Ronald Bending couldn't decide if he admired and loved his silver-gray Porsche 924 Turbo because it reminded him of Jane Holloway, or if he admired and loved the woman because she reminded him of the car.

Both had a smooth, elegant, pared-down look. No gaudy ornamentation. Nothing extraneous to function. Both built for speed. Both with bodies like Brancusi's 'Bird in Space.'

On the evening after Ernie Goldman had the nose problem, Bending decided he might cruise around, check out a few joints, and – who knows? – maybe find the great temporary love of his life. He framed a plausible cover story and called home. Luckily, Wayne answered.

'Hiya kid,' Bending said to his son. 'How's it going?'

'Okay,' Wayne said.

'Listen, tell your mother I can't get home for dinner. Big client in town, and I've got to wine him and dine him.'

'Sure,' Wayne said.

'This cat's from up north,' Bending went on glibly. 'Lots of bucks. Maybe he'll pick up the check.' He laughed heartily.

'Uh-huh,' Wayne said.

'So tell mother not to wait up for me. All right? Tell her I'll lock up when I get home.'

'Yeah,' Wayne said.

Bending hung up, wondering what was eating the kid. Growing pains, he supposed, and thought no more of it.

He showered and shaved in his office bathroom, changing to fresh underwear, socks, and shirt from a supply he kept there for just such occasions. Instead of putting on his suit coat, he donned a jazzy Porsche racing jacket and cap (with emblem) he had recently purchased.

It was finky, he knew, because he had never raced the Porsche in his life and didn't intend to. But the sharp nylon jacket and gold-trimmed cap were two more links to his marvelous machine. He inspected himself in the bathroom mirror, gave the cap a more rakish tilt. Crazy! He sallied forth, carrying suit coat and briefcase.

As usual, before he got into his car, he walked around it, inspecting the glossy finish anxiously for nicks, scratches, dents. It was his baby, and he spent a fortune on maintenance, following the manual religiously on periodic checkups and tunings.

He tossed suit coat and briefcase into the back. Sitting behind the wheel in his racing jacket and cap, he inhaled once again that wonderful new-car smell: leather, oil, machinery, money. The lighted dash looked like the control panel of a 747.

'Pilot to tower,' he said aloud. 'Taking off on south runway.'

Apparently he received a favorable response, for he gunned out of the parking lot, made a sharp turn, and headed for the Chez When. Where the action was.

He was so happy with his new racing jacket and cap, his freedom, with this incredible vehicle that responded nimbly to the lightest touch, that he had no awareness of the black Pontiac Grand Prix that picked him up when he left the parking lot and followed him south on Federal Highway.

'Lots of action tonight, Mr Bending,' the Chez When parking valet said, trotting forward to open the car door. Then, when Bending stepped out, 'Wow, will you look at the threads!'

'You like, Jimbo?'

'Wild,' the valet said admiringly. 'If you can't score in that getup, it's time for Geritol.'

Bending walked casually into the bar, didn't remove his braided cap until most of the creamers got a look at him. Then he found a vacant barstool, swung aboard, and ordered a bourbon, water on the side.

He had time for only one sip, hadn't even inspected the prospects sitting at the bar, when he felt a tug on his jacket sleeve. He swung around, and there was the superbutterball.

'What are you selling tonight?' he asked her. 'Cancer?'

434

'Listen,' she said, 'I'm sorry about that, pal. She wasn't due back until the next night. Honest.' Then, when she saw him looking about nervously . . . 'Don't worry, she's out of town for the week.'

'Uh-huh. What does she do for a living? All that traveling . . .'

The girl looked at him directly. 'She's on the convention circuit. Makes a good living.'

'I'll bet. She's beautiful. You swing both ways, huh?'

'Four ways,' she told him. 'Up, down, in, and out. Let me buy you a drink – to make up for what happened.'

He surrendered his barstool and stood at her shoulder. She really did want to buy him a drink, so he let her. But after that one, he paid.

They had a few more wallops and ignored what had happened the last time they met. They started talking nonsense again:

'I like your jacket,' she said. 'Are you a colonel in the Liechtenstein army?'

'Actually,' he said, 'I'm an admiral in the Swiss navy. But I have a confession to make: I'm not wearing a bra.'

'Doesn't it hurt when you jog?'

'Only downhill. You never did tell me your name.'

'Frank,' she said. 'And my girlfriend's name is Ernest.'

'What a coincidence,' he said. 'My law firm is Totter & Reel.'

And so on . . .

Bending wasn't sure he wanted to invest in a dinner again. But the girl was undeniably luscious . . . and available. She was wearing a wraparound skirt that fell open when she climbed onto the barstool. There were those creamy thighs.

She caught him staring. 'I told you she's out of town.'

'No,' he said regretfully, 'I can't take the chance.'

'Your place?'

'Impossible. I live at the YMCA.'

'How about a motel?'

He took a deep breath. 'Let's go have dinner,' he said.

Again, he watched with amazement while she demolished a two-pound lobster, french fries, asparagus, a small loaf of pumpernickel – and made two trips to the salad bar.

'Better have some dessert,' he advised her. 'I don't want the waitress thinking I starve you.'

'I'll work it off,' she assured him. 'On you. That Black Forest chocolate cake sounds good.'

He thought he'd take her to that grubby motel where he and Jane Holloway got it off. It was a deserted place, way out west past I-95. And it would be amusing if they got the same room. The same bed.

When Jimbo brought the Porsche around, Bending tipped him grandly, put on his glittery cap, and zipped up the racing jacket. Superbutterball looked at him admiringly.

'And the Mardi Gras hasn't even started,' she said.

They were talking tomfoolery again when they pulled out of the parking lot, and of course they didn't notice the black Pontiac Grand Prix that stayed well back, but made every turn they did.

At the motel, Bending went in to pay in advance and to register: Mr and Mrs Ben Cellini. He couldn't get the unit he wanted – it was occupied – but he was assigned another which the porcine proprietor assured him was 'just as comfy.'

Bending insisted on stashing the Porsche at the far end of the graveled parking lot, in the shadows of a stand of untrimmed bottle palms.

'I don't like to leave it under the lights,' he explained to superbutterball. 'Some smartass will try to hot-wire it or rip off the hubcaps.'

'Or someone you know,' she said shrewdly, 'might spot this cock-wagon and know you're shacked up here.'

'That, too,' he said laughing.

They found their unit. He unlocked the door and switched on the overhead light.

'I know it's not much, sugar,' he said, 'but stick with me, and I swear it won't be long before we have a Formica dinette set and a pop-up toaster.'

'You're the only pop-up toaster I want, sweetums,' she said. 'Lock the door. Then you show me yours, and I'll show you mine.'

While their preparations were progressing with much jollity and badinage, the black Pontiac Grand Prix, lights out, cruised slowly into the parking lot. It paused a moment, then started again and took up a position close to Bending's Porsche.

The driver and passenger, both wearing white T-shirts with sleeves rolled up above their biceps, settled down to wait.

'We'll give him fifteen minutes,' mustache said. 'He should be in the saddle by then.'

'Leave the motor running,' tattoo said. 'Just in case.'

'Who has the fun this time?' mustache said.

'Flip you for it,' tattoo said.

Inside the motel, superbutterball was doing her best to make up for what she called the 'indignity' suffered by Ronald Bending at their last meeting.

'All right, all right,' he said. 'I forgive you, I forgive you.'

While the fun and games were going on, the two men got out of the Pontiac. Mustache stood guard at the driver's door. Tattoo, who had won the toss, went to the trunk and took out an eight-pound sledgehammer.

He set to work on the Porsche with ferocious glee.

Ronald Bending stopped what he was doing and looked up. 'What's that?'

'What's what?' she said crossly. 'And why are you stopping?'

'There it is again,' he said. 'Sounds like someone's swatting an empty boiler with a baseball bat. Can't you hear it?'

'I hear it, I hear it,' she said, sighing. 'What's it got to do with us?'

Then came the unmistakable shatter and tinkle of broken glass.

'My God,' Bending said nervously, 'are they demolishing the place for a high-rise at this hour?'

The noise continued: the metallic bong and screech of tortured metal, the crash of falling glass. Bending got out of bed and began to pull on his pants.

'Where are you going?' she demanded.

'I'll just take a look around,' he said. He tried a grin that didn't work. 'That damned noise destroys my concentration.'

He thrust bare feet into his loafers, pulled on his nylon racing jacket.

'You stay here,' he told her. 'Lock the door behind me. I'll be right back after I find out what's going on.'

When he went outside, there were a few other men standing uncertainly in front of their units, looking around. The fat proprietor came stumbling, trying to get suspender straps over his balbriggan undershirt.

The noise had stopped. There was nothing to be seen. Bending began walking toward his Porsche, then trotting, then running. He stopped about ten feet away. The proprietor came wheezing up. And others behind him.

'Jesus H. Christ,' someone said with awe.

The body of the car had been demolished. Roof, doors, fenders, hood, side panels. Not only deep dents, but places where the metal had buckled and folded, and a few spots where the weapon used had penetrated completely, leaving jagged, paint-chipped holes. Even the hubcaps had been punished.

Every bit of glass was broken: windshield, windows, the big back plate. Headlights, taillights, parking lights were shattered. The sunroof had been hammered in, and now lay inside the car. Even the outside rearview mirror had been sheared off and lay broken on the gravel.

'I didn't see nothing,' the proprietor said hoarsely. 'I don't know nothing.'

Ronald Bending stood staring at his dream defiled. He felt the sting of tears. He tried to tell himself it was only a *thing*, but he didn't succeed. They had done more than destroy his wonderful machine.

It was the way he saw the world and his own life. The lark had soured. This was cruelty and menace beyond measure. He saw now the darkness and the danger. The message was clear: Death lurked.

Gone the fun and games. Vanished the beauty. Stilled the nonsense jabber. The beach, the creamers, the action, the sweet fucks. None of that was real. This was real. Ugliness, pain, and the black void.

They hadn't destroyed; they had created. Fear. He could never again look at sunrise or sunset without wondering if it might be his last. They had shoved his face in the mirror and showed him his own mortality. The tap dancer was vanquished.

'Who'd want to do something like that?' a voice asked.

'The pricks,' Luther Empt said wrathfully. 'Lousy pricks.'

Ronald Bending made no response. He was seated in an armchair in Luther's office. His knees were crossed; one foot jerked uncontrollably up and down. He was smoking one of his filter-tips. The ashtray beside him was filled with long butts, crushed and split.

'What did you do then?' Luther asked.

'Left it there,' Bending said. 'Got home by cab. The garage towed it in this morning.'

'Can they fix it, Turk?'

'I suppose,' Bending said, shrugging. 'The chassis is okay. But I don't want it. What's the point?'

Empt rose and poured Bending another stiff jolt of bourbon.

'Look,' he said, 'if you let this get you, they'll walk all over us.'

Bending gave him a ghastly smile. 'I've got to be honest with you, Luther. They hit me where it hurt.'

'It was just a *car*, for God's sake,' Empt said. Then he started selling, assuring Turk that if he stood fast, they could beat those cruds. He had a meet set up with Stone and Santangelo for next week, and once those bums saw the legal papers, they'd cave in. And –

'Luther,' Bending said, holding up a palm to interrupt the pitch, 'you may be right. I'm not saying you're not. But I'm getting out.'

'No balls,' Empt said angrily.

Bending didn't take offense. 'You're absolutely right. I'm scared shitless. If they can do that, they can do *anything*. And you know something else? It'll probably sound crazy to you, but I don't want to cruise anymore. I'm afraid I won't be able to get it up.'

'You're nuts!'

'Probably. But that's the way I feel. I'm sorry, Luther, but I'm getting out.'

'Not me,' Empt said furiously. 'I don't crawl for anyone. What can they do to me? Whatever it is, I can take it. Believe me, they don't know who they're tangling with.'

Bending sighed. 'If you say so. But think it over. These are not nice people, Luther.'

He drank his glass of bourbon. Just put his head back and belted it. Then he rose slowly, took a deep breath, tugged his suit jacket down. He looked about Empt's office vaguely.

'Well,' he said, with a honk of cold laughter, 'it was nice while it lasted. It just didn't last, that's all. Best of luck.'

'Yeah,' Empt said. 'See you on the beach Saturday?'

'Sure. I'm not going to curl up and die. Listen, if the weather holds, maybe we can have a cookout or something.'

'Count me in,' Empt said. 'Whatever you say.'

He watched Bending depart. The man wasn't standing so straight. He seemed hammered down, dented and broken.

440

Luther cursed aloud, and filled his glass with more scotch. He paced back and forth across his office. He had his own troubles.

He didn't want to tell Bending, but Ernie Goldman, that creep, had just come in at noon and announced he was quitting. Just like that. Shocked, Empt asked him how come.

'Uh, I got another job.

Empt asked him with whom.

'Uh, it's a new outfit, just starting up. In Miami.'

Empt asked how much they were paying.

'Uh, that's like, you know, confidential.'

Getting good and sore at these evasions, Luther asked what the hell he planned to do about his salary advances, which now totaled more than five hundred dollars.

And would you believe it, the nervous, trembling Ernie Goldman fished out a tattered plastic wallet and paid off on the spot, to the last penny.

Empt asked him where he got that kind of loot.

'Uh, I had a good day at the track.'

Which was, Empt knew, a lot of bullshit. The guy was lying for some reason. But that wasn't important. What was important was that Empt was losing the best tech he ever had, and it would be a pain in the ass replacing him.

He paused in his pacing to telephone May. He was going to tell her that he'd be over in an hour or so, and they'd go to that black joint and have a plate of ribs. But the phone rang on, unanswered. He wasn't bothered; he knew she'd be waiting for him.

He tried to push some paper, but he couldn't concentrate. What had happened to Bending's car . . . And to Bending . . . Ernie Goldman quitting . . . Luther Empt had a sweaty feeling that he was losing control, that he was being swept away by events.

He poured himself another scotch and resumed stalking about the office, carrying the glass. One thing was certain, he vowed: he was going to fight the bums. Holloway and

Bending could weasel out, but no one screwed Luther Empt and got away with it.

He had a lot of faults; he knew that. But lack of physical courage wasn't one of them. Holloway and Bending might be scared off; nothing and nobody scared Luther Empt. He could endure pain, and if it came to dying – well, he reckoned he could get through that, too, without whimpering.

Still, there were a couple of smart precautions he could take. He would keep his .357 Magnum with him at all times: on his person, in his car, in the office, at home. If they wanted to play rough, he'd give as good as he got.

Also, in the morning he'd go to his attorney and dictate a statement to be turned over to the cops or FBI in case anything happened to him. The statement would give the details of the porn deal and point a finger straight at Rocco Santangelo and Jimmy Stone in case Empt met a violent end.

Then, at the meeting next week, Empt would make certain Santangelo and Stone knew of the existence of the statement. That should upset their dirty little applecart! The statement would serve as Luther Empt's life assurance policy.

Relaxed by the whiskey he had consumed, and emboldened by the actions he was determined to take, Empt's confidence came rushing back. He cleaned up his desk, humming. He set out for May's apartment with excited anticipation.

On the way, just because he was feeling so good, he stopped at a florist and bought his sweet girl an angel-wing begonia in a nice ceramic pot with butterflies painted on the sides. May would love that, he knew; he could see her glow of surprise and delight. How she would fly into his arms!

He had to park almost a block away and walked back to May's place, carrying the plant wrapped in white, waxy paper. As he walked, he whistled a merry tune.

He mounted the stoop to her apartment. The door was open a few inches. He stopped whistling.

She was naked on the floor, legs spread, back propped against the sofa. Blood caked on her thighs. A dried rivulet from the corner of her mouth. One eye battered, purplish, a swollen pouf. Bruises on her breasts.

Empt glanced quickly around the apartment. Her torn clothes flung. Plants upset, dirt spilling onto the floor. He put his own gift aside, closed and locked the front door. He went down on one knee beside her. She looked up at him meekly, trying to open that puffed eye.

'Rape?' he said in his harsh voice.

She nodded.

He went into the bathroom, soaked a towel in warm water He came back, knelt close, began wiping gently: her mouth, thighs. The dried blood had to be rubbed.

'Let me,' she said, taking the towel from him. She ran it over her face, breasts, arms, legs. Then she stuffed the towel into her crotch.

'I'm dirty,' she said.

'Want to go to the hospital?'

'No.'

'Do you want a doctor? I can get one.'

'No.'

He was relieved at that, and ashamed for being relieved. He went into the kitchenette, found the Cutty Sark, poured half a tumbler. He brought it back to her. Sitting on the couch, he fed her the whiskey in little sips, wondering if that was the right thing to do if she was in shock.

'When did it happen?' he asked her.

'What time is it now?'

He told her.

'They left about a half-hour ago. They were here almost two hours.'

'They? How many?'

'Two.'

'White or black?'

443

'White.'

'How did they get in?'

'I let them in. They said they had a message from you.'

'What?'

'They knocked, and I said who is it, and a man said I have a message for you from Luther. So I unlocked the door and the two of them pushed in.'

'He said my name? He said Luther? Are you sure?'

'Yes. And when they left, they said to tell Luther they were here.'

He drank off the whiskey in the tumbler. He went into the kitchenette and refilled it. He came back to her and proffered the glass, but she pushed it away.

'No more. I feel sick.'

'Do you want me to call the cops?'

'No,' she said, 'don't do that.'

Again, he was relieved. He didn't want the cops either.

'What did they look like?'

'Young. Big. Wearing white T-shirts. One had a blond mustache. One had a tattoo.'

'Ever see them before?'

'No.'

'What did they do to you?'

'I don't want to talk about it.'

Suddenly it was important to him to know.

'Tell me,' he insisted.

She told him. In a slaty voice, the words more breathed than spoken. They tore her clothes off. They punched her. Kicked her lame leg. Raped her. Both of them. Sodomized her. Other things . . .

'Do you know them?' she asked him.

'The two guys? No.'

'How did they get your name?'

'Can you get up?' he said. 'I'll help you. You'll feel better lying on the couch.'

'No,' she said. 'I've got to go in the bathroom. I've got to take care of myself.'

'Oh,' he said. 'Yeah. Sure. Here, I'll help you.'

He lifted her to her feet, hands under her armpits. He supported her to the bathroom door, arm about her waist.

'You'll be okay?' he asked.

She nodded dumbly, went in, closed the door.

He went directly to the kitchenette sink, washed his hands thoroughly, dried them on paper towels. Then he tried to straighten the place: picked up her torn clothing, righted the overturned plants, even swept up the spilled dirt. Anything to keep from thinking.

May was in the bathroom a long time. He was getting concerned, but then he heard her moving about, heard the shower running, the toilet flush. He sat lumpily in the armchair, drank whiskey, waited.

She came out of the bathroom naked. He was surprised at that, and disturbed. He wished she had put on a nightgown or robe. Anything to cover herself.

'I took some aspirin,' she said. 'I hurt all over.'

'Are you going to be, uh, all right? You know . . .'

'I douched,' she said. 'And I'm on the Pill. So . . .'

She had pulled her long hair back tightly, bound it with a barrette. Her white face and body were scrubbed clean. Her skin shone. The darkening bruises stood out against the pallor like giant thumbprints.

'Can I get you something to eat?' he asked her. 'Or drink?'

She shook her head. 'I don't feel like it. I think I'll just get in bed and try to sleep. You don't have to stay.'

'I'll hang around,' he said. 'For a while.'

She stripped the coverlet from the couch, balled it up, threw it into a corner.

'They fucked me right on top,' she said matter-of-factly. 'So the sheets are clean.'

He hoped she would cover herself up, but she didn't. Just lay atop the sheet, small pillow under her head, thin arms folded across her punished breasts: a waxen corpse waiting for a shroud.

'Will you turn off some of the lights, please?' she said. 'It hurts my eyes.'

He switched off everything but the bathroom light, and left the door ajar so the big room was dimly illuminated.

He sat down again. He drank more whiskey, not tasting it. He stared at her, lying so still, so drained. Her arms were down at her sides now. Eyes closed. She said nothing, and he could not stop himself from thinking.

She was such a scrawny thing. Not his type of woman at all. Bones jutted. Those pancake breasts. Thin arms, and then that gimpy leg. No meat on her. Not really pretty. He imagined even her hair had lost its gloss. He wondered how he could have been physically excited by this broken bird.

His sweet little girl. His maiden. His virgin. No more. She had let those two guys use her like any two-bit whore. 'May I accommodate you?' She had accommodated them all right. Done whatever they wanted. Maybe even asked for more. It was possible.

It was all spoiled for Luther Empt. He didn't want to remember how he had felt about her, because then shame made his stomach flop. But that was all over now, all gone. Things could never be the way they had been.

He thought ponderously of how he might get away from her. He finally decided a hard, sharp break would be the best way to handle it. As far as he knew, she didn't know his last name, address, telephone number.

He'd just walk away from her. What the hell, she had been a hooker when he met her; she could take care of herself. Maybe he'd mail her a nice tip. That should make her happy.

He thought she might be dozing. He heard noises coming from her. Little sighs, little sobs. He rose cautiously, sidled toward the front door. He watched her, ready to return if she opened her eyes. But she didn't stir.

He eased the door open, slipped through, closed it gently behind him. He took a deep breath of cool night air.

He was beyond crying out at the cruelty and injustice of it all. What was it Turk Bending had said? 'They hit me where it hurt.'

7

Lucy came skipping into Levin's office, smile aglow. To his astonishment, he found himself recalling a quotation from *Cymbeline*: 'Golden lads and girls all must, as chimney-sweepers, come to dust.'

She was wearing painters' white overalls, a turquoise T-shirt, scuffed sneakers on sockless feet. The long, sunny tresses were braided into two plaits, tied with bows of green yarn. About one wrist was her bangle of seashells.

There was an exuberance in her manner that daunted him.

'How are you today, Lucy?' he said with a show of gaiety. 'I like your overalls! Very, ah, different.'

'We're all wearing them now, Doctor Ted,' she said, looking down at her costume. 'It's like, you know, a fad. Listen, can I ask you something?'

'Of course.'

'You didn't make my mother cry, did you?'

'Why do you ask that?'

'Well, the last time she was here, she came home, and she looked just awful. She had been crying. My goodness, I can tell. So I wondered if you made her cry.'

'No, Lucy, *I* didn't make her cry. But she told me something sad, and perhaps that made her cry.'

She looked at him with narrowed eyes, her head cocked to one side. 'Something sad, Doctor Ted? Something I did?'

He thought he might as well get to it. 'No, it wasn't anything you did. It was something she did that she's sorry

448

for now. She wishes it had never happened. Can you guess what it might be, Lucy?'

Eyes and mouth rounded to O's. She inched forward in the big armchair, sat on the edge so that her toes touched the floor. 'Oh!' she cried excitedly. 'That reminds me; I was going to tell you something. You remember how you liked those stories I told you? The ones I made up? Well, I made up a new story, and I said to myself, Doctor Ted would like to –'

'Lucy,' he said, interrupting her, 'can you guess what it was that made your mother sad? Something that she's sorry for now?'

She looked at him steadily. 'No, I don't know why she cried. It's certainly beyond me.'

'Do you remember that party you told me about? At your house. You wore a new dress and danced with your father for the first time.'

'Did I tell you about that?'

'Yes, you did.'

'Well, certainly I remember that party, although it was years and years ago. I was very young. It was a very nice party.'

'I'm sure it was. You were allowed to stay up an hour past your regular bedtime. Isn't that correct?'

'Maybe. I don't really remember.'

'But finally you went upstairs to your bedroom. You undressed and got into your pajamas. Then what happened?'

'I fell asleep,' she said promptly.

'That's not what you told me, Lucy,' he said gently. 'You said that you were so excited by the party that you lay awake for a long time.'

'Did I tell you that? Well . . . maybe.'

'And then?'

'Then? Then I fell asleep.'

'Did anyone come upstairs? Did you hear voices? Did you get out of bed to investigate?'

She looked at him. 'No,' she said.

It would have been too easy, he admitted, to make a breakthrough on his first attempt. He decided to come at her from another direction.

'Lucy, when you woke up the next morning, the morning after the party, do you remember having a dream?'

'A nice dream?' she asked.

'It could have been a nice dream,' he said cautiously, 'or it could have been a bad dream. Do you remember having any dream at all that night?'

'No,' she said in a small voice.

He sat back in his swivel chair. He wondered if other psychotherapists had the occasional urges he had: to grab a patient by the shoulders and shake savagely until the brain rattled and eyeballs rolled up into the skull.

He never did that, of course. And even if he did, he acknowledged it would probably be counterproductive. But still, he sometimes thought fondly of the days when priests and medicos scourged the demons from the bodies of recalcitrant patients.

'You don't remember?' he said softly. 'Are you telling me the truth, Lucy?'

She slipped off the edge of the chair and stood, tugging at one of her braids. She looked at him with a glazed smile he could not fathom.

'Doctor Ted . . .' she said.

He waited.

'I like you. I love you.'

She circled the desk slowly, came around to him. He turned in his swivel chair to face her. She came close, put her soft hands on his knees.

'Do you love me?' she asked in a seductive voice.

'There are many kinds of love, Lucy,' he began pedantically. 'There is the love your parents –'

'I love you,' she repeated, her small hands creeping up his thighs.

He had listened to the parents' description of her behavior and, intellectually, could understand their concern. But now, witnessing her aberration, being part of it, he could appreciate emotionally the intensity of their fears. His initial reaction was dread.

Transference was hardly a new experience for him. For any psychiatrist. But this passion was not for him, he knew. It was for what he represented. It could have been any of her father's friends, a teacher, a man who returned her smile on the street, the beach, anywhere.

He could have ended the incident immediately. He could have stood, stalked away. He could have buzzed for the receptionist. He could have banished Lucy immediately. But there was a chance . . .

He leaned forward, imprisoned her two little hands in his meaty paws. He held those hands lightly, drew her closer.

'Dear,' he said in a throaty voice. 'Darling.' He released one hand briefly to touch her hair, following the scenario she had remembered and related.

'I don't care,' she said in a singsongy voice, eyes glittering. 'I just don't care.'

Her tender child's skin was flushed. He could smell her sweet child's scent. The hands he gripped were boneless. Her body was without force or resistance. She was all compliance, willing, eager.

He opened his knees, let her move closer to him. Are you sure of what you're doing? he asked himself furiously. Are you absolutely *certain* this is the only way?

'Are you sure we're alone?' he asked, playing out his part.

'Hurry,' she said in a charged voice, her eyes hooded. 'Hurry.'

She stood, legs spread, waiting for him. But he sat rigidly, noting the trancelike appearance, quickened respiration, sweat on forehead and upper lip. He thought he detected a tremor in those grasped hands, a rise in skin temperature.

'Hurry,' she said. She tried to push her hands into his

crotch, but he held her fast. Her body writhed between his knees. She leaned up to him, mouth seeking.

'Hurry,' she said.

She was a small, warm animal trying to wriggle into him, mewling and nuzzling. He held her off as best he could, wanting to observe with a professional's detachment, but determined to push this as far as he could.

He bent forward to put his lips close to her ear. 'And then what did she do? Your mother?'

'He reached . . .' she recited in a disembodied voice. 'And she took off her panties. I saw . . .'

Her eyes were tightly shut now, the dream whirling. Her body had stiffened. Her body vibrated in a paroxysm of memory.

'And then?' he demanded.

'On her back. She was . . . On the bed. And he had, you know, his peter. They were making a baby. In her hole. I saw.'

'Everything?' he said sternly.

Her eyes flashed open. 'Everything!' she screamed. 'I saw everything! Hurry. Hurry. And he was moving back and forth. I thought he was . . . But he wasn't, because she wasn't crying. Oh! Oh! That's what she said. Oh! Oh! But he wasn't hurting her, I could tell. Once she laughed. I heard her laugh. So it was all right. You know? It wasn't bad. It was nice. And then she looked up and saw me. So I ran away. I went back to my own room. And I –'

She gave one convulsive sob, wrenched away from him, turned, vomited onto the floor at his feet. He stood quickly, held her as she bent far over and retched. Thick, ugly sounds came from her. Her small body was racked with spasms. She spewed in a gush.

'All right,' Levin said quietly. 'It's all right, Lucy.'

Still holding her shoulder with one hand, he was able to reach the intercom and buzz the emergency signal. Two short rings, one long. The door flung open, the receptionist came running.

There was confusion then. The receptionist brought newspapers to cover the sour mess on the floor. Then a maintenance man came grumbling with a mop and pail. Then the receptionist returned with a can of spray disinfectant that smelled vilely of wild cherry.

Dr Levin had led Lucy away from this scene. He placed her so that she faced the window, looking out. He put an arm about her shoulders.

'Would you like a glass of water?'

'I'm fine, thank you,' she said formally.

'We don't have much time left. Is your mother waiting for you downstairs?'

'Yes. In the car.'

'Well, before you leave, perhaps you'd like to use the bathroom and freshen up.'

She turned her head to look at him. 'You're not going to tell mother, are you?'

'About your being sick? Of course not.'

'No, not that. About what I told you.'

'No, I won't tell her that either.'

'She'd kill me if she knew.'

He smiled sadly. 'I don't think she'd do that. I think she'd be glad you told me. But I'm not going to repeat it, to your mother or anyone else.'

'I never told anyone,' she said sorrowfully. 'Not even Gloria, my best friend.'

'I know,' he said. 'It was a very hard secret to keep, wasn't it?'

She nodded, pulling at her braids. He moved around in front of her, sat on the wide windowsill facing her. He held her shoulders lightly.

'Lucy, there's a favor you can do for me.'

'What?'

'You know the homework you get in school? They give you homework, don't they?'

'Of course, silly.'

'Well, I'd like to assign you some homework, too.'

'What kind?' she said suspiciously.

'I'd like you to remember what you saw your mother doing the night of the party, and how it affected you. Do you understand? I'd like you to think about how you felt while you were watching, and how you felt about it later. Then, the next time I see you, I'd like to talk to you about it.'

'Okay,' she said chirpily. 'That's easy homework. I don't have to write anything out, do I?'

'You can if you like. I'd be happy to read anything you write about it. Or we can just talk about it like friends. We're still friends, aren't we?'

'Oh sure,' she said. 'I'm sorry I messed up your floor. I had a piece of pizza for lunch, and I guess it turned my stomach.'

'Probably,' he said, nodding. 'Our time is up, Lucy. I'll see you next week.'

'Can I tell you my new story, then?'

'Of course you can,' he said, walking her to the door. 'Now you tell the lady at the desk that you want to use the bathroom. Wash your face and rinse out your mouth, and your mother will never know what happened.'

'It'll be our secret,' she said with a mischievous grin. 'So long, Doctor Ted.' And then she was gone.

He went back to his desk to switch off the tape recorder. He lighted a cigar, not because he especially wanted it, but to blow a few mouthfuls of smoke into the air to dull that cloying wild cherry scent. Then he let the cigar go out.

He slumped tiredly into the swivel chair, head lowered, hands clasped across his belly. It had been a harrowing session. He looked down at his puke-spattered shoes. He knew significant progress had been made, but he was not particularly proud of himself.

8

Later, people recalled it as being an odd sort of day, choppy and chaotic. It had no form. Beach dwellers wandered about, talked, drank, sat down, stood up. No one seemed to know what to wear, what to do. A woman said, 'A rickety-rackety day,' and everyone knew what she meant, and agreed.

Perhaps the weather made it so. It dawned fair, turned foul, and then came rain squalls, periods of azure sky, thunder, a downpour, scudding clouds, balm again, high humidity, a chill wind, a searing sun, etc. Nature flaunted its whole bag of tricks.

That Saturday did not begin auspiciously for William Jasper Holloway. He was in the bathroom, shaving, when Jane came in and said, 'I want a divorce.'

Holloway set his razor carefully aside, gripped the sink with white-knuckled hands, and stared at his wife's reflection in the medicine cabinet mirror.

'That is not something you say to a man while he's shaving.'

She shrugged. 'Is there any good time to say it? You know this marriage just isn't working. No sex in – how long? Other things. I'll be happier if we break up, and you'll be happier, too.'

'Let me be the judge of that,' he said, happy already. But still remembering the early steamy days of their marriage when they came apart for each other.

'I'll move out on Monday,' she said. 'I think that's best. I'll go to a hotel. Your lawyer can talk to my lawyer.'

'But you won't talk to me?'

'No,' she said. 'What good would it do? I've thought about it for some time, and my mind's made up.'

'I know what that means,' he said bitterly.

'I'm sorry, Bill,' she said softly.

'No you're not,' he said.

He was too confused to clean his revolver that morning. It wasn't the thought of losing Jane that roiled him; it was the *trouble*. Lawyers, arguments, the settlement, the children, court appearances. Decisions demanded. His peaceful routine disturbed.

He didn't bother with breakfast, but filled an ice bucket with cubes and went directly to the living room bar. He poured a stiff vodka, took a gulp, and looked around. If he got to keep the house, the first thing he'd get rid of was all that depressing brown stuff.

He wandered out onto the beach with his second drink in a thick plastic tumbler so that people might think he was having a morning coffee. There were a lot of wanderers that morning. Everyone aimless and vacant-eyed.

Ronald Bending was standing on wet sand. His hands were deep in the pockets of his plaid Bermuda shorts. He was staring out at the crazy sea, charging every which way. Holloway went up to him and Bending turned.

'Morning, Bill,' he said.

'Jane wants a divorce,' Holloway said.

Turk looked at him. 'For real?'

Holloway nodded.

'Shit,' Bending said, and then he told Holloway what had happened to his car. He said he was getting out of the porn deal.

'Yes,' Holloway said, nodding, 'that's wise.'

'What are you drinking?' Bending asked, peering into the other man's tumbler. 'Seven-Up?'

'You know better than that.'

'Buy me one and then let's go dig up Luther. He better get out, too.'

So Holloway went back to his place, mixed himself a vodka and water, and a bourbon and soda for Turk, also in a plastic tumbler. The two men carried their drinks down the beach to Empt's home. It was drizzling then, but they didn't notice.

'This divorce,' Bending said. 'Jane's idea?'

'Yes.'

'I'm sorry, Bill.'

'I don't care.'

They climbed the coral rock steps to Luther's terrace and banged on the sliding door. He finally appeared, wearing a terry cloth robe and carrying a mug of coffee. He came out onto the terrace, looked at their tumblers.

'You're starting early,' he said.

'It's never too early,' Holloway said. 'Luther, we came to tell you that you better get out of the porn deal.'

'You're right,' Empt said unexpectedly. 'I decided last night that I'm going to take my money and vamoose.'

Bending looked at him curiously. 'What made you change your mind?'

Empt's eyes flickered. 'My lawyer convinced me that with you two guys out, I didn't stand a chance.'

They knew he was lying.

'You weren't threatened?' Turk Bending asked. 'Nothing like that?'

'Oh hell no,' Empt said boisterously. 'No one threatens me. No, it's just a business decision. I can use that money in my own place. Buy some new hardware. Expand.'

'The smart thing to do,' Bending said.

'I think maybe I'll get a jolt, too,' Empt said. 'Something to soothe the gut. I had a wet night last night.'

Holloway left Bending and meandered back to his own home. He was gloomy and jarred, ruminating on his ordinariness. The clouds were breaking; there were patches of sunlight; a few people were in the water, shouting.

Professor Lloyd Craner was on the terrace, sitting bolt upright, silver-headed cane clamped between his knees. He was sipping black coffee from a delicate bone china cup.

'Morning, professor,' Holloway said, taking a chair on the other side of the wicker table.

'Jane told me,' his father-in-law said. 'I'm sorry, Bill.'

'Well . . .' Holloway said. 'It happens.'

'Yes,' the old man said, and looked as if he might weep. He tugged angrily at his goatee. 'I don't like this – this breaking up. People should come together, not break up.' He sighed. 'Ahh, I'm a sententious old fool. Is there any chance of solving your, ah, problems?'

'Ask Jane,' Holloway said. 'I don't think so. When she makes up her mind . . .'

The professor nodded sadly.

'I hope,' Holloway said, 'that no matter what happens, we can continue to see each other.'

The grandee lifted his white eyebrows in astonishment. 'Of course. Understood. You're the only one I can beat at chess.'

'Not always,' Holloway said, smiling. He rose. 'I'm going to replenish my vitamins. May I bring you something?'

The codger considered. 'A small brandy perhaps. To revive my flagging spirits.'

'Be of good cheer,' Holloway said. 'Everything passes.'

'Unfortunately,' Professor Craner said.

At the same time, Wayne Bending, in his bedroom, the door locked, was packing a small knapsack with the few things he wanted to take when he made his escape. An extra pair of socks, pocket compass, jackknife, map of Florida, a condom that Eddie Holloway had given him, a few other trifles.

Wayne figured he'd have dinner with his family that night, kill a few hours, and then go up to his bedroom. He'd wait until everyone was asleep, and then he'd sneak out of the house. He'd go to A1A and thumb a ride north. Maybe he'd try New York first. If that didn't work out, he'd head westward for California.

*　　　*　　　*

Shortly before noon, during a period of endless sky and fulgent sun, the three men met again on the beach. Bending and Holloway were still dressed, but Luther Empt was wearing his rusty maroon swimming trunks, the drawstring cinched below his cannonball belly.

'I want to go in, but I don't want to go in,' he declared, eyeing the churning waves. 'It looks goddamn cold out there.'

'Go on,' Turk Bending told him. 'Be a hero. Do your hangover the world of good.'

'Yeah,' Empt said, 'I guess. Listen, what have you guys got on for tonight? Turk, the other day you were talking about a cookout or something. Is that still alive?'

'Okay with me,' Bending said. 'Bill, how about you?'

Holloway straightened and looked up. 'A party? Sure. Why not? A cookout if the weather holds, and if it doesn't, we'll move indoors.'

'Everyone brings his own food and his own bottle,' Bending said.

'Right,' Empt said. 'No one gets stuck for the whole tab. Who's going to throw this bash?'

'Me,' Holloway said. 'It's my turn.' He reflected that Jane would hate it, just *hate* it, and that gave him pleasure. 'I'll pick up paper plates and cups, and ice cubes, and all that stuff.'

'Great,' Bending said. 'Very informal. No one dresses up. Come as you are. About five o'clock, Bill?'

'Whenever,' Holloway said, shrugging. 'Let's just let it happen. But we need more bodies.'

'Good thinking,' Bending said. 'I'll do a Paul Revere up and down the beach and alert the natives. The Hopkinses, Sanchman, the Steins, Susie Burlingham – without bra, the Gardners – everyone.'

Holloway beamed. 'A *biiig* drunken orgy. Oh boy, now you're talking. I'll go get the supplies right now.'

He trotted away. They watched him go. Once he stopped, tried to leap sideways and click his heels. He didn't succeed and almost fell on the sand.

'He's acting nuts,' Luther said.

'Nah,' Bending said. 'He's just upset. Jane wants a divorce.'

'Shit,' Empt said. 'I'm sorry to hear it. I thought they were getting along okay. But you never know about people.'

'No,' Turk said, 'you never do. Listen, I'm going up and down the beach and tell everyone about the party.'

'And have a drink at every house.'

'That, too,' Bending said, grinning. 'Then I'll go back to Bill's and help him set up for this thing. You come over early and we can get greased before the mob arrives.'

'Will do,' Luther Empt promised, and after Turk left, he waded resolutely into the surf and then dived.

The water was shockingly cold for the first few moments. But then, as he swam determinedly outward, breasting the strong waves, his body temperature rose, the cobwebs were rinsed from his brain, and he began to glory in this muscle-stretching fight against the sea.

He stayed in for almost twenty minutes, swimming vigorously back and forth, parallel to the beach. He was not an expert; his overhand stroke was crude. But he had strength in arms, shoulders, back. It was good to dare the whole goddamned ocean and win.

He waded out, streaming, and chuffed up and down the strand to dry, with knees pulled high and elbows flapping. He dried quickly and went jogging toward his home, deciding he deserved a Bloody Mary after that stiff workout.

Eddie Holloway was ambling about the beach, wearing white briefs that looked to Empt not much larger than a jockstrap. Luther waved to him. Then, as he came up to his house, he met Lucy Bending, who was wearing a lacy coverup and carrying her sandals.

'Hi Mr Empt,' she said brightly.

'Hi princess,' he said. 'You look beautiful, as usual. I think you must be in love.'

'Silly!' she said, laughing delightedly. She looked at him. 'My goodness, you're really strong. I never noticed your muscles before.'

He sucked in his gut, flexed his biceps, did a burlesque imitation of a weight lifter. 'That's me – the circus strongman.'

'No,' she said with a curious smile. 'Really.'

He reached out to stroke her long, lustrous hair. 'What a princess! One of these days you're going to make some lucky young man very, very happy.'

'You think so?' she said archly.

'Oh yes. Well . . .' Suddenly he felt a stirring, a faint unease. 'Well, I've got to go get dressed. We're having a big party tonight at the Holloways'.'

'Oh!' she cried. 'A party! I love parties.'

'I do, too,' he said. 'I'll see you there. Your father is out now telling people about it. You tell your friends.'

'I will, Mr Empt,' she said. Then, as he moved away, she called after him, 'See you at the party!'

While Empt was telling Lucy about the party, William Holloway was telling Maria, the live-in maid. He hurried from the kitchen to escape her complaints. He got into his Mercedes carrying a fresh vodka and water.

Attached to the walnut dash of the car was a glass holder (designed for boats) affixed to a gimbal so the drink would never spill. Holloway placed his tumbler into the holder and set out for the supermarket, singing Neapolitan street songs in a not unmusical tenor.

He was wheeling his cart around the corner of the gourmet section when he collided head-on with a cart being pushed by Teresa Empt. Her cart contained six packages of chicken breasts.

They both laughed, and he told her about the party. She dawdled until she saw him safely out of the store, but he didn't know that. Then she took her purchases to the counter where Mike was working.

At home, Holloway stored the perishables away and went up to shower, feeling no pain. Not inebriated, mind you, but glowing and reasonably serene. Time was passing in a rosy dream, which was just the way he wanted it.

Jane was home and had heard about the party. To his surprise, she was wholeheartedly in favor of it – as long as she didn't have to help. He poured her a glass of white wine and then went into the kitchen to start things rolling.

Turk Bending drifted in to report that everyone he had contacted had eagerly agreed to attend, bringing their own food, drink, and guests. Then Bending had a drink and disappeared again. Luther Empt sent John Stewart Wellington over with a whole watermelon – a monster. Maria began to talk only in Spanish, which meant she had been nipping at the rum.

Holloway, moving slowly and not too methodically, set out tables and chairs, spread paper tablecloths, arranged paper plates and plastic cutlery, loaded the big brick barbecue with charcoal. During all these chores he hummed or sang aloud. It was his Italian day; he was particularly proud of his *Vesti La Giubba*.'

He had things pretty well under control by 3:00 P.M., when Wayne Bending came scuffling by, saying his father had sent him over to see if he could help with the preparations.

Holloway was delighted to see the boy. Opened a Coke for him. Gave him a bag of Cheez-Doodles. Sat him down at one of the poolside tables and joined him there.

'Well now, Wayne,' he said in what he imagined were the most understanding and sympathetic of tones, 'have you given more thought to what you're going to do?'

The boy looked at him directly. 'Still thinking about it, sir,' he said.

Holloway was shocked. Not at the reply, but because he knew, he *knew*, the lad was lying. And if he could lie so baldly to him, he who thought they had a special relationship, a special friendship, why then perhaps nothing was special at all.

He looked at Wayne, who was gazing up at the lowery sky. He thought it impossible that this youth felt nothing for him. He must have been touched by Holloway's interest and concern.

'Wayne,' Holloway said quietly, 'I want to help you. I've told you that several times. Isn't there anything I can do for you?'

'I'll be all right. I can take care of myself.'

'You can't!' Holloway cried. 'Where will you go? How will you live? You'll just make your family miserable. And me.'

'Yeah, well . . .' the boy muttered. 'Like I said, there's nothing for me around here.'

'Give me a chance,' Holloway pleaded. 'To get to know you better. Talk to you. Explain how things are. I don't want anything. I just don't like to see you throwing your life away.'

'Ah, shit,' Wayne said disgustedly. 'I know what's going on around here. You think I don't know? Who needs it? There must be better places than this. Where people don't dump on each other.'

Holloway wasn't certain what he meant. 'You mean lie to each other? Cheat?'

'Yeah. Like that. And pretend they're your friends, and then throw you over. It's all bullshit. I've had it.' He stood up suddenly. 'Listen, is there anything I can do around here?'

'What?' Holloway said, dazed. 'Oh, you mean the party. There must be something . . .'

He stared at Wayne, seeing a chunky lad with beautiful eyes. If, by some magical transplant, he could take all those young agonies unto himself, he would have done so, and gladly.

It would be at once his act of virtue, a wound, a sacrifice.

And, somehow, it would give significance to a life that Holloway now saw was without meaning or purpose.

'The party, Mr Holloway?' Wayne Bending said, breaking the silence and looking at him queerly.

'What?' he said, confused. 'Oh. Yes. The party. Well, I forgot to buy ice cubes. Could you bring over all you can spare from your house?'

'Sure.'

'I'll put them all in plastic bags in the freezer. By the time we run out, we should have more ready in the trays.'

'Okay, Mr Holloway. I'll go get them.'

He watched the boy shamble away. He thought of all the things he might have said. Should have said. About friendship, solace, compassion. About love. Instead, he had talked about ice cubes and putting plastic bags in the freezer.

Disgusted with himself, he hurled what was left of his drink, tumbler and all, into the swimming pool. Then he went into the house and mixed a fresh one.

There were brief spatters of rain that evening, but no one seemed to mind. Occasionally the clouds thinned and a crescent moon was glimpsed. It was cool enough for jackets and sweaters. The wind, blowing from the west, had a sweetish scent. 'Like incense,' someone said.

People began gathering early and seemed determined to stay forever. There was plenty of food, plenty of whiskey, beer, wine. Joints were passed. It was rumored that someone was carrying coke, but Jane Holloway couldn't find it. Just the same, she danced a demented Charleston on the pool verge.

If the party could be said to have one dominant mood, it was desperation. There were no fights, and no one jumped in the pool. Still, the adults seemed intent on abandon. As the evening gained momentum, restraint vanished, and even civility suffered.

The youngsters caught the temper, as if franticness was a communicable disease and they had been infected. Thin

464

voices rose to screeches and there were uncontrollable dartings between tables, throwing of food, wild horseplay on the lawn.

People ate when they pleased, drank from the bottle nearest to hand. They grouped, separated, traded jokes, flirted, cooked at the barbecue, brayed with laughter, wandered, mingled, assured each other this was the best beach party ever – and wasn't it fun?

Holloway and Bending had been drinking since morning, but they had achieved a plateau of intoxication that enabled them to function and join in the jollity. They were no more immoderate or oafish than the guests.

It was Luther Empt who presented a dark and surly face to the company. He sat by himself at a shadowed table, swilling straight scotch and occasionally muttering and scowling. His wife and mother avoided him, and eventually so did the others. The word spread: 'Luther's in one of his mean moods.'

Once, early in the evening, Lucy Bending came up to him, put a soft hand on his arm, and asked if he would dance with her. He glowered until he recognized who it was, and then his face lightened.

'Princess!' he shouted. 'You beautiful princess!'

'Will you dance with me, Mr Empt?' she repeated.

'Later, sweetheart,' he said. 'I can't dance to this fast stuff. When they play something nice and slow.'

'Promise?' she said.

'Cross my heart and hope to die,' he vowed, and leaned forward to kiss her cheek. But she moved to take the kiss on her lips. 'Oh, what a lovely princess you are!' he said with his raspy laugh, hugging her.

When she moved away from him, he stared after her. May was gone, and this sad, slow-brained man was just beginning to realize the enormity of his loss. Everything safe, warm, and light in his life had passed. He faced a dangerous, cold, and murky future.

Gertrude Empt and Professor Craner sat together, ate

steadily and quietly, and presented a studiously pleasant mien to the roisterers about them. They finished slices of honeydew, looked at each other, rose simultaneously.

'A nice party,' Gertrude said, 'but a little noisy. What about a walk on the beach?'

'Nothing would give me more pleasure,' he said gallantly.

'You're easily satisfied,' she said, taking his arm.

Jane Holloway, as usual, was surrounded by a circle of admiring men, all of whom she treated with cheerful contempt. Grace Bending was part of a small group of staid matrons discussing the problems of teaching their young children 'the facts of life,' and meanwhile keeping a cold eye on the antics of their carousing husbands.

Teresa Empt was having a difficult time avoiding the attentions of a moony Eddie Holloway. His cow eyes followed her everywhere. She finally found refuge with a limber young man, a guest, who talked of nothing but the fierce glories of skydiving.

Teresa listened attentively. After a while, she let her knee press against his under the table. His expression changed and he began to stammer. She smiled at him encouragingly and wondered if it was too soon to turn the conversation to the architecture of gazebos.

A little before midnight, moving with exaggerated caution, William Jasper Holloway navigated into his own kitchen. He was carrying an empty ice bucket. But the plastic bags in the freezer were depleted and the trays emptied.

He thought he could manage a quick trip to the Bendings' kitchen without misadventure. He set out through the gloom, moving slowly to avoid blundering into the palms and bougainvillea that separated the two unfenced lots.

Instead, he blundered into Wayne Bending, who was hurrying from the rear of his home, carrying a knapsack. It took a moment for Holloway to realize what was happening. He dropped the ice bucket onto the soft ground.

466

'Wayne . . .' he said in a choked voice.

'Don't try to stop me,' the boy warned. 'No one can stop me.'

'But you said . . . I told you I'd give you money.'

'I don't want your money. I don't want nothing from nobody.'

'Don't run away,' Holloway said, stumbling toward the boy. 'Please, please, please don't.'

'I'm going,' the lad said stolidly. 'You can tell my dad if you like. But I'll be gone by then; he'll never find me. I left a note.'

'A note?' Holloway said, groaning. 'Ah Jesus, a note!'

He felt something wrench inside himself: a crack, a split, and then a widening. He saw the failure of thought, not only to deal with this twelve-year-old boy, but to deal with himself. Reason was not enough.

He put his arms clumsily about the youth. He shoved his face forward, lips pursed.

'I love you,' he said. 'I love you.'

'What the hell's wrong with you?' Wayne shouted, pushing him away. 'You crazy or something?'

'I love you,' William Jasper Holloway said, gasping, heart cleft open. He tried again to take the lad into his arms. 'I love you.'

Wayne, cursing, shoved him violently. Holloway staggered back, sat down suddenly on the soggy earth.

'You creep!' the boy screamed at him. 'You're like all the rest.'

Then he turned and ran away into the darkness. Holloway sat there, feeling the wet of the ground seep into the seat of his pants. After a while he began to weep. 'You're just like all the rest.' He knew what all the rest were like.

He began talking aloud to himself:

'So all that stuff about living a virtuous life, enduring a wound, sacrifice – just blather.'

'No! No. I really felt that.'

'Bullshit. A stiff cock: that's what you felt.'

467

'That's cruel.'

'That's *true*. You betrayed him, and you betrayed your-self. He was right; you're just like all the rest.'

'We could have been friends.'

'Come off it! Stop deluding yourself. You know what you wanted. Face it.'

'I can't. I can't go on.'

'Very dramatic! But you'll go on. Just the way you always have. That will be your punishment.'

Still snuffling, wiping his eyes with the back of his hand, he climbed awkwardly to his feet. He felt the seat of his pants. Soaked through and, he supposed, stained. The final touch of buffoonery in a clown's life.

He rooted around in the dark, found the ice bucket, went stumbling toward the Bendings' kitchen door. It was open a few inches. Inside, the lights burned brightly. He heard voices and stopped, one foot on the sill.

He heard Luther Empt's slurred voice: 'Are you sure we're alone?'

And then the reedy, piping voice of a child: 'Hurry. Hurry.'

Holloway pushed open the door, peered cautiously around the jamb. Took one look. Then withdrew, jaw sagging, moving slowly backward until he was in gloom. He turned, threw the ice bucket from him, and began running frantically back to his own home.

He crashed through trees, tripped on bushes, trampled shrubs. Branches whipped his face. Once he fell, hurt his knee, pushed himself erect and charged clumsily on. He was weeping again, but noisily now, sobbing, coughing. His lungs burned, his rent heart pumped wildly.

He lumbered up the stairs, pulling himself along by the banister. When he came back down, carrying Eric, the gun unholstered and gripped purposefully, men and women were streaming into his brown, ugly living room, laughing, brushing rain from their hair and shoulders.

'Hey, Bill, where are you –'

'What are you –'

'Bill, what the –'

'Stop, Bill!'

But Bill didn't stop. He rushed out into the heavy drizzle, acknowledging the failure of reason, and wanting only to feel deeply, intensely, and let it take him where it would.

He heard the shouts behind him. He felt the wet on his face: tears and rain. But he could not stop now and, exultant, he went smashing back to the guilt that was his, and everywhere.

William Jasper Holloway burst in upon them and stepped close. Pointed his revolver. Emptied it into them. Saw them jerk and splatter. Explosions deafened him. Then he heard only clicks as he pulled the trigger again and again.

He flung the weapon away. Went rushing out again, dimly aware of people coming at him through the trees, baying like hounds. But he eluded them all, ran around the house to the beach.

Staggered through wet sand to the sea. Waded in without stopping. Plunged. Began swimming eastward as hard as he could. This time he was going to make it. Reach England. Portugal. Africa. Whatever.

9

'I called the husband,' Dr Theodore Levin said, staring at the nursery-rhyme animals painted on his office wall. 'I wanted to tell him how sorry I was about what happened. And there was a question I wanted to ask him that was eating at me.'

'How did he sound?' Dr Mary Scotsby asked.

'Terrible. Well, his daughter had just been shot dead, his wife was under heavy sedation, and his older son, Wayne – the boy I talked to – is apparently a runaway. So it's understandable the man isn't tracking too well.'

'What was the question you wanted to ask him?'

'You remember in the initial interview he told me about an incident that occurred during a cookout last Labor Day. Bending went into his kitchen – by the way, I think it's the same kitchen where the shooting took place – and he found Lucy seducing a man. Bending described him as a good friend. The newspaper stories said that a man, a neighbor of Bending's, had been shot to death at the same time Lucy died. I had to ask Bending if the murdered man was the same one he had caught with Lucy last year.'

'What did he say?'

'Yes.'

There was silence. She looked at him directly, but his gaze wandered: here, there, everywhere.

'It wasn't your fault, Ted,' she said quietly.

'You can say that, and I can say that, and it doesn't help. Time! If I had more time, I could have turned that child. I know I could have. And talking about guilt, I listened to all

470

the tapes again last night and picked up an error of omission. My error.'

'What was that?'

'When the wife told me about her sexual, uh, adventure the night of that party four years ago, I asked her if the man involved was the husband of the woman with whom Bending had disappeared. She said it wasn't, and I let it go at that. What I should have asked was whether he was the same man caught in the kitchen with Lucy four years later.'

'Why didn't you ask?'

'My delicacy will be the death of me,' he said with a sour smile.

'Ted, you're just guessing. You have no evidence that the same man was involved with both mother and daughter.'

'No evidence, no. But it makes sense, doesn't it? It would help explain Lucy's behavior, wouldn't it?'

'In a crazy kind of way.'

'You mean in a human kind of way.'

She sighed. 'Ted, I have a question: Did the husband know about his wife?'

'About the bedroom incident? I doubt it.'

'If he learned about it, how do you think he would have reacted?'

'It would be easy to say that, with his record of infidelity, he wouldn't give a damn. But I doubt that. I think knowledge of his wife's unfaithfulness would destroy him. He loves her, you know.'

'In his way.'

'Yes. In his way.'

Levin's gaze finally settled on her. His stare was so intense through those bottle-bottom glasses that she stirred restlessly.

'Why are you glaring at me?'

'Mary, let's get married.'

Silence. Finally . . .

'You're not joking now,' she said, 'are you?'

'No, I'm not joking. I wish I could tell you it's a mad,

471

passionate love, but you know me better than that.'

'Yes,' she said with a short, rueful laugh, 'I do know you. What is it then?'

'In espionage, there's a term they use. "Safehouse." It's a completely secure place where agents can stay and know they're free from danger and harm. It's a refuge, a hidey-hole. Mary, I need a safehouse. The world is too much with me. Everything's getting dark, and I'm frightened. First of all, for my own sanity. So you see, I'm asking you for very selfish reasons. I need a safehouse that offers shelter and protection. From the madness. I need your moral and emotional support. If I don't get it, I'm not sure I'm going to make it much longer. The sadness of being human is beginning to get to me. All our high hopes and dreadful defeats. Our weakness! I can't cope anymore. It's getting harder and harder for me to laugh.'

'Have you told all this to Al Wollman?'

'He tells me to pick up a creamer and get laid.'

'Yes, that sounds like Al.'

'But listen,' he said earnestly, 'I don't want you to think I'm asking you to marry me because I need a live-in shrink. Or nurse. I believe I can give you the same kind of support I want. What I'm hoping is that, between us, we can make a kind of – a kind of . . .'

'A kind of sanctuary?' she said.

'Exactly,' he said, relaxing. 'A kind of sanctuary. What do you say?'

'Yes,' she said.

10

It took three trips in Professor Lloyd Craner's old Buick to move his and Mrs Empt's clothes and personal possessions to their new apartment in the motel near the Intracoastal Waterway. It was almost 1:00 P.M. before the job was finished.

On the last trip, Craner stopped at a liquor store and bought a bottle of chilled champagne.

'To celebrate,' he said.

'What?' Gertrude asked. 'Total exhaustion?'

But her mood improved when the move was completed, and they were safely ensconced in their one-bedroom unit. The little apartment was jammed with their clothing, shoes, cartons. Gertrude's shell collection, and Craner's books. But neither was ready to start putting things in order.

They sat on the bed, and Craner poured champagne into two water tumblers.

'It's from California,' he said, 'but in a taste test by *Consumer Reports*, it was judged as good as or better than most imported French champagnes.'

She looked at him owlishly. 'That's the best part of living with perfessers; they know everything.'

He laughed. 'I admit I tend to get stuffy at times. I'm depending on you to cut me down to size.'

'You can count on me,' she told him.

They sipped the wine and agreed it was just what they needed.

'The cat's pajamas,' Mrs Empt said.

'The bee's knees,' Craner said.

473

And they both smiled, remembering.

'Gertrude, did you tell Teresa you were leaving?'

'Yeah, I told her.'

'What did she say?'

'She said, "How nice for you!" Then she said, "We must keep in touch." And I said, "Sure." Neither of us meant it. If I never see her again, it'll be too soon. And I guess she feels the same way about me. Did you tell your daughter?'

'She wasn't home. Jane is busy these days with some kind of a job that she's very secretive about. But I left a message with Eddie. I told him I was moving into my own place in a motel. He said, "Have a ball!" '

'The best advice I've heard yet. I gather that Jane isn't exactly pining away with Bill gone.'

'Not exactly.'

'Neither is Teresa with Luther dead.'

'How do you feel about it?'

She shrugged. 'At my age you've learned to live with everything. Especially death.'

'That's the way I feel about it. It's the Bendings I'm sorry for. Their shells aren't as thick as ours.'

They finished their glasses of champagne, and Craner poured more.

'You wouldn't be trying to get me drunk, would you?' she said. 'Just to take advantage of my weakness?'

'It's an idea,' he admitted. 'But actually, I'm trying to get up the courage to discuss something with you that we should have talked about before this. I'm willing to marry you if that's what you want, but we –'

'Are you crazy?' she burst out. 'Get married? What a nutty idea! We're both on Social Security. We get married and my benefits are cut. Our total income goes down. It's not worth it for a piece of paper.'

'I was hoping you'd feel that way. It's unfortunate that the laws of this great nation make it, ah inexpedient, and uneconomical, for people our age to marry.'

'Don't give it a second thought.'

'It won't bother you to live in sin?' he asked, tugging on his white goatee.

'Not if there's enough of it.'

'Well, then,' he said, beaming, 'I foresee a long and happy future for this illicit relationship.'

'I'll drink to that,' she said.

He poured the remainder of the champagne into their glasses, and moved closer to her on the bed. She pulled down the neckline of her muumuu to expose one brown shoulder. She batted her eyes.

'Kiss me, you fool,' she said.

And, laughing, he did.

TIMES OF TRIUMPH
by Charlotte Vale Allen

Spanning more than three decades in the turbulent
history of our century, Charlotte Vale Allen's magnificent
saga traces the life and loves of a woman born to
struggle against every adversity with dauntless courage
and unflinching love.

Leonie came to New York with all the world against her
and built her tiny eating-house into a mighty business
empire.

Gray, the London journalist who followed her across the
ocean, was the father of her children and the love of her
lifetime.

Through the First World War, the hard and hungry years
that followed, through love and pain and bitter sadness,
through the growing years of their son and daughter
destined to retrace their mother's footsteps into a Europe
once again torn apart by war – Leonie's life was a time
of triumph.

NEW ENGLISH LIBRARY

MEET ME IN TIME
by Charlotte Vale Allen

Meet Me in Time is a story about love, its intensity and destructiveness, its needs and satisfactions. It is also the story of the Burgesses, a brilliant, tormented family.

Gaby: bitter and unstable, cheated by the failure of her marriage and resenting the child she never wanted . . .

Dana: a talented playwright who recoiled from the truth about himself . . .

Glenn: the artist, haunted by her mother's death, expecting more love than anyone could humanly give her . . .

All three had dreams of fame, and passions that demanded fulfilment. All three shared the bittersweet inheritance from their mother, whose need to love had been overwhelming, and whose need to be loved was an inescapable legacy to her children.

Book Tokens

Give them
the pleasure of choosing

Book Tokens can be bought
and exchanged at most
bookshops in Great Britain
and Ireland.

NEL BESTSELLERS